A High Mortality of Doves

Kate Ellis

piatkus

PIATKUS

First published in Great Britain in 2016 by Piatkus
This paperback edition published in 2017 by Piatkus

1 3 5 7 9 10 8 6 4 2

A CIP catalogue record for this book
is available from the British Library.

ISBN 978-0-349-41306-8

Typeset in New Baskerville by M Rules
Printed and bound in Great Britain by
Clays Ltd, St Ives plc

Papers used by Piatkus are from well-managed forests
and other responsible sources.

Piatkus
An imprint of
Little, Brown Book Group
Carmelite House
50 Victoria Embankment
London EC4Y 0DZ

An Hachette UK Company
www.hachette.co.uk

www.littlebrown.co.uk

For Ruth Smith,
with many thanks for all
her reading and encouragement

Chapter 1

Myrtle

Stanley was dead. There was no doubt about it.

His mother had broken the news to his sweetheart, Myrtle, soon after she'd received the telegram. She'd staggered round to her house and waved the small piece of paper in her face, too shocked with grief to speak, too stunned to cry.

Not long after this, a letter arrived from his commanding officer, saying how he'd died bravely and felt no pain during his last moments on Earth. All the letters received by relatives said the same but nobody dared to challenge the thin comfort of the words because nobody could bear to disbelieve it. Myrtle Bligh certainly couldn't and neither could Stanley's mother who'd read the letter over and over until the fold in the paper began to fray and tear. And now she kept it safe in a biscuit tin, in pride of place on the mantelpiece like a holy relic.

The Stanley of Myrtle's imagination, the image she

thought of when she lay in bed waiting for the sleep that didn't come, had now become transfigured into a legendary hero. She saw him bathed in a halo of glory as he went over the top, falling gracefully and painlessly as the enemy bullet found his heart. In her imagination she saw his corpse lying on the grass of the battlefield – fresh green grass, never mud – quite unmarked apart from a neat, bloodless bullet hole in his khaki tunic. She saw his eyes closed in sweet repose and his arms folded piously across his chest. Resting in peace. She couldn't bear to think of that body she'd loved bleeding and torn apart by shells and shrapnel. And the letter had said his end was painless so she had to believe it.

She knew Stanley was dead because he'd spoken to her from the Other Side when she'd visited the medium in New Mills with his mother. She'd sat at the round table in the darkness, clasping the clammy hand of a man whose son was missing in action. Before that evening the only man whose hand she'd held had been Stanley, and it had felt odd to be doing the same with a balding stranger who smelled of sweat and fear.

As the medium, a fat woman in rusty black with a piping, little-girl voice, sank into a trance her voice suddenly deepened and she delivered her messages in the voice of a man: her spirit guide who told her that Stanley was smiling and blissfully happy on the Other Side. Everybody there received the same message. There had been no mention of pain. No fires of hell and damnation. The dead existed in eternal peace. And Stanley was amongst them.

It was impossible that Stanley was still alive. The army always told the truth about things like that and if they

2

weren't sure, they said 'missing in action'. Or 'missing, believed dead'. Some families in the village had received letters containing those terrible words. But if the letter said someone was dead, they were dead. Weren't they?

Only now she wasn't so sure. Not since she'd received that letter of her own that appeared to prove the first was a lie. It had been pushed through her door, her name printed in clumsy letters on the envelope. She hadn't recognised the writing but once she'd torn it open she'd known it was from him, and she put the change of handwriting, the roughly printed letters, down to some dreadful injury he'd sustained during those terrible years of war.

I am alive, the letter said. *Meet me in Pooley Woods at eight tonight. I'm in trouble so don't tell anyone. Bring this note with you, for if it should be found it would be the worse for me. S.*

Trouble could mean anything, of course, but she'd heard of men who'd deserted and were hunted down like animals. Cowards. She'd always hated cowards. When the men had marched proudly through the High Street that day, cowardice had seemed like the worst sin imaginable. Worse than murder. Surely Stanley, her wonderful sweetheart, sainted by his long absence, couldn't be guilty of such a thing. It was impossible.

Perhaps the words meant something else. Perhaps he'd been on some secret mission and there were still enemy spies out there pursuing him, even though the conflict was over.

She went through all the possibilities in her head as she peeled the potatoes on her mother's instructions, hardly aware of slicing into the starchy lumps before throwing them into the salted water. But at no stage did

3

it occur to her that she wouldn't go and meet him as he asked. If a miracle had occurred and Stanley had survived and returned to her, she wanted to know. She wanted to kiss those lips again. She wanted to marry him as they'd promised before he left. A small flame of hope had been reignited. How could she snuff it out now?

Without letting her mother know where she was going, she put on her coat and sneaked from their small stone cottage at the heart of the village, praying nobody would see her. It was almost dark and she felt nervous yet excited as the hard soles of her button boots clicked on the cobbles of River Street. Once she'd crossed the old stone bridge that spanned the river, she hesitated a moment when she saw a group of men entering the Cartwright Arms, their weather-beaten faces set with determination beneath their soft cloth caps. Working men in search of refreshment. She recognised some of them as men who'd worked on Wilf Fuller's farm with her dad ... before he'd gone away to France and never come back. She didn't want them to see her and she was relieved when they didn't look in her direction.

As she turned left down the High Street she cursed the heels of her boots, clicking so loudly and drawing attention. Not having been brought up to lie and deceive, she was unused to subterfuge. 'Tell the truth and shame the Devil' was one of her mother's favourite sayings. But if Stanley wanted secrecy, there must be a good reason.

It wasn't long before she reached the woodland on the edge of the village; the small area of trees amidst the fields that had always been the favoured place for courting couples and seekers of firewood. Pooley Woods had been her and Stanley's special place. They had met there so often to kiss – no more than kiss because that sort of thing would have to wait for their wedding night – and talk. But that telegram from the War Office had robbed her of the happy future she'd dreamed of: the wedding; the love-making; the companionship; the children. All gone. Until now.

Suddenly she was filled with hope; replenishing her spirits like water on a drooping plant. Her footsteps quickened as she heard the church clock chime. Eight o'clock. The time her fate would become clear.

As she entered the trees she heard a sound. A flutter of wings in the canopy of budding leaves above. A bird. She couldn't see it but she could hear its panic and she took a deep, calming breath. She walked on to the clearing where she and Stanley used to meet, telling herself there was nothing to be afraid of. She'd been in these woods a hundred times or more. But she'd never gone there alone before.

Then she saw him. A shape outlined in the dim dusk light filtering through the branches. He was standing quite still between two trees. Waiting in the shadows. He was watching her but he made no attempt to speak. She thought he was in uniform but she couldn't be sure. Suddenly she wasn't sure of anything any more.

She called his name. 'Stanley?' The word came out as a question because he looked different somehow. But it was a long time since she'd seen him and she'd heard war could do dreadful things to a man.

He began to move, walking slowly and awkwardly towards her. Stanley had been strong and he'd moved with the grace of muscular youth, but now his whole body had shrunk and his limbs seemed stiff, like an old man's.

'Stanley? Is it you?'

There was no answer. He was still an approaching shape, human yet not human, and she wished she could see his face but it was too dark. As she took a step back he stopped and held out his hand as if to reassure her.

Perhaps, she thought, he'd lost the power of speech. Perhaps he'd been so horribly disfigured that he couldn't bear for her to see. But she knew that even if he'd become a monster, she mustn't cry. She mustn't let him see her disappointment.

After a few moments she couldn't help herself. Overcome with pity and love she felt herself moving towards him.

'Stanley.'

She was a couple of feet away when she finally saw the face. It looked nothing like the one she'd expected. Instead of warm flesh, all she could see was a pair of painted, staring eyes and the parted lips of a life-sized doll. She couldn't suppress a gasp of horror at what he'd become. Her beautiful boy. Her Stanley. Her hand shook as she raised her fingers towards the face and when they made contact, she felt it hard and cold beneath her touch.

Then she felt a sudden pain in her chest and when she lowered her eyes she saw something dark and sharp protruding from her body. A sword, perhaps. Or a bayonet. The weapon of a soldier.

She gasped the question 'Why?' and fell to her knees in front of him.

Chapter 2

Flora

I am not at the centre these days. I hear news second-hand, whispered in the streets or in the hushed reverence of Father's waiting room. Even the news of Myrtle Bligh's death wouldn't have reached my ears so quickly had it not been for my own curiosity.

As soon as Sergeant Teague arrived at the house, I could tell by the look on his long, thin face that something bad had happened. I am not ashamed to confess that I tried to eavesdrop when he was shown into Father's surgery. I stood by the polished mahogany door, straining my ears to make out what was being said inside, and what I heard was so shocking that I knew it would shake even those hardened by the horrors of war.

Myrtle was found in Pooley Woods yesterday, and nobody has any idea what she was doing there. The gossips say that she went there to meet a young man, although the identity of her beau remains a mystery. He seems to be a phantom – but then so many of our young men are alive only in spirit these days while their earthly bodies rot in the fields of France.

There is some talk of a soldier being seen near the woods around the time she died but I can't believe it. The soldiers, those few who survived, shed their khaki eagerly as soon as they arrived home, like butterflies shed a chrysalis. Perhaps it was a ghost – one of those men who never came back revisiting a place of happier memories. I never used to believe in ghosts but these days I'm not so certain.

But one thing's for sure; it wasn't a ghost who ended Myrtle Bligh's life in such a savage fashion. Whoever killed her was flesh and blood.

My father, having viewed the body, knows the details of her death but he will not share them with me because he thinks them too shocking for what he calls my delicate female ears. I must listen and learn; glean fragments of information from the gossips and those with loose tongues.

Chapter 3

Although three weeks have passed since the discovery of Myrtle's body in Pooley Woods, the police appear to be as puzzled now as they were on the day she was found.

Like most of the village, I attended Myrtle's funeral and as I walk through the churchyard on my way back from delivering a bottle of Father's tonic to the vicarage, I can't help reliving that grim little ceremony. In my mind I still see the mourning flowers strewn around the grave as Myrtle's plain coffin is lowered into the earth and her inconsolable mother sheds bitter tears for her dead daughter. It rained that day as if heaven itself was weeping.

As I walk down the churchyard path a flash of white catches my eye. When I stop I see a dead dove lying on the grave of Emanuel Beech, one of Father's elderly patients who passed away last week. The bird's wings are spread over the mound of soil as if it is trying to protect old Emanuel's scrawny corpse from predators, and its snowy feathers lie stark like bone against the newly dug earth. The little beak gapes open but even death can't rob the dove of its beauty.

I stand there for a while with my eyes fixed on the lifeless thing until the chiming of the church clock reminds me that I have to be home. If I'm late Father wonders where I am and I can't face the inevitable questions.

Father is more anxious these days and I think it's because of what happened to Myrtle. Ever since her body was found he's been watching me, emerging from his study every time he hears a door open and interrogating me about my every movement. 'Where have you been, Flora? Where are you going? What time will you return?'

After spending the war at Tarnhey Court, taking responsibility for the life and death of men braver than me, I find Father's intrusion irritating. Nevertheless, I understand his concern. After all, Myrtle Bligh had been my contemporary, even though our relative stations in life meant that we had little to do with each other while we were growing up in the village. Of course all that changed once we both volunteered to do our bit for King and Country at Tarnhey Court and joined the VADs, those raw and inexperienced nursing auxiliaries who set aside their everyday lives and their squeamish natures to take care of the wounded. War and blood have been such levellers in our little community and Myrtle and I became colleagues for the duration, united in duty.

I confess I miss the work and our patients with their banter, born of brittle courage. Most of them were just boys, dragged suddenly into manhood by shells and bullets and their horrible disfigurements. At first the sight of their mutilated flesh robbed me of breath. But as I became accustomed to my duties, my heart and stomach hardened and I could look at them with no emotion but pity. Limbs missing, faces with no features, masses of blood and burned, mottled flesh; noses gone, eyes gone. Everything gone.

I must admit that Myrtle took to nursing those poor wounded shells of men much faster than I did. Sometimes she'd laugh at me and tell me that a doctor's daughter shouldn't be so alarmed by the sight of a bit of blood. She was right, of course. When I first walked through the imposing oak doors of Tarnhey Court and put on the simple blue dress, the snowy white apron and the white linen cap, I was a coward. And cowards aren't allowed to exist in times of war, so I hid my true nature and got on with it. Matron never knew and Sister never knew. Neither did my fellow VADs. Only Myrtle witnessed me vomiting into the sluice on that first day but, as far as I know, she never gave away my secret.

Now Myrtle's life has been cut short by a murderous attack and she sleeps her eternal sleep beneath the damp soil in the churchyard. They laid her beneath the old apple tree in the corner near the grey dry stone wall and there's talk that her family are saving up for a headstone. I find myself wondering what it will say. Maybe something like *Myrtle Bligh: born 1898 and taken from this vale of tears by a cruel murderer in 1919. May her soul be avenged.* But round here I reckon they'll choose something less brutal. Something sweet and sentimental. *Not dead, only sleeping* or *With the angels.* I doubt if her family will want to be reminded of how she met her end.

In spite of the time that's passed since Myrtle's death,

the tragedy is still the talk of the village and beyond. Every detail has now filtered down to eager ears: how she'd been stabbed through the heart and how a dead bird had been stuffed between her pretty, rosebud lips. A dove, possibly from the dovecote on the Cartwright estate. Or so people say.

They've been saying a lot of other things as well. The rumour of the soldier persists and there is talk that she had a secret sweetheart who may have been married. I don't know the truth of it because once Tarnhey Court was handed back to the Cartwrights and the patients, nurses and doctors left, Myrtle and I returned to our separate worlds – Myrtle to the tedium of the mill and me to the equally tedious task of looking after Father and his surgery.

I've often mentioned to Father that I should like to go away and put the skills I learned at Tarnhey Court to good use. I tell him I'd like to train properly as a nurse and work in some big city hospital but for some reason he won't countenance the idea. 'My dear girl, war puts us in some strange situations,' he says, scratching his sparse hair and consulting his gold pocket watch. 'But there is no need to prolong them now that we have the blessing of peace. The war was an aberration and it will never happen again.'

Father's a stubborn man and I know better than to argue. I will bide my time and strike when his defences are down. One day I'll get my way.

The police have been questioning some of the young men in the village about Myrtle's murder. Her sweetheart, Stanley Smith, was killed on the Somme and there have been no rumours of anybody replacing him in her affections so there is no obvious suspect. Through the network of gossips, I discovered that it was Jack Blemthwaite who found her body and there are some – no not some, many – who are saying that he was responsible for her death. You know what villages are like for whispers, veiled accusations from the self-righteous lips of the women in shop queues and outside church on Sundays. They gather round any scandal like crows around the corpse of a dead sheep and I learned long ago not to give any credence to their poison. Jack Blemthwaite is simple, you see, and folk always fear the different. Luckily his mother swears he was with her at the time they say Myrtle died. But the gossips say her statement is worthless: they claim that mothers will say anything. Mothers, they say, can't be trusted.

And there could be some truth in that because I've heard it said that my own mother couldn't be trusted. Maybe one day I'll discover why she went off without a word, leaving Father alone to care for me and John. The whisperers said she went off with a fancy man; a man who took a room at the Black Horse while he was visiting one of the mills on some unspecified business. But I was only young then and I've never managed to find out whether this story's true. I can't ask Father. I don't want to probe the wound which must still be raw, even after fourteen years.

I think I saw this alleged fancy man once. He was youngish and slim with a bowler hat and a small moustache that gave him the look of a large and prosperous rat. This was before the war so, for all I know, he might be dead now, his body blown to pieces in some Flanders trench. And I've no idea whether Mother is still alive because, after that night, we never heard from her again. As far as I can gather, Father returned from visiting a patient and found her gone, along with her valise and most of her clothes. The one thing she didn't take with her was a photograph of her children.

Whispers. Always whispers. Whispers wound like bullets. Only nobody calls a truce and nobody puts the names of the fallen on fine memorials in village squares.

The grass in the churchyard has been recently scythed and I breathe in the scent of it as I walk on towards the graves of some of the men I nursed. Men who were so sick from their terrible injuries that they had no hope of recovery. But we did our best for them, Myrtle and I and all the rest.

I pause by the graves of those poor young men and bow my head. Then, on impulse I return to old Emanuel's grave and pick the dead dove up by its wing. It feels light, as though it has no substance; a thing of air and spirit. I carry it to the apple tree and lay it in a little hollow in the bare brown earth underneath, not too far from Myrtle's grave. It seems right to leave it there somehow, as if it had passed away peacefully on a branch and tumbled to the ground.

My eyes are attracted by the array of wilting flowers that have been placed on Myrtle's grave. As I catch sight of the rotting blooms I can't help thinking of Myrtle as she was when I knew her. Petite with that sharp, pointed face of hers, always curious, always ready to chatter about other people's business. And now she is a decomposing corpse six feet beneath the ground.

The hands of the church clock are creeping forward and I know it's time to go. But, in spite of the chill in the air, I feel comfortable there in the churchyard. I like being near the dead.

As I walk away towards the old lych gate where the coffins used to rest on their final journey, I spot a figure on the other side of the churchyard wall. A tall, well-built young man with his cap pulled down over his eyes, as though he doesn't wish to be recognised. But everyone knows Jack Blemthwaite. He's unmistakable with his thick lips and his eyes bulging like gobstoppers. He looks strong. But he wasn't sent to war with the rest. He stayed safe at home in his mother's care, free from all danger. Some people in the village hadn't liked that.

I walk away quickly, back to the house. Father's evening surgery will be starting soon and he needs me.

Chapter 4

Annie

Annie Dryden had a secret but it wasn't one she could share with her husband, Bill. Not until she was sure at any rate. Mind you, Bill rarely spoke to her these days. When he returned home from his work at the blacksmith's each night, he'd sit by the fire, saying nothing while she fussed around him, preparing a dinner fit to fill the belly of a working man.

When she placed the food on the table in front of him he never uttered a word of thanks and he never asked her what she'd been doing during the day. It was the same with their three girls; he took no interest in their jobs in the mill, instead focusing on his own closed world of work and the Cartwright Arms. On occasions he came home the worse for drink, something he'd never done before the war. When their son Harold was with them he wouldn't have dreamed of it. Before that telegram came to say that Harold was missing believed dead, Bill had been a different man.

The letter had arrived with the lunchtime post while Bill and the girls were out of the house. At least Annie assumed it had come with the post. There was no stamp on the envelope so it might have been delivered by hand. Annie couldn't be sure.

When she saw it lying on the doormat she stared at it for a while before picking it up as though it was something fearful, a paper grenade that might cause untold damage. She rarely received letters and the sight of it reminded her of the one she'd received just over a year before; the one that had arrived a few days after the telegram that changed their lives. That momentous letter had been from Harold's commanding officer who'd expressed his deep sorrow. Some of the words he'd used weren't familiar to her as her reading wasn't good, and she hadn't been able to make out the signature. But she'd recognised the sentiment. Her son was a hero and she should be proud of him. Better a hero than a coward. Cowards were the lowest of the low and being the mother of a coward would have been the ultimate humiliation.

The news about Harold had left her stunned for a while but it hadn't dampened her spirits for long; especially once she'd convinced herself that the authorities had made a mistake. As far as she was aware, Harold's body had never been found. But rather than assuming he'd been blown to pieces by an enemy shell, Annie had become more and more convinced that he was still alive and she assured her sceptical husband that he was probably wandering, confused and with no identity, somewhere in France, having lost his memory. She reasoned that if he hadn't lost his memory, he'd have come home to Wenfield and his family and this assumption had kept hope alive, so much so that she kept his little bedroom, barely large enough to accommodate his single bed, as a shrine, untouched and ready for his return.

She'd stared at this latest letter for a while before opening it. Letters in the Dryden household usually heralded some official unpleasantness so she'd pulled out the sheet of paper with some trepidation and peered at the writing. Her eyes weren't too good these days, not close up, and she'd strained to see the words. The roughly printed letters swam in front of her eyes but eventually she managed to decipher the contents.

Dear Ma, it began. *I'm alive but I'm in trouble. Please meet me in the lane by Fuller's Farm at half past seven tonight. I'll explain everything when I see you. I don't want anyone in the village to see me and don't tell anyone, not even Pa and the girls. Please destroy this letter or bring it with you because if anyone finds it it'll be the worse for me. Please, Ma, do as I ask. I love you. Harold.*

Her heart lifted. She'd been right all along – her Harold was alive. But he said he was in trouble which could mean he'd taken the chance to desert when he'd gone missing. For a few moments her elation gave way to a crushing shame. How often had she chided others for their cowardice and now her own flesh and blood might be guilty of the same offence. But she'd soon banished the thought from her mind. Harold had probably been on some secret mission behind enemy lines. Most likely he knew something that still put him in danger. He was a hero. Of course he was.

Annie's main pleasure in life had always been the exchange of gossip and information, that thrilling feeling of knowing things others didn't. Even during the war there weren't many things that went on in Wenfield that Annie didn't know about, and her spirit was nourished by the secret sins of others. Even those of her so-called betters. But now she knew she had to keep her mouth shut and guard her new knowledge carefully. She wasn't going to share the contents of Harold's letter with anyone – not until the time was right.

When the girls and Bill returned home from work she had their dinner ready as usual, and as she bustled to and fro in the kitchen she couldn't help touching the letter carefully hidden in the pocket of her voluminous apron to assure herself that it was still safe. Everything had to be kept as normal as possible. Nobody must suspect a thing.

Just after Bill had gone out to the Cartwright Arms, Annie Dryden told her girls that she was going out to visit a neighbour and got ready, putting on her newest hat. And just after seven she hurried from the house, more nervous than she'd been on her wedding day.

This was the moment she'd been waiting for.

Chapter 5

Flora

Father hardly speaks at breakfast. He reads the newspaper as he's done every day for as long as I can remember, holding it high so I can't see his face. I remember Mother sitting in the chair opposite, her silence more eloquent than a thousand words of idle chatter. When Mother was here my parents rarely spoke to each other. Perhaps that's why she left us on that warm May night. Perhaps that's why she never came back.

A few weeks after Mother's departure, Edith moved in with us. Father required a housekeeper to run his household so, as Edith had been recently widowed and was in need of employment, she seemed the ideal choice.

I was eight at the time, a precocious child who took a great interest in the books in Father's surgery. My brother John was sent away to school, but since I was a girl, Father thought the presence of a governess was sufficient to meet my educational needs.

A succession of sad women, waif-thin and mildly shabby, had entered our old stone house near the centre of the village but none had stayed above a year. They were themselves daughters of professional men and clergy who had been unable to inveigle some man to the altar. I know them now for what they were and regret my rebelliousness and the trouble I no doubt gave them. For now I realise that they were my sisters in solitude. And since the war ended their ranks have been swelled by all those who lost potential husbands in the fields of France.

To return to Edith, it soon became clear that Father treated our new housekeeper a little differently from the governesses and the other servants. To my eight-year-old self Edith seemed old but now I know she can't have been more than twenty-two, the age I am now. She had freckles on her face and a generous mouth. And her fine hair, the colour of straw, was always escaping her hairpins, as though it sought freedom from the confines of conformity. She was beautiful, although I didn't recognise it at the time. But I am sure now that Father did.

Even though I was an observant child in those days, I knew little of the ways of grown-ups in matters of attraction. Now, however, I know why Father abandoned the worn tweed jacket he always wore at home once his visits to his patients were over and replaced it with a smarter new one he'd purchased during a rare visit to Buxton. He also started to use pomade on his hair and wax his moustache, something he'd never done in Mother's day.

His manner changed too when Edith was about. He became self-consciously polite, careful to say please and thank you and swift to compliment any meal she'd had a hand in. He smiled too much in those days. He'd never smiled when Mother was around.

Edith stayed with us for nine years then in 1915 she left us to do her bit for the war effort in a factory in nearby New Mills. I could tell Father missed her terribly but she can't have felt the same because she never returned to us after peace was declared. For a few weeks after she left us I used to see her in church on Sundays but she always avoided me and Father, sneaking out before us and vanishing through the graveyard as if she wished to escape an embarrassing situation. And then I heard she'd moved to New Mills to be nearer her work and I never saw her again. Sybil, our young maid of all work who happened to be one of Edith's many cousins, took over the housekeeper's duties when Edith left and these days Father rarely smiles.

Just as we're eating our breakfast we hear three heavy blows of our cast-iron door knocker. Knock, knock, knock. Like a portent of doom. Sybil hurries into the morning room, bobs a curtsey which looks like an afterthought, and tells Father that Sergeant Teague wishes to see him immediately on a matter of great importance. As none of Father's patients have yet arrived, she is instructed to make him take a seat in the waiting room.

In spite of the situation, Father doesn't hurry. He dissects his egg with studied concentration and sips at his tea. His large fingers are almost too big to fit into the dainty handle of his bone china cup and I find the way he hooks out his little finger in an attempt at refinement irksome. I'm curious about the sergeant's visit and my Father's lack of urgency irritates me. I know it's his way of exercising power; of demonstrating that he's at nobody's beck and call ... not even that of the local constabulary.

At last he drains his cup and stands up, dabbing his mouth with his napkin. He's hardly said a word to me over breakfast and he makes no comment as he leaves the room. But I can see that his body has tensed, as though he already fears what's coming.

Once he's out of the room I stand up and tiptoe out after him. The heavy mahogany door to the waiting room is shut. When I look around there's no sign of Sybil so I loiter by the door listening. Sergeant Teague is incapable of speaking *sotto voce* so every word he says is quite audible to anyone standing in the hallway.

'Wilf Fuller's dog found her lying next to a wall on the lane leading up to the farm first thing this morning. Will you come, Doctor?'

I can't make out my father's reply but the sergeant's presence suggests that this isn't a patient in need of emergency help. And when I hear Teague say the words 'it looks the same as the other one', I know immediately what he means.

I manage to hurry away before the two men emerge from the room. I don't want Father to know that I've been eavesdropping so I creep back to the morning room and when the door opens he finds me back in my chair as though I haven't moved in the meantime. Father's expression is hard to read so I tilt my head enquiringly. I need to find out what's going on.

'Is something wrong, Father?'

'Why should it be?'

'You look worried, that's all. Is it a patient?'

For a moment he doesn't answer. Then he looks me in the eye. 'It's nothing that need concern you, my dear.'

I feel anger rising like bile in my throat. During the war I nursed men who were hideously disfigured; men who were dying. I bandaged terrible wounds with cool efficiency. I assisted at operations and saw men's bowels exposed like sleeping snakes. I laid out the dead and mopped blood and vomit off floors. I saw men spewing blood; men whose limbs had been reduced to bleeding stumps; men whose faces had been burned away, reduced to nightmare masks. How can my father dismiss all my experience like this?

'What is it? Please tell me.'

'Very well,' he says with a sigh. 'If you must know it's a death. A violent death.'

'Let me come with you. I may be able to help.'

He smiles. The sort of smile one gives to an over-imaginative child. Indulgent and half-amused. 'From what the sergeant tells me this isn't a suitable sight for a lady.'

I rise from my seat. 'When I was nursing up at Tarnhey Court I saw things that would make most women faint with terror. Let me come. I can make notes for you. I can be useful.'

I can see doubt on my father's face and Sergeant Teague, standing behind him, looks horrified behind his whiskers, as though someone has suggested that a young child should watch a couple copulating. 'The doctor's right, miss. 'Tisn't a pretty sight.'

'I'll take the risk.'

I stride into the hall past the two men and take my coat off the stand. My hat is hanging there too and I press it onto my head and examine my reflection in the mirror, fumbling with the hat pin that would secure it to my hair, cursing my clumsy fingers. In the end I'm so hurried that my hat sits slightly askew. But I know that isn't important. I pick up my bag; inside is the notebook I always keep to jot down my observations. And my silver propelling pencil.

Father and Sergeant Teague are standing by the open front door and they exchange a glance when I join them. I half expect Father to protest but, to my relief, he's probably decided it isn't worth a battle.

Fuller's Farm is a fifteen-minute walk away and when we leave the house we ignore the stares of the women who stand in huddles outside the butcher's and the greengrocer's, their laden baskets hooked over their arms, and turn onto River Street where the stone cottages soon give way to open country. We eventually find ourselves on a narrow, overgrown lane where the ground is rutted from the passage of generations of farm carts. I know from experience that this lane is often muddy but it hasn't rained for a couple of days so my boots stay relatively unsullied as I walk slightly behind the men. My father's carrying the battered leather medical bag he's used ever since he qualified as a physician. How I long for some similar badge of office. But such things are denied me . . . for now.

Father never visited Tarnhey Court while the house was being used as a military hospital but once the war was over I made sure I told him what my duties entailed. The place was run by Matron with Dr Hexham and his assistant Dr Bone as medical officers in attendance, so there was no need for the services of the village doctor and he'd been left to care for his usual patients. I lived in at Tarnhey Court with the other nurses and I saw little of

Father – until he received the news about John and I was summoned home for a week to provide comfort in his hour of grief and need.

We walk on in silence until we reach our destination, a grim little procession, each dreading what they'll find at the end of the short journey.

Fuller's Farm stands in a hollow beneath a hill which rears up protectively behind the cluster of dark grey stone farm buildings, built so long ago they now form part of that undulating landscape of grey and drab green. Fat sheep graze lazily in the surrounding fields, oblivious to the drama being played out in the lane nearby. I can see a few early lambs too, wagging their tails as they feed. The only sound I can hear is bleating and birdsong. So normal.

And yet something is out of place in this bucolic scene. Next to the dry stone wall separating the lane from the field beyond, lies what I take at first to be a bundle of clothing. Then on closer inspection it becomes clear that it is – or rather was – a human being. A woman. Her skirts have been lifted over her head, concealing her face but revealing a chubby torso encased in a pair of greying bloomers and my first, inappropriate, thought is that she looks ridiculous, like something from a seaside postcard. But there is no humour in death.

A large uniformed constable is standing a couple of yards away, staring at the sheep in the field, doing his best to avoid looking at the thing on the ground.

'We had a quick peep at her face,' the constable says quietly when we arrive. 'But we put her clothing back how it was found.'

My father frowns. 'You should have made her decent. I don't know what you were thinking of.'

The sergeant looks sheepish. 'I just thought you'd like to see how . . .'

'I think public decency takes precedence. Hasn't the poor woman suffered enough indignity without lying there with her drawers on show for all to see?'

I take my notebook from my pocket and watch as Father squats down beside the corpse, as if he's about to take the pulse of some living patient. He hesitates before touching the dead, as if held back by some superstitious misgiving. But finally he reaches out his hand and gently lifts the woman's skirt away from her face, replacing it over her legs for decency's sake. I hear him gasp and I crane my neck to see over his shoulder.

I know her at once. Annie Dryden has been a bustling, plump presence for as long as I can remember. Always gossiping outside the butcher's shop with her cronies, a basket dangling from her arm. Annie had the reputation of being better than a telegraph as far as broadcasting unsavoury news was concerned. I've never particularly liked her with her sharp, currant eyes and her mean mouth.

My eyes are drawn to that mouth now. Stuffed between her thin lips is something white, as though in some fit of insatiable greed she's attempted to swallow something far too big to fit there. Most of the thing protrudes so far that it conceals her double chin. I recognise it for what it is.

'Looks like he's done it again, Doctor.' Sergeant Teague's words sound vaguely triumphant, as though he's enjoying the drama.

My father says nothing. He begins to examine what's left of Annie Dryden and I stand behind him, waiting for him to give his verdict.

'Do you have any idea when she died?' I ask.

Father looks round at me, surprised, as though he's forgotten I was there. 'I'd say she's been dead a while – probably sometime yesterday evening, although I can't be exact.'

'That fits,' says Sergeant Teague. 'Her husband reported her missing at midnight when he arrived back from the Cartwright Arms and found she wasn't home. She told her daughters she was going out to see a neighbour just after seven but none of the neighbours had seen her. Wilf Fuller found her first thing this morning when he came up here to check on his flock.'

'What about the cause of death?' I'm trying to sound efficient, professional. I want Father to forget I'm his daughter and think of me as a nurse ... someone worthy of his respect.

But he doesn't answer my question. Instead he looks up at Teague and asks him to arrange for the body to be taken to the Cottage Hospital. He needs to conduct a post mortem. As the sergeant hurries off to make the arrangements, I watch Father gently pull at the thing in Annie's mouth. At first it doesn't shift as though it's been thrust in there with some force, as if whoever did this terrible deed was anxious to stem the stream of poisonous gossip that habitually flowed from those torn and bloody lips. No, not torn. The slit of her mouth appears to have been enlarged neatly in order to insert the bird. With a sharp knife perhaps.

'It's a dove.'

'So it appears.' He holds the bird by one wing. The rear half of the creature is pristine white but the part that's been inside Annie's mouth is matted with saliva and crusted blood.

'It's exactly the same as Myrtle, isn't it?' I remark.

This time my father reacts to my words. He turns his head and glowers. 'Don't say a word about this to anyone will you, Flora. If this gets out it'll start a panic in the village and we don't want that.'

'But we can't ignore the fact that there have been two identical deaths. Surely people – women – should be warned to be on their guard?'

He gives me a curious look, as if I've said something vaguely outrageous. 'We don't want a lot of hysterical women flapping about, making a nuisance of themselves so it's best not to mention it. Besides, I expect the police will make an arrest very soon.'

'What makes you say that?'

'Well, it's obvious who's responsible for this atrocity.'

'Is it?' My heart begins to beat a little faster. I can guess what's coming.

Father straightens himself up. 'I blame myself for listening to his foolish mother. He should have been locked up in the asylum years ago. I should have insisted. If I'd followed my instincts, two women would still be alive.' He examines his pocket watch. 'We must go. I have arrangements to make.'

'I've taken some notes. Recorded my observations and sketched how her clothing was arranged. Do you want to . . . ?'

Father looks at me as if I were a backward child. 'I didn't want you to come in the first place and I doubt if your . . . ' He wrinkles his nose. 'Notes will serve any useful purpose.'

He stalks away and I have little choice but to follow.

Chapter 6

As we leave, Father walks so quickly that I find it hard to keep up with him and in the end I decide to abandon the effort. I know he'll soon be heading for the Cottage Hospital to make a detailed examination of Annie Dryden's corpse . . . just as he did with Myrtle's body. I'm familiar with the procedure. I know how he cut into Myrtle's flesh to discover the cause of her death. He didn't tell me his findings but I've heard it said in the village that she'd been stabbed.

There have been rumours that Myrtle had been violated before death. And, having seen how Annie was found, I can imagine how this particular piece of titillating speculation has spread. I could see no evidence that Annie's undergarments had been disturbed in any way but who was to say that the man hadn't been interrupted by something? Or that he'd intended to commit a terrible act and had been repulsed at the last moment by the sight of Annie's ample form?

Myrtle's youthful body might have proved more desirable, although I suspect desire has little to do with such violation. I suspect it's more an expression of power and control. Just as it must have been when Dr Bone cornered me for the first time at Tarnhey Court and tried to kiss me. I had argued with him earlier that day and as I pushed him away my instincts told me the kiss had no connection with any attraction he might have felt, rather it was his way of letting me know who was in charge. But it's a bold step from a stolen kiss to the abomination they say was unleashed on Myrtle Bligh's weak body.

These thoughts swirl around my head as I walk back to the village. Life and death. Power and lust. Grave matters for a day full of sunshine and shadows cast on the green hills round about by small clouds shifting over the rolling Derbyshire landscape like galloping beasts. As I reach the grey Market Square I'm so lost in my own thoughts that when I hear a voice bidding me good day, I jump with shock.

I recognise the voice at once and I turn to face the speaker. Roderick Cartwright is small for a man, barely a couple of inches taller than myself and many would call him handsome with his dark hair and warm brown eyes. He has his faults and weaknesses, I know that only too well, but there's always been a charm about him that few people can resist.

I say good day to him and when I continue walking he falls in beside me, speeding his pace to keep up.

'I hear they've found another body.'

'Who told you that?' I ask without turning my head to look at him. Roderick might be charming but he also possesses an air of entitlement endowed by his social position. Some people in the village call it arrogance but I think it's just the way he is.

'They're saying it's like the other one. That girl . . . what was her name?'

'Myrtle. Myrtle Bligh.'

'Of course, you knew her.'

I stop walking and turn to face him. 'Yes. I knew her. We were VADs together up at your house when it was a hospital.'

'I remember.' His lips twitch upwards but there's no warmth in his smile. 'Mama wasn't pleased about being thrown out of her home and sent to the dower house.'

'We all have to make sacrifices in time of war.'

Roderick suddenly looks embarrassed, as though he realises he's said the wrong thing.

'Of course. I didn't mean . . . We were glad to make the sacrifice really. Had to do our bit. Actually it was Papa who suggested it and . . . '

'I suppose it would have looked bad if Sir William hadn't suffered any inconvenience . . . especially when he spent so much time standing up in Parliament urging the young men of the country to go and fight.'

I know my words sound bitter but I don't really care. I've known Roderick Cartwright since the days when he was permitted to play with the children of the vicar and the local doctor. I know Roderick's weaknesses and his vanities and I know his fears. Sometimes I think I know more about him than I want to know.

'I joined up. Did my bit for King and country,' he says, suddenly defensive.

'Behind a desk in the War Office wasn't it?'

I see his cheeks redden. 'I wanted to go to the Front

but Father had other plans. I argued my case but . . . '

'But you're still alive, Roderick. Unlike all the men whose names are being carved on that new memorial.'

He looks like a dog who's just been kicked. 'That's hardly my fault.'

He's feeling sorry for himself, afraid that his cushy war will become common knowledge, and I'm suddenly filled with resentment as I think of all those who were sent to their deaths. 'When you came home in your officer's uniform everyone thought you'd been fighting in France so you were never called a coward. Not like some.'

'I wish I'd never told you about it now. I wish I'd let you go on thinking . . . '

'I promised not to tell anyone you spent the war in London and I always keep my word. Don't worry, your secret's safe.'

'But you still think I'm a coward. You still think I'm a lesser man than that brother of yours. It's not my fault, Flora. I'd have given anything to be on the front line.'

I'm starting to lose my patience with him. I've seen what the war did to all those young men. I know what it did to my dear brother John. If anybody wishes that on themselves, they're a fool.

He hesitates, as if he's about to make a confession. 'Besides, someone did find out – I don't know how, but they did. I had a hard time too.'

I ignore his words. And yet I feel a tiny twinge of pity for him. He needs no other accuser than himself. Having to live with the nagging feeling that somehow he's guilty of that most heinous of crimes, cowardice, is making Roderick Cartwright an unhappy man.

When we part he doesn't move from the pavement outside the post office and when I turn my head I see men pass him, touching their caps respectfully. If his secret becomes common knowledge that respect would vanish instantly and I have no wish to add to his misery. I realise I've been taking my own anger out on him and I regret it. Roderick Cartwright has always been a friend.

However, as I walk back to the house I hope he won't decide to follow me because I'm in no mood for company and certainly in no mood to sympathise with his insecurities. When I open the front door Sybil comes rushing into the hall and when I stand in front of the mirror to take off my hat I notice that her hands are shaking a little.

'Is something wrong, Sybil?' I ask. Gossip travels in this village like some dread disease with no respect for the feelings of those it infects.

'I've heard there's been another,' she says. I see terror on her pinched, pale face. But I decide to be open. Though brutal, the truth hurts less in the long run than deception.

'That's right. Another body's been found near Fuller's Farm.'

Sybil's hand travels to her mouth, clamping over it as if she's trying to stifle a scream. It reminds me of the dove that was stuffed into Annie's mouth. Did that serve to stifle something too? A lie perhaps? Or a secret the killer doesn't want to be brought into the light?

'Do you know who . . . ?'

'Annie Dryden.'

Sybil stands there gaping at me for a moment. As if Annie is the last person she'd imagined as the victim. 'How did she . . . ?'

34

Before I can answer I hear the kitchen door bell jangle in the distance. Once. Twice. Three times. The visitor sounds impatient. The kitchen door is Sybil's domain and she hurries to answer it. I pick up my hat from the table where I've discarded it and place it on the hall stand before entering Father's surgery, thinking the visitor is most likely one of the many tradesmen who turn up regularly at the house ... though there aren't as many as there were before the war. Butchers, bakers and greengrocers were all sent to fight and many haven't returned.

I'm grateful that the visitor has relieved me of the burden of answering Sybil's questions. I know she'd have kept probing until I revealed more details and I find the subject of Annie's murder distasteful. I walk up to Father's bookcase and select a book off the top shelf. Anatomy. I've always had an interest in anatomy. I carry the book into the drawing room and sit down but as soon as I begin to study the section on the workings of the heart, Sybil bursts into the room, wringing the white cloth of her apron in her agitated fingers like some wronged woman in a play. I ask her what's wrong.

'It's Jack, miss. My cousin, Jack.'

I've almost forgotten that Jack Blemthwaite is Sybil's cousin. But many of the people in the village are related in one way or another so it's often hard to keep track. 'What about him?'

'They've arrested him.'

'What for?' I ask the question even though I think I know the answer.

'They're saying he killed Myrtle ... and Annie. They've taken him to the police station.'

'Perhaps they're just questioning him, in case he saw something.' I know this probably isn't true but I feel obliged to say something comforting to put Sybil's unquiet mind at rest.

She shakes her head. 'No, miss. That was my mother at the door. She says he's definitely been arrested. *On suspicion.*' She pronounces the last two words as if they belong to some strange foreign phrase she's learned by rote.

'I'm so sorry, Sybil.' It's the only thing I can think of to say.

Chapter 7

I hear no more news until the evening. Father has returned from the Cottage Hospital, where he'd performed the post mortem on Annie's body, grim-faced and unwilling to discuss the matter. His evening surgery is better attended than usual and I can't help wondering whether the patients have come in the hope of a dose of gossip rather than a cure for their ills. Once surgery's finished he returns to the drawing room to find me reading a novel. I replaced the anatomy book before his return because I knew he'd be annoyed if he found me reading it and I'm in no mood for an argument over something so trivial. I would rather choose my battles.

We don't talk, our silence broken only by the hiss of the gas lights, an innovation of which my mother had once been so proud. The Cartwrights installed electricity up at Tarnhey Court just before the war and when I worked there I came to appreciate its benefits. But Father wouldn't hear of squandering money on such an extravagant luxury.

Shortly after the grandfather clock in the corner of the room strikes nine I hear a knock on the front door: it seems it's a day for visitors. I hear Sybil rush to answer followed by the mumble of a man's voice.

Sybil enters the drawing room after a perfunctory knock and bobs a half-hearted curtsey. 'There's Constable Wren to see you, Doctor.'

The constable's standing behind her, hovering on the threshold. I know Constable Wren by sight. For one named after the smallest bird in the British Isles it's always seemed incongruous to me that he's such a large man. Once Sybil's finished her introduction he steps forward, helmet respectfully in hand. His eyes are on Father and he probably hasn't registered my presence.

'I'm sorry to bother you, Doctor, but the sergeant says could you come to the station. Jack Blemthwaite's hurt himself.'

I watch Sybil's features rearrange themselves into a mask of concern. 'How bad is he?' she says. 'Only he's my cousin and . . . ' She takes a step back, as though she suddenly regrets her boldness. But I can't blame her. If I'd have been in her shoes I'd have wanted to know if my own cousin was badly hurt.

Wren turns to her and I see pity in his eyes. And compassion. I like him for it. 'He's cut himself bad and the sergeant reckons the doctor here should take a look at him.'

'It's a shame Blemthwaite didn't show such consideration for those women he killed,' my father mutters in a voice so low that I don't think Wren or Sybil can hear. At least I hope they can't.

While Father heads for his surgery to fetch his bag, I make for the hall and put on my coat and hat. I know it might cause another disagreement with Father but I'm determined to go with him. I want to see Jack Blemthwaite for myself and make sure he's all right. I don't have to ask Father why he's so convinced of Jack's guilt: he's always had an almost naive faith in the ability of the police to apprehend the right man. I myself can't share his certainties.

As it turns out, Father makes no effort to protest, almost as though he's accepted the fact that I will accompany him on the visit, just as I had when he was called to Annie's body. I'm hopeful that it's a step towards him acknowledging my experience as a nurse at last. Maybe a step towards him allowing me to follow my calling. But small steps do not make a whole journey.

The daylight's fading fast and the windows of Wenfield are aglow with the light from candles and oil lamps. In the village electricity is unknown, a force as magic and mysterious as the philosopher's stone. Few have drawn their curtains in the dusk and I can see inside the cottages. They are sparsely furnished with cheap china, won at fairs or handed down by relatives, standing in pride of place on mantelpieces, adding a spark of colour to the drab interiors. Even though they are built of the same solid grey stone, these dwellings seem so different from my own comfortable house with its sash windows either side of the gleaming front door and its servants' rooms in the upper storey. And more different still is Tarnhey Court, a fine Georgian pile with a pillared portico and ten bedrooms. But my memories of the Court aren't of luxury and grandeur; only blood, pain and suffering.

I walk beside Wren past the Cartwright Arms, a dingy establishment on the corner of the High Street and River Street with small windows and a painted sign hanging above the open front door. The pub's inner door is etched glass and as we pass I can make out the dark shapes of men drinking at the bar inside. There are two pubs in Wenfield – the Cartwright Arms and the Black Horse and the latter is considerably more respectable and provides rooms for travellers.

I notice Wren's eyes are drawn to one of the cottages we pass. It is separated from the Cartwright Arms by a narrow alleyway and stands a few doors away from the stone bridge that spans the river. I know the cottage that's caught Wren's attention belongs to the Dryden family and I see him bow his head respectfully for a second as we draw level with the door.

The thin curtains in the front parlour are closed across and light glows dimly through the cloth. Annie Dryden's husband, a burly, monosyllabic man, is bound to be in there with his three thin daughters – each indistinguishable from her sisters – going through the rituals of mourning; unable to take in the enormity of what has happened to his domineering wife.

It is dark by the time we reach the police station and the blue lamp outside has been lit, a reassuring reminder that the guardians of law and order are within, ready to protect the law-abiding and punish offenders.

But somehow I can't see Jack Blemthwaite as an offender. I have known him since childhood and on several occasions I have protected him from the jeers of bullies who can only display their strength by tormenting the weak. Even now I feel responsible for Jack Blemthwaite. Especially now.

Constable Wren leads the way into the building and greets the sergeant stationed behind the dark wood counter like an old friend. Doctor Winsmore has come to attend to the prisoner, he says, and a meaningful glance passes between the two men. Jack Blemthwaite has obviously been judged guilty even before his trial. The revelation that even a reasonable and sympathetic man like Wren is going along with it makes my heart sink.

We are led through a warren of corridors until we come to a wide flight of stone steps, leading downward to the bowels of the building. Wren walks slightly ahead of us in silence and when we arrive at an iron grille, he greets a tall grizzle-haired man standing on the other side with a bunch of keys dangling from his belt.

The barred door is unlocked and when it clangs shut behind us after we've passed through, I experience a moment of panic. This is what being a prisoner is like. No air. No light. No freedom. I feel slightly sick.

In spite of his injury, Jack Blemthwaite is still in his cell. He's lying on a hard, grubby mattress, sobs shaking his body. I can see his face is stained with dirt and tears and there is blood on his shirt. I can smell his sweat and something worse – the chamber pot in the corner of the tiny room is full to the brim. I turn to the officer on duty and ask if he can empty it. He looks as if he is about to argue but he does the job without a word. But as he passes the prisoner I see a look of sheer contempt on his face. Another member of the self-appointed jury that's found Jack guilty without the benefit of a trial.

My father opens his bag, careful not to meet Jack's gaze. Since our arrival, the prisoner has propped himself up into a sitting position and wiped his face with his sleeve. He suddenly looks hopeful, as if he thinks we've come to rescue him. He wipes his face again and I can see a line of mucus shining like a snail trail on the rough cloth of his shirt sleeve.

As my father searches in his bag, I step forward.

'How are you, Jack?'

He gazes up at me. He looks confused. Mystified. As though he has no idea what he's doing there. Jack is large and he looks strong and if his mind hadn't been damaged, he would have been considered handsome. But he's a child trapped inside a man's body and, although some children are capable of cruelty, I do not think Jack is one of them. His innocent and capricious mind hasn't developed much beyond the age of six. And surely a child isn't capable of doing what was done to Myrtle Bligh and Annie Dryden. Jack has always been gentle. He never even fought back against his tormentors.

'My hand hurts.' He holds up his wounded hand. Nobody has attempted to clean up the deep gash which runs from thumb to wrist. It must have bled badly and even though the blood has crusted I can still smell it. I know the scent of blood only too well.

'When can I go home?'

Jack sounds like a frightened little boy – a little boy with a man's deep voice. When I don't answer he meekly allows me to take his hand and examine the wound. I ask him how he did it and I see him glance at the constable who's standing in the doorway, having completed the unsavoury task of emptying the chamber pot.

'It was an accident. I fell over,' Jack says in a mechanical voice, as if his explanation has been rehearsed.

It is then my father takes over, cleaning and dressing the wound with cool professionalism while I pass him the necessary equipment. The opportunity for questions has passed but I can still give Jack an encouraging smile, just to keep his spirits up.

My father closes his bag, a signal to leave. But as we reach the door, Jack speaks again.

'I didn't do anything to Annie Dryden. They say I did but I didn't. Lady Cartwright will tell you. She asked me to clean out the dovecote and she came to see how I was getting on. I was there till it was dark then I went home. I told the truth but nobody believes me.'

I turn to the constable. 'What's the evidence against him?' I ask.

At first he looks as if he's about to tell me to mind my own business but then he relents. 'He was seen hanging about when Myrtle Bligh was murdered and now he's come up with this cock and bull story about Her Ladyship . . . as if she'd have anything to do with the likes of him. Don't you be taken in, miss. He's crafty, that one.'

'Has anybody spoken to Lady Cartwright?'

I see the man's face turn red. 'We didn't want to bother her, miss.'

'I'm sure Her Ladyship would rather be bothered than see an innocent man go to the gallows.'

I'll never forget the resentful expression on the man's face. And if he won't speak to Lady Cartwright, I will.

Chapter 8

I curb my impulse to visit Tarnhey Court that evening. My father points out that it's far too late to turn up unbidden on the Cartwrights' magnificent doorstep and after a few moments' consideration, I have to admit he's right. I need to win Her Ladyship over to my side. I have to persuade her that she can help me to avoid a terrible injustice.

However, I've known Hannah Cartwright since I was a young child and I'm not altogether confident of success. She's always seemed to me to be an ethereal creature with the distant, otherworldly manner of one who lives on another, higher plane of existence and a fondness for clothing herself in floating white. Her son, Roderick, has always spoken of his mama as if she is some revered mystic and there have been times when I've wondered whether she's perhaps a little simple. As for the kindness of her heart, I can't be sure.

When I arrive at Tarnhey Court the next morning I recognise the maid who answers the door as Sarah Cookham from Station Street. When war broke out she must have only been fourteen, too young to aid the war effort, and I hadn't realised that she now works for the Cartwrights. Last time I saw Sarah she was with her mother in the square, demonstrating against cowardice and handing out white feathers to any man suspected of not doing his bit. Now she has a slightly slovenly look and there's a stain on her starched white apron. Before the war the Cartwrights' staff had always been immaculately presented.

When I ask to see Her Ladyship she takes my name and shows me into the hall, leaving me standing while she disappears through a door I know leads into what the Cartwrights call the breakfast room. In my time as a VAD we used it for the storage of equipment and for the winding of bandages – yards of snow-white cloth that would soon turn red with blood. It had been inside that room that Dr Bone had made his first advances to me and the sight of the door revives the memory afresh. Dr Bone has returned to his practice and I still see him sometimes when I venture into New Mills or when he visits the Cottage Hospital here in Wenfield, which I know he does three times a week: Father says he comes over in the afternoon and leaves around eight just before the nurses settle their patients for the night. Whenever I see him nowadays he looks away, doing his best to ignore me. I take some pleasure in his embarrassment and hope it is brought on by shame.

As I wait, I look around the hall. During the Court's life as a hospital, it was painted a military grey but now it's powder blue and the sweeping mahogany staircase gleams with polish. When I lived there, all the furnishings had been removed, giving the place a spartan feel, but now it's packed with hall chairs, side tables, mirrors and glossy aspidistras in china jardinières. The Cartwrights have made a great effort to expunge all evidence of war and suffering from their home. I don't suppose I can blame them.

It seems an age before Sarah returns, her snub nose in the air. 'Her Ladyship will see you now,' she says as though she's doing me a great favour.

I follow her through the breakfast room into another corridor then she knocks on another door – the door to the drawing room. When I'm shown into Lady Cartwright's presence, Sarah stares impertinently as I sweep past her then she slams the door behind me.

I haven't seen Lady Cartwright for over a year, except at a distance in church. Each Sunday she arrives with the rest of her family immediately before the service is due to start. When everybody else is already sitting in their pews the Cartwrights process up the aisle, led by the church warden with his staff of office, and take their places at the front, acknowledging no one and leaving the church first once the proceedings are over.

Since the earliest days of my childhood, this ritual never changed and nobody in the village ever dared to challenge it until one Sunday in 1917 when the elder Bryce boy, home on leave from France, arrived at church late and found himself mingling with the Cartwrights' procession. He brazened it out, grinning at his sweetheart as he edged past Sir William and shot into one of the central pews, and the following week a number of the

46

younger people left before the Cartwrights could make their stately egress, barging their way out with a swift nod to the astonished vicar. From then on the family from Tarnhey Court have looked a little less sure of themselves at morning service. It's a subtle change, barely discernible, but I've noticed it.

I walk into the room to find Her Ladyship sitting on a chaise longue next to the tall bay window. She's a small woman whose dark wavy hair is streaked with grey. I have always thought her face resembled a skull with its large forehead and sunken grey eyes. Even in the first bloom of youth I don't think she's ever been a beauty.

When I was last in that room, it was a ward and the large windows provided our patients with cheering brightness. In my mind I can still see them there, the beds in rows, each with its little cupboard beside it for the boys' belongings. We always called them the boys: perhaps this helped to foster our sisterly – or occasionally motherly – feelings towards them. A lot of them seemed so young.

Now the room has changed. The narrow beds have long been banished, probably to some unvisited attic, and replaced with the family's original furniture. But the marble fireplace is still there ... and the yellow floral wallpaper that now looks a little shabby.

Her Ladyship looks up with an uncertain half smile of recognition, as though she isn't sure whether she's pleased to see me.

'Miss Winsmore,' she says. Her voice is high pitched and slightly lisping, like a young girl's. 'Roderick said he met you in the village. I trust you are well?'

'Very well, thank you, my lady.'

'And your father?'

'He's well, thank you.'

I wonder how long it will be before I can abandon the polite small talk and introduce the subject of Jack Blemthwaite. If I want the woman's co-operation and sympathy, it will take tact.

'I suppose there have been a lot of changes since you were last here.'

'There have indeed, my lady.'

'So noble to make such sacrifices for our poor wounded boys,' she mutters, gazing out of the window so I can't be sure whether or not her words were addressed to me. She has a distant look in her eyes, as if she's seeing the 'poor wounded boys' in her mind's eye ... although I suspect her image of them will be an idealised one. She has never been much of a one for reality.

'I hear the war memorial is ready. I've been asked to perform the official unveiling.'

'Good,' I say.

'I expect they asked me because of Roderick's service. The mother of a war hero,' she adds proudly.

I say nothing.

'To what do I owe the pleasure of your visit?'

I'm still standing there, not having been invited to sit nor offered any sort of refreshment. Not that I particularly want any but it would have been good to be asked.

'I'm rather worried about Jack Blemthwaite, my lady. You know Jack?'

'Poor Jack,' she says, waving her hand dismissively. 'Of course. His poor mother.'

'My lady, you've heard about Myrtle Bligh?'

I see her body shudder. She's wearing a loose yellow

silk dress that almost matches the wallpaper and it quivers with her like a jelly. 'Too horrible. To think there's a madman about. And after all we've suffered . . . '

'Another woman from the village has been found in similar circumstances. Her name was Annie Dryden?'

Her eyes widen in alarm. 'I hadn't heard.'

Her shock is clearly genuine but I feel I have no choice but to carry on. 'The police have arrested Jack Blemthwaite.'

Her hand flutters to her chest. 'Surely not. Jack's a gentle soul. A child.'

This is better. 'I know. And I think you may be able to help him. Annie Dryden was killed the day before yesterday, sometime in the evening. Jack says he was here until dark cleaning out the dovecote at your request. Is he telling the truth?'

She thinks for a few moments, and the effort of remembering makes her frown. 'Yes. He was here. I saw him when he first arrived. It was just after luncheon; around half past two. He came to the front door and asked to see me and I granted his request as a kindness. Of course it should have been a matter for the gardener but . . . '

I understand. The Cartwrights' gardeners, all six of them, went off to war and never came back. Now an old man from the village 'obliges' three times a week helped out occasionally by a young farmer's son who was sent back from the fighting because of his chronic asthma. No wonder the place is looking overgrown.

'What time did Jack leave?'

'He was definitely there when I took my walk in the garden before dinner just before seven. I decided to see how he was getting on. It was a fine evening and my

49

husband was out on constituency business of some sort so I was alone, you see.'

I wonder if this was an admission of loneliness. That she'd sought out company . . . any company. Even that of Jack Blemthwaite.

'He had a lantern but I told him to go as soon as the light faded. It was rather dirty in the dovecote and Jack seemed to be getting on with the job so I only stayed a couple of minutes. I told him to see Roderick when he'd finished to receive his payment. I was expecting Roderick back for dinner, you see.' A faraway look appears in her eyes. 'In the old days before the war one of the menservants would have attended to the matter, of course.'

'And did Roderick pay him?'

'You'll have to ask Roderick. He's out at the moment visiting one of the tenant farmers. I'm not sure what time he'll be back.'

'Thank you. If we can clear Jack's name . . .'

'Indeed.' She turned her head away and I knew I was being dismissed. It is said that Her Ladyship has been delicate since Roderick's birth and tires easily. From my nursing experience, I suspect that she only displays weakness when it suits her purposes.

As soon as I've thanked her for her time, she rings the dainty little bell that stands on the table beside the chaise longue and Sarah the maid appears. As she shows me out I ask her if she was aware of Jack Blemthwaite's visit but her answer seems guarded, with just a touch of insolence. Her Ladyship receives a lot of visitors and she can't remember them all. When I thank her for her help, I don't think she registers the irony in my words.

I remind her that I've often seen her in the village and

ask politely after her family. She says they're well and as I watch her expression, I see a hint of petulance there – as though she thinks she's too good for her present position. Her pretty, almost feline features are sharp . . . as is her tongue. I've always thought her an intelligent girl, and observant. She is the type of girl who'll go far in life, given the chance.

I'm halfway down the drive when an idea makes me retrace my steps. I can see the top of the dovecote peeping above the laurels at the side of the drive and I branch off down the path towards the walled garden. The gravel that would have crunched satisfyingly underfoot before the war is now thin and dotted with weeds. If it isn't attended to, the weeds will take over eventually and smother it like the road to Sleeping Beauty's castle. Nobody cares much about paths any more.

The dovecote in the corner of the garden is constructed in stone to match the house; a small round building with an old wooden door in the side and rows of holes above topped by a pretty glazed lantern roof. I can see white doves flitting to and fro, squeezing themselves deftly into the spaces.

I take a deep breath and open the door. The interior smells of bird droppings and as the odour hits my senses, the memory of my pain and humiliation in that place flashes through my brain like lightning. I hesitate then I force myself to step inside, my heart pounding. I can hear the soft coo of the feathered inhabitants who huddle on ledges around the walls and the lantern roof provides light, for which I'm grateful. I can tell that the interior has been cleaned out recently. I'm sure that Jack's incapable of thinking up such a lie and the state of the building seems to confirm his story. Now I have to persuade the police to share my view.

With some relief I leave the dovecote, closing the door carefully behind me, and when I reach the drive again I see Roderick walking towards me. He's dressed in a tweed suit – suitable attire for a visit to a tenant farmer – and he's carrying a jaunty walking cane. When he sees me he doffs his cap and smiles. This is my chance to confirm Jack's alibi once and for all.

'I've just been visiting your mama,' I say.

'I'm sure she was glad to see you,' he says, the smile still on his lips. 'Father went down to London first thing this morning and she wants for company when he's not here.'

'I'm afraid it wasn't a social call. You've heard about Jack Blemthwaite?'

The smile vanishes. 'I heard someone say he's been arrested. Hopefully this will be the end of the matter.'

'Your mother says he was here the evening Annie Dryden was killed. She says he was cleaning out the dovecote.'

'Someone had to do it. The place was in a terrible state and our gardener's on his own so he hasn't had time.' He pauses. 'When exactly was she killed?'

'The day before yesterday. Tuesday evening. She left her home just after seven. Jack was here then, wasn't he? Your mother says she saw him at seven and you saw him later, didn't you? He came to you to be paid?'

'Er . . . yes. I saw him when I got back just after eight. It was dark by then and I was surprised he'd stayed so long. I parked the car at the stables and when I passed the dovecote on my way back to the house he told me that Mama said I'd pay him. I handed over the cash and he left. But he'd been alone before that so I suppose he could have slipped out any time. Where did you say Annie Dryden was found?'

'I didn't. But she was in the lane by Fuller's Farm.'

'That's at least fifteen minutes' walk from here.' There is a short silence as he does his calculations. 'I'm sorry, Flora, but I can't put my hand on the Bible and swear he didn't sneak off and kill her between the time Mama says she spoke to him and when I paid him, and neither can Mama. You do understand?' He looks at me appealingly, reminding me of a dog that we used to own in the days before my mother left.

'Of course. I don't expect you to lie. It's just that I don't see Jack as a murderer. Do you really think he's capable of covering up the fact that he's committed a murder and using you and your mother as an alibi?'

'No, I don't. But I can't lie – I can only tell the police what I know.'

'I think he's being made a scapegoat. People have always tormented him because he's different. If you can't find someone to blame, Jack Blemthwaite'll do.'

'You might well be right,' he says reasonably. 'But there's really nothing I can do about it. I'm not going to perjure myself to protect him. If he is guilty and there's another death . . . ' He thinks for a moment. 'I really can't think of any way to prove he didn't do it . . . unless the killer strikes again while he's safe in custody.'

I know it's no use. And part of me realises that Roderick is right. I have done my best but I can't stop thinking of Jack Blemthwaite in that small, stinking cell, confused as a child without its mother. Hurt and puzzled as I was when my own mother left.

Chapter 9

Jack Blemthwaite has been committed for trial at the Assizes and he's been taken from the police station to be imprisoned in Derby until he appears in court. The very thought of his ordeal horrifies me. If the worst happens, Jack will hang by the neck until he's dead, but I'll do everything in my power to prevent it.

His mother's fled the village to stay with her brother in Stockport. I don't blame her because life would have been unbearable for her if she'd stayed. The jeering. Those whispers. The guilt by association. I confess there have been occasions when I've felt like weeping for her when I'm alone in my room but I haven't shared my thoughts with Father who is as sure of Jack's guilt as the rest of the village. Only Roderick Cartwright seems to share my doubts and I haven't seen him since the day we met up at Tarnhey Court.

The weeks pass and, as I venture into the village, I can

sense an easing in the atmosphere, like a slow relaxation after some terrible ordeal. As far as everyone's concerned, the killer of Myrtle Bligh and Annie Dryden is behind bars and poses no more danger to the women of Wenfield. But I can't share their certainty.

As the days lengthen it no longer seems like the season for death. More lambs are born in the farms round about and follow their devoted woolly mothers around the sloping fields. Buds swell on the trees and as the air turns warmer, the Earth becomes greener and new life appears everywhere.

I wonder whether Myrtle and Annie will soon be forgotten. Few people have spoken of them since Annie's solemn funeral when the church was packed with mourners who, I'm sure, hadn't particularly liked her in life. There is something strange about the funeral of someone who's died in such a way – Myrtle's had been the same. People speak in code, skirting round the brutality. At least with the victims of war, the painful truth can be enveloped in words of glory and courage. There was no glory in the way Annie Dryden died.

A week after Annie's burial, the new war memorial was unveiled at the far end of the High Street. A large crowd turned out for the ceremony and it was raining, which seemed appropriate somehow. Lady Cartwright and the vicar conducted their duties, protected by large black umbrellas and everybody sang heartily in spite of the weather. "Oh God Our Help in Ages Past" and "Abide with Me". During the interminable prayers, my eyes were drawn to the names. And one name especially.

John Winsmore. Lieutenant. We will remember them.

At least those words are true. I will never forget my

elder brother, John. His cheery face will always be in my memory. His unruly curls and warm brown eyes. His slightly crooked smile. His gently teasing voice; his laughter. Before the poison of war put an end to all that and the laughter stopped for ever. I stood at the edge of the crowd, the tears streaming down my cheeks mingling with the rain drops falling from the leaden sky as if heaven itself was weeping.

My big brother John made my childhood bearable after Mother left. I looked forward to him coming home in the school holidays like a prisoner looks forward to release. He encouraged my reading and my interest in science as well. Is it sinful to wish that Father had been taken by the war in place of my brother? Probably. I think I've probably committed a lot of sins since the war broke out and shattered the certainties of my life.

During the service I stood by Father's side, glancing at him every now and then. I saw him standing ramrod straight with no sign of tears blurring his eyes. But men don't show their feelings. And when they do, they are mocked and called cowards. I remember men I nursed at Tarnhey Court crying; sobbing for their mothers and their sweethearts. But there had been no mockery there. Only hands held and comforting words.

As I was walking home with Father, the Cartwrights' motor car swept past us, splashing my skirt as the tyres plunged through a puddle at the side of the road. I could see a figure wearing a peaked cap at the wheel and, for a split second, I thought it was a soldier. Then I remembered someone telling me that the Cartwrights had recently managed to acquire a chauffeur; a man injured at Ypres. I turned my head to peer into the car window and, as the man drove by, his eyes fixed on the road ahead, I thought his face seemed familiar but I couldn't place it. Perhaps it will come to me when I'm thinking of something else. It often works like that.

Roderick Cartwright was sitting with his parents in the back of the car. They looked like royalty gliding past in their shiny black Rolls-Royce. I suppose they are the nearest thing we have to royalty here in Wenfield. But, unlike the Royal Family, the Cartwrights made no acknowledgement of the crowd and there were no loyal cheers; only morose stares as the car drove away towards Tarnhey Court. In the whole history of the village, no monarch has ever deigned to visit us. We are too insignificant. The tide of history washes over us, eroding and changing our community with no thought to the lives of its people. It seems that we have no real influence over anything.

Things have been looking up of late. Since I accompanied Father to the scene of Annie Dryden's terrible end, he allows me to do a little more in the surgery. Grudgingly at first, then with more acceptance, if not gratitude. Many young doctors – like men in all other professions – died in conflict and there seems little prospect of him acquiring another medical man to help him in the practice in the near future. A helping hand – even my own helping hand – is often needed, even though I know it's not entirely welcome.

I kept the uniform I wore at Tarnhey Court – the blue cotton dress, the starched white apron with the red cross at the centre of the bodice and the white cap that covers my unruly hair – and I did wonder whether I should wear it while I'm bandaging wounds and delivering injections. But Father wouldn't allow it. Sometimes I go to the attic and take my uniform from the trunk where I placed it when Tarnhey Court shut its doors to the wounded. I take it down to my room and lay it on the bed. As I feel the cool cotton fabric and hold it to my face to smell that familiar scent of cleanliness, I shut my eyes and see the wards and the faces of the boys swathed in the white bandages which hide the horror of burned and mangled flesh beneath.

At times I sit on my bed and cry for them. Cry for those who died there at Tarnhey Court and for those who managed to survive, their future blighted by pain and disfigurement. Then I slip off my skirt and blouse and try on the dress. Blue was always my favourite colour in more innocent days but now I can't help associating it with suffering. The men wore blue uniforms in the hospital – hospital blues they called them ... amongst other things. I thought those ill-fitting uniforms made them look more like prisoners than the heroes they were.

Today I summon the courage to keep the dress on to go downstairs to breakfast and Father hardly seems to notice. To him it's just a plain blue dress. Only when I don the apron and the white cap he'll realise that I'm assuming the role of nurse.

When the time comes for surgery to begin I go upstairs to complete the outfit and when I come down, I see horror on his face. But I have prepared my argument. The patients will trust me more if I'm wearing the uniform of my chosen profession. As I expect, he's swift to point out that I hold no formal qualifications, which I take as an opportunity to argue my case again. Let me go and train in a proper hospital. Stockport isn't far away, or

I could go to Manchester, or even Liverpool, which I hear has a very fine training school. Let me gain my qualifications. My pleas are dismissed but I think I'm making progress. The more water pours over a rock, the more that rock is worn away and so I hope it will be with my father's stubborn opinion.

Yet in spite of his initial reaction, he allows me to help, calling the patients into the Presence and administering simple first aid. I consider this a triumph. There is much further to go before I reach my goal but I intend to persist.

After surgery finishes for the evening I feel tired. I step out of my uniform, folding it neatly away, and change for dinner. Then, after Father and I have finished dining on Sybil's mutton stew, I experience a sudden urge to get out of the house and walk in the fresh air. I see the look of panic on Father's face as he follows me into the hall and watches me as I put on my coat and hat. In an hour it will be dark but I promise to be home before then.

'Be careful, Flora,' he says with a gentleness that I've not heard in his voice since my mother left us all those years ago.

'Why? What harm can come to me?'

'Don't forget what happened to Myrtle Bligh and Annie Dryden.'

So that was it. In spite of everything he's said, he too has his doubts about Jack Blemthwaite's guilt. He fears the real killer is still out there, hungry for another victim.

'You don't think Jack's guilty then?'

Father doesn't reply to my challenge. But I see his cheeks turn red behind his whiskers. It will take courage for him to voice his doubts against the consensus of village and police opinion but I'm determined to ensure that he'll find it in him to prevent a terrible miscarriage of justice.

I must do everything in my power to make sure Jack Blemthwaite doesn't hang.

Chapter 10

Sarah

At first Sarah Cookham had wondered whether working at Tarnhey Court was her best option. These days lots of the girls were working at the mill or the factories round about but she'd never really fancied that sort of thing. As soon as she was old enough she'd done a short stint in a munitions factory during the war and she'd hated it.

At least Tarnhey Court was surrounded by hills and fields and the only sound she could hear there was birdsong and the soft cooing of doves; better than the deafening racket of machinery in the mills. She'd heard that before the war being in service had been akin to slavery but these days it wasn't so bad. With so many other choices available, staff were hard to come by now. Besides, she had an important ally in the house.

Letters for the servants were delivered to the back door, the front door being reserved for the Cartwrights' post – including important correspondence from the

House of Commons and invitations to social events. Each day Sarah checked the racks in the servants' hall to see if anything had arrived for her. In spite of living at the other end of the village, her mother was a prolific writer, conveying all the latest news and gossip even though Sarah went home at least once a week. She received other letters too, ones she generally ignored but was secretly pleased to receive. The fact that one of the young men who'd harboured ambitions to be her sweetheart in the months before she began work at Tarnhey Court still thought of her and made the effort to write was gratifying. Who knew how useful a devoted follower might be in the future ... especially now things had changed.

For a couple of months now she'd been feeling sick in the mornings and her usual monthly bleeding had ceased. She knew what those signs meant and she had plans to use the situation to her advantage. If she kept her head, her future could be bright. Money solved a lot of problems and she'd make sure she got her fair share. It was only right after all. For the first time in her life she knew she was in a position to wield real power. And she liked the feeling. She knew secrets: important secrets. And she intended to use those secrets to her advantage.

She was pleased that there was no sign of the housekeeper when she reached the servants' hall after finishing her morning duties. She looked in the letter rack and discovered that there were two for her today. Her mother had written as usual to tell her that her sister wasn't feeling well. She was worried and might call Dr Winsmore. It would cost money but it was worth taking the precaution, especially with all this influenza about.

Her address on the second envelope had been neatly

printed in black ink. Miss Sarah Cookham, Tarnhey Court, Wenfield, Derbyshire. She slit it open with her fingers and began to read. The letter inside was printed too so that she couldn't recognise the handwriting. She read the words.

Dearest Sarah. I'm alive. Meet me in Pooley Woods at eight o'clock tonight but don't tell anyone. I'm in trouble and I need your help. Destroy this letter or bring it with you because there'll be trouble if anyone finds it. Please don't tell anyone. Your loving brother, Peter.

She stared at the note for a while, stunned. Peter was dead. Peter was lying beneath the ground in France. But what if he'd swapped his identification with someone else and managed to escape? Anything was possible.

She could hear footsteps. The housekeeper was coming. She stuffed the letter into her pocket and hurried back to the still room. Her Ladyship would be wanting tea.

Chapter 11

Flora

The law grinds slowly forward and Jack Blemthwaite's trial still seems an age away. When I lie in my bed at night I think of poor, innocent, puzzled Jack in his prison cell. In my imagination I see it as a dungeon, the stone walls dripping damp and the air stale and so cold that his breath hangs in trails of white mist even though the weather has been warmer of late.

And then when I sleep, the dreams come; the dreams that began when I was working at Tarnhey Court. They make me wake with a start, bathed in perspiration. I hate the dreams. I've even come to fear them.

As there have been no more outrages, the village is more and more convinced of Jack's guilt and, as more weeks have passed, I fear Father has begun to share the general opinion once more. But I do not waver. I know Jack Blemthwaite is no killer.

It is Wednesday and, as it appears the good folk of

Wenfield have been deserted by their usual ailments, Father's surgery has finished early. Even so, he looks weary, just as he looked after he received the news of my brother's death.

While I busy myself with household matters, giving Sybil her instructions for our evening meal, Father vanishes into his surgery and I do not see him again until the telephone in the hall rings. Knowing that Sybil is still a little wary of the instrument, I answer it, expecting a request for Father's services from one of the few people in the vicinity who has access to a telephone of their own. I guess it must be either the Cartwrights, the police, or the landlady of the Black Horse, who installed an instrument in order to attract a more genteel clientele to her establishment.

I pluck the earpiece from its cradle and speak. Sybil has emerged from the back kitchen and watches me expectantly, almost as if she hopes the call will be for her. But I suspect she's merely curious.

The worried voice I hear on the other end of the line is male and local. 'Can I speak to the doctor?'

I hurry to Father's surgery and when I enter he looks up guiltily, as though I've caught him doing something shameful. But all I can see in front of him is a medical book, a volume I know well because I have occasionally consulted it myself. He closes the book swiftly but before he does, I see it's open on a page concerning mental disorders and his face turns red as he composes himself.

'Flora. What is it, my dear?'

'There's a telephone call. It's the police. Sergeant Teague. He says it's urgent. Very urgent.'

65

Father stands. He looks a little unsteady on his feet, as though he has had too much of the Scotch he keeps in the cut glass decanter in the dining room. But there's no sign of a glass. 'Please tell him I'll speak to him presently.'

I hurry to the hall to relay the message and I can sense the sergeant's impatience on the other end of the telephone line. I do not like the telephone myself. I prefer to see the face of the person I'm talking with. I prefer to know if they are telling me the truth.

Father eventually arrives in the hall and takes the instrument from me. He has now composed himself and I see no sign of the unsteadiness I witnessed in the surgery. I told myself he might have been napping and that I woke him suddenly. And as for the book, a doctor has to deal with many illnesses of the mind as well as the body. I saw such cases myself in the men I nursed and I heard the doctors once refer to it as one of the inevitable wounds of war. As if those poor men didn't have enough troubles with the physical wounds inflicted by the enemy.

I hover just out of sight in the doorway and listen. I can't see his expression from where I stand but I can tell the news is grave because of the guarded nature of his answers. He tells the sergeant he'll be with him presently and replaces the receiver on its cradle.

He stands quite still for a few moments and I watch him, not daring to speak. Then he turns and when he sees me he looks irritated.

'Are you eavesdropping again?'

'I happened to overhear,' I correct. 'What did the sergeant want?'

He hesitates for a while, as though he's wondering how

much it's safe to reveal. 'There's been a sudden death,' he says after a few moments. 'A young woman who works for the Cartwrights. She's been found in Pooley Woods.'

'Like Myrtle? Is it the same? What did the sergeant say?'

My father doesn't answer. He walks over to the hall stand and takes his coat from its hook.

'I'll get your bag,' I say before hurrying back into his surgery to fetch the big leather medical bag. I glance at the clock on the mantelpiece and see that it is half past five. I am starting to feel the first pangs of hunger but I won't allow the needs of my stomach to stop me going with Father. If we are late, Sybil can keep our dinner warm until our return.

I put on my coat and hat, pick up my own bag and look at Father expectantly. He gives me a small nod as though he can't be bothered arguing and leads the way out of the front door.

Pooley Woods hardly merits the name. It's a small patch of woodland on the edge of the village, standing between the grounds of Tarnhey Court and the Cottage Hospital. It is possible to stride through Pooley Woods in a hundred paces but, in spite of its size, it's been a favoured trysting place for village lovers, young and not so young, over the years. However, since the war, it is used more rarely because there are so few young men left. I myself played there as a child. But my childhood isn't something I care to think about too deeply.

I follow Father into the trees. It is light now but I know this green and friendly scene can become sinister in the hours of darkness.

I can see Sergeant Teague talking to Constable Wren.

67

They both look serious and stop speaking when they see Father and me approach.

'Where's the body?' Father says bluntly as I stand behind him, straining to see past the policemen into the trees. 'What time was she found?'

'Four o'clock,' Teague answers, his voice too audible for confidentiality. 'One of the hands from Hough Farm was taking a short cut through to the village and found her. He's gone to the station to make a statement.' He says the words with relish, as though he's assured himself of the farmhand's guilt.

'It is a woman?' Father asks. I can feel his impatience at the law's delays. He's a busy man.

Teague consults his notebook. 'The lad who found her identified her as Sarah Cookham – he knows her cause she used to walk out with his brother at one time. He says she works for Lady Cartwright up at Tarnhey Court. Parlour maid.'

'Has anyone spoken to this former sweetheart of hers?' I can't resist asking the question but it brings uncomfortable stares from Teague and his colleague Constable Wren.

'That won't be possible, miss. He died on the Somme. Will Tring.'

I curse my tactlessness. I know the Tring brothers. Bert Tring came back while his big brother, Will, stayed behind to lie beneath the battlefield.

'Finding her like that must have been a terrible shock for Bert,' I say.

Teague doesn't answer but he and Wren exchange a meaningful glance.

'You can't suspect Bert Tring,' I hear myself saying. I know Bert as a gentle soul, a sweet lad who wouldn't hurt

68

anyone. He must have been through hell when he served at the Front. I've heard he rarely speaks to a soul these days.

Once again the two policemen ignore me and begin to lead Father to where the body lies. I follow at a distance, my eyes focused on the undergrowth sprouting through last year's rotting vegetation. I can smell the scent of decay and new life.

Sarah Cookham's body lies in the centre of a small clearing. I hardly recognise the impertinent maidservant I met at the Cartwrights' but I know it's her. I stand slightly behind Father who's rummaging inside the bag he's laid on the stump of a tree.

I stare at the body. Sarah is wearing a dark-coloured coat which has been pulled up to reveal a pair of white cotton bloomers and the tops of her lisle stockings. Her head is visible and I can see a frivolously small hat clinging to her hair courtesy of a well-positioned hat pin. There's no sign now of the stained apron. She died off-duty. I see Constable Wren approach the body and pull down the coat to make her decent, trying his best to avert his eyes from her exposed underwear.

There is no sneer on Sarah's lips this time. Instead they've been extended, the sides cut to create a smiling gash. The wound looks straight and neat as though some sharp instrument was used to cut into the thin flesh. It is exactly the same as the others.

Something is lying beside the head. Something that once was white but is now bedraggled and half soaked with blood. I recognise it as a bird. A dove. Someone decided to remove the obscenity from the dead girl's mouth, probably out of respect.

I watch as Father squats down, careful not to dirty his

trousers on the rough ground. His lips are pursed with what I recognise as distaste as he conducts a brief examination. I can see a small gash in her clothing above the spot where her beating heart had been. The cloth around the gash is stiff with crusted blood and I know that, like Myrtle and Annie, she has been stabbed. And, from the look of the wound, she would have been face to face with her attacker when it happened.

My father straightens up and gives the order that Sarah should be taken to the Cottage Hospital – to the chilly room at the rear of the building with the small barred window which serves as a mortuary.

The constables are ready with their stretcher and I bow my head as they pass with their burden. Sarah's now been covered with a blanket, shielded from the gaze of the curious.

Once the body's been removed, I walk over to look at the bird. Its bloody feathers look sad and bedraggled. Whoever had done this hadn't only killed the woman, he killed the bird as well for its head lay at a strange angle as if its neck had been broken.

I watch Father leave Pooley Woods walking behind the two policemen who carry the corpse on its stretcher in a sad little procession. I know better than to follow for Father is not yet ready to allow me to witness the post mortem. But one day he will change his mind.

As I hang back, I see Constable Wren glance at me as if he wishes to make sure I'm safe. There is a murderer at large and for a split second I feel touched by his concern, before irritation takes over. After all I have seen and done during the war, I am no simpering child to be protected from unpleasantness.

I make a decision. I'll call at Tarnhey Court when things have settled to offer my condolences to Lady Cartwright. For a death in the household – even that of a servant – is a most distressing occasion.

I reach the side of the church and I am about to take the familiar road home when I see Father walking towards me.

'I thought you were going to the Cottage Hospital,' I say as soon as he's within earshot.

He looks annoyed, like a man whose plans have been thwarted. 'Sergeant Teague has made a telephone call . . . to London.' There is a note of awe in his voice as he pronounces the name of the capital.

'If the same murderer's responsible it means they'll have to release Jack Blemthwaite,' I say. 'Surely they can't think he's guilty now.'

Father shakes his head. 'I suspect that was the purpose of Teague's call. He's calling in a detective from London. Scotland Yard. He will let me know when he receives a reply. I am told the detective might wish to attend the post mortem so it's been postponed.'

I'd heard of Scotland Yard but until now it had been a distant idea, like some far-off country on a globe. You know it exists but you're never likely to see it for yourself.

The light is starting to fade as I walk home in silence by Father's side. I think of Sarah lying there like a doll thrown down by some petulant child. A lifeless plaything. No longer human. And I think that sometimes the suffering of this life is impossible to bear.

But I keep my silence and my thoughts to myself. For now.

Chapter 12

Albert

It usually begins with a telegram ... or a conversation on the telephone in his office at Scotland Yard. Or sometimes a letter. Today it was a telephone call from a Sergeant Teague from a Derbyshire village called Wenfield. Sergeant Teague, a nervous caller, spoke to the constable who answered the apparatus as though he was addressing a member of the Royal Family, humbly and careful to mind his manners.

In Albert's experience it was often like that with distant country forces. To some of them Scotland Yard seemed like some magical fortress manned with knights who were sitting there ready to ride out on white chargers and right wrongs throughout the land. It was either that or they resented the interference of cocky outsiders from the Smoke.

Inspector Albert Lincoln used to be cocky. But the war had changed all that. The shell that had blown off three fingers, leaving his left hand a red, shiny stump with a protruding thumb and forefinger, had also scarred his face and left him with a limp. His injuries had led to a return to Blighty and several months in hospital and, in those months, all his former bravado – the natural high spirits he'd possessed from childhood – had been knocked out of him and stolen by the thief of war.

He sat at his desk drawing on his half-smoked cigarette, staring at the notes he'd made while he'd been speaking to the sergeant with the barely comprehensible northern accent. According to the man three women had been killed in this small village in Derbyshire – in the High Peak. The name conjured images of snow-capped mountains in Albert's head. He hoped the place was accessible.

The sergeant didn't go into too many details on the phone. Albert had the impression he wasn't entirely comfortable with the new-fangled apparatus. He had the city dweller's amused contempt for the rural and he imagined Teague to be a stolid yokel, unblessed with imagination – or much intelligence come to that.

Albert had only ventured that far north once before and that was just before the war broke out in 1914 when he'd travelled to Cheshire to investigate the killing of a young child. The little victim had been more or less the same age as his own child; the child who had died of influenza as soon as the war was over, as though once one evil had ended it had to be replaced by another. He'd been determined to bring the culprit to justice on that occasion but his resolve to catch the Cheshire toddler's killer had been in vain. The identity of that innocent child's murderer had never been discovered, in spite of his best efforts. It was a failure that had stayed with him ever since. Even in the height of battle with shells and bullets whizzing towards his vulnerable body.

And now he was heading north again and all the arrangements had been made. Albert would travel up by train the next morning and he'd be met at the station by Sergeant Teague himself. As always, Albert was curious as to whether his mental picture of Teague would match the reality. He had been told that an inn called the Black Horse was the best place to stay in Wenfield and Teague had promised to arrange things with the landlady. He sounded as if he knew the set up at the Black Horse well and was putting business the landlady's way. Albert knew that was the way things often worked in these small communities.

He obtained his superior's permission to leave the Yard slightly early that evening and at seven o'clock he arrived at his home in Bermondsey. After opening his front door he walked through the silent house and found Mary in the kitchen. The house was cold. And shabby. Mary hadn't taken much interest in anything since Frederick's death. She went through the motions of life: cooking; cleaning; scrubbing floors; doing the laundry each Monday. He knew little of women's work but he assumed that was how she filled her time. They rarely spoke these days. Not since it happened.

When he'd first come back from the Front she'd turned her back to him in bed, as if his maimed body disgusted her and she couldn't bear to feel him near her. She'd never touched him since and sometimes he sensed she was angry. Angry with him for not being the well set up man she married. Angry with death for taking her only child. In many ways he was looking forward to getting away to Derbyshire. It would give him a chance to escape to another world even though, according to Sergeant Teague, three women had died there in the most brutal manner.

Mary looked round when she heard him enter the kitchen. 'It won't be long,' she said in a monotone, nodding towards the pan bubbling on the range. 'Sit down and I'll bring it.'

Albert did as he was told. There had been no warmth in her words, no greeting. And he knew she wouldn't even keep him company at the table. She'd have eaten earlier. Alone.

'I've got to go up north tomorrow,' he said as she ladled the grey-brown stew onto his plate. He looked at her and saw her shrug. 'It's a murder case. Three murders. Derbyshire. Little place called Wenfield.'

Years ago, before war and bereavement had changed her, she would have asked about the case, enjoying the vicarious excitement of crime at a safe distance. But not now. She made no comment, as if it was all the same to her whether he was there or not.

Once he'd finished eating she disappeared into the scullery without a word to wash the dishes, and he felt a pain of regret that was almost physical as he watched her go. They'd been content once. Almost happy.

He stood in the scullery doorway and watched her. Her dress was a fusty brown, too big for her now with all the weight she'd lost – brown to match the hair she'd tied up in a thin, unflattering knot. She'd rolled up her sleeves to plunge them into the mucky water. Her arms were thin, the flesh mottled red. He'd once suggested getting in a maid of all work but she wouldn't have it. She didn't want anyone else in the house. Interfering.

He had bought the *Daily Mirror* from a vendor near Scotland Yard on his way to work but hadn't had a chance to read it so he'd brought it home. He sat in his usual chair in the parlour and scanned the pages. As well as the usual reports of influenza outbreaks and the aftermath of war, there was a story about spiritualistic quacks – mediums and other such charlatans – who'd been preying on the bereaved, promising spurious comfort. He knew Mary had been visiting such a one – a woman who'd claimed that she could see Frederick playing in some heavenly garden. Perhaps he shouldn't have pointed out that the woman was a fraud. Perhaps he should have allowed Mary to believe in her and draw comfort from the deceit. He regretted his bluntness now, but at the time it had made him angry that somebody should profit from the tragedy of Frederick's death in that way.

After a while Mary joined him without uttering a word and sat sewing in the gaslight while he pretended to read. He could hear the clock on the mantelpiece ticking away the seconds. Each second an age, each minute an hour. Tick tick. But the one sound he wanted to hear, his wife's loving voice, stayed silent.

Mary went upstairs to bed first. She slept in Frederick's room these days as if they were no longer man and wife, making the excuse that she needed to be alone. She claimed she wanted to be close to their son, to feel his presence. He knew she slept with Freddy's teddy bear. He'd crept in while she was asleep and watched her clinging to the toy as if it contained the soul of its former owner.

Albert went to the room they used to share, undressed and lay on his back, staring at the cracks in the ceiling. He didn't know how he was going to face this for a lifetime.

He closed his eyes and tried to sleep. He had to be up early the next morning to catch the train up north.

He was almost eager to get away. And he felt bad.

Chapter 13

Albert Lincoln stood on the station platform watching the train chug away, breathing in the smoke-laden air as it vanished down the track, its chimney puffing white-grey clouds that trailed over the carriages like a thick sea mist. The rough stone of the little ticket office had been blackened by the soot of decades and a thin layer of dirt marred the white paintwork. But, in spite of this, it was a neat little station and the station master stood proudly at his office door, examining his pocket watch.

Albert looked around. Sergeant Teague had promised to meet him there and he was late. He would wait ten minutes then seek him out at the local police station. He was confident that it wouldn't be hard to spot the telltale blue lamp in such a small place. Wenfield was bound to seem tiny after London and, besides, he could always ask for directions. While he waited he took in his surroundings. The station stood at the edge of a village that was surrounded by hills and those hills, craggy at their peaks, were divided into large fields, not by hedgerows but by stone walls the colour of roof slates. His overall impression was of grey stone and sparse grass. And the sheep grazing on that grass looked grubby, as though they'd rolled in soot. There were lambs too, as yet unsullied by the smutty air, who followed their mothers around and gave the occasional leap of joy, as though they were testing out their small, woolly limbs for some future sporting event.

To his right he could see a trio of tall chimneys soaring into the air like huge pointing fingers; factories or mills of some kind built out of the same stone as the rest of the village. Their size dominated their surroundings like full-sized chairs in a doll's house. Smoke billowed from the chimneys and settled on the village.

Albert's ears caught the unfamiliar sounds of the valley. He could still hear the diminishing chug of his train as it puffed off into the distance and the faint hum of machinery drifting from the mills. Then there was birdsong and the bell on the church tower chiming the half hour. And the approaching sound of a single horse's hooves.

In spite of the presence of industry, this place was a haven of tranquillity after London. No omnibuses or motor cars; no cries from street vendors; no raised voices or human chatter. This was the countryside – a strange, alien world – but in this unlikely place three women had met a violent end. He hadn't been given all the details but he was sure that, once Sergeant Teague arrived, he'd give him chapter and verse.

He picked up his suitcase and started to walk towards

the station entrance. He'd been the only passenger to alight at that stop and he noticed that the station master was still standing in the doorway, eying him suspiciously, no doubt wondering what business this stranger in the black overcoat and homburg had in Wenfield. Before the war Albert knew he would have been a greater object of curiosity but now, with his pronounced limp and his scarred face, he was only one among so many. Few men had come back unscathed. At last, just as the station master stepped forward to examine his ticket, he saw a policeman in uniform, three stripes on his arm, hurrying towards him.

'Inspector Lincoln?' the policeman asked. Even though his voice was loud, it lacked confidence, as though he was afraid he had the wrong man.

'Sergeant Teague, I presume.' Albert placed his suitcase back on the ground and put out his right hand. 'How do you do?'

He saw Teague glance at the mangled hand dangling uselessly by his side. Then he grabbed his good hand and shook it heartily.

'How was your journey, sir?'

'Not bad,' was the best way Albert could think of to describe it. It hadn't been good but on the other hand it couldn't be compared to the troop trains where he'd stood crammed with hundreds of others like cattle. Cattle going to slaughter.

'We're putting you up at the Black Horse. I'm sure you'll be comfortable there. Landlord's a man called Joe Jackson. Poor chap's not so good since the war but his good lady runs the place like clockwork.'

'Pleased to hear it.' Teague's accent was so pronounced

that Albert had to concentrate hard to make out what he was saying. He told himself he'd get used to it. At least he hoped he would.

They walked to the police station down Wenfield's main street, lined with shops and houses, and Teague pointed out the Black Horse, the inn that would be Albert's home until his work here was finished. They turned left at an open market square and crossed an ancient stone bridge, finally arriving at the police station. Like the railway station, it was built in the rough blackened stone that was obviously indigenous to the area. In fact every building he'd passed, great and humble, had been constructed in the same material, including the tall square church tower he could see nearby. He imagined that even in death the people of Wenfield were laid to rest beneath this local stone. There would be no escape from it.

The weak sun was poking through the clouds, casting shadows on the surrounding fields, but Albert did up the top button of his overcoat. It was much colder here than in London. And as the chill in the air hit his face it made his wounded flesh tingle.

Once inside the police station Albert saw a large man standing behind a front desk that reminded him of a polished oak coffin.

'The superintendent's here,' the man at the desk whispered once the introductions had been made. 'He's come from Buxton specially to see you.'

Albert was about to say he was honoured but he thought better of it. He followed Teague down a corridor and into an office, the sort of utilitarian space that Albert was used to at the Yard. A man in the uniform of a superintendent was sitting behind a large desk and he rose when they came in. He was tall with grey hair, a smooth face and a military bearing, although Albert calculated that he'd probably have been too old to serve in the recent conflict.

Like Teague, the superintendent's eyes seemed to be drawn first to Albert's face then to his left hand. It was hard to know whether his gaze was sympathetic or whether he was assessing Albert's capability to do the job.

'Thank you for coming, Inspector,' the superintendent said after he'd invited both men to sit. 'I trust you had a good journey.'

Albert nodded, impatient to discover the details of the case he was expected to solve. He was soon to find out. The superintendent passed him a thick file and he opened it.

'Three murders. All identical. No witnesses. Women in isolated spots and in each case nobody knows what they were doing there. All were stabbed in the heart and found with their skirts raised, although there's no other sign that they'd been ... ' He cleared his throat. 'Violated. The strangest thing was what he did to their mouths. He slit them at the corners, presumably to make room for the birds he stuffed inside.'

'What sort of birds?'

'White ones. Doves.'

'I presume the birds were dead?'

The superintendent looked a little unsure of himself and consulted a notebook. 'Yes. Quite dead.'

'How were the birds killed?'

The superintendent took back the file and rummaged through it. 'It says here their necks were broken. It also says there is only one place you'd find white doves in this area and that's a dovecote at a house called Tarnhey Court near where two of the bodies were found. It's owned by Sir William Cartwright.' He gave a smug smile. 'But I think we can rule a man of Sir William's standing out of our inquiries.'

Albert had heard the name. Sir William Cartwright was a Member of Parliament who'd held some high position in the War Cabinet. Albert hadn't realised he had a home in such a distant spot. To him, Sir William was just a name glimpsed in the newspapers; a figure of stature so far above a humble detective in status that he'd never expected their paths to ever cross. But now it looked as though that situation might change.

'We had somebody in custody,' the superintendent said. 'A young man by the name of Jack Blemthwaite.'

'We were sure we had the right man.' It was the first time Teague had spoken.

'But now you're not?' Albert inclined his head to one side and saw Teague look at the superintendent.

It was Teague who answered. 'Everyone thought Blemthwaite did it. He isn't right in the head, see. Lasses used to be scared of him. He'd watch them.'

'So what made you change your minds?'

Another glance. Albert sensed that the topic was embarrassing. ''Cause there was another murder ... while Blemthwaite was locked up in Derby awaiting trial.'

'About as good an alibi as you can get.'

The superintendant gave Albert a quizzical look, as though he suspected he was being facetious. 'It wasn't an easy decision to call in Scotland Yard but the Chief Constable said we had to get to the truth of the matter.'

Before you became a laughing stock, Albert thought. But he knew better than to put those thoughts into words which would guarantee a lack of co-operation from the local force.

Albert stood up. 'May I read through the files to familiarise myself with the case?'

The superintendent passed the file back. 'That would be best. Sergeant Teague will take you over to the Black Horse. Nice establishment. Respectable.' The final word sounded like a warning, as though he suspected the man from London would favour something more exciting.

But Albert nodded. 'I'm sure I'll be comfortable.'

He picked up his hat and his suitcase before tucking the file underneath his arm.

'Good luck,' the superintendent said as he reached the office door.

Albert didn't reply.

Chapter 14

The Black Horse lived up to its reputation for comfort. Albert found the landlord, Joe Jackson, to be a large, brooding man who said little. But his wife made up for his silence.

'Are you here about these terrible murders, sir? Nobody's safe. I'm terrified to go out. Where are you from? London? I had some gentlemen from London staying here once: they had business at one of the mills. Of course Sir William goes to London all the time, him being in Parliament. He sometimes comes in here, you know. He says he likes the beer. Pint of best bitter for you, sir?'

Albert answered her stream of questions in monosyllables. And he accepted one pint, for the sake of politeness. However, he knew there wouldn't be a second. Too many eyes were watching him and as he left the bar and made himself comfortable in a settle near the window well away from his fellow drinkers, he was conscious of Mrs Jackson glancing anxiously in his direction as though she longed to continue her interrogation. He suspected she wouldn't be satisfied until she knew his life story. But he didn't intend to oblige her. There were things he wasn't inclined to share ... especially with strangers.

By the time he went up to his room his bladder was bursting and he was pleased, and rather surprised, to see that there was a water closet and a bathroom on the corridor opposite his door. Sergeant Teague had boasted that the Black Horse had all modern conveniences and it seemed he hadn't been lying. After visiting the WC with its green tiled walls, he unlocked the door to his small, spotlessly clean room. When he'd dumped his suitcase in there before going downstairs, he'd left the files on the bed and they were still there. However, there was now an extra blanket at the foot of the bed that hadn't been there before and he noticed that the files had been shifted towards the pillows. Someone had been in and moved them. He told himself it was probably the maid who'd deposited his blanket. But, even so, it had been foolish of him to leave them lying there like that. He wasn't usually so careless. Perhaps the long journey had tired him out.

However, he couldn't contemplate sleep without knowing what was in those files. First thing tomorrow he'd be taking charge of the case and he had to know everything. Every suspect. Every witness. Everyone who was connected in any way with the victims. His was to be the fresh pair of eyes.

He took his jacket off and began to read, making notes of the names as he read the witness statements. Once he'd finished he concluded that there'd been no solid evidence against Jack Blemthwaite, apart from the fact that he had a reputation in the village for being odd and simple. He had found the body of the first victim, Myrtle Bligh, and had run to the police station to report it right away. He had been in a distressed state, the report said. But this was hardly evidence of his guilt, especially as no blood had been found on his clothing. Albert had to concede that his alibi for the second murder, that of Annie Dryden, was dubious but he'd been in jail when Sarah Cookham was murdered. Nobody could argue with that.

The investigation so far had been a shambles. If the third woman hadn't been killed, Albert knew there was a chance that Blemthwaite might have been facing the hangman if he hadn't found a good barrister to defend him.

The truth was that once the local police had decided on Blemthwaite's guilt, they hadn't bothered looking at any other suspects. It was lazy, Albert thought. But he knew it happened.

That night he slept well, which was unusual as he normally found it hard to drift off to sleep in a strange bed. He'd been glad of the extra blanket because the night had been cold; far colder than he was used to. He awoke at six to the chiming of the church clock and lay there with his eyes open. Light was already seeping through the curtains, a different quality of light to that of London; more green and less grey. Like yesterday, the only sounds he could hear were the clop-clop of horses' hooves and the singing of birds. Wenfield had already woken up. And it was time he did likewise.

The landlady herself brought hot water to his room

and poured it into the blue patterned basin on the wash stand, enquiring how he'd slept. Was he comfortable? She sounded anxious so he assured her that yes, he'd passed a very good night.

Once he'd dressed he went downstairs for breakfast which he'd been told would be served in the saloon bar. Sure enough it was there, placed in front of him by Mrs Jackson. The plate was filled with eggs and bacon – a feast for a working man – and the woman stood back proudly as if she expected him to make some favourable comment.

A knife and fork lay either side of the plate and when he took the knife to cut up the bacon with his single hand, he saw Mrs Jackson's alarm, there for a moment then swiftly suppressed.

'I'm so sorry, Mr Lincoln. I never thought. Would you like some help?'

He knew she was being kind but he felt a stab of irritation. 'No thank you, Mrs Jackson. I can manage.'

She watched him for a few moments, as if she wanted to reassure herself that his words were true. Then he looked up and gave her a cold smile. 'Thank you,' he said and she hurried away as though she knew she was being dismissed.

Albert hadn't realised he was so hungry and his breakfast tasted good, quite unlike the meagre, half-hearted breakfasts Mary usually provided. She'd lost interest in food. She'd lost interest in everything.

When Mrs Jackson brought tea it was the colour of mahogany but it satisfied his thirst.

'Was that all right for you?' she asked as she took his empty plate.

The question was cautious, as if she feared causing more offence, and he suddenly felt bad about being short with her before. She wasn't to know how sensitive he was about his physical shortcomings. She couldn't know that he could no longer bear to look in the mirror because of the blemish the shell had left on his face.

He gave her a smile. It felt lopsided because of the stiffness of the scar tissue on the left side but he hoped it was reassuring. 'Sorry if I snapped at you before. It's just that ... '

'You don't have to explain, sir,' she said quickly, staring at the egg-stained plate in her hand. She had small hands, and smooth. Albert guessed that some unseen help in the inn dealt with the heavy work and the washing up.

He knew this was too good an opportunity to miss. There was nobody else about and he now had the chance to glean some local information. Call it gossip if you like, but he'd learned from other investigations that a lot can be learned from talking.

'Please sit down, Mrs Jackson.'

She put down the plate on a neighbouring table and pulled up one of the stout wooden chairs. The legs scraped on the stone-flagged floor.

'You know why I'm here?'

'Yes, sir. You've come about these murders.'

'Did you know the dead women?'

'Oh yes, sir. Mr Jackson and I know most folk round here.'

'Do you mind telling me something about them?'

She drew in her breath and paused for a few seconds, as if she was making a decision. 'I don't like to gossip,' she said in a low voice, glancing over her shoulder as she

89

leaned towards him. 'I mean, it's not right to speak ill of the dead, is it?'

'You want us to catch the murderer, don't you? If he's allowed to go free, all women are at risk, wouldn't you agree?'

Mrs Jackson nodded, seemingly convinced by Albert's argument.

'I knew it wasn't Jack Blemthwaite. He's a great soft lummox but there's no real harm in him. I've never known him hurt anyone. But some people say ... He's different, you see, and there are some who don't like that.' Her eyes were drawn to his left hand then she looked away. 'Anyway, I'm glad they know it wasn't him now.'

'The victims ... what were they like?'

She thought for a few moments. 'Myrtle was a nice girl. Not bright ... just ordinary if you know what I mean. She worked up at Tarnhey Court when it was turned into a military hospital during the war. Joined the VADs – nursing and that sort of thing. I reckon it was the most exciting thing that had ever happened to the poor lass. Her sweetheart was killed, you know. Lad called Stanley Smith. Nice lad – used to work for the blacksmith. She moved back to her mother's after the war finished but she was always close to Stanley's mam. There's talk that they went to these séances together ... to try and get in touch with Stanley.' She pressed her lips together. 'I don't hold with things like that myself ... interfering with things we aren't meant to understand.'

The thought of Mary's attempts to contact their little Frederick flashed across his mind and the memory caused a sudden pang of despair. 'I know what you mean. What about Anne Dryden?'

90

'Annie? Oh she was a different kettle of fish. The kindest way I can think of to describe her was a nosy old bat. She had a sharp tongue and she liked to know everyone's business. She wasn't particularly popular. And she drove her husband to drink if you ask me.'

Mrs Jackson was getting into her stride now. This was better than Albert had anticipated.

'Did she have any particular enemies?'

She sighed. 'Just because someone isn't popular, it doesn't mean they have enemies willing to kill them.'

Albert knew she was right. Annie Dryden might have been an unpleasant woman but, given the other deaths, her murder might not have been a personal matter.

'What about the latest victim?'

'Little Sarah. She worked as a parlour maid up at the big house – Tarnhey Court. Worked for Sir William and Lady Cartwright. I didn't know Sarah well but her mother's a decent woman.'

'Was Sarah up there during the war? Did she work with Myrtle Bligh at the hospital?'

Mrs Jackson shook her head. 'No, she was too young back then. She was only nineteen when she died, poor lass.'

'But she knew the other victims?'

'Most people round here either know each other . . . or know of each other, which isn't the same thing. I wouldn't have said the three were particular friends if that's what you're getting at.'

Albert took his watch out of his waistcoat pocket. It was time he left. He thanked his landlady and went back upstairs to fetch his coat, feeling he'd learned more during that brief conversation than he had when he'd pored over the case files in his lonely room.

Chapter 15

The post mortem was arranged for late that morning, after the doctor had dealt with those living patients who turned up at his surgery, and it was to take place in the mortuary of the Cottage Hospital on the edge of the village. It was something Albert viewed with trepidation. He'd seen terrible sights during the war but the prospect of watching a young woman being carved up like the Sunday joint made him feel slightly queasy. Not that he'd say as much to Sergeant Teague who walked to the hospital with him in silence.

After going through the files in his room at the Black Horse the previous night, Albert felt he was already sufficiently familiar with the case to make a few decisions. There were people he needed to speak to; people who, in his opinion, hadn't been questioned closely enough. The local police might be afraid of offending Sir William Cartwright and his family but he had no such qualms.

In his mind's eye he saw Sir William. Member of Parliament. Fat, sleek and prosperous, living in considerable comfort in Tarnhey Court and lording it over the village. He'd met his sort before and he hadn't cared for them. They were the type of people his superiors were always careful not to upset. And this made Albert angry.

According to the files, even though Sir William had been at home in Wenfield at the time of Myrtle and Sarah's deaths, and had been on his way back from a nearby constituency meeting when Annie Dryden died, he hadn't been questioned. Lady Cartwright and his son, Roderick, had given statements concerning Jack Blemthwaite's whereabouts at the time of Annie's death but they'd turned out to be useless. It had been perfectly possible for Blemthwaite to have run from the Cartwrights' dovecote to the murder scene and back again without Her Ladyship or her son being aware of it. Their statements, intended to put Blemthwaite in the clear, hadn't really helped him one bit.

Sarah Cookham's post mortem was to be conducted by the local doctor who had dealt with the previous two victims. This wasn't how things were done in London but Albert knew there was little choice. He just hoped the medical man was competent. In his experience, some weren't and they missed things. Important things.

The Cottage Hospital, in contrast to most of the local buildings, was built of harsh red brick and a sign carved over the main entrance announced that it had been endowed by Sir William Cartwright MP. Cartwright was clearly a local philanthropist as well as a Member of Parliament but even this didn't lighten Albert's suspicion. He'd known all sorts of nefarious deeds to be concealed behind good works. Sometimes he hated himself for his cynicism, but his instincts had often been proved right.

The small mortuary was tucked away at the rear of the building. It wouldn't do to alarm the patients by making its existence too obvious, Albert supposed. It was lined with white tiles with a slab in the centre covered by a white sheet. He could make out the shape of a human body beneath the undulations of the sheet; a small body. He suddenly felt desperately sad for this young life cut short.

The doctor was waiting for them. He was tall and stooped with a balding pate and a luxuriant moustache and he was dressed in a surgical gown, ready to begin work. Sergeant Teague appeared to know him well because the two men exchanged nods of greeting.

'Dr Winsmore, this is Inspector Lincoln from Scotland Yard.'

Albert saw that the doctor's eyes were drawn to his face first, observing the scarring before his gaze strayed to his hand. He seemed to be noting Albert's disfigurements with professional coolness. Since the war he was probably used to such sights, even in a little place like Wenfield. Albert had noticed the new war memorial as he'd walked from the railway station; the community here had had its share of casualties.

Winsmore didn't waste time on pleasantries. He whipped the sheet off the corpse like a magician revealing some miraculous illusion, and for a second Albert was shocked to see the young woman lying there, exposed and naked. She was small and thin. He could see her ribcage outlined beneath her small breasts and she looked so pathetic and vulnerable with her little patch of pubic hair on display that he had a sudden urge to cover her up again for modesty's sake. But he knew he had to watch as her body was violated a second time.

'Come closer, gentlemen, you can't see properly from there,' the doctor ordered. He sounded impatient, as though he wished to get the whole unpleasantness over with as soon as possible.

Albert did as he was told. He could see the victim's face better now. He could see the terrible grin created by the killer when he'd slit both ends of her mouth to widen it, presumably to insert the bird he'd read about in the report: the white dove stained with the victim's life blood. If it weren't for that she would have been pretty, he thought.

Winsmore pointed out the fatal wound. A neat stab wound a couple of inches in length just over where the girl's heart would have beaten in life. A single, well-aimed thrust that appeared to have been the cause of death. The mutilations to the face, the doctor surmised, had probably been inflicted after she'd been killed. At least, Albert hoped this was the case.

Albert had attended many post mortems in London and, what with that and his experiences of war, he was used to blood and internal organs spewing from battered corpses, but somehow this occasion seemed different; more obscene, if that was possible. As Winsmore worked he lowered his eyes. Watching would have seemed intrusive, voyeuristic. Like the time he and his mates had peeped through the hole in the wall to watch one of their comrades *in flagrante* with a French lady of the night while they were in Paris. But on that occasion it had been fun. A laugh.

After a while the doctor gave his verdict. 'I'd say it's identical to the others, gentlemen. No sign of ... sexual interference and the cause of death is a knife wound to the heart. A narrow blade, I'd say. Possibly something like a bayonet?'

'There are a lot of them around,' Teague observed glumly.

'Indeed.'

Albert saw the two men's eyes meet, as if in understanding. He'd been in this situation before, standing there in ignorance of the undercurrents of local knowledge swirling around him, the unspoken secrets kept between people who've been acquainted all their lives. It was an uneasy feeling, being an outsider. But it was one he was used to.

'So the three victims were definitely killed by the same man?' Albert asked. He needed to be sure.

'That's right,' the doctor said with confidence. 'No doubt about it.'

Albert looked Teague in the eye. 'Is there any chance the lad you arrested was responsible for the first two and someone's copied his modus operandi?'

Teague shuffled his feet like a nervous schoolboy caught out by his teacher. 'I doubt it. There were things we didn't make public; the way the clothing was arranged ... ' The uncertainty of his reply suggested to Albert that the local police's attempts at confidentiality didn't usually meet with absolute success.

'I take it Blemthwaite's been released?'

'It's being arranged,' said Teague.

Albert saw only one emotion on the man's face, and that was disappointment.

The doctor continued his work, cutting into the abdomen and lifting out the organs. After a while he broke his silence.

'What have we here? Oh dear. Oh dear, oh dear.'

'What is it?' Albert asked.

'Foolish girl,' the doctor said, shaking his head sadly. 'I'm sorry to have to tell you that she was pregnant. About three months' gestation.'

'In that case,' said Teague eagerly, 'we'd better make it our priority to find the father.'

Albert said nothing. He knew Teague would worry at this new discovery like a terrier because, in his simple world, the father must have killed her to avoid a scandal, perhaps copying the earlier crimes. But Albert intended to keep an open mind.

He was careful to thank the doctor before he left the mortuary. He needed to keep on the right side of the locals. In such a small, alien community, he needed allies, even people he wouldn't normally choose to work with. Besides, the doctor had seemed competent enough. He'd come across worse.

When he reached the cobbled street that ran through the length of the village, he looked round and saw that Teague was following a few paces behind. Albert could see a frown of disapproval on his face, as though he'd just tasted something nasty and was longing to spit it out.

'Something the matter, Sergeant?'

'No, sir,' Teague said quickly, as though he'd been caught doing something shameful. 'But I was just wondering. Do you want to go back to the station or . . . ?'

'I want to visit Tarnhey Court,' Albert said. From the look on Teague's face when he said it, he knew the man didn't like the idea. 'As far as I can see Sir William and his son were around at the time of all three murders but Sir William wasn't spoken to. Why was that, do you think?'

He saw Teague's face turn red, as though he knew he was being criticised for this neglect of duty.

'Sir William was at a constituency meeting in New Mills on the evening Annie Dryden was killed. Didn't get back till after nine.'

'Have you checked what time he left the meeting?'

'No but . . . Sir William and Master Roderick had nothing to do with it. They couldn't have.'

Albert stopped and swung round to face him. 'Nobody is above suspicion, Sergeant. Not even Caesar's wife if she happened to live in Wenfield. Do you understand that, Teague? Nobody.'

'But Sir William's a Member of Parliament, sir,' the sergeant said in a pathetic whine.

'They're usually the worst.'

Albert saw the look of shock on the sergeant's face at his lack of respect. But he'd had respect knocked out of him years ago. Vice wasn't confined to the lower orders.

'Are the Cartwrights an old family?'

Teague swallowed hard. 'I believe Sir William's grandfather made his fortune in the last century, sir. Before that, I wouldn't like to say.'

'After I've seen Sir William I intend to speak to the rest of his household.' Albert looked at Teague expectantly. 'Coming with me?'

The sergeant wasn't a man who hid his feelings easily. He wasn't comfortable with Albert's attitude but he knew it wasn't his place to question. He had no choice.

'Lead the way,' Albert said, realising he was rather

enjoying the situation. He knew he shouldn't rejoice in another's discomfort but he knew unquestioning acceptance of those said to be your betters was no longer appropriate. He had seen fallible officers lording it over privates with courage and integrity ... and he had also witnessed noble and brave officers being betrayed by lazy and self-serving men. A man's station in life was no longer any guarantee of his good character. All those certainties had vanished like gun smoke.

Albert saw Teague hesitate as they passed through a pair of grand stone gateposts, each with an eagle perched on top. The birds looked down on them as though they were sneering.

The drive leading to Tarnhey Court wasn't particularly long and soon Albert saw the house looming in front of him. It was large, but not ostentatiously grand. And it was built of the same local stone as the rest of the village; another building that blended with the rolling grey-green landscape. The laurel bushes fringing the drive looked rather overgrown. He supposed that, since the war, gardeners were thin on the ground.

Some gentry, in his experience, expected policemen to use the servants' entrance. But Albert was no servant to be ordered about. Never had been. He was the upholder of the law and he was there because three women had died.

It was obvious that the maid who opened the heavy front door had been crying. Her eyes were red and the area around them looked tender with rubbing. She wore a uniform that looked too big for her.

'Can you please tell Sir William that Inspector Lincoln from Scotland Yard wishes to speak to him.' Albert produced his card and handed it to the girl who held it between her thumb and forefinger as though it was something contaminated. Then she bobbed an untidy curtsey and invited them to wait in the hall. She'd see if the master was free to see them.

Albert was longing to say that Sir William had little choice in the matter but he held his tongue. It would be foolish to antagonise the most important man in the village on first acquaintance. He needed him to think he was still in charge. He wanted him off his guard.

He and Teague made themselves as comfortable as they could on two upright, unupholstered hall chairs, designed to keep unwelcome guests waiting in discomfort. Teague sat on the edge of his chair as if preparing for flight and the two men said nothing, not even small talk.

The girl appeared again, reminding Albert of a terrified small animal. But he told himself that her colleague, and perhaps her friend, had been murdered in the most terrible way. His thoughts kept straying back to the post mortem he'd witnessed but he tried to banish the image from his mind.

'Sir William will see you now, sir,' she said, bobbing another clumsy curtsey. She had the look of someone who was being trained up for the job but who hadn't quite got the hang of it yet.

They were shown into a room off the hallway, a masculine room with hunting scenes hanging on the dark red walls. The appearance of the man sitting in the worn leather armchair surprised Albert. Rather than being the sleek, well-fed creature of his imagination, Sir William Cartwright was a thin man of average height with sparse hair and an amiable face. He would have made an unremarkable country solicitor or perhaps a chief clerk of a provincial bank. He stood as they entered and offered his hand.

'I'm sorry to keep you waiting, gentlemen, but I received a telephone call from London.' He nodded towards the apparatus on his desk, a tall stick with a mouthpiece dangling from its side. He looked at the thing fondly, as a child would regard a new toy.

'I assume you wish to speak to me about Sarah. Tragic business. My wife is most distressed ... as are we all, of course.' He said the words with a politician's careful gravitas. The right phrase for the right occasion. Albert thought he sounded sincere, although these days, he never quite trusted anyone's motives.

'I'll tell you all I can, Inspector, although that won't be much. My wife deals with the servants and the day to day running of the house but she is indisposed at present. This unfortunate business has affected her nerves very badly. But I will answer any questions as best I can.'

He assumed a helpful expression and Albert decided to take advantage of his co-operative mood. He questioned him about his whereabouts at the time of each death and Sir William replied confidently. The only occasion he hadn't been at home was on the evening of Annie Dryden's murder when he'd been at a constituency meeting. They were welcome to check. Then Albert asked him whether he had seen any suspicious activity near the dovecote.

'It is in the walled garden at the side of the house and can only be seen from some of the upstairs windows,' Sir William replied. 'We don't keep dogs so any trespassers would most likely go unnoticed. It wasn't a problem when we had a full staff here but now since the war ... ' He gave a sad little shrug. 'My wife is alone a great deal so perhaps a dog or two would solve our dilemma. I'm often down in London, you see, and my son isn't always here.'

'A dog would be a good idea.' It was the first time Teague had uttered a word and Albert noticed his face had turned beetroot red, as though he feared he'd spoken out of turn.

'Especially with a killer at large,' Sir William said, lighting a cigarette. He flashed the packet at the two policemen but it was only Albert who accepted his offer. The gesture seemed to ease the tension. Three men with a common goal sorting out a problem over a cigarette. Or at least Albert thought that was the impression Sir William wished to give.

'My wife finds the suggestion that the killer came into the grounds to acquire the ... birds particularly upsetting.'

'That's understandable. Could he have obtained them anywhere else?'

'As far as I'm aware this is the only household in the area that keeps white doves,' Sir William said. 'There are plenty of pigeons, of course, but doves are a bit of a rarity.'

'Do they fly far from home?'

'It's possible, of course. In fact I told my wife this monster must have found them in the woods and killed them there. She suffers with her nerves so I prefer her to think the man responsible didn't set foot on our property.'

'Is it possible to speak to your wife, sir?'

'I'm afraid not. She's resting.'

'Were you aware that Sarah was pregnant?'

He watched the MP's face carefully but only saw shock and concern. 'No, I wasn't. These things happen, I suppose, especially since the war. No doubt there's some sweetheart who ... '

'Her family don't know of one.'

'As I say, since the war ... ' He sighed. 'The world has been turned upside down.'

'May we speak to your son?'

'He drove to Manchester in his motor car on business first thing this morning but I expect him back shortly.' He smiled and raised a warning finger. 'I know what you are thinking, Inspector. The young master and the serving maid. But I can assure you that Roderick is not responsible for the unfortunate girl's condition. I am absolutely certain he knows nothing of the matter.'

'What makes you so sure, Sir William?'

Sergeant Teague's mouth fell open at Albert's impertinence.

'I know my son and I would have recognised the signs. He showed no special interest in the girl, of that I am certain.'

'What time will he be back from Manchester?'

'I have no idea, I'm afraid.' Sir William took his gold pocket watch from his waistcoat and examined it ostentatiously. 'If that is all, gentlemen, time moves on and I have things to attend to.'

Albert knew when he was being dismissed. But that didn't prevent him from asking permission to question Tarnhey Court's servants.

Sir William readily agreed. After all, he had nothing to hide.

Chapter 16

Flora

'I met the detective from Scotland Yard this morning. He was in attendance when I conducted the post mortem on that unfortunate girl from Tarnhey Court.'

I look at Father, curious. He says the words casually, as though he's discussing some mundane domestic matter. He's been silent all through lunch and I'm surprised now by his sudden candour. Surprised and somewhat pleased.

'Do the police think the same man's responsible?'

My father suddenly looks flustered, like a man who realises he's let his tongue run away with him and revealed too much. 'Really, Flora, it is hardly a suitable subject for a young lady to be discussing over lunch.'

I am tempted to point out that it was he who'd introduced the topic but I say nothing. I learned long ago that there are times when it is futile to argue with Father. 'At least this means they'll have to release poor Jack Blemthwaite now ... doesn't it?'

Father grunts. 'I don't know why you concern yourself so much with that boy.'

'Because he's innocent, that's why.' Father's starting to irritate me. I had words with him last night about my wish to go to Manchester to train at the Royal Infirmary. I told him I'd written to the Matron there and that I'm awaiting a reply. I think now that it might have been a mistake to be so honest.

'Where's the detective staying?' I ask, hoping the change of subject will calm matters.

'The Black Horse. Where else would you expect? The Cartwright Arms is hardly a respectable establishment.'

Sybil shuffles in to take the lunch dishes. She looks nervous. Since the death of Sarah, she has been in a state of terror as though she suspects that somebody is stalking the village killing servants and she might be next. Father has suggested that I speak to her but I know that would be useless. She has an idea in her head, a fear that won't go away. I know what fear is like and how it saps the spirit.

'What's he like?' I ask once Sybil has left the room.

'Who?'

'The detective.'

Father sighs, as if my question is tiresome. 'He's from London. Injured in the war from the looks of it. But at least he's alive.' His eyes are drawn to the photograph on the mantelpiece, in pride of place like some image in a shrine. My brother, John, standing proud in his uniform. A lieutenant. An officer in his Sam Browne belt but looking so young. A child sent to die for his country.

I rise from the table. It's a fine day and I have no desire to stay indoors. Besides, Father is about to embark on his house calls so he has no need of me. That morning he allowed me to act as his receptionist and help him with routine medical matters but he still won't allow me to accompany him into the homes of his patients. Also, he is going to visit Lady Cartwright whose nervous condition has worsened since the demise of her unhappy parlour maid and he wishes to conduct the consultation in private.

I leave the room and once in the hall, I put on my coat and hat, looking in the mirror to ensure it sits straight on my hair. My hair is brown and thick and has always been a little wild. How I envied some of my fellow VADs at Tarnhey Court with their neat, straight locks. I was only too glad to hide mine beneath my nurse's cap, risking the wrath of Sister if too much stray hair escaped from beneath the white cloth.

Sybil enters the hall. She still looks frightened and I wish I could reassure her that the killer has no interest in her. But I know no words of mine will convince her. It's a pity she hasn't a strong sweetheart to walk out with and provide her with reassurance and protection. But as far as I know the nearest she's ever come to having a beau was when she made cow eyes at one of Wilf Fuller's farm-hands. But, like so many, that young man went to war and never came back.

'Your cousin Jack should be released soon. That's good news,' I say, trying to cheer her.

'Yes, miss. But that means the murderer's still around, doesn't it? He could be anywhere. He could be watching us now. Waiting till we go outside and . . .' She frowns, as if a terrible thought has just occurred to her. 'Are you going out now, miss?'

'That's why I usually put on my hat and coat.' I can't resist teasing her but it doesn't raise a smile. 'Look, Sybil,

I promise I'll be careful. And if I meet the murderer, I'll take him straight to the police station. An inspector's come all the way up from London – Scotland Yard – so I'm certain we'll be quite safe.'

She smiles and it feels like a small victory. Then she speaks again. 'I saw my cousin Edith yesterday,' she says, a note of caution in her voice. 'She came to Wenfield with her master in his motor car.' She says the final two words with some awe.

'She is still living in New Mills?'

'Yes, miss. She's working as housekeeper for another doctor now. It's a doctor as used to be at Tarnhey Court while you were nursing there, ma'am. You might know him.'

My heart begins to beat a little faster but I know Sybil cannot know my interest is anything more than polite. 'Do you know his name?'

'It's a funny one, ma'am. Dr Bone.' She gives a little giggle and sounds like a silly child in spite of her age.

'I remember Dr Bone,' I say calmly. 'He's a fine doctor. Saved a lot of our brave boys.'

She looks embarrassed as if she is ashamed of having mocked the name of such a noble creature.

'If you see Edith again, give her my special love, won't you?' Her mention of Edith has reawakened memories of our old housekeeper – my old friend – and I'm tempted to ask Sybil to contact Edith and ask her if she's willing to meet me when she's next in Wenfield. But, not being sure what passed between my father and Edith all those years ago, I say nothing. It's four years since she left and she's made no effort to keep in touch so perhaps it's best to leave things as they are.

107

Then Sybil speaks again. 'Edith asked after you – said she'd like to meet.'

It is as if she's read my mind. 'I'd like that,' I say, hoping Sybil will pass the message on.

She hurries off towards the kitchen and I make for the front door. I have seen the sunshine from the windows and have longed all morning to feel its warmth on my face. After leaving the house I walk down the High Street and as I pass, men touch their caps in greeting and women nod. I am known to all. The Doctor's Daughter. I wonder when I will cease to be someone's daughter and be known for myself, Flora Winsmore.

I walk down River Street towards the church, crossing the bridge over the flowing river. The water isn't high today because it hasn't rained for a few days, a rare situation around these parts where the hills attract rain clouds like magnets attract iron.

When I reach the churchyard I see the gravestones jutting up like blackened teeth on either side of the path leading up to the church porch and I spot a familiar figure standing, head bowed, a few yards to my left. I recognise Roderick Cartwright at once. I have seen him in that particular place before, beside a grave I know doesn't belong to a member of his family. But friends can be just as dear. Perhaps more so.

He looks up and sees me but there's no smile of greeting today. And no gentle mockery in his eyes.

'I was just . . . '

'I know,' I answer. He looks relieved that there's no reproach in my voice.

After a long silence he speaks again. 'They say Jack Blemthwaite's out of jail. There's talk that him and his mother have gone to stay with a cousin in Glossop.'

'Well he couldn't have killed your parlour maid, could he?'

'The man from Scotland Yard visited my father earlier. Asked him a lot of questions.'

I was suddenly curious about the man who'd had the temerity to question Sir William Cartwright MP. 'What's he like?'

'I didn't see him. I was in Manchester. Only got back half an hour ago and decided to come out here for a walk. I needed some fresh air.'

'Me too,' I say, feeling a sudden bond between us. Perhaps to both of us, Wenfield is like a cage and the hills around our green, confining bars.

'Father said the inspector was asking after our whereabouts when Sarah was killed. I hope that doesn't mean he thinks we had anything to do with . . .'

'He probably asks everybody the same questions,' I say quickly.

He lights a cigarette with his gold lighter. I can see his initials engraved on it in fancy letters: RC. It looks like a gift and I wonder if he received it from his parents.

He waves the cigarette packet in my direction but I shake my head. I tried smoking when I was working at Tarnhey Court but I can't say I particularly enjoyed it. The men always offered their fags around to us as a gesture of sharing, of generosity, and it seemed churlish to refuse. We used to smoke them during our breaks, standing outside on the terrace well out of Sister's view. I think the men liked to think they could give us something, however little, in return for the loving care we gave them.

I see that Roderick's eyes have been drawn once more to the grave. The headstone hasn't yet been tainted by soot and time. I can read the carved name from where I'm standing. *James Carr. Born 1897 died 1918. Taken too soon.* I remember James. He grew up on the Cartwrights' estate, the son of the head coachman, and he went away to war, an eager volunteer. Then, by some stroke of luck – if you can call it that – he was wounded and shipped back to Blighty, ending up being treated at Tarnhey Court. It was unusual for men to be sent to a military hospital so close to their home but he'd worked for the Cartwrights, helping his father as a stable boy, and I'd always wondered if strings were pulled. I remember his halo of fair curls, his physical beauty that sent the local girls' hearts aflutter. But, as far as I remember, he'd had no special sweetheart.

'You miss James,' I say.

He nods. 'His father taught me to ride. Harry Carr was a good man. James's death killed him as well. The war did for both of them.'

'You and James were close.' I watch his eyes and when I see a flicker of something I recognise as grief I find myself warming to him again as I did when we were children. Perhaps Roderick has suffered like everyone else in spite of his cushy posting behind a London desk.

When he doesn't reply I touch his sleeve. 'His name's on the war memorial. At least he's remembered.'

'What good is that when he's six feet underground?'

He begins to walk away and I follow.

'Perhaps we can walk together,' I say.

He slows his pace and waits for me to catch up.

'Did the inspector say anything else?' I ask as we're crossing the bridge.

He stops and gazes down at the river. A duck floats by,

110

bobbing on the water like a toy. 'He asked about the dovecote. Apparently it's the only place the birds could have come from ... the birds found with the bodies.'

'I hear they were stuffed into the victims' mouths.'

'Why would he do that?'

'How should I know? Perhaps he's a madman.'

'The dovecote's never locked and it can't be seen from the house so anybody can get in there. My mother's taken to her bed. Father says the idea of a murderer prowling around our grounds has taken its toll on her nerves. He's thinking of getting dogs.'

'That's a good idea,' I say. 'Do you think the doves have some meaning?'

'They must do or he wouldn't have done it, would he?' He sounds a little impatient now, as though he thinks my question foolish.

We walk on in silence until I speak again. 'Now they know it can't have been Jack Blemthwaite, I wonder if the inspector has any other suspects.'

Roderick gives a bitter smile. 'All I know is that he wants to speak to me. Not that I can tell him anything.' He looks at me. 'Killing women is hardly my thing.'

We part at the gates to Tarnhey Court and I head for home. In my absence the afternoon post has arrived and a letter is sitting on the hall table. My name is on the envelope, the handwriting neat and sloping. *Miss Flora Winsmore.* I feel a thrill of excitement as I pick it up and start to slit the envelope open, hoping it's from the Matron of the Manchester Royal Infirmary inviting me for an interview. But when I read the letter I discover the contents are more personal and I see the words *Yours sincerely, Edith Barton* at the bottom. I hadn't expected Edith to get in touch so soon and I realise that this must have been her intention when she spoke to Sybil. I am pleased of course, but I can't help wondering why she wishes to re-establish contact now. After all, she's only been living three miles away and there's been no word from her since she left my father's employment four years ago.

I read the letter and discover that she wants to meet me. I know she now works for Dr Bone and I assume that, through her cousin Sybil, she knows about my work at Tarnhey Court during the war. She must be aware of my connection with Bone and I wonder if she has some concern about him she wishes to share with me.

My memories of Dr Bone are not pleasant ones and, even though he was a hard-working and proficient surgeon, the thought of him as a man still makes me shudder. It was only the good company of the patients and staff, and the fact that I rarely found myself alone with him after what happened, that made his presence there bearable. The thought of Edith keeping house for him is not a comfortable one. I hope he treats her as a gentleman should. The Edith I know is no shrinking violet so I trust she would not allow him to take liberties.

She wishes to meet me at Miss Forrest's tea shop in the High Street. It is a suitable place for ladies to meet and yet I find myself there very rarely. Our appointment is tomorrow and I write a hasty reply which I shall give to Sybil to post.

I look forward to our meeting. It will be good to see Edith again and hear how she does. And I know that curiosity will force me to enquire about Dr Bone. I do not like that man.

Chapter 17

That night I dream of Tarnhey Court. I dream that it is night and I am on duty, sitting at the desk at the end of the ward with all my patients lying in their neat little beds. Everything is still and silent. No sounds of the country night; no screaming foxes or hooting owls. No sounds from the men; no snores or snuffles; no calling for 'nurse' in the long hours of darkness. I pick up the lamp on the desk and begin my rounds but every man is lying on his back with his arms neatly folded over his chest. I begin to cover their faces with their sheets because I know they are all dead, every one. But I feel nothing. No panic and no shock that my patients have all died on me in the night. I go about my grim business calmly until a figure appears in the doorway. Dr Bone in his white coat. He fills the door-frame, looming there like an ogre in a fairy story, and I am in the centre of the ward when he starts to move towards me, gliding like a phantom across the floor.

I stand there paralysed until he is close to me. I can smell his breath; brandy and tobacco. And I feel the warmth of his body as his hands tear at the buttons of my uniform. He is stronger than I am and any attempt to push him away is useless. I feel his hands lift my skirts but I cannot scream and the dead men in the beds cannot come to my defence.

I wake, sweating and heart racing, before I can experience the well-remembered moment of pain – the moment of shame and betrayal that I have tried so hard to expunge from my conscious memory. Then I lie there for a minute or so, too shocked to move. I have had that same dream several times since the war finished and each time its effect is the same. I know it will take me fifteen minutes or so before I can compose myself and face Father at breakfast. But at least it's not as disturbing as that other dream I have on occasions.

I wash and dress slowly, taking deep, calming breaths and wondering if it was Edith's letter and her association with Bone that triggered this latest nightmare. I hope my coming meeting with her won't stir up painful memories again. Some things are best forgotten.

I help Father in his surgery as usual. I like to think he is coming to appreciate my work, perhaps even to consider me indispensable. I am able to lift the burden of many routine medical matters from his shoulders now that I am there to clean and bandage wounds, give injections and deal with other minor complaints. And yet it is still my dearest wish to train in some big hospital, to become a Sister one day with real responsibility for the patients in my care. In optimistic moments I know that, in time, I'll persuade Father to agree. In others I realise that since John's death, I am all Father has and this means he'll always be reluctant to let me go.

Lunch is served by Sybil as usual. She is a fair cook, even though she displays little imagination in the kitchen. When I praise her she blushes as if some suitor has made a naughty suggestion. Then, while Father is out of the room I ask her about her cousin, Jack Blemthwaite, although I don't mention my coming appointment with Edith. There will be plenty of time for that.

Sybil seems to have more than her fair share of cousins but Jack is a cousin on her mother's side while Edith is on her father's. She confirms that what Roderick told me is true: Jack and his mother have gone to stay with yet another cousin in Glossop, four and a half miles away, until all the fuss dies down. Jack, she says, is nervous about returning to the village where he's been blamed for such terrible things and I tell her I understand and to pass on my good wishes if she sees his mother. She agrees and gives me a tight little smile, as if she considers it our secret.

After lunch I put on my hat and coat and tell Father I am going for a walk while he calls on his patients. He seems preoccupied and says nothing. I do not intend to mention Edith's name.

Once past the square, I walk down the High Street, passing the Black Horse on my right. The sight of the inn reminds me of the inspector from London. From Scotland Yard. The very name conjures thoughts of mystery and adventure and I wonder what the man is like. Father has met him, of course, but he said little about him. Wenfield is not a large place so I'm bound to meet him sooner or later. I wonder how I'll recognise him then I realise he'll probably be in the company of Sergeant Teague or one of the other policemen at the station. All I have to do is to look for a stranger who looks out of place in the village.

Miss Forrest's tea room is a most respectable establishment. In spite of Mrs Jackson's best efforts to make the Black Horse an island of gentility, ladies usually choose to meet at Miss Forrest's with its chintz curtains and snowy lace tablecloths while the Black Horse has come to be regarded as the place where businessmen from Wenfield's three mills – the men who pass for captains of industry around these parts – gather to talk commerce over lunch or dinner. And since the war ended, people from Manchester, having started taking the train out here to enjoy the countryside, also seek refreshment there. I wonder if there will be more of them as the war becomes a distant memory.

I push the tea room door open and a bell rings, bringing Miss Forrest gliding from the back with an ingratiating smile of greeting and a leather-bound menu. I ask for a table for two and Miss Forrest leads me to one by the window. I thank her and a girl dressed in black with a starched white cap and apron steps forward to take my coat on her employer's instructions. I nod to some of the other women in the room; the mill manager's wife sipping tea alone in the corner and Mrs Bell, the vicar's wife, who is sitting with her elderly mother. As her mother peers myopically at a menu, Mrs Bell looks up, smiles and gives me a discreet wave. She is an amiable woman. And one of the few who shared my opinion of Jack Blemthwaite's innocence.

I have arrived five minutes early and Edith is exactly on time. I watch as she enters, setting the little bell

116

ringing again and when she sees me she smiles shyly, as though she's not quite sure of her reception.

I return her smile as she approaches the table, followed by the girl in the starched apron who is preparing to take her coat.

Once Edith is settled in her seat I study her closely. She has hardly changed since I last saw her; in fact she looks well and a little plumper than I remember. I notice a few grey hairs amongst the gold but, other than that she has retained her beauty, which is more than can be said for most women of her age around here. I can't help wondering whether Dr Bone finds her attractive. Or perhaps it's just youth and innocence that excites him – or the despoiling of those fragile things.

'How are you, Flora?' she asks once we have ordered tea and scones from the starched girl.

Now that we are together, we both seem to be lost for words but I try my best to answer.

'I am well. Father is well.'

'And my cousin Sybil is looking after you?'

'Very well. She's become a passable cook.' I smile awkwardly. There is so much I want to say but the way must be cleared with small talk first.

'I was so very sorry to hear about John,' she says gently, putting her hand on mine.

'Thank you. But I don't think there's a family in the village who hasn't lost somebody.' I could have added 'apart from the Cartwrights' but I don't.

'It is such a relief that the war is over, don't you think?' I see anxiety in her eyes and wonder if there's somebody she herself has lost; whether she met somebody after she left our house to go and do her bit in the New Mills factory.

117

'Yes, it's a great relief.'

'Sybil told me that you nursed during the war.'

'I joined the VADs and worked up at Tarnhey Court.' I pause for a moment. 'It made me realise that nursing is what I want to do. Proper nursing. I've written to a hospital in the hope of getting a place to train.'

'Your father must be so proud of you.'

'Not exactly. He disapproves of a woman having a career of her own.'

Edith frowns. 'Times are changing, Flora. He has to realise that.' She hesitates. 'I hardly dare ask this, considering how many young men we've lost, but is there a sweetheart?'

I shake my head and for a few moments I sit in silence. Then I tell her what she wants to hear. 'There was a young man; one of the patients I nursed. He was an officer from Manchester ... a district called Didsbury. Once he was discharged we corresponded for a while but then ...' I hesitate as though the subject is still painful. 'I received a letter from his mother to say he went back to the Front and he was killed the day after he arrived. She'd been told that he died bravely with no pain. The letters always said that. When we heard about John those were the exact words they used.'

Edith assumes a sympathetic expression and squeezes my hand. 'It's been a difficult time for all of us.'

'You lost somebody too?'

She shakes her head. 'There was nobody,' she says simply.

'You work for Dr Bone now?' I can't resist the question. The more I know about him the less my imagination will transform him into a monster. I want him to be ordinary. Weakened and harmless.

'As soon as the war ended, so did my employment in the factory and when I heard that a doctor was looking for a housekeeper I applied for the post. It wasn't as if I didn't have experience of such work.'

She smiles as though she's happy in her work. But I wonder how she can be.

'Dr Bone has recently set up a practice in New Mills and he visits the Cottage Hospital here in Wenfield three times a week.' She hesitates. 'He worked at Tarnhey Court during the war so your paths must have crossed.'

'Yes.' I don't feel inclined to elaborate on my experience of the man. I don't wish to shock Edith. This fresh reminder of his visits to the Cottage Hospital and his regular presence in Wenfield disturbs me and I wonder if I should be more on my guard. But if he travels by motor car, he might not linger in the village.

'I'll ask him if he remembers you.'

I feel a sudden panic. 'No. Please. I was only a humble VAD so I'm sure he won't.'

She looks at me curiously, as though she's sensed something is wrong and I regret the vehemence of my words. But she says nothing more on the matter and changes the subject.

'These murders at Wenfield have been the talk of New Mills. I believe they've called in Scotland Yard. Is that right?' She says the words with relish, as though she was enjoying a mystery by Sir Arthur Conan Doyle. But this is no fiction created to entertain. These women's deaths are real.

'Father conducted the post mortems.'

'Of course. Have you met the policeman from London?'

I shake my head and realise how much I long to meet

him, to encounter somebody from the outside world who has no connection to Wenfield with its petty disputes, prejudices and loyalties. I want to know about his life in London, that place I've only heard about in stories. London can be reached by the trains that stop at Wenfield station ... but it might as well be on another planet. Perhaps I will go there one day. I am only twenty-two so there is time yet. I don't plan to spend all my life in Wenfield.

'I hear no news of the Cartwrights where I live,' Edith says.

'It was their parlour maid who was murdered. Lady Cartwright was very shocked ... understandably.'

'What about Roderick? How is he?' She tilts her head to one side and gives me a knowing look.

'He survived the war.'

'Good. You and Roderick were always close when you were growing up and I always wondered whether you and he ...'

I shake my head but I say nothing.

'So many young men gone,' she sighs. 'We have to grab our opportunities with both hands. Don't let them pass you by, will you, Flora?'

I see now that she thinks I am at risk of being an old maid as so many others are condemned to be. I hardly like to tell her that I don't really care.

We eat our scones and drink our tea, making conversation. I discover that she has travelled to the village with Dr Bone in his motor car. Today is one of the days he works at the Cottage Hospital and, with all this influenza about, he's come earlier than usual and plans to go back to New Mills to take his evening surgery before returning to Wenfield later. I ask Edith if he knows she is meeting me but she shakes her head. She told him she was meeting a friend but she didn't name names and I feel relieved. She carries on talking, praising her doctor and his winning ways with his patients and I listen politely, my lips pressed tightly together lest I am tempted to blurt out the uncomfortable truth. Then something she says catches my attention.

'To think that he was over this way on the evenings those women were murdered.'

'He might have seen something.'

'The police never came to ask him.'

'Perhaps he should tell them he was here.'

'I'm sure he would have done if he had any information.' There is something smug about her answer, as if she has complete confidence in his natural honesty. She has clearly only seen a good side to the man. I was unfortunate enough to experience the bad.

'Do you intend to call on Father?' I ask.

She hesitates and I see her face flush. 'I think it's best if I stay away.'

I feel a little disappointed. I realise now that Edith was good for Father and I suspect he misses her. I remember standing outside the drawing room and hearing voices – Edith's and my father's. I heard him asking her to be his wife but I couldn't make out her reply. A couple of days after that she announced she was leaving to do her bit for the war effort and I wondered then whether his clumsy proposal was the reason she fled our house – for that is how it seemed to me at the time. If she couldn't return his feelings then, I can understand why she's too embarrassed to see him now. She has chosen to work for Dr Bone and

I wonder afresh how she feels about her new employer. Is there an attraction there? But she gives no hint. The matter must remain a mystery.

It is time to part. We pay the bill, splitting it evenly, and the starched little waitress brings our coats. Miss Forrest bids us goodbye with an obsequious smile and says she hopes to see us again soon.

Once we're outside in the street, Edith says she's walking to the Cottage Hospital to wait for Dr Bone. She tells me she'll stand beside his motor car until he emerges from the entrance as arranged. She does not wish to be late and inconvenience him in any way. He is a busy man.

We begin to walk down the High Street. I don't know whether we'll arrange to meet again because I suspect her curiosity about my present welfare has now been satisfied. I think how I once came to regard her almost as a mother; how I was so hopeful that marriage to my father would keep her with us forever. Five years ago we were happy. Five years ago the young men of the village were alive and looking forward to a future with their wives and sweethearts. A lot can change in five years.

We part at the crossroads with a handshake, not a kiss. She's chosen to turn right, a route that avoids passing our house, and I watch her disappear down the street. Then I see something that makes me catch my breath. A familiar figure is walking towards her, carrying a large leather bag. It's inevitable now that Edith and my father will meet.

Even from twenty yards away I can recognise the stiff hesitation of embarrassment. But Father lifts his hat to her and continues walking. I see her glance over her shoulder at him before continuing on to keep her appointment with Dr Bone.

Father is walking my way but he doesn't appear to have seen me. I retrace my steps and nip into the doorway of Miss Forrest's tea room just as Mrs Bell, the vicar's wife, is on her way out, supporting her elderly mother's arm. We exchange pleasantries and I enquire about the vicar's health. He's been a martyr to gout for many years and I learned from Sister during my time at Tarnhey Court that a poultice of potato juice is sometimes efficacious in such cases. However, when I suggested this remedy to Father, he ignored me and the vicar still suffers.

I myself suggested the remedy to Mrs Bell after church one Sunday but I don't know whether she has tried it. And why should she? To the village I am a chit of a girl unqualified to offer advice to anybody. I am just the daughter of the village doctor and a mother who was no better than she should be; a woman who abandoned her family for another man.

I look up the street and see that Father is no longer there so I wish Mrs Bell and her mother good day and hurry off. I have preparations to make before evening surgery and I need to think. Edith's talk of Dr Bone has unsettled me.

I am almost at the house when I see a motor car approaching. A small black model, similar to my father's. I only have to cross the cobbled street to reach my front door but instead I stand there watching, peering at the vehicle. The weak sun reflects off the glass so I can't see the driver's face but I can make out two figures in the front seats; a man and a woman. And as it comes closer, I see the woman is wearing a hat like Edith's. Which means the man must be Dr Bone. As it draws level with me I can see their faces at last and I step back and put up a hand to shield my own, pretending I am brushing off an insect. But to my horror Edith has seen me and she says something to her companion. But his eyes don't stray from the road. He will not look at me.

I watch the car disappear down the street and the memory returns like an unexpected blow. Dr Bone used to take a great interest in the dovecote while we worked at Tarnhey Court. That's where he took me that night and my humiliation was accompanied by the soft cooing of those innocent white birds.

Chapter 18

Albert

The servants at Tarnhey Court all told the same tale. They'd heard nothing, seen nothing and they were saying nothing. Nobody had been aware of any interference with the dovecote, but that was hardly surprising because, according to the housekeeper, a military band could have been marching up and down in there and nobody would have been any the wiser.

The last person to be interviewed was the Cartwrights' chauffeur, a man called Sydney Pepper. His quarters were above the old stables, now home to two motor cars – Sir William's Rolls-Royce and his son Roderick's little Morgan. Pepper's job was to drive Sir William and Lady Cartwright in the Rolls. Their son, Master Roderick, preferred to drive himself, although he still expected his vehicle to be cleaned and polished to a sparkle.

They found Pepper in the stables where two horses, a carriage and a governess cart shared their space with the

Cartwrights' two vehicles. The chauffeur wasn't tall but he was built like a prize fighter. His hair was cropped as short as a convict's and the scar on his forehead added to the impression of a man in a permanent state of belligerence. His manner, however, belied his appearance. He was nervous. Obviously so.

As soon as Sergeant Teague saw Pepper, he was all for taking him down to the station for further questioning but Albert advised caution. He wanted to find out more about the man first and confirm the alibis he'd been given before he took any drastic action.

Pepper claimed that he'd been in the stables cleaning Sir William's Rolls-Royce at the time Sarah Cookham was killed. According to him those bloody doves that fly around the estate played havoc with the Rolls's shiny black paintwork. Always shitting on it, they were. They might look pretty but they were bloody vermin. Sergeant Teague had written down his words verbatim without comment.

When Albert asked him if he'd ever been tempted to kill any of the verminous creatures, he nodded eagerly. Then, realising he might just have incriminated himself he backtracked swiftly, saying he'd never actually harmed one in spite of the provocation.

After some thought he said he remembered Master Roderick coming into the stables that evening while he was cleaning the car. He thought he'd left a packet of fags in the Morgan but when he looked they weren't there so he left. He hadn't engaged the chauffeur in conversation and he wasn't sure whether he'd remember. But they could try asking.

Pepper's alibi for Myrtle Bligh's murder was equally

vague. He had been on his way to the Cartwright Arms when he changed his mind. He had a stomach ache and couldn't face the landlord's beer which wasn't always kept as well as it should be. Nobody had seen him on either occasion. And when he was asked whether he'd been aware that Jack Blemthwaite was cleaning out the dovecote around the time of Annie Dryden's murder, he shook his head. Sir William had taken the Rolls over to New Mills, choosing to drive himself, so he'd gone to the Cartwright Arms at opening time and he'd never seen the daft lad, he said – even earlier in the afternoon. For all he knew, Blemthwaite might have been lying. He might not have even been there at all because Lady Cartwright lived in a world of her own and she might have got the day wrong. You couldn't really rely on anything she said.

Albert recognised this as a clumsy attempt to shift the suspicion back to the original suspect. But he'd been around too long, heard too many lies, to fall for it.

Finally, just when the questioning appeared to be over, he returned to the subject of Sarah Cookham's murder. It was a tactic he'd used before – let the suspect relax then hit them with the hard interrogation.

As soon as Sarah's name was mentioned again, Pepper's manner changed. He fidgeted and avoided Albert's gaze. On the evening they said she was killed he'd cleaned the Rolls as he'd already said. Then for the rest of the time he'd been alone in his lodgings above the stables. He had no witnesses but he swore he didn't kill her. He hardly knew the indoors staff and he never had much to do with the maids.

Albert couldn't help wondering why Pepper's answers

to his questions sounded so unconvincing and evasive. It was possible the man had a criminal past and didn't like the police. But it was also possible that he'd been involved somehow in the women's deaths. And if Sir William was right and the son of the house hadn't been responsible for Sarah Cookham's pregnancy, to Albert it seemed feasible that the chauffeur might have taken a shine to her.

As the interview drew to a close, Pepper, who'd been nervous at first, was looking positively terrified.

'Look, I know I haven't anyone to back me up,' he said. 'But I'm telling the truth. I don't know nothing.'

'Were you the father of Sarah Cookham's baby?' Albert asked.

Suddenly Pepper relaxed. He unclenched his fists and bowed his head. The tough man had gone, diminished into a shadow. 'Chance'd be a fine thing,' he said with a sigh of resignation.

Albert looked at Teague and saw the sergeant fingering the handcuffs in his pocket. But Albert thought he knew what might be coming. He'd been at the Front himself.

'What do you mean?' he asked gently.

'Had my tackle shot away at Wipers, didn't I? I can't do it no more. Doctors'll tell you.'

'I'm sorry,' said Albert. 'It must make you angry.'

'There's a lot worse off than me, I suppose.' He looked away, bitter now. Albert suspected he'd once valued his virility. His injury had been the cruellest one of all.

'Can we have a look at your rooms?' said Albert.

'Why? I ain't done nothing.'

'Just routine,' said Albert.

Pepper mumbled something Albert couldn't quite

128

make out before nodding towards a set of stone steps in the corner. 'Up there. But you won't find nothing.'

Albert made his way upstairs, Teague following. When he glanced back he saw that Pepper had started polishing the Rolls, as though he needed something to occupy his hands.

'What do you think, sir? Do we arrest him?'

Albert didn't answer. Even though Pepper could be ruled out as the father of Sarah's baby, his wounds didn't prove he wasn't the killer. What if his injuries had left him angry and vengeful? Did this give him even more of a motive? He thought of the way the bodies were found, the skirts raised as though they'd been violated. But, according to the doctor, there had been no sexual interference so perhaps the killer was incapable of finishing the act. But, in spite of his suspicions, he needed proof. Jack Blemthwaite had been arrested without any real evidence ... and Albert didn't intend to make the same mistake.

Pepper's room was large but dark, lit only by one round window set high in the wall. The walls had been distempered years ago but now they needed another coat. However, the room was arranged with military tidiness, the small bed made to a standard that would satisfy the most exacting sergeant major and nothing out of place.

Teague started to search through a neat pile of books lying on top of the chest of drawers in the corner of the room and Albert told him to be careful to leave everything as he found it. He saw Teague roll his eyes and carry on, taking a photograph album from the bottom of the pile and flicking through the pages.

'What have you got there?'

'Photographs. Want a look . . . sir?'

Albert took the album from him, expecting to see the usual posed family portraits; the man's parents, perhaps. Or a woman who had once been his sweetheart. But instead he saw a series of group pictures. Soldiers in uniform posed in rows. He recognised Pepper on the front row, sitting cross-legged at the end, his officers on chairs in the centre of the row. Pepper had a pair of stripes on his sleeves. He'd been a corporal.

He turned the page and saw another group. This time the uniforms were different. But Albert recognised the clothing immediately as the uniforms of a military hospital. Hospital blues. Albert remembered them well. The men were sitting in rows again, some with missing limbs, some sporting crutches and others in wheelchairs. At both ends of the picture stood nurses in spotless white aprons and caps. The nurses looked as young as most of the men. A generation blighted by injury, suffering and death.

Something about the photograph looked familiar but he had to study it for a few moments before he realised why. He recognised the facade in the background as the front of Tarnhey Court. Sydney Pepper had been there as a patient during the war and he'd returned to work there as a chauffeur. He wondered why he hadn't mentioned it. But then he'd never asked.

He pocketed the photograph without knowing quite why. There were several similar ones in the album so he hoped Pepper wouldn't realise it was missing. He'd been given the impression that the chauffeur was new to the area, a stranger. But now it turned out he had been resident in that very house before. The convalescing men would have been able to visit the village so had he met the victims there? Had he chosen them then? Brooded and imagined what he would like to do to them when he regained his health? It was a possibility that had to be considered.

Albert stood and watched as Teague continued his search. And when the sergeant squatted down to see beneath the bed he saw a look of triumph on his face as he removed something from the dark gap between the springs and the floorboards. A bayonet. Teague held it up like a trophy.

'This could be the murder weapon. We've got him, sir.'

Albert couldn't deny that he experienced a frisson of excitement. But he suppressed it swiftly. A bayonet was a common souvenir of war and lots of men had kept them – including himself. His too was hidden; he'd placed it at the back of his wardrobe at home. Mary said she felt safer knowing it was there.

'Can you see any bloodstains on it?'

Teague shook his head, disappointed. 'Clean as a whistle. But he was a soldier; he'd know to keep his weapons in good order. Do we bring him in?'

Albert considered the question for a while. 'Not yet. I want to speak to Roderick Cartwright before we do anything else.' He heard a half-hearted protest from Teague but he ignored it. 'Roderick was definitely around on the evening of Annie Dryden's death and I want to see what he has to say for himself about Pepper's claim that he was there at the time of Sarah Cookham's murder too. Let Pepper think he's in the clear for now. Put the bayonet back where you found it.'

Teague looked as if he was about to argue but after a

few seconds he did as he was told, although Albert could tell he wasn't happy about it. Eventually he spoke. 'If another poor woman gets killed ... sir ...'

'I'll take that risk,' Albert said quickly. But as soon as he'd uttered the words he began to have doubts. Was Teague right? If it was Pepper and he struck again, how would he feel if the life of an innocent soul was lost as a result of his stubborn pride?

'Very well,' he said with a sigh. 'We take the bayonet to the station and tell Pepper what we're doing.'

Teague gave a smug smile, as though he'd gained a small victory over the man from Scotland Yard. Then, without a word, he retrieved the weapon and tucked it under his arm like a sergeant major's swagger stick.

Albert followed him out, suspecting he'd just lost face. But what was that over a human life? For four years life had been cheap. Now it was precious.

Chapter 19

Albert was told that Roderick Cartwright had taken his car and driven to Manchester again. It seemed Roderick spent a lot of time there these days and Albert was beginning to wonder if he was avoiding him deliberately. When he'd telephoned Tarnhey Court from the police station, the housekeeper had informed him that Master Roderick intended to spend that night at his Manchester club but he should be back the following morning. Albert felt frustrated but there was nothing he could do till tomorrow.

It was seven o'clock when he left the station to return to the Black Horse, taking some files with him to read during the evening. He wanted to go through the statements given by the staff at Tarnhey Court and look for discrepancies. He also wanted to see whether there was someone in the village he should be looking at more closely. He needed to get to know the characters who lived there and the resentments that, no doubt, festered in that small community ... and he wanted to find out whether there was anybody whose mind might have been so damaged by the war that they were capable of committing this dreadful atrocity. Many had been left with scars nobody could see.

Sergeant Teague suggested that they had a word with the vicar, the Reverend Bell, the next morning and Albert had to acknowledge that it wasn't a bad idea. The man would be aware of people's troubles. Maybe he'd even know their deepest secrets.

Albert was making his way back along the street when the world around him began to spin. It was a feeling that had become familiar since the shell had exploded, knocking him off his feet and sending burning fragments hurtling towards his face. He had hit his head against the side of the trench. Hard. And he'd lost consciousness only to wake and find that his hand was a bleeding stump and he could no longer walk.

He did his best to keep upright, knowing the feeling would soon pass. But, in the meantime, his aim was to get back to his room without losing his dignity. He put out his right hand to steady himself against a wall but then he realised he'd just started crossing the street. He stumbled and put out his damaged hand to save himself then he felt a pain on the side of his face as he hit the cobbles. The side bearing the still tender scars that ached in the cold and damp and itched in the heat.

He lay on the ground, half aware of running footsteps and voices. In his dazed state it took him a few seconds to realise why the voices sounded so strange. Then he realised that it was the accent, so different from that of his native London. He found it hard to understand what they were saying to him but he could make out the words 'hurt' and 'doctor'. He tried to protest that he didn't want to make a fuss but they weren't listening to him and he was soon being hauled to his feet, supported by two men whose breath smelled of beer. In spite of his insistence that he wanted to go to the Black Horse, they appeared to be taking him in the opposite direction, half carrying him between them towards a large stone house just off the main street. He could feel something warm dripping down his face but it took him a while to realise that it was blood.

One of the men lifted a large brass door knocker in the shape of a lion's head and let it fall three times. Albert knew it was useless to argue that he'd be fine on his own, especially now the blood was dripping down his cheeks. When he put up his right hand to wipe it away, he felt it damp and sticky on his flesh.

The door opened to reveal a thin woman in the plain black dress of a servant. She was clearly used to such occurrences because she ushered them calmly into a side room lined with chairs and told them the doctor was out on a house call. 'Did they want to wait or go to the Cottage Hospital?'

But before a decision could be made another young woman appeared in the doorway. She was taller than the first girl with wavy brown hair that she'd attempted to tame into a bun. Her eyes were large and green and Albert, in his dazed state, thought her beautiful.

'I'll see to this, Sybil,' she said to the girl in black. She spoke with the authority of the lady of the house and Albert wondered if she was the doctor's wife.

She sat down beside him, thanking his two escorts and giving them a nod of dismissal. Their duty was done.

'The doctor's not here at the moment but I can dress your wound. It doesn't look too bad,' she said, touching the scarred flesh gently. 'How did it happen?'

'I fell in the street. Those two chaps picked me up and brought me here.' He wasn't going to admit to feeling faint. He didn't want this woman to fuss and insist that he wait to see the doctor.

He was grateful when she asked no more questions and told him to follow her through into the next room. When he arrived he saw it was a doctor's surgery with a couch and folding screens against the far wall and a monumental desk in the centre.

The young woman opened the door of a glass cabinet, took out a bottle and some white dressings and told him to sit. He made for the patient's chair beside the desk but she pointed to the couch.

Once the wound had been cleaned to her satisfaction, she began to speak. 'I haven't seen you before. Are you here visiting one of the mills?'

'No.'

'You're from London, aren't you? I can tell by your accent. I nursed a few boys from London during the war.' She smiled at the memory.

If she was a nurse, that explained why she was so adept at dressing wounds and so unaffected by the sight of blood, Albert thought.

'Were you nursing at the Front?'

She gave him a rueful smile. 'I'm afraid my father wouldn't allow that.'

'Your father? You're not married to the doctor then?'

136

'No, he's my father. There you are. All done. No stitches needed. It looked worse than it was.'

He put a hand up to his face and felt the dressing. It was smaller than he'd expected and he began to feel faintly embarrassed, as if he'd caused a lot of fuss about nothing.

'Come back tomorrow and I'll change the dressing for you.' She gave him another smile.

He held out his hand. 'Albert Lincoln.'

'Flora Winsmore. Pleased to meet you.'

She took his hand. Most people focused on his damaged one, but she didn't. She looked him straight in the eye and he liked her for it.

'Thank you, Miss Winsmore. I'll see you tomorrow.'

'You never told me what you're doing in Wenfield.'

'Didn't I? I'm normally at Scotland Yard. I've been called up here to help your police.'

'About the murders,' she said.

'Yes. About the murders.'

She said nothing more, as though the subject of murder had subdued her spirits. But that was hardly surprising, he thought. The women of the village must have been living in fear since the outrages began, always wondering who would be next. Looking around suspiciously whenever they went out. Imagining it could be them.

He said goodbye and the maid saw him off the premises. But when he was out in the street he glanced back at the house.

That night he slept well. Strange, he thought when he awoke the following morning, that he never dreamed of Mary these days. Sometimes he felt guilty about it.

As he lay in bed the next morning listening to the

sounds outside in the street, his right hand travelled up to his face and he felt the dressing there. The area was sore and he cursed himself for showing such weakness.

He stared up at the cracks in the ceiling for a while, wondering if he was fit for the task that had been entrusted to him and nursing the ache of self-doubt that had plagued him throughout his life. But then his mind wandered to Flora Winsmore. He was due to see her later that day to have his dressing changed and he realised that he was contemplating the prospect with more eagerness than was appropriate. He shut his eyes and tried to force himself to think of the case, to go over in his mind all the things he planned to do that day, but Flora kept intruding.

Eventually he swung his legs out of bed and stood up, steadying himself with his good hand. After a swift wash he dressed and prepared himself mentally to go down to breakfast. Mrs Jackson seemed a pleasant woman but he didn't feel like making polite conversation when he had so much on his mind. And he hoped she wouldn't ask about his face. When he'd arrived back the previous evening he'd hurried up to his room to avoid being seen but now a public appearance was inevitable. He practised the lie he would tell. He was good at lies.

He took his watch from his waistcoat pocket and saw that he was late. But he was hungry so he didn't intend to miss breakfast and he knew that they could cope at the police station until he arrived.

Mrs Jackson had clearly been waiting for him to come down because as soon as he reached the foot of the stairs she emerged from the kitchen door carrying his hot breakfast.

'Oh dear, what have you done to your face?' she asked with a concerned frown as he sat down at the scrubbed wooden table.

'I tripped over a kerbstone and fell in the street.'

The words came out easily and he could tell by the look of sympathy on her face that she'd believed him. And there was something else too; disappointment perhaps that his explanation hadn't been more dramatic. Wrestling a crazed killer to the ground perhaps, or being punched by a desperate robber.

'Miss Winsmore dressed my wound.'

It was hard to read Mrs Jackson's expression as she placed his breakfast in front of him. 'The doctor's daughter?'

'That's right. She told me she worked as a nurse during the war.'

'I believe she did. I don't know her well but she seems a nice enough young lady. I expect her father's glad to have her at home. He lost his only son in the war, you see. And his wife ... ' She stopped speaking, as people do when they think they've said too much.

'What about his wife?'

'Oh, it was a long time ago ... when John and Flora were young.'

Albert waited, looking at her expectantly, knowing from long experience that people can never resist the urge to fill a silence. She looked round, as if she was afraid she might be overheard.

'He was staying here. His name was Nerrist and he was in Wenfield on business. He told my husband he was an engineer and he was visiting one of the mills, something to do with machinery for making cloth. I think he was from Liverpool or thereabouts.'

Albert guessed where this was leading but he wished she'd get to the point.

'Anyway,' she continued. 'He met Mrs Winsmore, the doctor's wife, and word has it they started meeting secretly in Pooley Woods. Next thing we know, he finished his business in Wenfield and when he went back to Liverpool the doctor found his wife had upped and left as well without a word. No note for the children. Nothing. Disgraceful, that's what I call it. How can a woman leave her little ones like that?'

'What was Mrs Winsmore like?'

Mrs Jackson thought for a while before replying. 'She was from Manchester – the doctor met her while he was working in a hospital there – and I got the impression Wenfield wasn't exciting enough for her. She came from a wealthy family by all accounts and her parents were dead so she was left comfortably off. She was always beautifully dressed and I've heard she liked balls and fancy dinners. I expect she wanted more out of life than being married to a village doctor.' She sighed. 'But we can't always have what we want in this life, can we?'

'It can't have been easy for the doctor, bringing up two children on his own.'

'It wasn't until Edith came that things settled down. Edith Barton was a young widow and she went there as the doctor's housekeeper. She became like a second mother to those children but she left to do her bit once the war started and I believe she's living in New Mills now. Nice woman.'

'And the children's mother was never heard of again?'

'Not that I know of.'

They had been talking so long that the runny fried egg on Albert's plate was starting to congeal, so he gave Mrs Jackson a dismissive smile and began to eat. But she hadn't finished.

'Mind you, there are those that say she never left.'

Her words caught his interest but his mouth was full so before he could ask the inevitable question, she'd bustled off in the direction of the kitchen. Perhaps it would be a topic of conversation for another morning, he thought. Something more intriguing than the usual small talk about the weather.

He arrived at the police station half an hour later and was greeted by a solemn-faced Sergeant Teague.

'Nothing new to report, sir,' he said with disappointment.

'Well I wouldn't have expected our man to turn himself in overnight,' Albert said lightly. 'I want to speak to Roderick Cartwright as soon as he's back from Manchester.'

'If you're sure, sir. Only Sir William's an MP and a magistrate and ...'

'I don't care if Sir William's the King himself. Roderick Cartwright was around at the time of at least two of the murders, he knew the last victim and, as far as I can see, he hasn't been questioned properly. I was told that he'd be back sometime this morning. And if he isn't we keep going back until he is.'

Teague looked alarmed at his boldness. All his life he'd been used to treating the Cartwrights like royalty. But history showed that there had been times when even royalty had revealed their dark side.

It was unlikely that Roderick would have returned

from Manchester at such an early hour but there were other things to do in the meantime. He wanted to speak to the vicar in the hope that he'd be willing to share his local knowledge. And perhaps it would also be worth having a word with his wife as she wouldn't be bound by the restrictions of her husband's spiritual position.

Albert decided to seize the opportunity to continue reading through the files that lay on the desk that had been allocated to him in the little tiled office off the station's main corridor. Sydney Pepper was still on his mind and, on top of one of the files, he found the photograph he'd taken from the chauffeur's quarters. He began to examine the faces: first the men, then the nurses standing at each side of the group.

He recognised Flora Winsmore at once. She looked so young in her uniform; the starched apron and the crisp white cap folded and pinned to conceal her wavy hair. There was a calm competence in her expression. And pride. It was her job to care for these men and she did it well.

As he studied the picture he noticed something strange. The faces of some of the men didn't look quite right. They weren't scarred and disfigured like his own. On the contrary, they looked flawless; so perfect that there was something vaguely inhuman about them, although he couldn't quite figure out why this was.

At least, he thought, he'd have something to ask Flora Winsmore when he saw her again. She'd be able to tell him all about the people at Tarnhey Court ... and about Sydney Pepper. She'd have seen him at his most vulnerable. She'd know his weaknesses.

However, that morning the vicarage was his first port

of call. He was tempted to go alone but Teague was lurking around his desk looking hopeful so he decided that including the local man was probably wise. The wind had just got up, stinging his raw cheek and shaking the branches of the trees that surrounded the churchyard. Albert held on to his hat with his good hand as Teague knocked at the vicarage door.

The Reverend Bell's maid answered. She was in her fifties with grey hair arranged in a tidy bun beneath her starched cap. She peered at them over her spectacles as Albert introduced himself.

Soon he was sitting beside Teague in the vicar's study perched on the pair of upholstered dining chairs kept in there so that the vicar's visitors could sit in tolerable comfort and drink tea. The Reverend Bell himself was a round-faced man with a fringe of brown hair around his shiny bald pate. He assumed an amiable expression and sat with his head tilted expectantly, waiting for them to begin.

'You know why we're here?' said Albert.

'I presume it's about these dreadful murders.' He glanced at Sergeant Teague. 'I heard that Scotland Yard were being called in. Since poor Jack Blemthwaite has been proved innocent . . .'

'Quite. I don't think the police have spoken to you yet, have they?'

'No.' He arched his fingers and his lips tilted upwards in a small, secretive smile. 'It seems I haven't been regarded as a suspect. Is that about to change?'

'I'm not sure,' said Albert, earning himself a killing look from Teague. 'I'm afraid I don't believe in ruling anybody out until I know otherwise. If His Majesty himself had been around these parts at the times in question, I'd be interviewing him as well.'

'Quite right, Inspector. The police should go about their business without showing fear or favour.'

Albert noted that Bell had a rich, mellifluous voice, perfect for delivering those long sermons. Or perhaps his weren't long. Perhaps he left his audience wanting more – always a wise option but not one that was open to a policeman.

'You were acquainted with all the victims, I take it?'

'I was.'

'What were they like?'

'They had little in common if that's what you mean. I can only describe Myrtle Bligh as very young and easily led. She was the sort who'd go along with anything suggested by a stronger nature. Annie Dryden liked to poke her nose into other people's business, I'm afraid, and didn't always make herself popular as a result. As for Sarah Cookham, I only knew her very slightly because she was a Methodist – not one of my congregation – but I have heard it said that she had a sharp tongue and big ambitions.'

'Did you know she was expecting a child?'

The vicar raised his eyebrows. 'Poor girl. Do you know who the father was?'

'That's what I hoped you'd tell me.'

'I'm sorry, Inspector, I can't help you there. In fact I've told you everything I know about the unfortunate women.' He leaned forward. 'I do pray that this tragic business is over and that your presence here will mean the killer, whoever he is, won't have the audacity to commit another outrage.'

'We can but hope. You must know the people of Wenfield pretty well. Do you have any suspicions? Is there anybody you think we should be keeping a special eye on?'

The vicar thought for a while. 'There are so many men here and elsewhere who have seen horrors beyond our imagination and who knows how that might have affected their minds. When you catch this man, it might be that he is not responsible for his actions. But that, of course, will not be the view of the authorities and he will almost certainly hang for his crimes. As for my suspicions, I am aware of nothing that could lead you to your killer. I'm sorry.'

In view of his observations about the men damaged by war, Albert found himself wondering whether Bell would have shared any suspicions if he had them. He seemed the sort of man who'd give the Devil the benefit of the doubt.

'Do you know Sydney Pepper – the chauffeur up at Tarnhey Court?'

'I'm afraid not. I don't think he has ever attended church.'

'What about Roderick Cartwright?'

The vicar's face clouded for a second, then he resumed his normal amiable expression. 'Yes, he attends church with his parents. Charming young man.'

But Albert had seen that look, there for a moment then gone. There was something about Roderick Cartwright that the vicar wasn't willing to share. But he wasn't inclined to press the matter just at that moment.

'By the way, where were you at the times of the three deaths?'

145

Again Teague looked horrified at the question but the vicar himself seemed quite relaxed as he answered, consulting his diary and providing an alibi for each occasion; a visit to a sick parishioner, a confirmation class and a meeting of the parochial church council. He told them they could confirm the appointments with the people involved and his wife and maid would vouch for him the remainder of the time. Albert would go through the motions of checking but all his instincts told him that Bell was telling the truth.

They returned to the police station and after an hour Albert suggested to Teague that they pay another visit to Tarnhey Court. He ignored the sergeant's suggestion that they should make an appointment so the family wouldn't be inconvenienced and walked ahead of Teague down the main street passing houses and shops: a baker's, a butcher's, a tea room with neat tables occupied by hatted ladies, and a chandler's with brooms and buckets hanging outside and a smell of creosote wafting from its dark doorway. Women walked with baskets on their arms, heads down against the wind as if they feared for their hats, and several men loitered outside the Cartwright Arms, waiting for opening time. Some of these men were elderly but others had the look of returned soldiers; strong, restless and without regular employment to keep them occupied.

It was an ordinary day in Wenfield but he had to remind himself that any one of those men could be a killer. He found himself studying the faces, looking for signs of guilt, even though he knew this was futile. A murderer, in his experience, rarely looked like a murderer. Many killers he'd known in the course of his career had seemed like mild-mannered nonentities. Ordinary men – and occasionally women – whose appearance belied an extraordinary darkness in their souls.

They passed the doctor's house and turned into Tarnhey Lane, passing Pooley Woods to their right. When they reached Tarnhey Court and Albert marched up the drive to the stables, he was conscious of Teague lagging behind. It was only when the sergeant saw they weren't making for the house that he caught up.

'Are we speaking to the chauffeur again, sir?' Teague asked hopefully. 'Are we going to make an arrest?'

'It's not Pepper I'm interested in this time. He can wait. I want to check if Roderick's car's here. If he's back from Manchester I intend to speak to him.'

Albert knew Teague wasn't happy about the prospect but again he ignored the sergeant's misgivings. The garage door was standing open and his spirits lifted when he saw Roderick Cartwright's Morgan parked there next to Sir William's Rolls-Royce. Sir William had been adamant that Roderick had nothing to do with the maid Sarah's pregnancy. But something about that young man had put the vicar on his guard. And he wanted to discover what it was.

The maid who answered the front door sniffed when she saw the identity of the visitors, but she stood aside to let them in and said she'd see if Master Roderick was at home. Once more they were shown into the drawing room but today there was no sign of Sir William Cartwright . . . or his wife for that matter. While they were waiting, Albert walked slowly around the room, taking in the paintings on the walls. He had already been told that the Cartwrights weren't an old family but there were enough portraits of ancestors to convince the casual visitor that they had a long and distinguished pedigree. However, the people in the pictures bore no resemblance whatsoever to Sir William and he knew these things could be purchased easily when scions of impoverished aristocrats auctioned off the family belongings. Ancestry by the yard. If he was right about this, the Cartwrights were deceivers. But was this their only deception?

It was a full five minutes before Roderick Cartwright appeared. He shook hands and apologised for keeping them waiting. The young man was all charm on the surface but Albert thought he could detect an uneasiness beneath his apparent confidence. He was nervous and Albert wondered why.

Roderick invited them to sit and asked if they'd like tea. Albert refused. He hadn't come there in search of refreshment.

Albert began to ask questions. Where had Roderick been when the three women had been murdered? The answer came smoothly. He'd been at Tarnhey Court on each occasion.

On the evening of Myrtle's death he'd been at home playing records on the new gramophone in his room, a new technological innovation that was his pride and joy: his parents would vouch for him. When Annie died, he had been visiting one of the tenant farmers before going for a drive in his motor car. He arrived home around eight when he paid Jack Blemthwaite for his work in the dovecote. They could check his stories if they wished. He spoke with such confidence that Albert almost believed him. Almost but not quite. There was something too glib about his replies, as though he'd practised them over and over in the privacy of his room until he was word perfect.

But when Albert asked about his dealings with Sarah Cookham, Roderick's manner changed. It was a small change, almost imperceptible, but Albert was used to observing suspects and he could see it.

'No, Sarah and I were never ... close like that,' he said. 'And I certainly wasn't the father of her child.'

'You know she was pregnant?'

'My father told me. To tell the truth, I wasn't attracted to the girl. I thought her a little ... ' He searched for the appropriate word. 'Sly. If I were to choose a mistress from amongst one of the servants, it certainly wouldn't have been Sarah.'

Albert raised his eyebrows. 'You've been intimate with your family's servants in the past?'

'No. I mean, none of them have been pretty enough.' Roderick gave a nervous smile and Albert found it hard to know if he was telling the truth.

'Have you any idea who the father of her child could be?'

'I knew nothing of her private life. She was a servant. Besides, I was away for three years during the war so I've no idea what went on here in my absence. You must ask the other servants.'

'We have. They say Sarah was secretive. She never spoke of a sweetheart so they assumed it wasn't just some young man from the village she was walking out with. That's why we thought it might be you.'

'I assure you it wasn't. I'm afraid you have to look elsewhere for Sarah's lover.'

'Where were you on the evening she died?'

'Here.'

'Did you leave the house?'

'I believe I went out for a walk but I didn't go anywhere near Pooley Woods. And before you ask, I spoke to nobody while I was out. I have no witnesses because I wished to be alone.'

'Is there any particular reason for this desire for solitude?'

'I wanted to consider my future.' He gave a long sigh. 'My father wishes me to train as a lawyer then, perhaps, to follow him into Parliament, but my inclinations lie elsewhere. I have acquaintances in Manchester who wish me to go into business with them.'

'What kind of business?' Albert asked, aware that Teague would probably think his bold question too impertinent.

Roderick hesitated for a few moments. Then he leaned towards Albert, as if he was about the share a confidence. 'We wish to open a new theatre in Manchester. As well as plays, we plan to show films. That's where the future lies, I'm sure of it. Coming from London, you must be aware of that.'

'I am indeed, sir.' Albert stood. 'Thank you for your time. And if you can think of anybody who could confirm your whereabouts on the evening of Sarah Cookham's death, that would be most helpful.'

A worried look appeared on Roderick's face. 'I'll try but I fear nobody saw me.'

Albert moved towards the door, Teague following like an obedient dog.

'What do you think, sir?' Teague said as soon as they were outside. He hadn't uttered a word throughout the interview and this was the first time he'd broken his silence.

'I think he's hiding something.'

'About Sarah?'

'As Shakespeare once put it, he doth protest too much, methinks.'

He saw Teague glance at him with fresh admiration. There was nothing like a few quotations from the Bard to impress the likes of Sergeant Teague.

'His alibis for all the murders seem rather vague,' Albert said. 'We need something more solid if we're to eliminate Roderick Cartwright from our inquiries.'

'But why would he do it, sir? What's his motive?'

'Who can fathom the mysteries of the human mind, especially after this war.'

Albert looked down at his left hand. He'd come back from the fighting changed forever. Perhaps Roderick Cartwright had too but in ways that weren't visible to a stranger. Perhaps there were things going on in that young man's head even he couldn't guess at.

Chapter 20

Albert had always liked to use his time efficiently and, as he needed to visit the doctor's to get his dressing changed, he planned to question Flora Winsmore about her time at Tarnhey Court while he was there.

He found he was looking forward to seeing Flora again, rather more than he thought appropriate for a married man. But no doubt she had a sweetheart somewhere, he told himself. Some young doctor she'd worked with during her time at Tarnhey Court perhaps. A man who'd stayed in Blighty to care for the wounded instead of allowing himself to be used as cannon fodder on the Front. Someone wiser than himself.

He went to the doctor's alone because this wasn't something he wanted to share with Teague. The man was stolid and unimaginative and his presence had begun to irritate Albert. However, he'd discovered during previous cases that local knowledge is essential. Not everywhere was London and not everyone thought like Londoners. Besides, the locals seemed to trust Teague and that was worth a lot. Albert needed him whether he liked it or not.

When he reached Dr Winsmore's door he knocked and waited, fingering his dressing and feeling suddenly like a shy suitor – which, he told himself, was ridiculous. After a while the door opened and the maid led him through to the chair-lined room where he'd waited the previous day. He sat down, his heart beating fast, and watched the door. Soon she'd appear, his ministering angel. Her gentle fingers would tend to his wounds.

But when the door opened it was Dr Winsmore who stood there. Instead of a surgical gown, today he wore a tweed suit and looked every inch the country doctor. Albert's heart sank as the man approached with his hand outstretched.

'I believe my daughter tended your injuries yesterday. Come through to my surgery.' The man seemed a little impatient as he led Albert through to the adjoining room.

'I'm sure there is no need to bother you, Doctor,' Albert said. 'It's a trivial matter and Miss Winsmore ... '

'Nonsense, man,' the doctor said gruffly. 'Now that you're here I might as well take a look.' He removed the dressing and tutted. 'Nasty cut. And on top of all that scarring as well. Is it painful?'

'A little.'

The doctor took a wad of cotton wood and dabbed on some stinging liquid. It hurt a lot but Albert wasn't going to let him know that.

'Where did you get that?' the doctor asked, nodding towards Albert's left hand.

'Going over the top. Shell exploded next to me. Lost three comrades. They told me I was lucky.'

'That's one way of looking at it.' Winsmore carried on working in silence. His fingers weren't as deft as Flora's and they felt clumsy on his tender flesh. 'At least my daughter can dress a wound,' the doctor mumbled after a while. 'She wants to go away and work in some hospital. Have you ever heard the like?'

'Nursing is a noble vocation. You must be very proud of her,' Albert replied.

The doctor's answer was a sceptical grunt.

Once the dressing was changed, Albert asked the question that had been on his mind since he entered the surgery. 'I'd like to speak to your daughter. Is she at home?'

A spark of worry suddenly appeared in the doctor's eyes. 'What do you want to speak to her about?'

Albert almost told him to mind his own business but he suspected this wouldn't increase his chances of getting his own way. 'It concerns a police matter I hoped she could help me with. I need some information about Tarnhey Court and what went on there during the war.'

'Why?'

'I'm afraid that's confidential.' He gave the man an apologetic smile but thwarting the doctor's curiosity with the use of his official position had given him a thrill of satisfaction.

The doctor gave another grunt and rang the bell at the side of the fireplace. After a few moments the maid appeared and dropped a little curtsey.

'Sybil, will you tell Miss Flora that a gentleman from the police wishes to speak to her.'

154

Sybil scurried away and the doctor invited Albert to take a seat beside the desk.

It wasn't long before Flora appeared, giving a tentative knock on the open door.

Albert stood and smiled reassuringly but when the doctor stayed where he was he feared the father intended to stay there as a chaperone which was the last thing Albert wanted.

It was time for decisive action so he turned to the doctor. 'Would you mind if I spoke to Miss Winsmore alone? I'm afraid some of my questions involve confidential police matters.'

For a moment it looked as if the doctor would refuse to move but, after a few moments' hesitation, he stood up. 'I'll be just outside,' he said to his daughter, shooting her a warning look.

As soon as he'd left the room, leaving the door slightly ajar, Albert went over and shut it. What he had to say wasn't for inquisitive ears.

Flora sat and looked at him expectantly. His memory of the previous day hadn't deceived him. She was beautiful but not in the usual sense. There was a liveliness about her, an intelligence, and that was something he'd always admired in a woman. Mary had been like that once … many years ago when they'd first met.

'How's your face?' was the first thing she asked.

'Your father's done a sterling job,' Albert replied.

'Good. I was told you wanted to ask me some questions.'

He took the photograph he'd found in Pepper's room from his pocket. 'When you said you'd nursed during the war, you didn't mention you'd been at Tarnhey Court.'

'Didn't I?'

'So many places were used as hospitals that I never thought ... I'd like to ask you about one of the men you nursed.'

'Which one? There were rather a lot.'

'His name's Sydney Pepper.' He pushed the photograph towards her. 'There he is. He works at Tarnhey Court now as a chauffeur.'

A look of realisation passed across her face. 'Sydney. Of course. I thought I recognised him.'

'Have you spoken to him recently?'

'No. When I saw him he was driving Sir William's Rolls-Royce. He looked so familiar but his name escaped me. Poor Sydney,' she said, a faraway look in her eyes. 'Before the war he worked in a factory that made motor cars and when I was nursing him he used to talk about them a lot. I expect his job suits him well.'

'A happy ending?'

'You could say that.'

'But ... ?'

'He suffered dreadful injuries.'

'What kind of injuries?'

She bowed her head. 'His groin. The poor man can never have children. He was engaged before he went off to France but ... '

'She didn't stick by him?'

'She wrote to him while he was in hospital saying she couldn't marry him. She couldn't face seeing his injuries.'

'Do you think she was wrong?' He didn't know why he asked the question. It wasn't relevant. It was too personal.

Flora gave him a curious look. 'I wouldn't like to judge.

156

But he took the rejection badly. He changed ... became very bitter. The cheerful lads were always the easiest to nurse, no matter how severe their injuries. It was seeing a man's spirit destroyed that was hardest to bear.'

'Do you think his fiancée's behaviour might have made him want to avenge himself on women?'

She turned her face away and Albert could sense her reluctance to incriminate her former patient, a man she had cared for and brought back to health.

'Could his bitterness have turned to anger – violence even?'

She looked at him and when he saw fear in her eyes he knew he'd hit on the truth. 'He lost his temper at times but I can't blame him. Fate dealt him a terrible blow and ...'

'Was he ever violent?'

The question hung in the air between them for a few seconds before Flora spoke. 'Yes. One of the ward maids spilled his tea and he hit her across the face. Sister had to ask one of the doctors to give him something to calm him down.'

'I'd like to speak to the girl he hit. What's her name?'

Another silence.

'Please. What's her name?' He saw tears welling up in Flora's eyes. 'What's the matter?'

She took a deep breath. 'Her name was Myrtle Bligh.'

Albert could tell from her expression that she felt like Pepper's betrayer. She, who had once nursed him and dressed his wounds, had been the one to condemn him to the gallows.

'You did right to tell me,' he said.

'Please go now,' she said softly.

He left the house without another word. And as soon as he returned to the police station he gave orders that Sydney Pepper was to be brought in for questioning. Also the chauffeur's bayonet was to be retrieved and placed in a cupboard in Albert's temporary office for safety so if Pepper was their man, at least the killer wouldn't have his weapon of choice to hand.

He sat down at his desk to think. Pepper had no alibi and he was known to have a violent temper. He'd probably harboured a resentment against women but was incapable of rape so this fitted with the fact that the victims' bodies hadn't been violated. He'd also known the first victim, Myrtle Bligh. He'd assaulted her and had had to be restrained. Albert could imagine the hatred festering within him and the possibility that some twisted logic made him blame the whole of womankind for his shattered life.

Sir William Cartwright would have to make do without a chauffeur for the time being. Sydney Pepper was the best suspect they had.

Once Pepper had been brought to the station and locked up in the cells, Teague was keen to begin the questioning. However, Albert advised delay, saying that a time of contemplation might lead to a confession and that would save them all a lot of trouble. But as he said the words, he was suddenly struck by a desire to extend his stay in Wenfield. He was in no hurry to get back to London and Mary. The thought of entering his own house and having to speak to his wife again brought on an ache of reluctance in his heart followed by a pang of guilt that he felt that way.

His mind kept returning to Flora Winsmore as though

some demon inside him was holding her image up beside that of Mary and tempting him to compare the two women. He tried to distract himself by telling Teague that he wanted to return to Tarnhey Court and make a more thorough search of Pepper's rooms.

As the two men left the police station the clouds that had gathered over the hills were starting to darken and Teague observed that it would rain before long. While they were walking Teague couldn't resist speculating about Pepper's guilt. It sounded to Albert as if he'd already made up his mind that they had their man, although he'd heard the sergeant had been just as certain after Jack Blemthwaite's arrest. And on that occasion he'd been completely wrong.

When they arrived the Rolls-Royce was parked in the stables but the Morgan had gone. Roderick Cartwright was out and about again. The room above the stables hadn't changed since their last visit. Everything was back in its allotted place. Perhaps this was a legacy of Pepper's years in the army.

'Let's get these cupboards searched properly,' Albert said. 'And that wardrobe.'

The first time they'd been in there they'd both been careful to leave everything as they found it, but now Pepper was under arrest consideration for the suspect's home wasn't a priority. The only important thing was that they didn't miss any vital piece of evidence. Albert searched through the cupboards while Teague saw to the drawers, throwing out their contents onto the floor.

'Hope you're going to put all that lot back again when we've finished,' Albert said as he approached the large wardrobe in the corner.

'Why? Pepper won't be worried about it . . . not where he's going.'

Teague was making assumptions, which Albert found irritating.

'He won't be going anywhere if we don't prove our case. Found anything yet?'

'Not a thing. I think we should have these floorboards up.'

'All in good time.'

He opened the wardrobe and saw that the clothes inside were hanging neatly on good quality wooden hangers. Pepper was a man who still took pride in his possessions, in spite of the terrible traumas he'd been through.

'Didn't I see in one of the reports that a soldier was seen near the woods on the night Myrtle Bligh died?' said Albert as he turned to face Teague.

'It was just a rumour . . . never confirmed. The witness had been in the Cartwright Arms since opening time,' he added meaningfully.

Albert ignored the insinuation. 'Pepper's army uniform's still here – all smart and pressed. Or someone might have seen him in his chauffeur's uniform and mistaken him for a soldier. Where did that story come from?'

'We never found out, sir. It was just one of those stories that gets about. A friend of a friend saw something . . . you know the sort of thing.'

'It might be worth trying to pin it down . . . find the witness.'

There were drawers in the bottom of the wardrobe and Albert started to open them, expecting to see more clothing, shirts and underwear perhaps. But he was surprised to see a face looking up at him. Or rather it wasn't a complete face; it was the top half a face, the forehead and nose with one realistic glass eye behind a pair of spectacles. The mouth and chin were missing. It was painted the colour of flesh. Beautifully tinted. A realistic work of art.

Albert recognised it at once for what it was: a portrait mask created by an artist to fit snugly over a casualty's face and conceal horrendous injuries and he now knew why some of the faces on the photograph they'd found in Pepper's room had looked so flawless. He'd seen such a mask before on a colleague at Scotland Yard; a man whose chin had been blown off by a hand grenade. The unfortunate man had lost the power of speech and he'd been assigned desk duties but his chin had been painted so skilfully that, on first sight, it would have fooled the casual observer. As he stared down at the fragment of a man's face, he wondered how it had come to be here and why it wasn't being worn by the man it had been made to help. The sight of that human face brought back memories of unspeakable pain and he closed the wardrobe door.

'Found anything, sir?' Teague asked.

'Nothing that helps us. What about you?'

Teague shook his head. If they had hoped to find a killer's diary detailing his crimes and the pleasure he took in committing them, they had been disappointed.

As Albert followed Teague out of the stables, Flora Winsmore once more intruded into his thoughts. Perhaps she could explain how Sydney Pepper came to be in possession of a portrait mask that clearly belonged to another man.

He needed to speak to her again.

161

Chapter 21

Flora

I keep remembering Sydney Pepper as he was when he was admitted to Tarnhey Court. I recall the day when he arrived in an ambulance and was carried through the front door on a stretcher as so many of them were, moaning with pain, his blood staining the blanket the ambulance men had thrown over him.

Sister was never kind to the ambulance men – she said they were conshies and didn't deserve to breathe the same air as our brave lads. She said they should have been at the Front fighting for King and Country. But I said nothing because it wasn't my place to question the motives of others back then.

When I saw what that shell had done to Sydney's body, I was almost sick. I remember breathing deeply as I tried to force the nausea away but when I inhaled all I could smell was the metallic scent of blood. I came to know that smell so well while I was at Tarnhey Court; I even became used to it. And it certainly wasn't as bad as the stench of gangrene.

I feel no better about betraying Sydney Pepper to the police. I lay awake all last night wondering if my words might have set that poor man off on the road to the gallows and now I have a headache and an uneasy conscience. Father says that if the man's innocent no British jury will find him guilty. He has great faith in the police, the British justice system and what he calls 'twelve good men and true'. Myself, I'm not so sure.

Perhaps I should mention to the inspector that Dr Bone is often in the village. But that might be taken as a suggestion that he should be treated as a suspect and the inspector might ask me how I came to form my opinion. I couldn't bear him to find out about that unfortunate incident at Tarnhey Court; that day my innocence was lost.

Two letters have arrived in the early post and Sybil has placed them on a silver tray in the breakfast room as usual. One is addressed to me and has a Manchester postmark. The other is for Father and the postmark is smudged so I can't quite make it out.

I am tempted to tear my letter open there and then before Father enters the room, but instead I slip it in the pocket of my skirt. If it is what I suspect, I don't wish him to see it and I know I'll have to do my best to hide my excitement and my nervousness. My future could depend on this letter.

Once Father has joined me and we are both seated at the breakfast table, Sybil enters the room carrying the food. I bid her good morning but Father is too busy opening his post to acknowledge her. I watch him tear his letter from its envelope and I see his face turn a worrying red behind his moustache. The letter contains something that alarms him.

'Is something the matter, Father?' I ask, putting down my cutlery.

Father is still staring at the letter in horror and I ask my question again. He pushes the letter to one side and assumes a calm expression. 'It's nothing. Just some nonsense. Nothing that need worry you, my dear.'

I know he lies because I can see fear in his eyes. Then I watch him screw the paper into a ball and throw it in the direction of the fire Sybil lit earlier in an attempt to alleviate the morning chill. It lands at the edge of the grate, safe from the feeble flames.

Before I can enquire further he leaves the room without touching his breakfast and once he is out of the room, I take my own letter from my pocket and tear it open. It is from the Matron of the Royal Infirmary thanking me for writing and saying that I might be invited for an interview in due course. I experience a glow of excitement and I am aware that a smile has come involuntarily to my lips. I watch the door for Father's return, knowing that I must keep the matter to myself for the time being, but when he doesn't return after a couple of minutes I begin to feel uneasy. It is not like him to abandon his food.

I wait a little longer and when he still doesn't appear I leave my seat and hurry to the fireplace to retrieve the letter from the grate. I have been watching the fire and I see that, even though the flames are now more established, they haven't yet reached the ball of paper. I bend over to pluck it out and once I have it in my hands I flatten it out.

I see there is no signature, and there is one question printed there:

YOU MURDERED YOUR WIFE – WHERE WERE YOU WHEN THE OTHERS DIED?

Chapter 22

I have kept my father's letter. I have it in my dressing table drawer amongst my undergarments; somewhere I am confident he will not venture to look because it is best if he thinks it destroyed. I think of those terrible words; surely nobody can think that my father has any connection with the recent outrages? It is true that on two occasions he was out of the house visiting sick patients but it is unthinkable that he could do such a thing. And the mention of my mother upsets me. She left of her own accord and I tell myself the note is a malicious lie. I've heard of others who've received such letters accusing them of awful things. It leaves a bitter taste but I must try to ignore it.

I keep my letter from the Matron in the same place. I have read her letter over and over many times since its arrival and each time I experience a sense of excitement. How good it would be to live in the nurses' home with my fellows and watch my patients as they recover. But I must put such thoughts aside for a while. There is no sense in confronting Father with my plans and risking an argument before things are more certain.

Father is out on his rounds and I am in the drawing room talking to Sybil about household matters when there is a knock at the door and she rushes to answer as she always does. I strain to hear and I can make out a man's voice which I recognise at once as that of Inspector Lincoln. As I stand up and smooth my dress, ready to receive him, I feel a tingle of anticipation passing through my fingers. Perhaps his wound needs more attention. Or perhaps it is me he has come to see, using his injury as an excuse. I dismiss the thought, take a deep breath and fix a smile of greeting to my face when I see the door open.

He enters the room and my eyes are drawn immediately to the left side of his face; the shiny blotchiness of the scarred flesh. He has discarded his dressing now and I can see the redness of his wound scabbing over and well on the road to healing. When he smiles at me I feel a glow of warmth even though there is still a chill in the air and I'd told Sybil that a fire was unnecessary.

'I see your wound's healing nicely, Inspector,' I observe after inviting him to sit.

'Thank you, yes. But that isn't why I'm here.'

He has a large leather bag with him that he carries carefully, as though it contains some delicate treasure. He places the bag on the floor and opens it and, unable to contain my curiosity, I crane my neck to see what's inside.

He lifts out an object which I recognise at once. A mask created skilfully to conceal terrible mutilation and

167

restore a man's face to its previous appearance. It is a mask that would save a brave man from enduring the revulsion of his fellows. I know of men who went into the village before such masks were fitted only to return with accounts of how people had averted their eyes in horror and how children had pointed and run away as if they'd seen a monster come to life. The masks had given them back their identities, their dignity and their lives.

'Masks like this one were made for some of our patients at Tarnhey Court,' I say. 'The ones whose faces were ... ' My eyes are drawn to his own mutilations, mild compared to some I'd seen. I wonder if he too had been offered a mask to conceal them. But they probably weren't judged severe enough.

'I know what it is. I wondered if you recognise it.'

'Where did you get it?'

'I'm afraid I can't say.'

I feel a little hurt that he isn't willing to confide in me. I'd felt a closeness, an intimacy between us when I'd dressed his wound but perhaps I was deluding myself. I'd felt attraction before. I'd even felt it for Dr Bone before his behaviour shattered my romantic illusions.

'I'm sorry,' he says, giving me an apologetic smile. 'It's a police matter, you see. Confidential. But I'd be very grateful for your assistance.'

'Of course. How can I help?'

'It's likely this came from Tarnhey Court. Can you tell me who it was made for?'

He hands me the mask and I cradle it in my hands, feeling it cold against my fingers. Such masks are created out of copper, coated in silver then painted with enamel and finished with varnish. I see there is a space left for one good eye to peep through but the other eye is glass, painted on the reverse. The eyebrows are painted delicately and the lashes created from fine strips of tinted metallic foil. This one is designed to cover the top half of the face and was attached to the wearer's face by a pair of spectacles which had served to hold it in place. It is so skilfully executed that at a distance it would be hard to tell that it was false. I know that face but the name refuses to come to me so I close my eyes in an effort to remember.

'You know who it belongs to?'

I study the mask, hoping the sight will jog my memory. And after a while an image emerges from the mist. A young man who must have been handsome before war changed everything. He'd been a lance corporal, tall with fair curls, but when I knew him he was very sick. I suddenly recall his name. George Smart. Lance Corporal Smart. I say his name out loud and it conjures him again, lying helpless on his bed.

'Where is he now?'

I look away. The memory hurts. 'He appeared to be recovering well – that's why the mask was made for him. But then after a few weeks, infection took hold and ...'

'So why would someone keep his mask?'

'Where did you say it came from?'

'I didn't.' He smiles at me as if he knows I'm trying to catch him out. For a few moments he doesn't speak, as though he is considering the matter. 'But I don't suppose it'll do any harm to tell you. We found it at Tarnhey Court ... in the chauffeur's quarters above the stables. Can you think how it could have come into Stanley Pepper's possession?'

The mention of Pepper's name tugs at my conscience again. 'I remember Stanley was there at the same time as George Smart and they used to smoke together outside on the veranda. I think they became good friends so the most likely explanation is that he kept the mask as a memento when George died.' I pluck up the courage to ask my next question. 'Do you really think Sydney killed those women?'

'I'm afraid I can't discuss that.' To my surprise he sounds genuinely sorry.

'I don't think he did it. I know I told you he hit Myrtle but ... I'm sure he ... '

I can see sorrow in his eyes, as though he pities my innocence and I suspect that he's convinced himself of Pepper's guilt. 'You nursed him back to health,' he says. 'It's understandable that you don't wish to believe him capable of something like that.'

What he says is true. I can't deny it and I don't try to.

He bows his head and sits in silence for a while, as though he is wrestling with some great dilemma and when he speaks his words surprise me.

'Miss Winsmore, I need your help. I know nobody here and I need some background information. If you are willing to share your knowledge of the village and its people ... their histories and their quarrels ... it would be enormously useful.' I see him swallow hard. This request is not easy for him to make. 'I would be most grateful for your assistance. A little advice here and there might make all the difference to my inquiries.'

'What about Sergeant Teague?'

He smiles, suddenly more confident. 'The trouble with local officers is that they see everybody from a policeman's point of view. And people tend to watch what they say when they know the police are around, even people who have nothing to hide. On the other hand, as the doctor's daughter, you're known and trusted. You see things others don't. Am I right?'

I realise he's been flattering me but I like the warm glow his words give me. I am trusted and he thinks me intelligent enough to read the motives of my fellow human beings. Or maybe he thinks I am duplicitous enough to spy on them.

'Of course it's vital that any conversation between us is conducted in private without the prospect of interruption.'

I see him glance towards the door. I know he fears Father will return any moment and I feel a sudden thrill of excitement. He wants to take me into his confidence. I'm important to him.

'We can't talk here,' I hear myself saying. I see him watching me but it's hard to know what he's thinking.

'Then can you suggest somewhere suitable?'

I think for a few moments, only too aware that if I'm seen with him it will be all round the village by tomorrow morning and I would be labelled either a loose woman or a collaborator ... or both. But I know a place where privacy is guaranteed. I suggest the little stone boathouse by the river. It is on the Cartwrights' land but since the war there are no gamekeepers or outdoor staff to patrol there. There is only Sydney Pepper who is languishing in a cell at the police station and not in a position to bother us. And the fact that he is in custody, the inspector says, means that I needn't fear walking alone. I take this to mean that he's convinced he has the right culprit this

171

time and, I must admit, Pepper's a more plausible candidate than poor Jack Blemthwaite. I tell the inspector that I often take an evening walk after dinner and I'll meet him there at seven.

'Your wife must be missing you, Mr Lincoln,' I say as he puts the mask carefully away in his bag. I watch his face for a reaction and I see a brief flash of panic in his eyes.

Then he turns to me. 'I'm widowed,' he says.

I mumble my condolences but he looks away.

I see him to the front door, surprised at how much I am looking forward to seeing him later. But I tell myself firmly that it is a professional matter. A police officer from Scotland Yard needs my help and I'm to provide him with useful local knowledge. Nothing more.

I watch as he walks off down the street in the direction of the police station. I imagine that when he gets there he'll interrogate Sydney Pepper about the mask. I try to imagine the scene and how Sydney will react. He was never an easy patient at Tarnhey Court and I can't help thinking that the unpredictability of his nature will go against him with the police. Will they understand how war has scarred his mind as well as his body? But surely Inspector Lincoln will, if anybody does. He's suffered too.

I step back to shut the door when I look up and see a man walking towards the house. My stomach lurches but before I can shut out the sight of him, he is there in front of me, staring into my face. There is no escape and I find myself wishing that the inspector hadn't been so quick to leave.

'Dr Bone,' I say. I know my voice sounds strained, as though it doesn't quite belong to me. 'Father is out. Can I give him a message?'

'What time will he be back?'

Bone is tall with a slick of dark hair. Many at Tarnhey Court used to call him handsome – quite the heart-throb – and I know he has that opinion of himself. Now I'm conscious of an arrogance about him, as though he thinks himself above the rest of us. I know others saw it but I was too innocent and impressionable back then to share their misgivings. He stands before me now, all charm, just as he used to at Tarnhey Court – until that evening when the pretence slipped and he revealed his true nature. Now as he smiles at me, it is as if he has forgotten what happened between us and he expects me to have done the same. But I can never forget.

'I expect him back at any moment.'

He looks at me expectantly, as though he wants to be invited in to wait. Courtesy demands that I admit him but everything in me screams against it. But I bow to convention and utter the words. 'Won't you come in, Doctor? My father shouldn't be long.'

'How are you, Flora?' he asks.

I make no reply as I usher him into the drawing room, almost colliding with Sybil in the hall. I ask him to excuse me and instruct her to take over and ask the doctor if he would like some refreshment. A cup of tea perhaps. Then I flee upstairs and fling myself on my bed, tears shaking my body. I don't want to be near the man and the very thought that we are under the same roof fills me with revulsion.

To my relief I hear the front door open. Father is home from his rounds so Bone will soon be gone. A few minutes pass then I hear a soft tapping on my door. It is Sybil and she has a message from Father. Can I go downstairs and have a word with him and Dr Bone?

173

She must have seen the horror on my face because she asks me what is wrong. Is it something to do with the policeman from London who called before? I tell her no. The policeman hasn't upset me in the least. I ask her to please tell Father that I feel unwell.

But this answer fails to satisfy her. I've never thought of Sybil as a particularly intuitive creature but I can tell she suspects something's amiss. And she worries at it like a dog with a bone.

'What's wrong, miss? You look so upset.' She sits down beside me on the bed and takes my hand. Her action surprises me but I find it comforting. I feel I need a friend. A confidante. If Edith had been there, she would have taken on the role but she isn't. Since my days at Tarnhey Court, Sybil is all I've had.

'I don't want to go down there. I'd rather not have to speak to Dr Bone.'

'Why ever not? He seems such a nice gentleman.'

Her naivety causes my anger to rise and before I know it, I've blurted out the words.

'He's no gentleman – quite the opposite.' I sit there, frozen with horror at what I've just said and I know I've probably set Sybil's imagination racing. It was stupid of me to reveal so much but I compose myself, knowing I must rescue the situation.

I instruct her to go downstairs and give my apologies, hoping she'll have the wit to act normally. I imagine her staring at Bone as if he is some monster come to ravish her. I hope she won't betray my indiscretion.

But when Sybil opens the bedroom door I see Father outside on the landing and he stands aside to allow her to pass.

174

'A word if you please,' he says, glowering on the threshold. There is something stiff and controlled about his words, as though he is trying his best to control his temper. 'I asked Sybil to fetch you down a while ago so I've come upstairs to see where you are. Dr Bone and I want to speak to you.'

'I'm feeling unwell, Father,' I say.

He stares as though he finds the sight of me distasteful. 'I couldn't help overhearing what you said to Sybil.'

I catch my breath and when I stand up my legs feel unsteady. I walk over to the window and stare out at the hills. I don't know what made me abandon my self-control in that way and I feel the embarrassment afresh.

'I don't know what's wrong with you, Flora, saying something like that to a servant. I just hope it doesn't get back to Dr Bone. I'm ashamed of you, Flora, I really am.'

He pauses and looks as if he is about to spit at me. 'Perhaps you're more like your mother than I thought,' he says in a hiss before turning to go.

I can't find words to say in my defence. He thinks I am some foolish girl who slanders an innocent man on a whim. And the mention of my mother has shocked me. It's the first time he's uttered her name since she left us.

He turns back to me with contempt in his eyes. 'I'll go downstairs and tell Dr Bone you're indisposed. Three more cases of influenza have just been admitted to the Cottage Hospital and we were wondering if you would use the nursing skills you learned at Tarnhey Court to help out there because one of the nurses has fallen ill. But it seems we'll have to manage without you.'

When he leaves the room, shutting the door behind

him, I fling myself on the bed and tears of frustration fill my eyes again. This was my opportunity to prove myself to Father and I've thrown it away. I cry for a full half hour and when I hear Father go out, I take the anonymous note he received downstairs and burn it on the drawing room fire.

Chapter 23

Father's at the hospital and I don't know what I will say to him when he comes home. I know I'll have to face him and I feel completely wretched. But what did I expect? Bone was always going to triumph because people will never believe that a respectable, professional man like him can be anything less than a saint. I try to put all thoughts of him out of my mind as I set off for my walk but I fail.

I'd been looking forward to meeting Inspector Lincoln at the boathouse but now my stupid error has tainted everything. What caused that foolish moment of indiscretion? I know my best avenue of revenge would have been to let Bone know he had made no impact on my life: that what passed between us has left no scar.

I eat dinner alone and Sybil serves it in silence. I would have liked to ask her to eat with me but that's not the way things are done in this house. Even in Edith's day when she'd seemed to be growing so close to Father, she'd always eaten alone. I wonder if she still does so now that she works for Dr Bone.

As I put on my coat and hat in the hall, Sybil emerges from the back room. 'Are you all right, miss?'

Her question stirs up my feeling of foolishness once more but I can't blame Sybil. I can't take my own mistakes out on her for I know she means well.

'Has your cousin Edith said anything to you about Dr Bone?'

She suddenly looks wary. 'Only that he's a nice gentleman. She says she likes working for him.' For the first time it strikes me that she might think my damning verdict on Dr Bone had been born out of spite or resentment.

'Do you know what time your father will be back?' she asks timidly, watching me as though she's afraid of saying the wrong thing. Perhaps she imagines that she too might become the victim of my sharp, lying tongue. If only she knew the truth about Dr Bone and myself. But that is something I can never share with a living soul.

'He'll probably be late home. More cases of influenza have been admitted to the Cottage Hospital.' I'm trying to sound as though nothing is amiss but she still looks at me with those uncertain eyes.

'In that case I'm minded to go and visit my aunt in Glossop this evening. Would that be all right, miss?' she asks nervously. 'If I hurry I'll be able to catch the train.'

'Of course. You go. Will you be seeing your cousin Jack?'

'Yes.'

'Give him my best wishes, won't you?'

She nods and hurries off as if she's glad to be out of my company.

I wait until she's gone and set off at half past six. I'm early so I take a circuitous route across the square towards the Cartwright Arms. I see the pub windows are aglow with gas light and a group of men are making their way inside like moths drawn to a flame. Most of them are elderly; men who were too old to be sent to the Front. Most ignore me but some touch their caps as I pass. I acknowledge them with a small nod, polite but distant. I wonder what they'd say if they knew the truth about me.

Miss Forrest's tea shop is all shut up and the blinds are drawn so that I can't see the tables inside. She lives above the shop and I can see a light in the upstairs window. How she loves to gossip. She's always been like that from as early as I can remember. A word over the scones here and a snippet of juicy information over a tea cup there. I heard there used to be a time when Mrs Bell, the vicar's wife, refused to go in there because of the poisonous talk but now she seems to have relented. I like Mrs Bell. She's one of the few women in the village who treated me with sympathy after Mother left, unlike many others who saw her defection with the man from the Black Horse as an opportunity for entertainment; a little vicarious excitement in their little lives. They used to whisper behind Father's back but I knew all too well what they were saying. I was a child and they didn't think I understood their vinegar words. But I did.

There are a few people abroad and I greet them with a good evening as I pass. Some, I know, are on their way to the Methodist church where there is a regular midweek meeting. The women are smart in their hats and some walk alone, newly emboldened now that word has got out that the police have the murderer behind bars.

I too feel confident as I retrace my steps to the square and turn right to walk out of the village along the road leading to the Cottage Hospital. When I reach the hospital I see lights blazing in the windows. Father is in there with Dr Bone and I could be with them if I hadn't yielded to the temptation of indiscretion. I curse my impulsiveness afresh. I've forgone a chance to convince Father of my capabilities and I've placed Sybil in an embarrassing position, not to mention my father who has to work alongside Bone with my foolish words echoing in his mind. And yet, I am not at fault. Why should Bone escape with his reputation untainted? But in future I'll exercise self-control. I'll watch, wait, and achieve my vengeance with a cool heart.

I'm contemplating my dilemma when I hear footsteps behind me and I'm seized with unexpected fear. It seems that all my boldness is a sham; a mask like those boys used to wear to hide the horrors beneath. I swing round and see one of Wilf Fuller's sons, a big lad of around sixteen. He hurries past me with a quick 'good evening, miss' and vanishes down the path to the river. I hope he isn't making for the boathouse and I'm relieved when I see him continue towards the gates of Tarnhey Court. I take the footpath beside Pooley Woods. It's a lonely spot even though it is only a short walk from the village centre. But I have every reason to trust that Inspector Lincoln's presence will offer complete protection. It is the thought of going home again that fills me with dread. I wonder if Father will bring Bone back with him. What will I say to the man if he does?

I meet nobody else and soon I reach the river bank where all I can hear is birdsong and the bleating of sheep in the fields round about. The river is flowing fast. It never dries to a trickle as the water flows from the rain-soaked hills that surround us. It is deep here but it runs so clear that I can see the pebbles beneath. It looks cold and refreshing. On rare hot days in summers past we children used to paddle in the shallows further along the bank, performing a strange dance of pain as we braved the sharp stones that cut into our bare feet. Some of the boys used to take off their clothes and swim, careful to hide their shock when the cold water hit their warm, bare flesh.

When I reach the boathouse I'm relieved to see that the inspector is there already waiting for me, his back turned, gazing at the view of the hills. All this green wilderness and fresh air must be a novelty for him after London. I wonder if he likes it or finds it dull.

I say hello and he swings round to face me. He thanks me for coming, as if I am doing him a favour. After the awkwardness of my day, his greeting cheers me and when he pushes open the boathouse door I follow him inside. The door is rotting and it judders at his touch and I notice that a few of the old window panes, opaque with the grime of years, are broken. The interior smells damp and is empty apart from an old rowing boat and a coil of damp rope in the corner. The place conjures memories of my childhood. John and I used to play in here with Roderick Cartwright and the vicar's children. I can still see our initials carved on the far wall. Back then it was our den, our private place. I wonder if it has always been this shabby and tumbledown. I don't remember it this way. To our young selves it had been a palace of adventure.

The inspector, suddenly businesslike, produces a notebook and pencil and asks me to write down the names of anybody I think he should be speaking to. I jot down the names of some men I know to have violent tendencies; men who are reputed to fight or beat their wives. Further down the page I list those men who've returned from war; those whose personalities, so I've heard, have been changed by their experiences or injuries. I feel my hand shaking a little as I write, aware that his eyes are on me. When I hand the list back to him he reads it in silence.

'Is there anybody you particularly favour?'

'You asked me who I think you should speak to and I really can't say any more. I don't want to get anyone into trouble,' I say quickly. 'I take it you're not convinced that Sydney Pepper is your man?'

'If Sergeant Teague had his way, he'd be taken over to Derby to stand trial at once but in my opinion it never hurts to consider other possibilities. May I call you Flora?'

'I don't see why not.'

'I'm Albert.' He extends his hand and I take it. It feels warm. He holds my hand for a little longer than necessary but I make no attempt to take it away. He's standing close to me now and I can almost feel the warmth of his body. And when he leans forward to kiss me, I lift my head towards his like a flower seeking out the sunlight.

Then we spring apart, the moment gone.

I leave the boathouse, my face burning with embarrassment, hardly understanding the feelings that tentative kiss has kindled inside me. Albert follows me out and offers to walk back with me. I hear anxiety in his voice and I'm not sure whether he's worried for my safety or if he regrets his boldness. I refuse his offer, hiding the turmoil I feel inside, and say that, as the whole point of our meeting is secrecy, it wouldn't be wise for us to be seen together. I wonder if meeting him like this has been my second mistake of the day. But it doesn't feel that way now. With hindsight, I fear I might regret it but I can't help feeling glad that his lips touched mine.

I don't see Father again that night but I hear him come home at eleven when I am in bed. I lie awake wondering whether he is alone down there but I can't hear any voices so I assume Bone has returned home to New Mills. I wonder if Edith will be waiting up for him.

I find myself thinking about the influenza patients. Did any die? Could I have made a difference if they had? I curse myself once more for my stupidity and it's only the memory of my encounter with Albert that cheers me a little. But once the case is solved he will return to London and I'll be alone. Before going to sleep I re-read the letter from the Matron. I have never longed to escape from Wenfield more than I do now.

That night I have the dream again: the same dream I've had on and off for so many years. I'm standing at the top of the stairs and I sense a dark presence behind me, holding me back. Down below in the hall I can see something – a pile of clothes ... or is it a person? I'm staring down and then I feel myself being lifted, flying from the scene. I try to scream but no sound comes out. Then I wake, my heart pounding and perspiration pouring from my body. I haven't had this dream for over a year but since Myrtle's death, it's started again.

The next morning when I come down to breakfast

I'm relieved to find that Father has already left the house and that Sybil seems less wary as she bids me good morning. Instead she looks at me with pity as she places the food in front of me, as though she knows I've embarrassed myself with my impulsive words. She knows I'm in disgrace.

'Sybil. What I said yesterday ... about Dr Bone. Can we forget all about it?'

'If you say so, miss.' She gives me a weak smile but I reckon she's curious. I know I would be if I was in her place.

'How's Jack?'

She looks relieved by the change of subject. 'He used to be so chatty but ... I don't think being in prison did him any good. My aunt said he don't talk much at all now. She's worried about him and I can't blame her.'

'I'm sorry.'

'Still, he's better off there where folk don't torment him like they used to do here.' She hesitates and I know she has something to tell me. I see her glance round nervously as if she's afraid someone will overhear. 'I think I saw somebody – last night when I was walking home from the station past Pooley Woods.'

'Who was it?'

She hesitates. 'I thought it was a man ... but now I've had time to think about it, I reckon it must have been a ghost.' There is a mixture of fear and excitement in her eyes, as though she's relishing the dramatic potential of the situation. Sybil's always had a superstitious and over-imaginative streak so her words don't surprise me.

'Why do you think it was a ghost?'

She looks uncertain now, as though she realises that

184

what she's said might be taken as foolish. 'There aren't any soldiers in uniform around now, are there? Not since the war ended.'

I know she's right about this fact at least. After the horrors of the past four years, men who aren't serving in the regular army have been only too glad to discard their uniforms; their reminders of the horror of conflict.

She blushes. 'That's what made me think it was a ghost, miss. One of the lads who didn't come back.'

'Do you think you should tell the police?'

'Oh no, miss. If it was a ghost I'm going to feel daft if they come to ask me questions, aren't I? Maybe it's best to say nothing.'

The telephone rings before I can reply. Sybil's carrying a tray of breakfast things so I relieve her of the task of answering. When I lift the receiver I hear a woman's voice and to my surprise, I recognise it as Edith's. And it is me she wishes to speak to.

'Are you all right, Flora?' she asks. 'I hear you've been unwell.'

So news of my diplomatic illness has got back to her. Bone has been talking about me. The very thought makes me shudder.

'I'm much better today, thank you.'

'I thought you might be at the hospital. Doctor Bone has left all his patients in the care of his assistant and rushed over to Wenfield to help your father.'

Her words remind me that Father's patients will soon be calling to see him, disappointed when they don't find their doctor there ready to listen to their symptoms and complaints. Unlike Dr Bone, he's never employed an assistant and I suspect he plans to return from the hospital for a couple of hours to take his surgery. But, in the meantime, it will be up to me to deal with them as best I can.

'I couldn't go yesterday because I wasn't feeling well,' I lie. 'And Father left for the hospital first thing this morning so I'll be needed here to attend to any patients who turn up to see him while he's away.'

There's a moment of hesitation before she speaks again. 'So you won't be free today?'

'Father said he'd be back to take his surgery this morning so I should be free later.'

'Can we meet at Miss Forrest's again?' I can hear anxiety in her voice and I wonder why.

'If you want.' I feel suddenly nervous. What if Dr Bone's said something to her? What if he's decided to get his version of the story in first? The thought fills me with revulsion. But I have to know so I promise to meet Edith and in the meantime I carry out my morning's tasks automatically, my mind barely registering what I'm doing. By the time Father returns four patients have had their dressings changed and only five are waiting. I slip easily into the role of receptionist and once the patients have left, I tell Father I'm going out.

He raises his eyebrows. 'I thought you'd be begging me for the opportunity to help us at the Cottage Hospital.' When I say nothing he speaks again, his face solemn. 'A woman died last night. Wilf Fuller's daughter-in-law. This particular strain of influenza seems to hit the young particularly badly. And two more cases were admitted this morning – both farmhands from Barrow Farm up in the peak. The poor lads are very sick. They got through the war and ...'

'Am I still needed?' His words have made me ashamed. I've put my qualms about Bone above my duty. 'I can come in this afternoon if you wish.'

He considers my offer for a while before speaking. 'Two of the nurses are sick and the others are exhausted so if you can make yourself useful ...'

I can tell it pains him to ask. I nod.

'I'll have to do my usual rounds this afternoon so you'll be working with Dr Bone.' He watches my face but I'm careful not to betray my feelings.

'I'm sure I'll manage.' I wonder how much he's guessed. I wonder how well my father really knows me.

Feelings of excitement and dread mingle in my mind as I keep my appointment with Edith. I now have a chance to prove myself to Father but it'll mean working with Bone again. I won't let him stand in my way. Not this time.

I expect to find Edith waiting inside the tea room but instead I see she is standing outside with a group of other women. The blinds are down, exactly as they were when I passed last night, and a woman I recognise as the wife of a clerk from one of the mills is rapping on the glass shop door.

Edith sees me coming down the street and walks over to meet me.

'The tea room's closed and there's no sign of Miss Forrest. I fear she might have been taken ill. This outbreak of influenza ...'

'Perhaps we should ask the police to make sure she's all right,' I say with a worried frown, looking up at the windows above the tea shop. 'If she's lying up there ill and helpless ...'

As luck would have it, Constable Wren appears at that moment. He sees the little crowd gathered outside the shop and makes his way over with a cheerful 'Everything all right, ladies?'

Edith and I watch as the women flutter around him like birds, each keen to explain the situation. Eventually we see him knock on the door and when there's no reply he hits the pane with his truncheon and the ladies start at the tinkle of shattering glass.

Nobody speaks as the constable enters the tea shop, taking charge of the situation. We wait until he emerges from the shop and see that his expression is solemn, like a doctor about to break bad news to a nervous patient.

We hear him speak to the assembled gathering, now swelled by more women who, after sensing excitement while shopping at the butcher's opposite, have come over to see what's going on.

'There's no sign of Miss Forrest, I'm afraid. Perhaps she's gone away.'

'She never goes away,' someone says. 'And I was here yesterday. She would have said something.'

Edith looks at me. I can tell she senses that something is wrong and I share her misgivings. There's a lot of influenza about so perhaps Miss Forrest went out that morning and was taken ill, I suggest. Perhaps someone will find her. This explanation seems to satisfy Edith who asks if my father is home. I tell her he'll be out on his rounds and that I've promised to go and help out at the hospital later that afternoon. I suggest we go home and she agrees after asking me what time Father is expected back. From the anxiety in her question I can tell she doesn't want to meet him.

Once we're back at the house Sybil makes us tea. Edith is delighted to see her cousin and they chatter for a while about family matters before Sybil disappears back into the kitchen to attend to her duties. I find it difficult to believe now that Edith was once in her place. Her time spent working during the war has endowed her with such new confidence and independence that I can barely imagine her in the role of a servant. I wonder how Dr Bone treats her. He isn't married so the thought suddenly flashes across my mind that they might have become close – just as I used to hope she'd become close to Father.

I hardly like to ask about her relationship with Dr Bone. In fact I've resolved not to raise the subject of her employer at all. So I'm surprised when Edith mentions him as soon as we're alone.

'I asked Dr Bone whether he saw anything when he was over here on the days those women died but he assures me he didn't.' When I say nothing, she continues. 'But since I asked him he seems a little ... preoccupied. As though something's worrying him.'

'You think he knows something about the murders?' I say, suddenly bold.

'Of course not. The very idea's laughable.' She gives a dismissive little laugh, mocking her doubts.

'He might have seen something and doesn't want to say anything in case he's wrong. Some people don't wish to appear foolish.'

She considers my suggestion for a moment and nods slowly. 'You could be right.'

'Perhaps you should ask him again.'

I see her face redden. It's clear she doesn't wish to push

the matter. 'I don't like to. He might think I suspect him of something.'

'Do you?'

'Of course not. You know Dr Bone. He'd never do anything like that. The idea's preposterous.'

I let her live with her illusions and say nothing.

'But he's definitely had something on his mind. Perhaps it's connected with his work.'

'He doesn't confide in you?' I remember how Father used to spend cosy evenings by the fire with Edith – her darning and sewing and he reading in companionable silence. Sometimes I'd hear them talking and laughing softly as if they were sharing some private joke. At times it sounded like the conversation of lovers.

'Not really.' She sounds uncertain. 'He's a very private man.'

I sit forward in my seat, suddenly alert. 'You think he has secrets?'

Edith takes a sip of tea and changes the subject.

Chapter 24

I have changed into my clean uniform. The blue cotton feels cool on my skin and the starched apron and cap make me feel efficient and professional – a nurse to be trusted. I reach the Cottage Hospital and as I enter the building by the main door I look up and see Sir William Cartwright's name emblazoned above me. I follow Father's directions and when I reach the ward I'm greeted by a Sister, the kindness of her manner belying the severity of her features. She says she is pleased that I can help out and asks me about my nursing experience. To my relief my answers seem to satisfy her and she puts me to work at once emptying bed pans into the sluice. It is work I am used to and I tackle it cheerfully. It is good to feel useful again, even if the task is menial.

There are two other nurses besides Sister and they both look exhausted. One tells me she's been awake all night because there have been three new admissions.

And when I have dealt with the bed pans, I am asked to take the patients' temperatures.

There are some very sick people in the ward – all men as the women's ward is down the corridor. I recognise some of them from the village but others are strangers from the outlying area. Many of them are young; men who've survived the horrors of war only to be laid low by infection. As I record the patients' temperatures, I am alarmed at how the fever has taken hold and how the sweating patients writhe with delirium. One of the nurses says there have already been several deaths. I do not know how nature can be so cruel.

When Dr Bone enters the ward, I busy myself mopping the brow of a young man I do not recognise. But the doctor spots me and stares, as though he wishes to speak to me. But I have no wish to speak to him.

I reach the bed at the end. The man lying there is quite still and his temperature is high but almost back to normal. Sister has told me he has passed the crisis and will live. He is in his forties, older than many in the ward, and his face is familiar to me. His name is David Eames and in war he was a lieutenant serving on the Somme. But in peace, he was and still is an artist living in an isolated house about a mile from Wenfield. I remember him telling me that it had been his uncle's house and that he'd inherited it some years ago. He shares the place with his younger sister, having chosen to move there and pursue his passion for art after his wife died in childbirth in 1913. At Tarnhey Court I saw the sketches he made of his fellow patients and was impressed by the way he could capture the essence of his subjects. He always said he likes to work in oils when he could get the materials, and

192

since the end of the war I know he's harboured ambitions to make his name as a portrait painter.

It upsets me to see David so ill because he enriched my life during those difficult years. While he was convalescing from his wounds at Tarnhey Court we discussed art and books – things I'd never been able to talk about with Father or any of my contemporaries from the village. I used to sit outside with him and we'd talk as he helped me roll bandages. In those contented hours he taught me such a lot and, to my regret, I haven't seen much of him since the war ended. Father disapproves of me visiting him alone and, with one leg missing, David finds it hard to come into Wenfield so we've drifted apart as people do. And now I'm relieved to see that my old friend is recovering and out of danger.

He is asleep and I watch his chest rise and fall as he breathes. He looks older than I remember but, unlike others, his face is unmarked by war. And yet at Tarnhey Court he'd used his formidable skills to help those who bore the terrible scars of battle. As well as being an accomplished artist, David's also a sculptor and I know he took great pride in being able to give disfigured men their faces and their dignity back in the workshop near the old kitchens he'd been given to perform his miracles.

Albert asked about the mask he'd found in Sydney Pepper's accommodation but he never asked me who actually created it and I didn't think the information was relevant. Besides, I'm reluctant to draw David to the attention of the police, even though I know he has nothing to hide.

David's eyelids are flickering open and I stand over him smiling, hoping the sight of a friendly face will cheer him and aid his recovery. When he sees me he looks confused for a moment, as though he thinks himself back at Tarnhey Court. Then I take his hand and he smiles. 'Little Flora,' he says. His voice is still weak. 'What are you doing here?'

I explain and ask him how he feels.

'Better. Much better. I want to get back home to my work. Has my sister been to visit? According to the nurses I've been unconscious so ...'

I tell him I don't know but I promise to ask Sister.

He beckons me close to him and when I lower my head towards his, he speaks in a whisper.

'I heard someone saying Sydney Pepper's killed three women. Is that right?'

'The police think so.'

'Sydney was a troubled soul,' David says softly. 'It doesn't surprise me. Not really.' Then he grabs my hand, as if what he has to say is urgent. 'He's here. Flora. I've seen him. You will take care, won't you?'

I know who he means. And I promise him I'll take the greatest of care. I won't put myself in danger again.

I hear Sister's voice calling me and when I turn I see Dr Bone standing beside her. He is looking straight at me. And the smile on his lips has not spread to his eyes.

Chapter 25

Albert

Another woman was missing from the village and Albert Lincoln had a nagging feeling that the affair wouldn't end happily. He'd spent all that morning making inquiries; trying his best to find out all he could about the woman's life and relationships. And so far he'd only discovered things about her that he didn't particularly like.

The missing woman's name was Emmaline Forrest and she was the proprietor of a tea shop on the High Street. A most respectable establishment where the ladies of Wenfield felt relaxed enough to gather during the day for tea, buttered toast and, more excitingly, cakes.

Miss Forrest was a businesswoman and she was a spinster who'd resided in the village for many years, inheriting her shop from her father who'd run it as a tailor's establishment – quite high class, he was told. Nobody seemed quite sure of the lady's exact age – there are some questions it's not polite to ask – but the consensus of opinion seemed to be that she was in her forties.

As far as Albert could gather, although there'd never been any hint of scandal about Miss Forrest herself, she loved to believe the worst of others. For favoured customers, her tea shop was a well of secret information and certain ladies used it as a repository of knowledge about their fellow villagers. He couldn't help wondering if Flora Winsmore was amongst their number – but he thought not. He imagined she was more likely to be the subject of their gossip. Just as her mother had been before her.

When Mrs Jackson had told him about the doctor's wife's defection he'd been tempted to ask her for more details, anything that would give him an insight into Flora's life, but the last thing he wanted was to stir up the viper-tongues of the village. Some things were best forgotten. However, from what he'd learned so far about Miss Forrest, he had the impression that she never forgot. Or forgave.

With Sergeant's Teague's help, he'd reached the conclusion that Miss Forrest was respected but not liked, except by her inner circle of cronies. Lady Cartwright, of course, was above a visit to the local tea shop but that didn't prevent gossip about her family flowing like tea amongst the fussy lace table cloths. Albert had come across such premises before in the course of his career. He thought them as poisonous as the vilest public houses in the roughest alleys of London.

Miss Forrest appeared to have no relatives, neither did she have any close friends that anybody knew about. Her life was her tea shop and she was queen of the hive. Her absence was certainly out of character and this made him concerned for her safety.

It didn't seem to occur to Teague that she might be the killer's fourth victim – after all, they had Sydney Pepper behind bars now. But Albert feared the local police had been too quick to assume they'd got the right man, just as they had in the case of Jack Blemthwaite. He knew that the evidence against Pepper was more substantial and yet he wasn't entirely happy. If it turned out that Miss Forrest had fallen prey to the killer, this would mean that they were wrong again and this time it would be his responsibility. He was the man from Scotland Yard. He was supposed to be in charge. He'd made mistakes before and he knew how it felt. On one occasion he'd even sent an innocent man to the gallows, only to find out his mistake the following year when the real killer confessed. He couldn't bear to think of such a thing happening again.

Miss Forrest lived in the rooms above her shop. A parlour, two bedrooms – although one contained a jumble of old furniture and was clearly unused – a small kitchen and a little bathroom with the luxury of a separate lavatory. The place was furnished with good solid pieces, probably inherited from her tailor father. It wasn't an ostentatious home but it was comfortable.

As Albert stood there in her bedroom with its narrow single bed, it occurred to him that she must be a lonely woman. He wondered whether she'd once had a sweetheart. Nobody they'd spoken to so far had mentioned a man in her life, past or present.

It wasn't until three o'clock that Albert ordered a search of the area for the absent woman. He wanted things done discreetly for now to avoid public panic so he sent as many constables as he could muster to Pooley Woods. Two out of the three previous victims had been found there. It was the killer's favoured hunting ground.

After giving the order, Albert stayed alone in Miss Forrest's rooms for a while because he needed time to think. He was still learning about the people of Wenfield; their enmities, their alliances and their preoccupations. After London they seemed like some distant tribe with their own customs, almost their own language as sometimes he found it hard to understand what was being said. At that moment there was only one person in the village he would willingly spend time with, and that was Flora Winsmore. He thought of their meeting the previous night with a mixture of excitement and guilt. Before they met he'd told himself that she was merely the bridge between him and the community he'd been sent to investigate but that kiss still lingered in his mind. He'd woken in the early hours still feeling it on his lips and, to his shame, he'd allowed himself to imagine, to enact, the most desirable outcome there alone in his narrow bed.

Afterwards he'd lain exhausted with guilt and regret pressing on him like a weight. He'd forced himself to think of Mary but each time her face flashed across his mind he felt more wretched. It was Flora Winsmore he wanted beside him in that bed, not his wife's scrawny body. He told himself he mustn't see Flora alone again; that he had to forget the idea of her being his interpreter of Wenfield. It had been a foolish, selfish notion which could only cause grief and Flora's family had been hit by enough scandal when her mother ran away from her husband and children all those years ago.

He knew that he'd be neglecting his duties if he didn't

make a search of Miss Forrest's rooms, just to check whether there was any clue to her whereabouts, so he began to look in the cupboards and drawers. It was an easy task because she kept them so tidy, and after he'd sorted through the neat piles of underwear and linen in the bedroom he moved to the parlour.

In the top drawer of a small bureau in the corner of the room, he came across some notepaper and a fountain pen, together with a stack of envelopes which suggested she was a keen letter writer. A couple of letters lay at the front of the drawer, already addressed but, as yet, unsealed. Albert picked one up and drew out the contents. It was a note printed in capitals with no address above and no signature at the bottom.

WHY DOES YOUR WIFE SPEND SO MUCH TIME ALONE WITH THE ORGANIST? it said. Albert studied the envelope and saw that it was intended for the Reverend Bell and that the address, like the letter, was printed. Anonymous.

The second was addressed to a man whose name was unfamiliar and suggested the recipient had an unnatural affection for his niece.

There was only one conclusion Albert could reach: Miss Forrest was either a mischief maker or a blackmailer, although, as no money was mentioned, he suspected the former. He stuffed the letters in his pocket and sat down, wondering if they could bring charges against the woman when she turned up. The letters were poisonous so there was nothing he'd like more.

Albert had been in the flat above the tea shop for over half an hour, laid out on Miss Forrest's chaise longue with his eyes shut, when Sergeant Teague poked his head round the door. He'd been going over the possibilities of the case in his mind, trying not to allow thoughts of Flora Winsmore to intrude, but he knew what station talk was like. It would no doubt be reported back that the inspector from London had been enjoying forty winks whilst on duty.

'What is it, Sergeant?' Albert asked, doing his best to sound alert.

'They've found Miss Forrest, sir. In Pooley Woods like the others.'

Albert felt light-headed as he stood up. After what he'd found, he hadn't really expected the matter to end like this so Teague's words had shaken him.

'You're sure it's her?'

'Absolutely sure, sir. The local lads all know her by sight.'

'What about the ...'

'The bird, sir? Yes, it's there like the others, stuffed into her mouth. By the way, sir, Sarah Cookham's funeral's at half past three at church. Thought you might want to go along and pay your respects.' He saw a cautious look on the sergeant's face, as though he feared Albert would dismiss the suggestion.

But Albert nodded. 'You're right, I should go. But first I ought to see Miss Forrest's body. I hope it's not been moved.'

Albert saw Teague's face turn red. 'Surely she should be moved as soon as possible, for decency's sake?'

Albert gave an exasperated sigh. 'I want everything left as it is. The scene's not to be touched.'

'But we should make her decent. That's what we did before,' the sergeant said in a self-justifying whine.

'I don't care what you did before. I'd better get over there and make sure my orders are obeyed. And I want a photographer to take pictures.'

Teague opened his mouth, about to protest, but Albert clapped his hands together. 'Come on, there's no time to lose. I want to see her exactly as she was found.'

Albert allowed Teague to get down the stairs before he followed him out. The broken glass in the tea room door had now been boarded up and the place made secure so he let the door shut behind him and walked down the High Street in the direction of Pooley Woods. As they passed through the square he noticed people standing in clusters, casting him nervous glances. Fear spreads fast in a small place like Wenfield.

He spotted Mrs Jackson from the Black Horse outside the butcher's with a basket hooked over her arm. She caught his eye and stepped forward as if she was about to speak to him but then she backed away when she saw the determined expression on his face. He swept past her with a curt nod. It would be best, he thought, if the details of the grim discovery weren't made public just yet. Ideally he'd have liked to keep things quiet for as long as possible. But he knew that would be difficult.

Grim-faced and silent, he followed Teague to the little area of woodland on the edge of the village. The sergeant huffed and puffed in front of him as though the briskness of the walk was too much for him.

When they reached the trees Albert spoke. 'Is there a photographer in the village?'

Teague shook his head. 'Not in Wenfield but there's Mr Ventnor's Photographic Studio in New Mills. He does weddings and . . . '

'Go back and phone the station at New Mills, will you? Tell them to call on Mr Ventnor and tell him his services are needed.'

Teague hesitated for a moment before setting off back to the police station. From the look on his face, Albert knew he thought his request bizarre. But he didn't care what the sergeant thought. He'd have things done his way.

As he entered the woods alone he could hear voices nearby so he followed the sound and soon found himself at the edge of a small clearing. There was quite a crowd ahead of him gathered around something on the ground. He knew what that something was without having to see it.

He made his way slowly towards the centre of activity, looking and listening, taking in his surroundings. It was a lonely location, dark under the sheltering canopy of trees and smelling of damp earth; not the sort of place where a woman on her own would venture for a stroll. She must have come here for a reason; possibly to meet somebody.

Albert had read the reports and there'd been no mention of any sort of note being found on the bodies or any hint that the victims had been in touch with their killer to arrange a meeting. But Myrtle Bligh, Annie Dryden and Sarah Cookham had all gone to unexpected places, alone and without explanation, to meet their deaths and he was annoyed that, so far, this factor hadn't been considered by the local police. The assumption had been made that the killer had leapt out on them to launch a murderous attack. Nobody had asked what the victims had been doing there in the first place.

He felt in his pocket for the anonymous notes. Who else had received the latest victim's venomous little communications? he wondered. Is that why she'd died in that place? Had the others been involved in the business of revealing the darkest secrets of their fellow villagers too?

'Right,' he said. 'Let's see what we've got.'

The small crowd of uniformed officers parted to allow him through and he saw that somebody had covered the body on the ground with a sheet. He bent down and when he flicked the sheet to one side he was relieved to see that the victim hadn't been moved. She still lay on her back, her knees bent up and her black skirts raised to reveal a pair of pink bloomers. Her open eyes protruded in astonishment and her mouth was stuffed with what appeared at first sight to be a white feathery ball, streaked with dried blood. Her mouth had been slit open at the sides to accommodate the thing he knew would be a dove. One of the birds from the Cartwrights' dovecote.

'She's not to be moved or touched until she's been photographed.'

He saw the constables exchange glances.

'I've sent for a photographer from New Mills. I'm hoping he'll be here soon. Has the doctor been called?'

'Someone's gone to fetch him, sir,' said Constable Wren. He looked uneasy. 'It isn't right to leave her like this, sir. It isn't respectful. And we should take that thing out of her mouth.'

Albert's instinct told him that Wren had a point. But he needed to glean all the information he could from the scene. He decided on a compromise. 'I want the bird left where it is but you can cover her up again with that sheet till the doctor arrives,' he said, knowing that failing to respect local sensibilities would lose him allies. This wasn't London where people could live anonymously. These men were acquainted with the dead woman. She might not have been popular but they greeted her in the street and saw her in church on Sundays. She was more to them than a lump of meat.

They were about to replace the sheet when he raised his hand to stop them before squatting beside the body. He stared without touching and noticed that, even though she looked as if she'd been the victim of a sexual attack, her substantial underwear appeared to be undisturbed. The motive, he guessed, was humiliation rather than violation. The killer had revelled in the woman's loss of dignity. He could see the blood crusted on the black cloth of her bodice and the small tear where the weapon had been thrust into her chest. He wondered if she'd taken a while to die. If that was the case, her killer must have watched her death throes and stayed at the scene to arrange her body. Taking his time and revelling in the cruelty. He could see the bird protruding from her bloody lips. There was some meaning behind all this, he thought. Someone was trying to convey a message of some kind. But what that message was, he had no idea.

He heard a familiar voice. Dr Winsmore had arrived. Albert stood up, steadying himself with his good hand and turned round, half hoping that Flora would be with him. But the doctor was alone and he looked exhausted.

'I've just come from the hospital – this influenza outbreak,' he explained as he stared down at Miss Forrest's mortal remains. 'I thought you had the culprit locked up. You let him go?'

The question sounded more like an accusation. Dr

Winsmore was assuming Sydney Pepper was guilty and that Miss Forrest's death was a result of police incompetence.

'Pepper's still in custody.'

Without another word the doctor bent down and lifted the sheet off the dead woman. Then he stood back to study her. 'It looks exactly like the others. I thought at first it might be someone who's copying the killer but there are too many similarities; details that haven't been made public.'

Albert saw Winsmore frown at the dawning realisation that Sydney Pepper was, in all probability, innocent and the killer was still at large amongst them. From now on the whole village would be watching their neighbours with suspicion. If Pepper, the outsider, wasn't responsible, it might be someone they knew well; someone they'd grown up with.

'All the constables have been sworn to secrecy about the manner of the victims' deaths,' Albert said. 'But I wouldn't rule out the possibility of loose tongues in public houses or the sharing of tittle-tattle with a curious wife who promised to say nothing then promptly passed on the juicy titbits with her friends.'

Teague, who'd been listening closely to the conversation, butted in. 'Aye, you're right. Gossip spreads round these parts like those grassfires we get on the peaks in dry weather.'

Albert nodded, knowing that nothing could be ruled out, not even Sydney Pepper's guilt.

'Had Miss Forrest any particular enemies that you know of?' Albert asked Teague while the doctor was making his examination.

'No, of course not,' he said automatically. 'She was a dried up old spinster but ...' He fell silent for a few moments, as if he was considering Albert's question afresh. 'Well, I suppose women go to her tea room to gossip ... and not all of it's pleasant, as far as I can make out. The wife goes in there from time to time – not regular, you understand – and she says some of the talk can get a bit ... poisonous, if you know what I mean.' He glanced at the body. 'But I don't like to speak ill of the departed. It's not right.

'Is there anybody in particular she was gossiping about?'

Teague shook his head. 'I don't know. But I can ask Mrs Teague if you like.'

'Thank you. That might be helpful. Have you heard about anyone receiving letters – anonymous letters?'

Teague shook his head.

'Well, if you find anything out, please let me know at once.'

Teague touched his helmet in a sort of salute. Then Albert heard the doctor speak. 'In my opinion she died sometime last night. Things are busy at the hospital so I won't have time to do the post mortem till tomorrow.'

Albert said it couldn't be helped. Influenza was a terrible thing. A killer. Back in London he'd known it claim the young and healthy – an invisible killer he couldn't catch and send to the hangman.

He took his watch from his pocket. In an hour and a half Sarah Cookham would be buried in the churchyard and he wanted to be there. In the meantime he had to decide whether Sydney Pepper should be released. His instincts told him there was no longer any reason to detain him, but some little nagging voice inside his head still counselled caution.

After half an hour the photographer arrived. As he was the proud owner of a motor car, a gleaming little black model, his journey from nearby New Mills had been swift. In London they had regular police photographers to record the scenes of crimes but here they had to make do with this cheerful man with dark curly hair and a permanent smile. It was immediately clear that the man was more used to putting nervous brides and sitters at their ease than photographing corpses and when he was shown the body the smile vanished and he looked as if he was about to be sick. But, to his credit, he went about his business as instructed and promised that Albert would receive the resulting pictures as soon as they were developed.

After he'd finished Albert gave permission for the body to be moved to the Cottage Hospital. According to Dr Winsmore, there had been three deaths there during the night so the little mortuary would be rather crowded.

Time was running out. He had to be at the church for Sarah's funeral. He hated funerals. He hated death and all its trappings. He had seen too much of it already.

Chapter 26

There was quite a crowd outside the church waiting for the coffin to arrive. It seemed most of the village had come to say their farewells to Sarah Cookham, the Cartwrights' parlour maid. Whether they'd come out of grief, respect or morbid curiosity, Albert couldn't tell.

As he made his way up the stone path to the church door, passing the grey graves that stood like sentries either side of the route, he saw the Reverend Bell waiting at the lych gate, his snow-white surplice flapping like a flag of surrender in the wind. The sky was as grey as the headstones now and he feared a downpour wasn't far away. He suspected it rained a lot around these parts.

The coffin arrived in a shiny glass hearse pulled by four jet-black horses with large black plumes of feathers on their bobbing heads. Albert thought it rather an ostentatious conveyance for a servant's coffin. Perhaps her employers had paid for it; a gesture of generosity for her final journey. It pulled up outside the lych gate and the coffin was borne to the church with the crowd watching in silence. Behind the hearse was a Rolls-Royce that Albert recognised at once as belonging to Sir William Carwright. He watched as Sir William and his wife emerged from the back while their son, Roderick, vacated the driver's seat, having assumed Sydney Pepper's duties for the day. All three were dressed in mourning black and wore suitably solemn expressions as they made their way into the church to take their places in the family pews at the front.

The Reverend Bell shouted the words of the funeral service in a rich bass voice but the wind snatched away the odd phrase here and there. Albert, however, knew the words by heart. *I am the resurrection and the life, sayeth the Lord.* The congregation formed a ragged line behind the coffin and followed it into the church, the men taking off their caps when they reached the porch.

Albert looked around for Flora Winsmore but he couldn't see her, or her father. He imagined they'd be busy at the Cottage Hospital dealing with the influenza outbreak but he still harboured hopes of seeing her. During the service his mind kept wandering to their meeting at the boathouse, to how it felt to have her body close to his when their lips met in a kiss, but he forced himself to pay attention to what was going on. News of Miss Forrest's death had obviously spread because the Reverend Bell made oblique references to another friend who'd been taken from our midst only last night in similar tragic circumstances. He noted the tutting and head shaking of the congregation, as though they couldn't quite believe the evil that was slithering its way through the place like a ravenous serpent.

While the vicar droned on about the tragedy of Sarah's untimely end and the fruits of human wickedness, Albert watched the faces of the people in the pews. To a man and woman they looked subdued and respectful. Only a woman he took to be Sarah's mother, a widow as he remembered, and her three daughters were making a conspicuous display of grief, sobbing loudly into their handkerchiefs. He'd heard from Teague that the woman had lost a son in the war and he felt for her. If the opportunity arose, he intended to catch her afterwards, express his condolences and assure her that he would do all he could to apprehend her daughter's killer.

He was sitting at the side of the church near the centre of the nave, trying to look inconspicuous while he watched the congregation. His pew was at right angles to where the Cartwright family sat, the best seats in the house, and this afforded him a good view of the family as they listened to the words, stood to sing the hymns and knelt in prayer.

Lady Cartwright looked as if her thoughts were miles away and she was hardly aware of what was going on, while Roderick Cartwright fidgeted nervously with his hymn book as though he was longing for the whole thing to be over. Albert fixed his eyes on the trio. Sarah had been pregnant and he didn't know whether he'd believed Roderick's protestations of innocence. He was as sure as he could be that the young man was hiding something.

The congregation stood for the final hymn. *Abide with Me*. As Albert mouthed the familiar words it reminded him of war and memorials. The Glorious Dead. It had been sung at every service of remembrance he'd been to and he knew the words by heart. He looked down at his mutilated left hand. Had it all been worth it? He wasn't sure of anything any more. Only that he needed to see Flora Winsmore again. The thought of Mary sitting silently at home, staring into the distance, engulfed in mourning, brought on a pang of regret so strong it was almost painful. Flora represented life while Mary ... He hardly dared to think about it.

Lady Cartwright had moved her head back slightly which meant Albert now had a clear view of Sir William Cartwright's face and what he saw surprised him. His head was bowed, as though he didn't wish to be observed but Albert could see tears glistening on the MP's cheeks and he saw him take out a silk handkerchief and dab his eyes discreetly. His wife beside him was singing, her hymn book held high in gloved hands, seemingly oblivious to her husband's grief. She'd hardly looked at him throughout the service and her son, too, seemed to be ignoring his father, as though something unpleasant had passed between them earlier that day.

Albert couldn't help wondering whether the bad feeling had anything to do with the dead servant they were there to bury. Had Roderick's unsuitable attachment caused a rift in the Cartwright family? Or had the young man been telling the truth when he'd denied having any sort of relationship with Sarah Cookham? All of a sudden Albert had an urge to stand up, to take the vicar's place and demand whether anyone in the congregation knew who'd been responsible for the victim's pregnancy. But he fought the impulse. He hadn't come all the way up from London to cause a public scandal by his unsuitable behaviour.

Before he knew it the service was over and everybody had filed outside to the churchyard and gathered around the open grave. As the coffin was lowered in he noticed that the Cartwrights had positioned themselves at the back of the crowd and they were edging away as if they were keen to rush off as soon as they decently could. All the colour had drained from Sir William's face. He looked like a man who'd received a terrible shock.

It was natural, Albert thought, that he should be upset by his servant's death but his reaction did seem a little excessive. Albert wondered whether Lady Cartwright had her suspicions about her husband's dealings with Sarah. And whether she'd regarded the girl as her rival.

A soft drizzle had begun to fall and a few large black umbrellas had been unfurled. Now they were outside, Albert made the most of this opportunity to study the rest of the congregation, concentrating on those hanging at the back. He'd known killers attend their victim's funerals before, as though they couldn't resist seeing the culmination of their handiwork. But today he was disappointed because most people there seemed to be ordinary villagers come either to pay their respects or out of curiosity.

He heard the final hollow thud of earth being thrown down on the coffin lid and followed the Cartwrights out, surprised that they hadn't even stayed to shake the vicar's hand or convey their condolences to the dead girl's relatives as etiquette demanded. They made straight for the Rolls-Royce and once more Roderick took Sydney Pepper's place at the wheel. Before Albert had a chance to catch their attention the car had driven away in the direction of Tarnhey Court. It was only a short distance but he supposed their social position meant they couldn't be seen to walk like all the rest. There were some things war hadn't changed.

He lined up with the others to express his sympathies to Sarah's mother and sisters who wore the stunned look of people who were longing to awake from some dreadful nightmare but feared they never would. There was nothing Albert could think of to say that he hadn't said before a thousand times to the bereaved – that hadn't been said to him and Mary when their son, Frederick, died. His words were hardly original but he hoped they sounded sincere.

He walked slowly out of the churchyard, the memory of Sir William's intriguing behaviour at the funeral still at the forefront of his mind. He knew he might not be altogether welcome at Tarnhey Court but he had a job to do. And if he ended up offending a Member of Parliament, so be it.

But first he called in at the police station to bring himself up to date with the latest developments, only to find that there weren't any. Miss Forrest's body had been taken to the Cottage Hospital and Mr Ventnor the photographer was going to let them know when his pictures were ready. Constables were out taking statements in the village. They were doing all they could, Constable Wren explained nervously as though he suspected the man from Scotland Yard would be expecting more.

Albert thought it best not to tell the men at the station where he intended to go. He suspected they might interpret his visit to the Cartwrights as malicious harassment of the village's most prominent inhabitant. Maybe it was, he thought. He'd met too many people like Sir William and his son during the war and, with some honourable exceptions, their behaviour had done nothing to raise his opinion of his so-called betters.

He left the station alone and walked to Tarnhey Court. The drizzle had cleared up and the sun was making a weak attempt to peep through the grey clouds. As he passed through the gates, the overgrown laurels formed a gloomy tunnel over the drive. He could see the roof of the dovecote peeping above a high stone wall and, on impulse, he made straight for it. He opened a gate and found himself in a walled garden and when he approached the dovecote in the corner he saw that the door was standing open. He slowed his pace, wondering whether anybody was inside. But before he reached his goal he saw Roderick Cartwright emerge from the small building. And as soon as Cartwright spotted him Albert noted that he looked shocked ... and perhaps guilty.

'Mr Cartwright. Can I have a word with you?'

Roderick swiftly composed himself but it was too late. Albert had already noted his discomfort.

'I saw you at Sarah's funeral.'

'Of course I was there. She worked for us.' The words sounded defensive.

'Did your family pay for the hearse?'

'That's none of your business.'

'Did they?'

'My parents believe in treating their staff well. It was the last thing we could do for her.' He'd shut the dovecote door behind him but he turned his head slightly and glanced back at it. 'I was just having a look inside the dovecote. Things have been rather neglected since the

214

war and I was assessing how much work needs doing.' He smiled. 'And if it was our doves that the killer . . . '

'You were looking for clues?' Albert asked, half amused.

'I'm hardly Sherlock Holmes but I was curious to see whether anything had been disturbed.'

'And has it been?'

'Not as far as I can see. I heard about Miss Forrest. Terrible business. Does it mean you're going to release Sydney? I've heard Miss Forrest's death was similar to the others so if the same man killed her that suggests Sydney's innocent, doesn't it? And my parents are missing his services.' He tilted his head to one side, awaiting an answer.

'Do you think we should release him?'

Albert's question was obviously unexpected. Roderick looked confused. 'Me?' He thought for a few moments. 'Well, I think he'd be quite capable. He's always struck me as an angry man after what happened to him in the war . . . '

'How do you explain Miss Forrest's death then?'

'She was a poisonous old bitch who used to spread her venom to anyone who'd listen. I should imagine she made a lot of enemies.' Roderick spoke with feeling.

'You included?'

Roderick's face turned red. 'I meant in the village. We didn't have much to do with her up here. Anyone could have used these murders as an opportunity to get rid of her, don't you think?'

'I think you have a vivid imagination.'

Albert took the letters he'd found in Miss Forrest's flat from his pocket, careful to let Roderick see only the envelopes, not the contents. 'Have you ever received anything like this?'

Roderick's face turned red and after a few moments he nodded. 'Vicious, vile things – anonymous of course. Father had one too. I burned mine and so did Father. It was all lies, of course, but sometimes you have to put up with that sort of thing when you're in the public eye.'

'What did his say?'

'He never showed me.'

'What about yours?'

'I'd rather not say.'

'Did the writer ask for money?'

Roderick shook his head. 'I don't think blackmail was the intention. I think they were just to let people know their secrets weren't safe – that someone knew.'

'Any idea who sent them?'

'I can take a few guesses but I can't be sure.'

'Is your father at home?'

Albert saw the relief on Roderick's face – the relief of a suspect who thinks the attention of the police is about to be focused elsewhere.

'Yes, he's in if you want a word with him. But he's going back to London later so you'll have to be quick.'

'Thank you.' Albert turned towards the house. Then he turned back. 'By the way, where were you last night?'

'I was here. At home. My mother will vouch for me. I was in all evening.'

'And your father?'

'He was here too. We all were.'

Albert knew he was lying. But whether he was lying about himself or his father, he couldn't be sure. He started to walk down the path that led back to the drive and when he reached the gate something made him turn round again. He saw Roderick Cartwright re-entering the dovecote and shutting the door behind him. There was something furtive about his movements, as if he was afraid of being observed.

Albert retraced his steps, sticking to the grass at the side of the path to avoid the gravel that might crunch beneath his feet and betray his presence. He reached the dovecote and stood quite still, listening. He could hear Roderick speaking in a low murmur. Somebody was in there with him. But then he'd never actually said that he was inspecting the building alone.

He was tempted to open the door and confront him but instead he decided to go to the house to have a word with Sir William. However, Roderick Cartwright's actions had made him curious so he stood for a while shielded by a blossoming apple tree and eventually he saw the dovecote door open again. Roderick emerged followed by a man who looked like a gardener, young and scruffily dressed.

They had the look of conspirators, as if it hadn't only been repairs they'd been discussing.

Chapter 27

Sir William had displayed a politician's propensity for never answering a straight question so Albert learned little during their meeting. Yes, the family had paid for Sarah's funeral. It was the least they could do as her own family could never have afforded such a dignified send off. He had found the service unexpectedly moving, he said when Albert had asked about his emotional reaction in the church. The death of such a young person was always a tragedy.

The owner of Tarnhey Court said all the right words and yet the watchfulness in his eyes and the smoothness of his replies made Albert doubt his truthfulness. In fact, he reminded him of a con man he'd once arrested in Soho.

Sarah had been a nice girl and her fellow servants thought highly of her. No, she had no regular follower, as far as he knew, and he didn't wish to speculate about the identity of the baby's father. He admitted that he'd received an anonymous letter but claimed that its contents were malicious nonsense although, conveniently, he couldn't recall the exact accusation. He'd just glanced at it and burned it right away. He was always happy to help the police but unless the inspector had any more questions ... After all, he was a busy man.

Albert recognised this as a skilfully executed dismissal but there was little he could do about it. Besides, it was getting late so he thanked Sir William and prepared to return to the police station.

He left by the front door, shown out by Sarah's replacement. But when he was halfway down the drive, he heard running feet behind him. He turned to see the young maid who'd shown him out trying to catch him up.

'Sir,' she said breathlessly, her hand on her chest as if to still her thumping heart.

Albert waited patiently while she caught her breath. 'Can I help you?'

'It's Mrs Banks.'

'Who's Mrs Banks?'

'The housekeeper,' she said as though she was surprised he didn't know. 'She sends her compliments and says can she have a word in private.'

He followed her back to the house, noticing that she kept looking round as if there was something secretive about the meeting she'd just facilitated between the policeman and the housekeeper. They entered the house by the back door and Albert found himself in a world of dull green paint, pictureless walls and uncarpeted floors. It seemed colder here and darker, almost as if all the sunlight had been stolen by the people upstairs who lived in its warm glow while those down here toiled in this dull, colourless world. So close and yet so distant.

The maid showed him into a cosy little parlour where a pair of comfortable armchairs were arranged around a neat fireplace and a snowy cloth covered the table in the corner. One wall was lined with tall cupboards with a fine display of sparkling china on the glazed shelves above. A framed pious motto above the fire announced that God sees all our sins.

One of the armchairs was occupied by a stout, grey-haired woman wearing black. As she stood up to greet him, Albert saw that she had a kind, intelligent face. She looked like a woman who wouldn't miss much of what was happening around her and his first thought was that she'd probably make an excellent witness. He was suddenly filled with fresh hope.

She introduced herself as Mrs Banks, the Cartwrights' housekeeper. She'd only been with the family since they moved back into Tarnhey Court after the war, she told him. She'd been housekeeper to a family in Buxton before then but she wanted to move closer to her sister in New Mills.

Albert listened carefully while she spoke and he wondered why she was giving him this brief biography. He was soon to find out.

'You see,' she said. 'It isn't as if I've been with the family a long time and watched Master Roderick grow up. I think the truth needs to be told, don't you?'

'Undoubtedly,' Albert replied. He suspected she was clearing the way for a revelation about her employers, making the excuse that there was no long service to guarantee her loyalty. He waited for her to continue.

'I'm not one to spread scandal or gossip but some things are wrong and I don't like people using their power and status to take advantage of gullible girls.' She sounded quite indignant which, from his point of view, was good.

'Was Sarah Cookham gullible?'

'She was. She was a silly girl and when I told her he was taking advantage, she wouldn't listen.'

'Are you talking about Roderick?'

She gave him an exasperated smile. 'Roderick? Oh no, it wasn't Roderick. He's a sweet boy under all that bluster. Even though there are things about him he wouldn't want to be made public.' She looked at Albert meaningfully.

'What do you mean?'

'That's really not for me to say. And the last thing I want is to get him into trouble. Forget I said anything. Please.'

Albert assured her he would and she nodded warily, as though she wanted to believe him but couldn't quite bring herself to do so.

'So who made Sarah pregnant? One of the servants? The gardener? I saw a young man in the garden earlier.' He thought of the young man he'd seen with Roderick in the dovecote. He was young and good looking. Just the sort of man Sarah might go for.

'He's not the gardener. He just helps out. And it definitely wasn't him.'

He sat and waited for Mrs Banks to continue and after a few moments she spoke again.

'I caught them together once,' she said almost in a whisper. 'It was very embarrassing and he asked me to say nothing. Normally, he can rely on my complete discretion of course, but with Sarah dead . . . '

She paused and Albert waited patiently. He knew her reticence meant that she wasn't about to accuse some lowly gardener and he suspected he knew what was coming. But he wanted to hear her say it.

'It was Sir William.' She exhaled, as if uttering the words had been a great effort. 'I'm in his employ and I feel disloyal but I think the truth is more important, don't you?'

'Yes. I do. Please tell me everything you know.'

'As I've just said, I caught them together. I was delivering fresh linen to the bedrooms one morning and I thought Sir William and Lady Cartwright were downstairs in the breakfast room. I entered Sir William's bedroom and, to my horror and surprise, he was in there. And he wasn't alone. He was . . . embracing Sarah. And they were kissing. I shut the door again quickly of course and I'm not sure whether they knew I was there. Nothing was ever said.'

'You think he was the father of her child?'

'From then on I watched her very closely and I couldn't help noticing that she'd disappear from time to time whenever Sir William was home from London.'

'Did you see her with anyone else – any young men?'

She pursed her lips together. 'When I was first in service followers weren't permitted to call at our employers' houses but since the war things have become rather . . . slack. But I was never aware of any young men calling on Sarah – which was surprising because she was a very pretty girl. Then when I caught her with Sir William I realised why. She had bigger ambitions . . . although I

222

don't know what she expected would happen. Sir William was hardly going to abandon his wife to run off with a parlour maid, was he?'

'Some girls can be very naive,' Albert said.

'I blame all these romantic novels. Always had her nose in one, she did. And now the poor girl's six feet underground. I saw you at the funeral.'

'I was trying to be unobtrusive.'

She smiled. 'Will you speak to Sir William?'

'I just have ... but I'd be neglecting my duty if I didn't have another word in light of what you've just told me.'

'You won't say it was me who told you about him and Sarah, will you?'

Albert shook his head. He had no desire to see this woman dismissed from her job for telling the truth about what she'd seen. 'I promise you I won't say where the information came from.'

She seemed reassured by his answer and offered him tea, as though she didn't wish to be alone to contemplate her indiscretion. But he declined. He wanted to speak to Sir William again before he went off to London. And when he said he'd leave the house and call at the front door so it wouldn't look as though he'd been talking to someone below stairs, Mrs Banks expressed her gratitude.

He walked round to the front door as promised and knocked. The maid who'd conveyed Mrs Banks's message opened the door, looking rather surprised to see him back. But she said nothing and hurried off to tell Sir William that he wished to have another word.

After a couple of minutes she returned with an apologetic look on her face. She was sorry but Sir William had gone off to catch the London train ten minutes ago. Master Roderick had taken him in the motor car.

Albert thanked her and made for the railway station. But when he arrived there, the train had already gone. And there was no sign of Roderick Cartwright or the shiny black Rolls-Royce.

It was almost six o'clock and he was beginning to feel hungry so, after calling in at the police station to see if there were any new developments and hand in the anonymous letters as evidence, he returned to the Black Horse.

Mrs Jackson greeted him with the news that his dinner would be served in half an hour if he wished. As he thanked her, a sudden wave of tiredness engulfed him and he told her he'd go to his room until his meal was ready. Most of the time the damage war had done to his body didn't bother him but sometimes his weakness and vulnerability overwhelmed him and he had to rest. In those distant days of youth and strength, he'd never imagined he'd ever feel this way. He was thirty but there were times he felt like an old man.

He was about to climb the stairs to his room when Mrs Jackson came hurrying after him flourishing an envelope in her left hand. 'This came for you by the lunchtime post, Inspector.'

She handed over the letter and Albert recognised the handwriting at once. Mary had written to him. She'd never been a keen letter writer and he wondered what had prompted her to put pen to paper this time. He stuffed the letter in his coat pocket and made for his room. As soon as he'd shut the door behind him he sat down on the bed, tore the envelope open and began to read.

Dear Albert, I'm writing to tell you that I'm staying with Mother. She's got this terrible influenza that's going around and I need to take care of her. I didn't want you to get back home and find I wasn't there so I thought I'd better let you know. Your wife, Mary.

There had been no assurance of love at the close. No expression of affection in the bare words. Her words were as cold as his feelings.

He shut his eyes and once more thoughts of Flora flooded unbidden into his head. The thought of her caused him to relive that kiss in the boathouse and he felt a sudden stirring of desire. It was the kind of desire he hadn't felt for Mary since before Frederick's death when something inside her had died too. He'd tried to tell himself that it wasn't Mary's fault; that her indifference sprouted from her grief. But the prospect of being back with his wife in that cold house of mourning made his heart sink.

Perhaps it would be best to avoid Flora Winsmore in future. Every time he saw her he was overwhelmed by temptation. Besides, he hoped he'd soon be able to bring the killer of Sarah Cookham and the others to justice. It was just a matter of asking the right questions and getting the evidence that would make the solution fall into place. And once he'd succeeded, he'd leave Wenfield for good and never think of Flora again.

He returned the letter to its envelope and stuffed it back into his jacket pocket. At least if Mary was fully occupied nursing her mother, he didn't have to feel awkward about being away and leaving her on her own. As he made his way downstairs good smells were coming from the bar and his hollow stomach rumbled at the thought of Mrs Jackson's dinner.

It was meat pie, swimming in rich gravy with creamy mashed potatoes to the side. Mrs Jackson's menu might be limited but her food was tasty and well cooked. He ate hungrily while she looked on with satisfaction, commenting when he'd finished that she liked a man who enjoyed his food.

There was apple pie for pudding, drowned in a thick custard the colour of spring primroses. Mrs Jackson once more looked gratified when he expressed his appreciation. And as she returned to ask him whether he'd like a fresh cup of tea to wash down his meal, she looked as if she was in a talkative mood. The food had perked him up and he was now inclined to make the most of his opportunity. This was a chance to gain a bit more local information and when Mrs Jackson returned with the pot of tea he invited her to fetch an extra cup and join him.

She blushed at the invitation but sat down beside him, alert as though she was hoping for some privileged insight into his investigation. However, he wanted to tap into her knowledge rather than the other way round.

'I went to Tarnhey Court today,' he began. 'It's a fine house. I believe it was used as a hospital during the war.'

She nodded. 'That's right. Some of the poor lads used to come in here once they were well enough to be allowed into the village. A lot of them had terrible injuries – burns and the like – and a few of them used to wear masks painted to look like their faces. Some of them were so good you couldn't tell from a distance but, even so, I used to wonder what they looked like underneath.' Her face suddenly reddened, as if she realised she'd said something tactless. 'Oh, they were really bad. Far worse than . . . '

Albert smiled reassuringly. He knew his smile was lop-sided these days because of the scarring. 'I know what you mean. Did you see much of Roderick Cartwright during the war? Was he injured or was he one of the lucky ones?'

She leaned forward and looked around as if she feared someone might be listening, even though the saloon bar was empty. 'Oh he was definitely one of the lucky ones,' she said in a loud whisper. 'It soon got about that he hadn't been sent to the Front like the other lads from round here and rumour had it that his father got him a cushy billet behind a desk in London. As you can imag-ine it caused a lot of resentment, especially when the telegrams started to arrive saying lads had been killed ... or were missing believed dead. Left a bitter taste, it did. Some didn't take kindly to it at all.'

'What did they do?'

'Well I heard from Mrs Jones who used to be house-keeper for the Cartwrights before Mrs Banks that when he came home on leave he used to get letters – anony-mous letters. When the hospital took over the Cartwrights moved out of Tarnhey Court and went to the dower house on the other side of the village where Sir William's mother lives. Whoever sent the letters knew exactly where he was and when.'

The mention of anonymous letters caught his atten-tion. 'So it was someone who knew what the family were up to. Any idea who it was?'

'Between you and me there were a few of them. Like a witches' coven they were. If they even got a sniff of cowardice ...'

'So other people got these letters?'

227

'Oh yes. And white feathers. My Joe ... Mr Jackson ... they gave him one when he was sent home with shell shock. In a terrible state he was. They were going to send him back but thank God the war finished before they could.'

From what Albert had seen of Mr Jackson, he seemed a quiet, introspective man. He cursed himself for not recognising the all-too familiar signs. After all, he'd seen enough cases of shell shock during the past few years. Injuries to the mind were as common as those to the body.

'Who was it who gave these feathers out?'

'Do you want me to name names?'

'It might be helpful.'

Mrs Jackson considered the question for a few moments before she spoke. 'Like I said, there were a few of them and unless a man had obvious injuries,' she nodded towards Albert's left hand, 'he was fair game. I don't like to speak ill of the dead but I reckon the worst of them was Miss Forrest. Mrs Bell, the vicar's wife, stopped going into her tea shop because of the spiteful talk and so did I. I've never set foot in the place since but Mrs Bell's all sweetness and light and Christian forgiveness so she'd started going in again recently. Very creditable, I'm sure, but I'm not that saintly.'

'Who else was involved?'

'Annie Dryden ... her that was murdered. Then there was Caroline Bartlett, the chemist's wife. It was easy for her. She's only got daughters – no sons to be needlessly slaughtered at the Front. There were others too. Miss Trace at the haberdashery and quite a few of the wives from the village. They called themselves the Society for the Abolition of Cowardice. SAC for short. They used to put up notices round the village. They put one on the church notice board once but Mrs Bell tore it down. They were a mixture: old and young and a few silly girls joined in too. Easily led.' She rolled her eyes.

Albert nodded. This might explain why one of the letters he found was aimed at discrediting Mrs Bell.

'You say Miss Forrest and Annie Dryden were heavily involved. What about Myrtle Bligh and Sarah Cookham?'

She gave a knowing smile. 'Sarah might have been one of them – I'm not sure. But I don't know about little Myrtle.' She leaned forward. 'So that's how your mind's working, is it? You think these women were killed because they sent a white feather to the wrong man ... maybe someone who killed himself because of what they did?'

This was exactly what he was thinking. 'Can you think of anybody who fits that description?'

She straightened her back and looked at him defiantly. 'As I matter of fact I can. You're looking at her. After my Joe got a nasty little note with a white feather enclosed, he tried to hang himself in the stables at the back of the pub. Luckily our pot man found him and he was cut down in time. A doctor from Tarnhey Court was here in the saloon bar at the time and he saw to him and we put him to bed. He was really good, Dr Bone was. He understood, you see, and he said if he had his way, those poisonous bitches would face the courts. Fat chance. Nobody wants to be seen as unpatriotic, do they? Not many people understand ... not even now the war's over.'

'Is Dr Bone still in the area?'

'He has a practice in New Mills and I believe he comes here to work at the Cottage Hospital a few days a week. I expect he'll be there a lot with this terrible influenza out-break. He's such a lovely man – did a lot of good up at Tarnhey Court during the war. Those boys couldn't sing his praises highly enough.'

'What about your doctor here ... Dr Winsmore?' He couldn't resist asking the question and he knew it was inevitable that he'd try to steer the conversation round to the doctor's daughter. He felt the urge to talk about her. And this way, he could do it without arousing suspicion.

'Poor Dr Winsmore. I told you all about his wife, didn't I?'

'Yes. Do you know whether the doctor ever tried to find her after she left?'

'Not that I know of. When it happened he went into his shell. Never spoke about it. Which is hardly surprising, is it?'

'You said there were some people who said she never left.'

She waved her hand dismissively as though she was embarrassed about saying too much. 'Oh it was just one of those things people say. You know how it is.'

'What about the man Mrs Winsmore went off with?'

'Mr Nerrist? He was about your height. Shock of black hair. Blue eyes. Good looking lad always ready with a joke. Cheerful, I'd say. I thought he was a nice young man. Until I found out what he'd done.'

'The affair ... could that have been just another story that got round? Was there any evidence?'

'They were seen together. They even had tea at Miss Forrest's ... bold as brass.'

'That doesn't necessarily mean they were lovers.'

'Well the doctor never denied it, even to the vicar. I

was talking to the Reverend's housekeeper and she overheard the vicar asking the doctor about it.'

Albert suppressed a smile. For a woman who said she didn't like to gossip, Mrs Jackson seemed rather an expert. 'You said Mr Nerrist lived in Liverpool. Do you have his address?'

Mrs Jackson looked wary. 'Why?'

'No particular reason. I'm just curious.'

This answer seemed to satisfy Mrs Jackson who hurried off, returning a couple of minutes later with a large, leather-bound book. Albert recognised it as the register he'd signed when he arrived. She searched through the pages and stopped at a page marked 1905. There it was. Martin Nerrist. And the address was in the Liverpool district of Allerton. He took out his notebook and wrote it down.

Asking Flora Winsmore if she'd ever attempted to contact her mother would make a good excuse to see her again.

Chapter 28

Flora

I am enjoying my work at the hospital, even though Dr Bone is there much of the time. I see him watching me and I wonder what he is thinking. Is he sorry for what he did? Or does he wish to humiliate me further? I avoid him as best I can and make sure I am never alone when he is about.

The murder of Miss Forrest is the talk of the nurses and they say they are afraid to venture out after dark. The activities of the killer have created such an atmosphere of terror that each woman imagines herself as the next victim. There was great relief when Sydney Pepper was arrested but, as he was in custody at the time of Miss Forrest's death, it seems that his innocence has now been established which means the killer is still free to walk the streets and prey on his selected victims.

There is talk amongst the nurses that Sarah Cookham's funeral was a lavish affair, paid for by Sir William

Cartwright. Some take it as evidence of the Cartwrights' generosity to their staff but I've never known them be so generous before, not even to the families of those staff killed in the war. However, I think my thoughts and share them with nobody. I do not wish to be a gossip. I know the pain sharp tongues can cause.

Pepper had been the ideal scapegoat for the murders but he has now been released from the cells beneath the police station and is a free man once more. I wonder how Albert Lincoln has borne the humiliation of arresting the wrong man. The truth is, I think of Albert often. And I think of the warmth of his body as we stood there in the boathouse and that handsome, damaged face I kissed so readily. I know I must focus all my thoughts, all my attention, on my sick patients, but Albert keeps intruding. He is a widower and I keep thinking of the grief he must have felt at the loss of his wife. I too have known loss and this is a bond between us. And he didn't mention any children so I assume he is alone in the world. Alone and free.

There is so much to do on the ward that time passes quickly but the day is punctuated by Dr Bone's rounds and I see him looking at me. I refuse to meet his eyes, knowing I must behave in a professional manner at all times. There is no room for my own emotions when the patients are depending on me.

David Eames is still here on the ward but I am happy to say he's recovering well, although he's still too weak to return to the isolated cottage he shares with his sister so we will care for him here at the hospital until he regains his strength. I pass the time of day with him whenever I can. A cheerful nurse who takes an interest in her patients, Sister says, is as good as a tonic. David seems worried about the murders and asks me if I have any news of the police investigations. I assume he's worried for his sister so I tell him what I can, which isn't very much.

David's sister, Helen, visits this afternoon. I have met her only once before and I thought her a little strange then. She is a handsome woman; tall with striking auburn hair and a generous mouth and she is what some call highly strung. David told me once that she too used to be an artist and that she'd once been muse to a man who had made quite a name for himself in the artistic world. Then a few years ago she'd had what David described as a nervous breakdown and attempted to slash her wrists: David said you could still see the scars and he's always been very protective of her, as though he regards her as his responsibility. When I enter the ward during visiting time and see her sitting at his bedside, clasping his hand, I think her beautiful.

She looks up and sees me watching but does not smile. Then I see David whisper something to her and she looks away as if I'm invisible.

'This is Helen, my sister,' David says when I approach the bed. 'I think you met once when I was at Tarnhey Court.'

'Yes, we did,' I say. 'It's good to see you again, Helen.' I see no reaction on Helen's lovely face, not even a slight change of expression.

'Helen's very nervous with this killer about,' David says. I sense he's embarrassed by his sister's lack of greeting but I smile to reassure him that I understand. 'She has to cycle back to the cottage alone, you see.'

'I'm sure she'll be all right in daylight,' I say. 'I've met

234

the inspector from Scotland Yard who's come here to take charge of the case. He seems a very capable man.' I feel myself blush. 'I'm sure they'll make an arrest soon.'

Helen turns her head towards me at last. Her green eyes are wide and anxious. 'You don't understand. I can't be in the cottage alone. Someone broke into David's studio a few weeks ago when we were out. They smashed the glass in the door and took things.'

'What things?'

'Two of the masks David made at Tarnhey Court during the war.'

'Is that all?'

She doesn't answer my question. 'He made them for his comrades, didn't you, David? And when they died he kept them as mementos. They're works of art. Beautiful.'

David nods sadly, recalling his dead friends. Remembering how he took plaster casts of their faces and, using old photographs, modelled their original features carefully before fashioning the masks to cover the damaged parts of their faces and lovingly matching their skin tones in paint. His work began once the surgeon's work finished and I used to watch him recreate those faces and give men back their self-respect.

'It was annoying,' he says. 'But it could have been worse. At least they didn't break into the cottage.'

'Why would someone want the masks?' I ask.

Helen puts her face close to mine. I can smell her breath and it isn't as pleasant as her looks. 'What if it's the killer who broke into our cottage? What if he's taken the masks to conceal his true identity?'

'Have you told the police about the break in?' I ask.

Helen shakes her head.

'You should.'

Helen's eyes widen with fear. 'If it was the killer, it means he knows that David had the masks and he knows where we live.' There is an edge of hysteria in her voice and she looks at her brother as if she is pleading with him to protect her. 'I don't want to stay there on my own, David. But I've nowhere else to go.'

David looks away and I sense his frustration. He is used to caring for his sister but illness has rendered him temporarily useless. I place a comforting hand on Helen's arm. 'David's getting better every day and he'll be able to go home soon. Just take care and lock your doors. Don't forget, the killer's never attacked anyone in their own home so I'm sure you'll be safe.'

I know she isn't listening. All my attempts to reassure her have been in vain.

'I'm going to stay at the Black Horse until you come home,' she continues, fidgeting with the cloth of the hospital bedspread. 'That'll be best. They're bound to have a room. Nobody visits Wenfield unless they have to. Especially with this influenza outbreak ... and a murderer at large.'

'I'm going off duty as soon as visiting is over,' I say to her. 'I'll walk to the Black Horse with you if you like.'

I expect Helen to make some small show of gratitude but she gives a dismissive wave of her hand. 'As you wish.'

Half an hour later Helen and I are walking side by side through the village square towards the Black Horse. She has no overnight things with her and I imagine this sudden abandonment of her cottage has stemmed from a moment of panic and she hasn't thought the matter through. Helen, I guess, is like that: I've heard there have been times when her impulsiveness has caused embarrassment. But I can still feel some sympathy for her – and the loving brother who takes such good care of her.

When we reach the Black Horse I take her inside where we're greeted by the taciturn Mr Jackson who says he'll fetch his wife, adding that she's the one who deals with the rooms. He asks us to wait in the saloon as it's more suitable for ladies and when we push open the etched glass door we find ourselves in the company of a group of suited businessmen, probably visitors to one of the mills, who glance up at us appraisingly then resume their discussion about the price of raw materials and machinery. As we wait in the window seat, my attempts to make conversation with Helen are met with monosyllables. Eventually I give up and watch the door, hoping Albert will come in, surprised at the strength of my desire to see him.

The door opens but it is Mrs Jackson who appears. She is a woman who exudes capability and she greets us with an enquiring smile. I explain that Helen requires a room and when I say why, Mrs Jackson is all sympathy.

'Of course, dear. I understand perfectly. I wouldn't like to be out in the wilds on my own with all this going on,' she coos. 'I have a nice quiet room at the back if that suits.' She quotes a price and Helen nods absentmindedly as though money is the last thing on her mind.

Helen turns to me. 'I'll need a few things from the cottage. Can you see to it?'

She addresses me as if I'm a servant and I'm unsure how to reply. My inner pride prickles with indignation for a few moments but then I tell myself I'm doing this as a favour for David and agree to her imperious demand. She gives me the door key and Mrs Jackson calls the girl who helps with the meals, instructing her to show Miss Eames up to room five.

I am left alone with Mrs Jackson for a few minutes and we exchange pleasantries. Then she asks me to sit beside her in the seat recently vacated by Helen. She has something she wishes to say. Something of a delicate nature.

I know Mrs Jackson to pass the time of day with but we have never been close so I wonder what news she wants to impart. For a split second I'm afraid she might have heard news of my meeting with Albert in the boathouse and I wonder if she wishes to warn me that he is a notorious womaniser ... or, worse still, a married liar. I am relieved when I discover it is nothing of the sort.

'I was speaking to Inspector Lincoln, the man from Scotland Yard,' she begins. She looks embarrassed, as if she fears that what she's about to say will reflect badly on her. 'And the subject of your family came up.'

'He was asking about me?' If he is trying to find out about me, perhaps this is good news.

She hesitates. 'No, my dear. He was asking me about your mother ... her disappearance. I'm not one to gossip and I didn't know whether to say anything but I thought you should know. Perhaps I should have told your father.'

'No, Mrs Jackson, it's best not to bother him. What did you tell the inspector?'

She frowns as though she's making a great effort to recall exactly what was said. But she doesn't tell me much and I suspect she's trying to make it sound as if she was more discreet than she actually was.

She says she told him the address of the man my mother was supposed to have absconded with but she doesn't offer me the same information and I don't embarrass her by insisting. If Albert knows where the man is, perhaps I can persuade him to tell me.

'Thank you for telling me,' I say.

'If you ask me, it wasn't right what your mother did. Joe and I weren't blessed with children but if we had been, I could never have upped and left them like that.' She put her hand to her mouth as though she feared she'd said too much. 'I'm sorry, my dear. I really shouldn't have said that. Your mother might have had her reasons. You never know what's going on in other people's lives, do you?'

Mrs Jackson's words touch me in a way I hadn't expected. Since Mother left us I've smothered my grief at her loss. When John and I were young we clung together against the world while Father nursed his own disappointment. My brother and I became so close that we knew what each other thought before we said it. We both loved Edith and it upset us when she left us. Then John joined up, returning for a while to recover from his unseen wounds before going back to the Front. After that I never saw him again and half of me died when that telegram came. They sent a plaque too, something to acknowledge his bravery and our loss. Father has it hidden away in a drawer somewhere but he never looks at it.

It suddenly occurs to me that Mother might not know John is dead and finding her suddenly takes on a fresh urgency. Even after what she's done, she should be told. She should feel the loss of the son she gave birth to. It would be her punishment.

I have the keys to Helen's cottage safe in my pocket and I tell Mrs Jackson I'm going to fetch Miss Eames's things for her. I sense that she's curious about Helen Eames but she asks no questions. I leave the saloon at the same time as the group of smartly dressed men and one of them holds the door open for me to go out first. I thank him politely and step out into the street.

I see Father's car outside the house which means he's home from his afternoon rounds. I open the front door just as Sybil emerges from the kitchen and she greets me with an enquiring look.

'How are things at the hospital, miss?'

I know she's worried about the influenza outbreak. Some of her many relatives have succumbed but, fortunately, all have recovered. And yet the threat is still there, hanging over young and old, the healthy and the ailing. Especially the young and healthy it seems.

'Two new cases were admitted today,' I answer. 'So I'll be going back tomorrow. Is my father home?'

'Yes, miss. He's just got back from his round. Mrs Bligh's youngest has the influenza,' she said solemnly. 'After losing Myrtle . . .'

'Let's pray for a swift recovery,' I say piously.

Sybil nods and vanishes back into the kitchen. I watch her disappearing back and wish there was something I could say to reassure her but I have no comfort to give. I open the door to Father's waiting room and when I find it empty I give a token knock on his surgery door and I hear him say 'come in'.

He's sitting at his desk as though he's waiting for a patient, his stethoscope lying on the blotter in front of him. He looks up but he doesn't smile.

'I said I'd go up to the hospital later,' he said. 'Any news?'

I know he's asking whether there have been any more deaths at the hospital in his absence and when I shake my head I see a look of relief pass across his face.

'Sybil tells me the youngest Bligh girl's sick.'

'She doesn't seem very bad but often the patient appears to be past the crisis and then they take a turn for the worse. Her mother's very distressed as you can imagine ... after Myrtle. But, in my opinion, she doesn't need to be admitted to hospital ... not yet.'

I stand in front of his desk like a naughty schoolgirl summoned to the headmistress's study. He invites me to sit but I prefer to stay where I am. I can see his expression better from here.

'I've been to the Black Horse.'

I see a momentary flash of alarm in his eyes, swiftly hidden behind a benign smile.

'I hope you're not becoming a toper, my dear?'

I return his smile, letting him think I find his feeble joke amusing. 'Of course not. There's a patient at the hospital. His name's David Eames and he was a patient at Tarnhey Court during the war. He's an artist and sculptor and he made portrait masks to conceal facial injuries.'

'I've heard about it – in fact I've seen the results. Very realistic.'

'Well David – Captain Eames – lives in a cottage up in the hills with his sister and she's nervous about being left alone there with this killer about. She thought it best to take a room at the Black Horse while her brother's at the hospital and I offered to help her.'

'Very commendable.' He looks slightly puzzled, as though he is unsure where the conversation is going.

'While I was at the Black Horse I spoke to Mrs Jackson. She said the inspector from Scotland Yard has been asking questions ... about Mother.'

The colour drains from his face and I think of that horrible, poisonous letter. That crushing statement followed by a single question: YOU MURDERED YOUR WIFE – WHERE WERE YOU WHEN THE OTHERS DIED?

'She gave the inspector the address of the man they say Mother went off with. He was from Liverpool. Did you know that?'

He shakes his head but I don't believe him.

'Did you ever try to find her?'

He hesitates before answering. 'There was no point. She'd made up her mind.'

'You had me and John to care for. Surely you could have persuaded her to come home ... for our sake.' At the mention of my dear John's name I feel tears pricking my eyes. I blink them away. I won't give in to emotion. I just want the truth that has been kept from me all those years and, if possible, I want to hear my mother's version of events. I can't believe she would have left us without a thought.

Father gives me a strange look. 'I presume her new fancy man was more important to her than her children. If I were you, I'd forget all about her. I have.'

'You should have tried to find her.'

He regards me with pity. Mother hurt him badly, just as she hurt me and John. Perhaps he's right. She made her choice so perhaps I should forget about her. But I can't put her out of my mind. When I close my eyes she's there, laughing and beautiful. A butterfly in a cage.

As I leave Father to his thoughts, I'm certain that he knows more of the matter than he admits. Perhaps it's just that he feels the shame of a cuckold and has no wish to relive that part of his life. If this is the case, I can't blame him. But I need to know.

I put my hand in my pocket and my fingers come into contact with Helen's keys. I'm not needed at the hospital until tomorrow so I decide to go now while I have nothing else to do. I'm still waiting for a letter from the Royal Infirmary and I'm disappointed when it doesn't arrive in the afternoon post. I comfort myself with the thought that these things take time.

I could walk the mile or so to David's cottage but I decide to use my bicycle. It's not that I'm nervous about walking alone down the narrow lanes lined with waist-high dry stone walls but two wheels are quicker than two legs. My bicycle is kept in the shed at the back of the house and I wheel it out of the garden onto the path before mounting. The spring sun is peeping out from behind the clouds and as I ride through the village I feel the breeze against my face. During the war when I lived in at Tarnhey Court, I rarely used my bicycle because I was fully occupied with my work but now it allows me a certain level of freedom. Perhaps one day I will own a motor car so I'm not at the mercy of our unpredictable elements. One day.

I pedal on, leaving the confines of the village and out into the countryside. I can hear sheep bleating in the fields as though they're engaging in some deep ovine conversation. I see the mother sheep tailing their playful lambs, keeping them close. If only all mothers were as devoted.

All of a sudden the sight of a familiar figure makes me stop, hopping off the saddle and wheeling the bicycle along the lane. Albert touches his hat and at first I think he looks pleased to see me but then I notice that his brow is furrowed by a worried frown.

I speak first. 'What are you doing here?'

'I wanted to see where Annie Dryden was found.'

I look round and point to a spot a few yards down the track, next to a dry stone wall. 'It was just over there. I came here with my father to take notes.'

'So you saw her?'

I nod my head. 'Yes. I saw her. And what he did to her.'

'According to the post mortem he didn't do anything.'

'That's not how it looked. Her clothing was . . . '

'Perhaps that's what he wanted people to think. Where are you off to?'

I explain about David's illness and Helen's nervousness at being left on her own in the cottage they shared. 'I'm going to the cottage now to fetch Helen's things. She didn't want to go there alone.'

'But she's happy to let you run the risk.'

'Helen's . . . ' I search for the word. 'Highly strung. I'm not.'

This time he smiles. 'No. You're one of the most sensible women I've met.'

'I don't know whether that's a compliment.'

'I meant it as one.'

I feel my face burning then I remember I have something to tell him. 'David and Helen's outhouse was broken into a few weeks ago.'

I have Albert's full attention. 'I don't remember any-body at the station mentioning this.'

'They didn't report it.'

'Why not?'

'I don't know.'

'Was anything taken?'

'When David was a patient at Tarnhey Court during the war he used his talents to make masks for men with terrible disfigurements.'

'I've seen an example. Sydney Pepper had one. It belonged to a friend of his who died.'

'Anyway, David uses an outhouse at the cottage as a studio now and a couple of the masks he kept there were stolen during the break in.'

'I'd like to talk to him.'

'I'm sure that'll be possible,' I say. 'He's recovering well.'

'Was he in hospital at the time of Miss Forrest's murder?'

I know why he was asking and it's a relief to be able to answer yes. David Eames, a man I regard as a friend, had been delirious with fever in the Cottage Hospital when Miss Forrest had met her gruesome end. His innocence is guaranteed.

'Once I've taken a look at this murder site, I'd like to see the scene of the break in. Do you mind if I come with you?'

I feel a thrill pass through my body but I force myself to smile calmly and tell him that I hadn't been looking forward to visiting David's empty cottage alone so I'll be grateful for his company. But isn't he needed back at the police station?

'The local lads are doing the legwork,' he says, his eyes fixed on mine as though he's trying to read my thoughts. 'I'm here to think and I do that best out of doors,' he says, sniffing the air. 'It's good to get the smoke of London out of my lungs for a change.'

'You like our countryside?'

'There are lots of things I like about Wenfield,' he answers, still watching me. I feel my cheeks burning. 'Sometimes you can tire of life in a big city,' he says.

'I can't wait to experience it.'

He doesn't answer. I prop my bicycle up against the stone wall and walk back with him to the spot where Annie Dryden was found. When I point it out he stares at the ground, then he looks around, taking in the whole scene.

'You knew Annie Dryden,' he says. 'Did this place have any significance for her?'

'I don't think so. Although her son used to work for Wilf Fuller – he farms this land.'

'Does Annie's son still work here?'

I shake my head. 'He died at Passchendaele. Or rather he was reported missing, believed dead.'

Albert stands there staring over the wall at the sheep-filled fields and I can't tell what he's thinking.

'Could she have been on her way to visit Wilf Fuller?' I suggest.

'Mr Fuller's been interviewed and he says he has no idea what she was doing here. He claims he didn't know her particularly well . . . only to say hello to in the village. What do you know about him?'

I shrug my shoulders. 'Wilf's well regarded. His wife's a nice woman but they keep themselves to themselves. They've got two daughters and a son.'

'The son survived the war?'

'Too young to fight. He's only fourteen and the girls are younger. I really can't see the Fullers having anything to do with Annie's murder.'

He nods as if he was happy to accept my opinion and I feel relieved that my words won't make the Fullers the focus of police attention. I retrieve my bicycle and as I continue on towards David's cottage Albert catches me up and walks by my side.

We walk in silence for a while and the lack of conversation feels comfortable somehow, as if we're old friends content in each other's company with no need for words.

But after a while I can't contain my curiosity any longer. 'You were asking Mrs Jackson about my mother.'

'I apologise for my inquisitiveness,' he says. 'After all, the matter has nothing to do with my case.' He pauses. 'I'm afraid I was just curious. I want to know more about you.'

'And what have you found out?'

'Only that everyone in the village made the assumption that your mother ran off with a young engineer from Liverpool who was here on business. He was staying at the Black Horse and his name was Martin Nerrist.'

'What exactly did Mrs Jackson say about him?'

'She said he was good looking. Dark hair, blue eyes, always ready with a joke. Bit of a charmer by the sound of it.'

'Did she tell you they met at the hotel? Did she say they were lovers?'

'She said they were seen together in Miss Forrest's tea rooms. That's all.'

'So there's no evidence they were having an affair?'

'Only that when he left the village, so did she.'

'That's not exactly evidence.'

'Not the sort that would stand up in court,' Albert says lightly.

'I need to find her.'

He turns to face me, placing his hand on my arm. The touch sends a thrill through me and when he removes his hand I want the contact to continue. 'Is that wise?' he says, frowning as though he's concerned for my safety.

'I need to know why she left. I need to tell her about John.'

Albert looks at me with sympathy, as though he understands. We carry on walking and when we reach the cottage I ask him the question that's burning into my mind. 'Will you give me Martin Nerrist's address? If I can talk to him ... find out exactly what happened.'

'It was fourteen years ago. He might have moved. Or he might not have come back from the war.'

'Liverpool isn't far. I can get there and back in a day on the train.'

'What about the hospital?'

I suddenly realise I'm getting carried away. Perhaps it's the excitement of being with him. 'I'll have to wait until things are quieter.'

'I don't suppose I can stop you.'

'Do you want to?'

'Not particularly. She is your mother after all. Besides, it's hardly a police matter.'

'So you'll let me have the address?'

Albert hesitates. Then he takes out his notebook and scribbles something down. He tears the page out and gives it to me.

248

'Thanks,' I say. 'I promise I won't tell anyone where I got it.'

He looks as if he suddenly regrets his decision but I distract him by producing David's keys from the pocket in my skirt. First of all we make for the studio, a large brick outhouse at the back of the cottage with extensive windows to let in the light. One of the panes in the half-glazed door appears to have been replaced recently, suggesting that this is how the thief gained entry. I unlock the door and look round. I have been here several times before and some of the paintings I saw then are still here, stacked up against the walls. A half-finished clay sculpture of a woman's head stands in the centre of the room alongside a large landscape of hills and fields; a local scene.

Albert circles the studio slowly, opening cupboards and picking things off shelves. In one cupboard he takes out a portrait mask with a triumphant flourish. It's half-finished and my heart lurches as I remember that its intended recipient died of his wounds before it could be properly fitted.

When we leave the studio I lock the door carefully and Albert turns his attention to David and Helen's cottage. Once inside I climb the narrow wooden staircase that leads to the two bedrooms. I've never been upstairs before and I feel like an intruder as I take the little leather suitcase from the top of Helen's wardrobe and begin to pack the things she might need. The undergarments I find in the drawers are silk, the best quality, but faded and well worn.

As I fill the suitcase I can't resist the temptation to look through her drawers and wardrobe. The clothes hanging there are past their best, but good quality like the under-wear. And I'm surprised to feel rough khaki amongst the fine fabrics. David's old uniform is hanging at the back of the wardrobe and as I brush my hand against the stiff, scratchy cloth, I wonder why he hasn't stored it away in an old trunk like most other men have done. Something best forgotten. It also puzzles me why it is in his sister's wardrobe rather than his own. Perhaps she keeps it there as a reminder of his survival. But she isn't the sort of person I can talk to about such a personal matter.

I hear a sound behind me and when I turn I see Albert standing in the doorway, blocking out the feeble light from the small landing window.

'Have you finished in here?' he says as our eyes meet.

I close the suitcase and lift it off the bed. The bed is large enough for two and I imagine Helen entertaining lovers here. I have always thought of her as a woman who cares nothing for convention. She was once muse to an artist . . . but she paid a high price. The scars on her wrists are still visible.

Albert enters the room and lifts the suitcase. After taking it out onto the landing he returns and places his hand on my shoulder and I suddenly want him to kiss me. I want him to do what Dr Bone did to me in the dovecote at Tarnhey Court. I never thought I'd want to repeat that painful, humiliating experience again – but I know that this time it will be entirely different.

He hesitates, brushing back my hair and studying my face. I stand on tiptoe and we kiss, gently at first then with increasing passion. And then my body welcomes him as we fall, kissing, on to Helen's bed.

Chapter 29

After taking the suitcase to Helen at the Black Horse, I return home and shut myself in my room, telling Father I'm going in there to read. I lie on my bed, fingering the empty space beside me and imagining Albert there, nursing our secret, hugging it to myself.

I know he shares my feelings and that my love is returned. This sensation is new to me. It changes everything. And yet as I lie here it seems that nothing has changed.

I listen for a knock on the front door, hoping it will be Albert. But each time it's one of Father's patients. I want to run to the police station. I want to take him in my arms in front of Sergeant Teague and Constable Wren and claim him. This feels like a form of madness and I know that, for a while at least, I must be discreet and say nothing. I must be patient.

Then I fall into a sudden panic. What will happen

251

when he has to return to London? Will he ask me to go with him? The prospect of a new life excites me. Perhaps I could train as a nurse at one of the capital's great hospitals. I grin like a simpleton at the very thought.

I must think of other things. To my disappointment Father tells me at breakfast the next morning that my services aren't required at the hospital that day; one of the sick nurses has now recovered and no new cases of influenza have been admitted overnight. I greet the news bravely, offering to step in again if I'm needed, but I sense that Father's relieved. I still wait for the post each day and there is still no news from Manchester. However, I tell myself that, after recent events, that might be a good thing. I remember Edith telling me when I was a child that when one door closes, another opens. Perhaps she is right.

I feel restless and I wonder whether I should swap my role of nurse for that of visitor and visit David Eames at the hospital this afternoon. But Helen will no doubt be there and I don't particularly want to see her. She makes me uneasy, although I can't say why. I don't think she likes me and I know she'd like me even less if she knew what had happened in her room between me and Albert. When I think of our audacity I smile again. I can't stop smiling. Once breakfast is over Father asks me why I'm so cheerful and I can't think of an answer. Perhaps I should make more effort to conceal my feelings.

The telephone rings and Sybil answers. 'Doctor Winsmore's residence.' I presume it'll be somebody wanting Father's services but as I begin to climb the stairs, I hear Sybil saying that the call is for me.

I take the mouthpiece from her, hoping it's Albert. My

heart races and I feel my hand shaking as I prepare to speak. But it isn't Albert's voice I hear. It's Roderick Cartwright and he wants to see me. I conceal my disappointment and tell him I'll come to Tarnhey Court but he says it would be best if we meet somewhere else. He suggests the dovecote as it's out of sight of the house. I hesitate for a few seconds before agreeing. The secrecy makes me nervous. So does the location.

When I tell Father I'm going out, he tells me to take care. If Sydney Pepper's innocent it means the killer's still out there, waiting for prey. I assure him that no harm will come to me in the village and I promise him solemnly that I won't stray into any lonely places. As I put on my hat I turn to see that he's followed me into the hall. He looks worried, as though he doesn't believe I'll stick to my word. Perhaps he's guessed I'm hiding something but I tell myself this is nonsense. How can he know?

I am thinking how I can engineer a meeting with Albert once my meeting with Roderick's over. Or will he contact me? I'm beginning to tire of the uncertainty already but I must exercise patience and self-restraint.

When I leave the house several women in the street greet me with a prim 'Hello, Miss Winsmore.' And I think one of them looks at me strangely, as if she sees there's something different about me. But it must be my imagination and once I pass through the gates of Tarnhey Court I see nobody.

Father's words begin to echo in my head. This is a lonely spot; somewhere only the Cartwrights and their servants go. In the years before the war there were more servants – and guests too – but now the place has a deserted, neglected feel, as though the family has lost interest.

I make my way towards the walled garden and the dovecote, wishing I'd insisted on another meeting place but it's too late for that now. My stomach lurches as I see a figure emerging from the laurels. A man in uniform. I take a few steps back and then I recognise him as Sydney Pepper wearing his chauffeur's uniform. He obviously realises I'm frightened because he stops a few feet away from me and takes off his cap.

'Sorry, miss. Did I startle you?'

I feel foolish and force a smile. 'A little. But it's quite all right, Sydney,' I say. 'Are you well?'

'As well as I can be, miss.' I detect a hint of bitterness in his words.

I wonder whether to explain my presence then I decide it's none of his business and besides, I know Roderick might appreciate my discretion.

I walk on, aware of Pepper watching me as I push open the old wooden gate to the walled garden. I hope Roderick will be waiting because I don't want to be in there alone.

I am relieved when I see him pacing up and down out-side the dovecote, a half-smoked cigarette dangling from his fingers. When he sees me he throws the cigarette to the ground and the narrow grey plume of smoke drifts upwards. He gives me a nervous smile. He looks worried.

'Thanks for coming,' he says before lighting another cigarette. He offers the packet to me but I shake my head.

I see a white dove fluttering into the dovecote, return-ing home. Roderick glances up at it.

'What is it?' I say. 'Is something wrong?'

'We've known each other a long time, Flora. I can trust you, can't I?'

'Of course you can.'

After a short silence he speaks again. 'That man from London's been round. He's been speaking to Mrs Banks, our housekeeper. I was on my way down to one of the store rooms and I happened to pass her parlour door. Stupid old bitch couldn't keep her mouth shut.'

I raise my eyebrows. 'What were you doing downstairs in the servants' quarters?'

He looks away. 'Don't ask.'

'You were in the garden store, weren't you?'

He doesn't answer and I know I'm right.

'You're taking a big risk, Roderick. Is it wise to carry on your liaisons so close to home?'

'Probably not. But he's rather nice. I can rely on you not to say anything, can't I?'

'Do you need to ask? I've known your secret for a long time and I've never spoken of it to anyone. I never would.'

He steps forward and gives me a hug. But when he draws back I see that he still looks worried. 'I think Mrs Banks might have told the London man about me.'

'Does she know?'

'She lives here so she might have guessed. I'm afraid the London man might have me down as a suspect.'

'Why should he?'

'Because the women who died were the ones who were spreading all the gossip. I haven't mentioned it before but I had an anonymous letter – so has Father – so if the police think I have something to hide . . .'

'My father had a letter too,' I say, a little relieved. 'You're not the only one. Besides, surely you wouldn't kill anyone to stop it coming out that you prefer men to women? That's ridiculous.'

'No it's not,' he protests. 'Don't you realise I could go to prison if the police found out ... and it could ruin Father. And it's not only my ... preferences I'm thinking of. Those women were the same ones who found out I spent the war behind a desk and put it about that I was a coward. Miss Forrest kept giving me white feathers. And I found one under my pillow as well – I think Sarah put it there.'

'You wouldn't kill anyone because of that, surely. Anyway, you were in uniform so how could they know where you were posted?'

'I think Sarah must have got wind of it and spread it around. And there's something else. I overheard Mrs Banks gossiping to that policeman. She said Father and Sarah were having an affair. Poisonous bitch. If it wasn't so hard to get servants these days I'd tell Father to get rid of her.'

'Is it true? Were they having an affair?'

'I don't know. He's hardly likely to confide in me, is he? But he has been acting strangely since she died.'

'Do you think your mother suspects anything?'

'Mother lives in a world of her own so I doubt she'd have noticed if they were fornicating on the rug in front of her.' He throws what remains of his cigarette onto the ground and stamps it out with a violence that surprises me. 'I'm sorry to drag you into all this, Flora, but I needed someone to talk to. Someone who understands me.'

He looks at me with pleading eyes; those eyes that used to melt my heart when we were young and ensure that he usually triumphed in all our games. Roderick has always known how to use charm to get his own way.

'Do you think it's possible my father killed those

women?' he continues. 'Could he have killed them to cover up the fact that Sarah was his real target? She was pregnant and she was the type who'd make trouble. She could have ruined him.'

I smile. His words sound ridiculous. 'I can't see it somehow.'

'Father was here in Wenfield on each occasion. And those doves can only come from here.' He sweeps his hand towards the dovecote then he takes his cigarette packet from his pocket and lights another. 'The man from London thinks it must be someone from this house. So if it's not Sydney ... And it's not me ...'

'Everyone brought up in the village knows about the dovecote. And I can't imagine Sir William stalking women and ... and doing what the killer does to them.'

'Perhaps that's what he wants you to think. Father's clever. Cleverer than me. I inherited Mother's brains.'

I watch his face, unable to fathom out why he seems to be trying to incriminate his own father. 'I still can't believe it,' I say. 'Any more than I believe you're the murderer.'

He reaches out and takes my hand. 'Thanks for the vote of confidence. You'll keep your ear to the ground, won't you ... tell me if they're saying anything in the village. I believe you've been seen talking to that inspector.'

'Who told you that?' His words make me uneasy. They mean Albert and I must have been seen together and I wonder how much people know – and what conclusions they'll come to.

Roderick taps the side of his nose. 'It was Charlie ... my, er, friend. He saw you meeting up near Fuller's Farm and walking off together. Don't worry. Charlie knows how to keep his mouth shut. He's had lots of practice.'

I don't feel reassured. But I plan to get away from Wenfield tomorrow. I'm going to catch the train first thing in the morning and go to Liverpool. I'm going to find Martin Nerrist . . . and hopefully my mother.

Chapter 30

Albert

Albert took Mary's letter from his pocket and read it through again. In his mind he saw her in her mother's house, tending to the sick old woman, running up and down the narrow uncarpeted staircase at her beck and call. He knew Mary would go about her filial duties with morose efficiency. She rarely smiled now. Not since they'd lost Frederick. He imagined her spooning soup into the invalid's mouth or sitting in her mother's small back parlour, mending in the gas light. The Cartwrights, he'd noticed, had electricity but he and Mary hadn't been able to afford such a luxury on a policeman's wages.

His thoughts kept returning to Flora. He couldn't help it. When he'd been with her it was as though Mary didn't exist and now the memory of his infidelity made him uncomfortable. His marriage to Mary was so brittle that it hadn't taken much to shatter it; only the promise of that warmth and love that had been denied him since the loss of Frederick had forced him and Mary apart. His love for his wife had withered over the past months like a plant without water.

But he knew that he was married to Mary for better or worse and the remorse he felt about lying to Flora about it was eating into him. He knew he should be eager to leave Wenfield and temptation behind but he couldn't force himself to feel like that, however hard he tried. Flora was here and there was nothing to go home to London for.

He did his best to put the dilemma out of his mind and asked Constable Wren to telephone Tarnhey Court to see whether Sir William had returned home. Wren seemed nervous about making the call and Albert guessed he was reluctant to bother the local gentry he'd been brought up to revere. Albert, however, had no such qualms. He was determined that the Cartwrights would be treated like everyone else.

He was pleased when Wren reported that Sir William had returned from his trip to London and when he told the constable that he was going to Tarnhey Court to have another word with the MP, he was mildly amused by the look of alarm on the man's face. Then he announced that he'd go to see Sir William alone because he didn't want to scandalise the local officers more than necessary with his lack of what they considered to be appropriate respect. Besides, he hoped the walk in the fresh air would give him the opportunity to clear his head and think about his problems, personal and professional.

As he walked the rain held off, although the dark clouds gathering over the hills suggested that situation might not last long. When he arrived at Tarnhey Court he saw the Rolls-Royce parked outside the house. Sydney Pepper was standing beside the car, polishing the driver's door with a yellow duster and as soon as he heard Albert's footsteps on the gravel he straightened up, touching his cap respectfully. There was a spark of panic in his eyes, as though he feared Albert had come to re-arrest him.

'Bloody birds,' he said nervously, nodding towards the car door. 'Always shitting on the paintwork. Those doves might look pretty but they make a hell of a mess.'

'Must be a problem,' said Albert, feeling obliged to put the man at his ease after the ordeal of his brief imprisonment. 'Don't worry, I don't need to speak to you again ... unless you have something new to tell me.'

Pepper shook his head vigorously and returned to his task but as Albert approached the front door he looked back and saw the chauffeur watching him, as if to check that he hadn't changed his mind.

When Albert was shown into Sir William's presence by the maid he'd seen the other day, the Member of Parliament looked completely relaxed. Wren's phone call had prepared him for the visit and Albert feared now that it might have been a mistake to forewarn him. But he knew that his first question would come as a surprise – at least he hoped it would.

'I've been hearing rumours that you and Sarah Cookham were having an affair,' he said calmly, as though he were asking about something mundane like his preference for milk and sugar in his tea.

A brief flash of panic appeared in Sir William's eyes, swiftly suppressed. He sprang to his feet and strode over to the door. He opened it, peeped out into the hall to check for eavesdroppers then closed it again before turning to face Albert. 'Where on Earth did you hear that?'

'I'm afraid I can't say. I need to know if it's true.'

After a few moments of silence, a knowing smile appeared on the MP's lips. 'We're both men of the world, Inspector. I'm sure I can rely on your discretion.'

There was a hint of threat in his words. The ghost of a possibility that, were Albert to cause embarrassment, word of it might reach the ears of his superiors in Scotland Yard. Albert had come across men like Sir William before and knew that nothing is ever spelled out in their world. But that didn't make the threat any less real.

'If it turns out not to be relevant to my inquiry, I assure you the matter will go no further.'

Sir William took a deep breath. 'Very well, Sarah and I ... It was a moment of madness on my part. My wife's not a well woman and ... we all give in to temptation from time to time, don't we?'

Albert looked away, hoping that Sir William wouldn't be able to see how his words had touched him. Who was he to judge this man when he'd done something similar? He tried to tell himself that Sarah's vulnerable position made Sir William's fall from grace worse than his own but this didn't make him feel any better.

He carried on. 'You were the father of her child?'

'So she claimed.'

'You didn't believe her? You think there might have been someone else?'

'She was no blushing virgin, I assure you.'

'But you felt responsible enough to provide her with a lavish funeral.'

'It was the least I could do, given the terrible

262

circumstances of her death. Such a tragedy.' The politician had taken over from the man again.

'I'm afraid I'll have to check your whereabouts at the times of all the murders.'

'I think you'll find that's already been done.' The veneer of Sir William's politeness was beginning to wear thin. 'But check again by all means. Now if that's all, I'm expecting a call from the Home Office.'

Albert knew when he was being dismissed and he suspected the mention of the Home Office had been intended to intimidate him, to make him realise what an important man he was dealing with. Sir William hadn't expected his affair with Sarah to come to light and he'd done his best to bluff it out. Short of arresting him, there was nothing more Albert could do at that moment so he left, saying he might have to return. He too could issue threats.

He was shown out by the maid who led the way silently, scurrying down the hall like a frightened mouse. He saw her jump when a door to the drawing room opened to reveal Lady Cartwright who was standing there dressed in a diaphanous white gown. She looked like an ageing bride; Miss Havisham without the cobwebs.

'Inspector. Will you talk to me?'

'Of course, Lady Cartwright. What can I do for you?'

She beckoned him inside the room and he followed, waiting for her to take a seat on the sofa at right angles to the empty fireplace before sitting down on the matching sofa opposite.

She came straight to the point. 'I saw him.'

'Who?'

'The soldier.'

'Which soldier?'

'I was walking in the walled garden because it was a fine night and I wanted some fresh air before bed. I saw him standing by the dovecote. He must have been a ghost, mustn't he?'

'When was this?'

She named the night of Miss Forrest's death – around nine o'clock. 'It was misty but I could see his face.'

'Can you describe him?'

'I can do better than that, Inspector. I recognised him. It was Simon Plunket from Porlack Hall – it's about five miles away. The Plunkets are a very good family and I've known his poor mother for years. He was brought here to Tarnhey Court when he was wounded, you know. His face was terribly disfigured by shrapnel.' She paused. 'He passed away during an operation to amputate his leg. And now his ghost's trapped here. Perhaps I should ask a medium to release his troubled spirit.'

'What makes you so sure it was him?'

'I've told you. I saw his face and I knew him at once. He looked a little strange. He had staring eyes – like a doll or one of those waxworks I saw once in London. But he was in his uniform . . . '

'Uniform? What kind of uniform?'

'I wasn't close enough to see but he was definitely an officer and poor Simon was a captain.' A concerned frown appeared on her face. 'Do you think I should tell his mother?'

'I think that would only distress her. Is it absolutely certain that Simon Plunket's dead?'

'Of course. I attended his funeral myself. Roderick was away doing his bit,' she said proudly. 'And my husband

was in London so it was left to me to represent the family.'
She shook her head. 'To get all this way home and then
to expire on the operating table ... But they did say he
was horribly disfigured.'

Disfigured enough to need one of David Eames's
masks, Albert thought.

Suddenly he wanted to speak to Eames and find out if
he made one for Simon ... and, if so, what had happened
to it.

Chapter 31

Albert needed to question David Eames and he was tempted to visit Flora on the pretext of asking her about the Cottage Hospital's visiting hours. But he told himself that might not be wise so he traipsed back to the police station instead. Since his conversation with Sir William, his conscience had been nagging him and he knew this was the right choice, even though some wheedling, whispering voice in his head was telling him otherwise. His feelings about what happened at David Eames's cottage were confused. One moment he felt deep shame and the next he longed to see Flora and repeat the pleasure that had so long been denied him.

He told himself that if he could solve the case quickly and return to London, it would be best for everyone concerned. The identity of the killer still eluded him but there was a boldness about the perpetrator's actions; an arrogance which made Albert hope that over-confidence would lead to him making a bad mistake.

He asked Wren to call the Cottage Hospital but he said it wasn't necessary. His mother had been a patient there a few months ago and he'd visited her every day so he knew the times off by heart. Seven to eight. And the Sisters made sure those times were strictly observed.

It was six o'clock and hunger was gnawing at Albert's stomach so he decided to return to the Black Horse. As he ate dinner alone in the saloon bar, he kept thinking of Flora and how her mother's alleged lover had stayed in that very place, possibly ate at that very table. These days Flora Winsmore intruded into his mind on the slightest pretext, no matter how hard he tried to concentrate on the case. He put his hand in his pocket, feeling Mary's letter, knowing that what he'd done had been wrong and impulsive and that he should put an end to it now. He was so distracted by his thoughts that he barely tasted Mrs Jackson's meat pie followed by jam roly poly. But that didn't stop him complimenting her on the food as she cleared the table.

He walked to the hospital to see David Eames, wondering whether this particular line of inquiry was a waste of time. Lady Cartwright was hardly a reliable witness. She could have imagined the soldier at the dovecote and given her conjured phantom the face of her friend's lost son. People wanted to believe that their beloved dead were still present and, to a suggestible mind, a tree or shrub might take on the form of a late loved one in the shadowy darkness.

But he reckoned it would do no harm to ask so he found the correct ward and eventually drew up a chair at David Eames's bedside.

He was relieved that the man was well enough to speak to him and he noted the look of surprise on the patient's face when he introduced himself.

'How are you?' Albert began as he sat down. The chair provided for visitors was hard and uncomfortable, no doubt to discourage the patients' friends and relatives from lingering too long and getting in the nurses' way.

'Not so bad. They say I'll be out in a couple of days.'

'That's good to hear. You did some good work during the war, I believe.'

Eames pushed himself up on his pillow. 'Good work? I was shipped home to Blighty after two weeks out in France. Lost a leg on the Somme so I didn't have much of a chance to make any difference out there ... good or bad.' Albert could hear a note of bitterness in his voice.

'I'm talking about the portrait masks you made at Tarnhey Court.'

David looked him in the eye. 'How did you hear about them?'

'I'm sure your efforts were very much appreciated,' Albert said, avoiding the direct question.

He saw Eames looking at the burned side of his face. 'I could have helped you with that,' he said bluntly.

'I know. But there were a lot who were much worse than me. It's right they took priority. Do you mind if I ask you some questions?'

'Not in the least. How can I help you?'

'While you were at Tarnhey Court did you make a mask for a Simon Plunket – a captain?'

'Yes, I did. When I realised they couldn't just patch me up and send me back to the Front I had to think of another way of using the talents God gave me to help the war effort. I found I could give men back their identities.'

'What if someone's stolen those identities?'

Eames looked puzzled. 'What do you mean?'

'Someone might use your masks to gain ... anonymity. I believe you had a break in and a couple of masks were taken.'

'Who told you that?'

'I've been talking to Flora Winsmore.'

'You know Flora?' David's eyes lit up at the possibility of them having discovered a mutual friend and Albert was embarrassed by the innocence of his question.

'Yes. We've met. Was one of the stolen masks the one you made for Simon Plunket?'

'As a matter of fact it was.' His expression changed as realisation dawned. 'You're here to investigate those murders, aren't you? You think my break in had something to do with what happened?'

Albert hesitated. Eames had been in hospital at the time of the last murder, which ruled him out as a suspect. He had to share what he knew with him if he was to learn more. 'Someone claims they saw Simon Plunket on the night of one of the recent murders.'

Eames was quick to understand. 'And you think they saw someone wearing his mask? Simon had terrible injuries. The mask I made for him almost covered his entire face so it would be quite recognisable as him.'

'Who knows you kept the masks in your studio?'

'It was no secret. Most people who were at Tarnhey Court would have known I kept them, I suppose.'

'Anyone else?'

'My sister, of course. And Dr Winsmore. And various friends.'

'Who?'

David suddenly looked uncomfortable. 'I have quite a few visitors. Roderick Cartwright's involved with a theatre in Manchester and he sometimes asks my advice about artistic matters; scenery and all that.'

'What about his father?'

'Sir William has visited once or twice. I rent my cottage from him, you see. He took a great interest in my work at Tarnhey Court, which is hardly surprising as it's his family home.'

'Anybody else?'

'Sydney Pepper's been to the cottage a few times. He's a troubled man and he likes to keep in touch with his old comrades from Tarnhey Court days. He says he has happy memories of the place ... the way he was cared for. Now he's out in the big wide world on his own I think he feels lost.'

'Is that all?'

'Dr Bone visits on occasions, just to see how I'm getting on. He amputated the leg so I expect he feels responsible.' He gave a bitter smile. 'And the vicar drops round for a Scotch from time to time. Nice chap – not one of those holier than thou types. Doesn't try too hard to convert me. I make my cottage sound like Piccadilly Circus, don't I, but I assure you I manage to spend plenty of time alone with my thoughts and my work.'

'What about your sister?'

'Helen doesn't entertain much these days. She's not been well.'

'And you've no idea who could have taken the masks?'

'None whatsoever.' He reached out and touched Albert's shoulder. 'I don't like to think of my work being used for something like this. I made those masks for a reason . . . to help.'

'Don't you worry, sir. We'll catch him.' Albert realised his assurance probably rang hollow. He'd been there in Wenfield a while now and he still had no inkling of the killer's identity. The inquiries the local police had made into the activities of Wenfield's male inhabitants had drawn a blank. Most of them had watertight alibis for the times of one or more of the murders but someone in that small community was lying. He just needed to find out who that was.

Now at last he felt he was making progress and that, if Lady Cartwright was to be believed, he could narrow down the list of suspects to those who knew what David Eames kept in his studio. If he was right, the break in at Eames's cottage was no opportunistic crime and the use of the uniform and mask suggested a good deal of planning.

As he left the hospital he couldn't help looking for Flora. But there was no sign of her. Perhaps she wasn't on duty or she was working in another ward. He told himself it was a good thing she wasn't there. The sooner he forgot about what had happened between them, the better.

But when he was on his way to the Black Horse, he saw her riding her bicycle along the street in the dusk, a silhouette at first . . . then recognisable. When he stood in her path she came to an abrupt halt.

'That was a stupid thing to do. I could have run into you.'

'I'm sorry.' He couldn't think of anything else to say as

271

the realisation dawned that he wanted to be with her more than anything else.

'Did you want to talk to me?' There was a hint of uncertainty in her voice, as though she was sharing his doubts about the wisdom of what they'd done.

'I've just been to see David Eames in hospital,' he said. 'I take it his sister's still staying at the Black Horse.'

Flora nodded. 'I've just been to see her. She says she's too nervous to go back home. David asked me to keep an eye on her. How was he when you saw him?'

'Recovering.'

'I hope you didn't treat him as a suspect because David isn't capable of . . .'

'No. I just wanted to talk to him about his break in.'

A look of relief passed across her face. 'Could he throw any light on it?'

Albert shook his head.

He'd intended to tell her that what had happened was wrong. To apologise and say it had been a moment of insanity; a temporary loss of control that would never be repeated. He'd resolved to admit that he'd lied and tell her about Mary. But now they were there face to face, all those intentions were vanishing like morning mist. 'Can we meet again?' he heard himself saying. 'What about tomorrow?'

'I'm not free tomorrow,' she said. 'I'm going to Liverpool to try and find the man they say my mother went off with. I need to know what really happened to her, Albert. I need to know where she is . . . if only to tell her John's dead. Whatever she's done, she's got a right to know that.'

'Would you like me to come with you?'

272

She shook her head. 'I'd rather go alone.'

'But we'll meet soon?'

Flora didn't answer. She was preparing to mount her bicycle again when she appeared to change her mind. She had something to say but he could sense her reluctance as though she wasn't sure whether she was doing the right thing.

'This might be nothing . . .'

Albert knew that when people said that, useful information often followed. He waited for her to continue.

'I know the housekeeper of one of the doctors who works at the Cottage Hospital. He has a practice in New Mills but, with this influenza outbreak, he's been here in Wenfield a lot recently.'

'What are you trying to tell me, Flora?'

'Edith, his housekeeper, told me that he was in Wenfield when those women were killed. He was here in the village on each occasion.'

'Are you sure?'

'I can only repeat what she told me.'

'What's his name?'

'Dr Edward Bone. He worked at Tarnhey Court during the war. It probably means nothing but I thought I'd better mention it.'

Albert took the bicycle from her and wheeled it to the side of the road where the gap between two stone houses formed a narrow alleyway. Feeling reckless, he propped it up against the wall before leading Flora into the darkness of the alley. He drew her to himself with his good arm and kissed her tenderly, all thoughts of Mary obliterated by the moment.

Chapter 32

Flora

I barely slept last night. Perhaps it's my uneasy conscience. Did I do right telling Albert about Bone? One moment it feels like a betrayal, the next a sort of justice.

Or perhaps it was the thought of my journey to Liverpool. It probably isn't prudent but I have to know whether my mother's still alive. And if she is, I have to tell her that John didn't come back from France. I wonder if the news will break her heart. I wonder if it will cause her to regret the way in which she abandoned us. Surely it must do. The mother I knew wasn't so unnatural that she wouldn't care whether her only son lived or died.

I've been trying to imagine what Martin Nerrist would be like and in my mind I always see the young man described by Mrs Jackson. Dark-haired, good looking with bright blue eyes and a ready smile. An attractive man. Then I tell myself he'll have been through the war so, if he survived, he'll be changed. Fourteen years older and possibly damaged in mind or body or both. His glorious youth will have vanished and, even though the man tore my young life apart, the thought of such a downfall makes me sad.

Over breakfast I tell Father that I am catching the train to Stockport to do some shopping. I'm surprised that he looks rather pleased. Perhaps he thinks shopping is preferable to professional ambition.

Father's been bringing Roderick Cartwright into the conversation a lot recently, and I wonder if this is a clumsy hint. When we were younger he often used to say that Roderick would be a suitable match for me and now it seems the subject has been resurrected. But I'm not in the least bit tempted to tell him the truth about my potential suitor because I have a fondness for Roderick born of years of acquaintance and I'd never willingly put him in danger by sharing his secret with others. His relationship with Charlie – and the other men he's told me about – is his own business and nobody else's and the thought of him being arrested for his inclinations makes me feel sick. So I nod and smile whenever Father mentions him and let him live with his illusions.

I catch the train and change at Manchester. As I sit in the carriage I begin to feel nervous. Setting off on a quest to find the truth about my mother had seemed like a good idea back in Wenfield but now all the confidence I felt is vanishing. I have a name and an address in the suburbs that is fourteen years old and I'm afraid that, unless I'm extremely lucky, this won't be enough.

I arrive in the city and, after Wenfield, I'm shocked by its filthy grandeur. I step out of the station and hear sea gulls crying overhead like souls in torment. I see a respectable looking woman waiting outside the station, presumably for a friend or relative, and I ask her the best way to get to Allerton. I am relieved when she knows the area and tells me it is best to catch the train to Mossley Hill station and walk from there. I do as she suggests and plan to ask again for directions when I reach the station. The people here seem friendly and I hear a lot of Irish and Welsh voices chattering away. There are also black and brown faces. I've seen a few when visiting Manchester but never in Wenfield. I feel as if I've entered a different world; a world full of possibilities and excitement. And I like it.

Perhaps my mother is here living amongst these people. Perhaps I'll find her today. My heart beats faster as the train arrives at the little station. Mossley Hill. It sounds as if it's in the countryside and, after the city centre, it seems a peaceful and prosperous place, filled with budding trees and fine villas.

I ask the porter for directions and he instructs me to take the road opposite the station. His voice has the hint of an Irish accent and he has black hair and blue eyes, just like Mrs Jackson's description of Martin Nerrist but he must be at least fifteen years Nerrist's junior. For a moment I'm tempted to ask if he knows the man but then I realise such a question would be foolish so I thank him and follow his directions.

The road is most respectable, with large brick-built villas on either side. Motor cars stand outside some of the houses, indicating the affluence of their owners. This isn't how I imagined Nerrist's address. I'd been expecting something shabbier.

I reach my destination. Number thirty-eight with a

name carved on the gateposts. The Laurels. It is a large semi-detached house, about fifty years old, with a green front door and decorative green gables. A sleek black motor car stands on the gravel drive. If Martin Nerrist still lives here, he hasn't hit hard times.

I stand at the gate staring at the house for a while before summoning the courage to approach the front door. After tugging on the bell pull I wait, my heart pounding in my chest. But what is the worst thing that can happen? I find Nerrist has moved out years ago . . . or I am sent away as an embarrassing reminder of past follies. Either way, I am in no danger.

I hear footsteps within the house and the front door opens. The maid who stands there, looking at me enquiringly, wears a black dress with a clean white apron and a snowy cap on her greying hair. I ask if I have the right address for Mr Nerrist and, to my surprise, she asks who's calling and invites me to wait in the hall. I say my name and take a seat, thinking that perhaps he won't want to see me when he realises who I am.

The wait seems endless, although it doesn't last more than five minutes, and when the maid returns, I stand up, my nervous fingers rubbing at the cloth of my skirt.

'Mr Nerrist will see you now, Miss Winsmore. If you'd like to come this way.'

I hadn't expected this to be so easy. I had expected a long search ending in failure and a disappointed journey home. Now I'm so nervous that I think that might have been preferable to facing the man who took my mother from me. I follow the maid into a drawing room bathed in sunlight streaming in through a large bay window. A man stands up as I enter. He is well built with grizzled hair and his eyes are cornflower blue. He smiles and invites me to sit. Fourteen years have added grey to his hair and inches to his body but, other than that, he is the man Mrs Jackson described.

'Miss Winsmore, how can I help you?'

There is a note of caution in his voice, as though he suspects the purpose of my visit but daren't ask directly. I look round. The room has a woman's touch. But is that woman my own mother?

'This is rather embarrassing,' I begin. He is listening intently, willing me to continue. 'I understand you worked in a village called Wenfield in 1905.'

'It's a long time ago,' he says. 'That time before the war seems very distant now. I was in France, you see, but I was lucky enough to return unscathed.'

'But you remember Wenfield?'

'Oh yes, I remember.' From the tone of his words I guess that his memories of my village weren't exactly happy.

'You knew a woman called Julia Winsmore.'

I see his face colour at the mention of her name. 'Yes. I did.'

'You and Julia became lovers.'

He bows his head as though he is ashamed. 'Who told you that?'

'Please. I just want the truth.'

He looks up. 'Yes, we were lovers. It sounds so sordid now but it didn't seem so at the time. You haven't told me your Christian name, Miss Winsmore.'

'It's Flora.'

As he sits back I see a variety of emotions pass across his face: hope; shame; curiosity. I wait for him to speak again.

'Then you must be her daughter. She used to talk about you and your brother ... John, is it? Why have you come? Is Julia all right?'

The question shakes me. All my expectations have suddenly been overturned. 'That's what I came to ask you.'

'Me? What makes you think I'd know?' His shock sounds genuine.

'She left Wenfield with you.'

'You've been misinformed, Flora. May I call you Flora?'

I nod and wait for him to continue. I find myself liking this man, in spite of my preconceptions.

'I won't deny that I was very attracted to your mother. She was a beautiful woman. And restless. She told me she felt stifled by life in Wenfield and she said she'd often told her husband, your father, she wanted to move to the city.'

'I don't remember.'

'Perhaps you were too young. She'd been brought up in Manchester, you see, and wasn't used to life in a small village. I was working at the mill with no friends in the vicinity and she was lonely and frustrated by village life so we struck up a friendship. We used to meet in a little tea room and talk about all sorts of things.' He smiled fondly at the memory. 'But mainly the advantages of life in the city away from the pettiness and the nosiness of a small community. She used to think people were watching her all the time ... judging her. She never minded being seen with me. I think it amused her to give the village gossips something to get their teeth into.'

As I sit listening to him I see my mother smiling at me, saying I was her darling girl and telling me never to get

279

trapped in a cage. I was too young to know what she meant back then but now I understand. My plan to train as a nurse would have delighted her. It might delight her still. If I can find her.

'What happened?' I ask.

Nerrist looks at me, puzzled. 'My work in Wenfield came to an end and I left. Julia and I agreed to meet in Pooley Woods. Do you know it?'

'Yes.' I wonder whether to tell him about the murders but I decide that the subject isn't relevant to the matter in hand. Besides, I don't wish to distract him – not until I find out what happened to Mother.

'We'd meet there and go to a little boathouse Julia knew.'

I flinched at the memory of the boathouse. My mother had met her lover there and a generation later, I'd met mine. Did that mean Mother and I were alike?

'We'd arranged to meet in the woods,' he continues, bowing his head like a penitent. 'I'd finally persuaded her to come back here to Liverpool with me – with you and your brother, of course.'

'You'd asked her to leave my father?'

'She was always talking about escaping and I thought that's what she wanted. I'm an engineer and even then I was becoming well established in my chosen profession.' He swept a hand around the room. 'And I'd inherited this house from my grandfather so I had the means to support her. I made it quite clear to Julia that I was in a position to give her and her children a home. It would have caused a great scandal in Wenfield, of course, but here nobody knew her and I could have put it about that she was a widow.' He gave a distant smile. 'I was going to

280

say we'd met and married in a frenzy of romance and I took her poor fatherless children under my wing. Nobody would have been any the wiser.'

'What about my father?'

'I'm rather ashamed to say we didn't give him much thought. I'm sorry.'

I can tell he is genuinely remorseful. He must have been young at the time, much younger than my mother, and he'd seen the situation from the point of view of romantic youth, not yet coloured by the realities of life. He had thought to rescue my mother from the prison of her village existence but his good intentions had paid no heed to the feelings of those around her.

I asked the question that was eating away at my mind. 'What happened that night? Did she meet you?'

'I waited for her but she never came. I just presumed she'd changed her mind; that she'd liked the fantasy but backed out when she realised the implications of what she planned to do. I didn't dare to call at her house and run the risk of facing her husband so I never saw her again and I've had no word from her for fourteen years.'

The door opens and a woman enters. She is small with fair hair and an amiable, freckled face. Nerrist stands to greet her and she gives me an open, welcoming smile.

'I didn't know we had a visitor,' she says.

'My dear, allow me to introduce Miss Flora Winsmore. Miss Winsmore, this is my wife, Dorothy.' He turns to his wife. 'I met Miss Winsmore's family when I was working in Derbyshire many years ago and she's been good enough to pay me a call.'

'How lovely,' Dorothy says, all innocence. 'You must stay for lunch, Miss Winsmore.'

'Thank you, Mrs Nerrist, but I really must be going. It's been delightful to meet you.'

I stand to leave. I can't make polite conversation over lunch, deceiving this likeable innocent woman. I have discovered nothing here apart from a deepening mystery. If my mother didn't leave Wenfield with her lover that day in 1905, where did she go? And where is she now?

Martin Nerrist escorts me into the hall and when we reach the door he speaks in a low voice, as though he doesn't wish his wife to overhear.

'I'm so sorry, Miss Winsmore, I really have no idea where Julia is. If you find her, will you write to let me know? Please.'

He still cares about her, even after all these years; even though he seems happy with his pretty wife. I say I will and we shake hands.

My mother's lover has no idea what became of her and I'm beginning to fear what I'll discover if I continue my search.

Chapter 33

The journey back to Wenfield seems to take hours and the train is packed and smoky. I know the smell will linger in my hair and clothes and I fear this will make Father curious about where I've been. Maybe he'll think I've been frequenting public houses but I don't care. I've just found out that everything I ever believed about my mother was a lie and now I want to know what really happened to her. And where she is now.

I arrive home at half past five to find a letter waiting for me. Sybil brings it to me as I'm taking off my coat and hat, saying she recognises the handwriting. It's from her cousin, Edith, she says and she hangs around waiting for me to open it and satisfy the curiosity she makes no effort to conceal.

But, to her disappointment, I put the letter in the pocket of my skirt and say I'll read it later. I feel grubby after my long journey but I know it's important that nobody finds out where I've been. I ask Sybil where Father is and she tells me he's visiting a patient and is expected home shortly. I'm dreading sitting opposite him at the dinner table, knowing what I now know. And part of me feels like a Judas for having met and liked his rival for my mother's affections.

I retire to my room to wash before dinner and I change my white blouse as the cuffs and collar are black with soot. Once that's done I sit on the bed and take the letter from my pocket. I slit the envelope open carefully, take out the letter and spread it out on my quilt.

My dear Flora, it begins. *I have some wonderful news to share with you. Can you call on me tomorrow at the above address? I can't wait to tell you but please say nothing to your father until we've spoken. Would twelve noon suit? If this is inconvenient, please telephone Dr Bone's surgery and leave a message for me. Your loving friend, Edith.*

I read it through several times, hoping to find some clue to what Edith's wonderful news might be. I've always thought of Edith sailing through life like a swan, serene and untroubled, but the excitement behind the words in her letter is palpable.

Father's surgery will be over by the time Edith suggests so I have no reason to refuse her invitation. I wonder why she asks me to say nothing to Father and that night I lie awake speculating.

When I rise the next morning I venture out to the baker's because Sybil is fully occupied complaining to the woman who does our laundry about the state of Father's shirts. I leave her to it, put on my hat and coat and leave the house with Sybil's wicker basket swinging on my arm.

As I walk I think of my mother. She hated this village

284

and felt crushed by the people and their petty concerns. The only people she ever seemed to have time for were the Cartwrights. However, I'm not sure if this stemmed from some snobbish desire to mix with her social superiors or because their horizons were wider than those of her other neighbours. As I always assumed that Martin Nerrist was the cause of her absence, it never occurred to me that the Cartwrights might have had any connection with her fate. I am certain that Roderick knows nothing – if he did, he wouldn't have been able to keep it to himself all these years. But I'm not so sure about Sir William and his wife. How well do I really know them?

In the village it would seem to a passing stranger that all was well. People are going about their business as usual and it's hard to believe that a killer might be amongst them; a killer who's already claimed the lives of four women in the most horrific way. Perhaps war has hardened people to death and tragedy. After the terrors and violence of the front, cold-blooded murder no longer has the power to shock.

I reach the war memorial and pause there as I always do, my eyes drawn to John's name. I want to kneel. I want to finger the precious letters and feel their hard depression carved into the cold stone. The letters look sharp and newly chiselled now but over the years I know those names will weather and smooth until they're barely legible. And yet John will always be there in my head and in my heart. I've heard some say that the ghost of a soldier haunts the outskirts of Wenfield but John is my very own ghost. I feel him by my side; I hear his footsteps behind me in the dark. My dearest sweetest, gentle brother. The brother who always watched over and protected me.

I tear myself away from the memorial and as I walk away I feel it calling me back. But it is an inanimate lump of carved stone. The souls of those men are elsewhere. The vicar assures us they're in heaven. I hope he's right.

I see a figure emerge from the front door of the police station and turn in the direction of the Black Horse. It's Albert and he's alone so I walk slowly to meet him, trying my best to seem casual, as if we're two acquaintances who encounter each other by chance. When he spots me he stops and waits for me to catch up but I can't read his expression. He might as well be wearing one of the masks David Eames made for all the emotion he betrays.

He raises his hat politely as though he barely knows me; as if he's forgotten what passed between us in Helen Eames's bedroom. I hide the turmoil I feel inside and conjure a friendly smile.

'I wanted to see you,' I say.

'I'm not sure it's wise,' he says, looking around as though he's afraid we're being watched.

'Why not?'

'I'm here to work. To catch this lunatic. If my superiors find out I've been . . . '

'How would they find out?'

Another long pause. 'I'm sorry, Flora. Perhaps when this murderer's finally behind bars . . . '

'Then you'll be going back to London.'

For the first time the mask slips and I see emotion pass across his face. Confusion maybe. Or pain. 'None of us knows what the future holds.' He looks round again before his right hand brushes mine, grasping my fingers and squeezing them gently. I can't help looking at his mutilated left hand. It seems the war is always with us.

'I've got something to tell you,' I say in a whisper. 'Can we meet later? Is Helen still at the Black Horse?'

'I spoke to her at breakfast this morning. Her brother's being discharged from hospital tomorrow so she'll be going back home then.'

'So the cottage is empty this evening?' I do my best to keep the eagerness I feel out of my voice.

For a brief moment he looks reluctant, as if I've suggested he undergo some dreadful ordeal. Then he relents. 'Very well. I'll meet you there at seven.' A shadow passes across his face as though he's remembered something unpleasant. 'I don't like to think of you going there on your own ... not with this killer still at large.'

'I'll cycle there. Don't worry.'

'I can't let you do that. Meet me at the gate to Tarnhey Court. I'll walk with you.'

'Someone might see us.'

'Not if we're careful. Do as I say. I insist. I've seen what this man does. I know what he's capable of.'

His concern touches me. And as we part I glance back and see him disappear into the Black Horse, the place that reminds me of Martin Nerrist and his time in Wenfield. And, by association, I'm reminded of my mother and the mystery of her disappearance. I wonder if she's alive somewhere – and, if she is, whether we'll ever by reunited.

I spend the rest of the morning in a daze, anticipating that evening's meeting with Albert. I experience the thrill of guilty pleasure. I now have a secret – not one as potentially devastating as Roderick Cartwright's, but a secret none the less. Dr Bone has a secret too – one I suspect he'll do anything to conceal. I fear it wouldn't be judged as harshly as Roderick's but in my mind it's so much worse. Roderick's forbidden love for members of his own sex has never hurt anybody. His secret's never stained another's life and I often wonder why the law judges it so harshly.

When I arrive home with the loaf and potatoes I went out for weighing down my basket, I leave the provisions in the kitchen for Sybil and change my clothes to help Father in his surgery. It's the usual parade of minor injuries and sore throats but Father is careful to examine each patient, alert for signs of influenza. Father's visiting the Cottage Hospital after he's completed his rounds. One new case has been admitted, one woman has died and three people, including David Eames, have almost recovered. I ask if I'm needed but he says no.

Once surgery is over I change my clothes again, put on my coat and secure my hat to my hair with three hat pins, just to be sure. It's time for me to cycle over to New Mills to see Edith. I know Dr Bone won't be there because I asked Father if he'd be at the Cottage Hospital and, to my relief, the answer was yes.

As I ride my bicycle I find myself wishing I lived somewhere flat. Here the landscape is so hilly and the effort of cycling up the steep inclines can be exhausting. Whenever the road proves particularly steep, I dismount and push my bicycle along, remounting on the brow of the hill then freewheeling down the slope with the air rushing past my face. When I reach New Mills I raise my hand to my head to feel my hat, only to discover that it's now held on precariously by a single pin. Fortunately the other pins are still in the hat so I pause to rectify the damage and make myself look respectable.

I cycle past shops, churches and houses with small

front gardens, all built from the same local stone as Wenfield so that the town looks as if it's been hewn from the landscape. Dr Bone lives in a fine double-fronted house right at the edge of town; the last house before the buildings give way to patchwork fields with a fine view of the peaks beyond. Those peaks are topped with snow throughout the winter but now spring is established, they glow green and grey in the weak sunshine.

I wheel my bicycle up the garden path and when I reach the front door I raise my hand to ring the bell. Then I stop, suddenly afraid. What if Bone hasn't gone to Wenfield? What if he's changed his mind? Edith, in her innocence, would have no reason to warn me.

To my relief Edith answers the door herself. As she approaches I can see through the glass that there's a smile on her lips, as though she's nursing some delicious news she's longing to tell to the world. There's a radiance about her that I haven't seen before and I wonder what her news can be.

She opens the door and invites me into a parlour at the rear of the house, a spacious, pleasant room flooded with daylight. It's a woman's room with floral curtains at the window, ornaments cluttering the windowsill and shelves and a vase of spring flowers stands on the table by the window. When she was with us Father gave her a dark back room to use as her parlour. Dr Bone has done considerably better.

As she invites me to sit and rings for tea she can hardly contain her excitement. When the tea arrives she pours from the silver tea pot and hands me the bone china cup. The best bone china. When Edith was our housekeeper, Father kept the best for important visitors.

My last conversation with Albert is on my mind and I wonder if he's followed up my hint about Dr Bone.

'I believe the police are interviewing all men who were in Wenfield at the time of those terrible murders,' I say innocently. 'Didn't you say Dr Bone was there?'

'Yes, but if he'd seen anything suspicious, I'm sure he would have told the police.' She leans towards me, her eyes glowing with happiness. 'I said in my letter that I have some exciting news, Flora. You haven't asked what it is.'

'What is it?' I ask. Something about her excitement suddenly makes me uneasy.

'You're one of the first to know.'

'To know what?'

'I'm getting married.'

'That's wonderful,' I say automatically. 'Who's the lucky man?'

I sit there dreading her answer. I see the best room, the fine china and I think I know why she, a servant, has been so favoured. I hold my breath, waiting.

'It's Dr Bone. He's asked me to do him the honour of becoming his wife.'

This is the answer I've been dreading and her innocent pleasure appals me. I sit there, the tea cup half raised to my lips, knowing that I have no choice. I have to destroy her blissful little world. It would be unfair to do otherwise.

'Edith, you can't.' The words come out in a whisper.

She looks confused. Then she smiles. 'You've misheard, my dear. Dr Bone's asked me to marry him.'

I lower the cup onto its saucer with a loud chink of china. 'You can't.'

'Can't what?' She looks worried, as if she fears I've lost my senses.

'You can't marry him. He's not who you think he is.'

'What on Earth do you mean?'

'There are things about him you don't know.'

'What things?' She looks frightened now, as if she has a premonition that her comfortable, hopeful world is about to be shattered.

'Something happened when we were at Tarnhey Court during the war. Something terrible.'

She puts down her own cup and stares at me. 'Tell me. Please.'

I take a deep breath. I don't want to do this. I don't want to spoil Edith's happiness and rob her of her future security. But I can't allow her to go ahead with a marriage to a man who's not worthy of her.

'When I was working at Tarnhey Court he ... molested me. He ...' I can't finish the sentence. Saying the words will make me relive my ordeal and I can't face that.

I see Edith's hand go up to her mouth as if she's trying to stifle a gasp of horror. Then, when she lowers the hand, I see a look of hostile disbelief on her face. 'When was this?'

'Shortly before the war ended. Please, Edith, don't tell him I told you. I just thought you should know the sort of man you're planning to marry.'

'You're making it up.'

The anger I feel suddenly produces a rush of courage. 'He ... assaulted me, Edith. I was taking a break from my duties in the walled garden at Tarnhey Court when he joined me in the dovecote. We'd always been on friendly terms and I thought nothing of it. But he grabbed me and pushed me against the wall. I was shocked then I felt his hands pushing my skirt up and then . . . '

She looks shocked by my bluntness but it comes as a relief to blurt out the secret that's been festering inside me all this time.

'I don't believe you. You must have led him on.'

I look at her with sadness. This was the reaction I'd expected if my secret ever came to light. That's why I've never told anybody before. That's why it's taken the thought of Edith being allied to such a man to make me speak out.

'You know me, Edith. Would I lie?'

'Perhaps you're jealous. Perhaps you want Edward for yourself.'

'Do you really believe that?' I look at her with pity. Love and a desire for a cosy, secure life can make us blind.

'You'll be saying he's responsible for these murders next.'

I say nothing and allow her words to settle as she considers the possibility that perhaps he is. A man who'd do what he did to me could be capable of anything.

I see her shock turn to anger. Soon she'll tell me to go: she'll say she never wants to see me again and I will have failed in my mission.

Then she says something that jolts me. 'You're a fine one to make false accusations when your family has got a nasty little secret of its own.'

For a few moments I take in what she's said. 'What secret?'

'Don't tell me you don't know.'

'Know what?'

'What happened to your mother.'

My heart begins to pound.

'If you start slandering Edward, perhaps I should tell the police what I know about your father. The good doctor.' The final words are said with heavy irony.

'What do you mean? Tell me. Please.' I feel a warm tear trickling down my cheek. I hadn't expected our meeting to turn out like this. I'd thought that when I told her my story, she'd be shocked by her intended's ungentlemanly behaviour and call off her engagement at once. But I had miscalculated. And now it seems I'm about to receive a shock of my own.

She turns her face towards me and I see her expression soften. 'You deserve to know the truth,' she says quietly. 'She was your mother, after all.'

'How can you know what happened? You weren't even there. You didn't come to live with us until a year after she vanished.'

I can see pity in her eyes. 'Your father and I became close during the time I worked for him and he ended up asking me to marry him.' She gave a bitter little smile. 'History repeats itself, doesn't it? Anyway, I said I couldn't accept him because his wife might still be alive. Bigamy's a crime and we could both have ended up in prison. Then he said there was something I needed to know ... something that happened in the past. I thought it would be something trivial, an indiscretion when he was a medical student perhaps but ... '

I watch her. Her anger has been replaced by sorrow. She drains her tea cup and asks me if I'd like more. I'm surprised at the normal gesture punctuating this strange conversation.

'He said he wanted to be completely honest – that if we were to be married, there should be no secrets between us. He told me his wife had threatened to leave him and go off with some engineer from Liverpool. They'd been having an affair ... making him a cuckold was how he put it. It was such an old-fashioned word and I remember it made me laugh, not realising what was coming.'

'What did he tell you?'

'He told me he killed his wife. She went to her room to pack her suitcase and as she was about to go downstairs he grabbed her to try to stop her going. He said she lost her balance and fell down the stairs and when he checked her pulse, he found out the fall had killed her. He swore it was an accident but he was afraid nobody would believe him.'

Her words stun me. I stare out of the window at the trees swaying in the spring breeze, unable to speak, unable to think.

'It's high time you learned the truth about what happened to her, Flora,' she says gently. 'There have been too many secrets ... too many lies.'

I turn my head towards her. 'What did he do with her body?'

'He said he buried her in the garden. He showed me her grave.'

'The flower bed near the apple tree?'

'How did you know?'

'He's always tended that bed lovingly ... like some sort of shrine. We have a gardener who helps out once a week but Father won't allow him near that part of the garden.' I catch her eye. 'I wasn't lying about Dr Bone, you know. It's the truth.'

'I think you both gave in to temptation but I can't believe Edward forced himself on you. He's not like that. He's always behaved like a perfect gentleman towards me ... and all his patients say the same. I think you gave in to your carnal desires, Flora ... and now you feel ashamed. I can understand that.'

I'd never thought Edith a prig and her use of the phrase 'carnal desires' surprises me. I doubt if she'd have picked it up during one of the Reverend Bell's kindly sermons. Perhaps the vicar of her new parish favours a more fire and brimstone approach.

'I won't have you blaming Edward for your own weakness,' she continues. 'It takes two.'

I see her looking at me with a mixture of disapproval and pity. In the cheap novels I've known her to read, a heroine who has fallen from grace in such a way would most likely end up dying in the gutter or repent and spend the rest of her days doing good works. But I refuse to feel any shame for an event that was no fault of mine.

'So you'll go ahead and marry him?'

She doesn't answer my question. Instead she asks me one. 'What are you going to do about your father?'

'I don't know. Have you told anyone else?'

'I've kept his secret for fourteen years. What purpose would it serve if I betrayed his confidence now?'

'Why didn't you say anything at the time?'

'To tell the truth, Flora, I felt sorry for him. Dr Winsmore's a kind man and a good doctor and I believed he was telling the truth when he said your mother's death was an accident. If I'd involved the police, he might have been arrested ... even found guilty of murder. How could I have lived with myself if they'd hanged him? Let the past stay in the past, Flora. We've survived a terrible war. Let's make a new start . . . all of us.'

I'm grateful that her anger has passed and for the first time I notice the diamond ring on the third finger of her left hand. It is slightly too large and she turns it round and round nervously, as if to reassure herself that all is still well.

I take my leave, knowing that a great shadow has fallen between Edith and myself. And I know, although she hasn't said it, that if I pursue my accusations against Edward Bone, there is a chance her tender conscience will force her to tell the truth about Father. As I cycle home to Wenfield I feel defeated.

I'm also dreading seeing Father again. Even if Mother's death was a terrible accident, he still covered it up. And what if it wasn't an accident? What if Edith was misled? What if my own father is a murderer?

I think of Albert. How can I be with him while I'm harbouring such a great secret about my own parents? But I know I must maintain my silence for the sake of Father's life.

Chapter 34

I go to my room at bedtime but I do not undress. I sit on the bed summoning courage for the task ahead. I have put on an old skirt and, as I peep out of the window, I see that it is a fine night. It hasn't rained for a couple of days so the ground should be dry.

That night I creep from the house. There is only one way to find out the truth of what Edith told me and I know the task will be distasteful. But I tell myself that by now there will be no blood, no rotting flesh. Just dry bones . . . like the skeleton that dangles from the frame in Father's surgery.

I know the flower bed is out of sight of Father's bedroom window so I sneak downstairs and take an oil lamp from the little room beside the scullery. I light it and carry it out of the back door into the cool night air. I know I'll find a spade in the little brick shed at the bottom of the garden so I walk there on tiptoe, glancing back at the house every so often, hoping a light won't appear at any of the windows.

The shed door creaks as I open it and I freeze, fearing the noise has alerted Sybil or my father. I wait, breath held, but all is quiet and after a couple of minutes I retrieve the spade from its resting place and carry it over to Father's flower bed.

There are no weeds here. Father keeps it pristine, almost like the gardens at Tarnhey Court used to be before the war. I find a patch of bare soil amongst the neatly trimmed perennials and I begin to dig down. I've put on my oldest boots and I know that by the time I've finished they'll be caked in soil. The lantern is resting on the ground and I lift it to see into the hole I've dug. Nothing. I dig down further but I can see no telltale glow of white bone against the darkness of the soil.

I dig in a different space. Then another. I dig down deeper and the unaccustomed effort makes me perspire. I know my hands and skirts are getting covered in soil but at this moment I don't care. I can always make up some tale for Sybil. She's not the inquisitive type and I know she'll accept whatever fiction I care to tell her.

When I've been working for an hour or more, I begin to fill the holes in carefully, fetching a rake from the shed to give the illusion that the soil hasn't been disturbed.

I am now satisfied that Edith was lying.

Mother isn't there.

Chapter 35

Albert

Sergeant Teague gave Inspector Lincoln an enquiring look. 'We've already taken a statement from Dr Bone for the evening in question. He left his motor car outside the Cottage Hospital and stayed the night there then in the morning he walked straight from the hospital entrance to his motor car and drove back to New Mills. There was no need for him to walk through the village or go anywhere near Pooley Woods and he was quite clear that he didn't see or hear anything suspicious. Why do you want to speak to him again, sir? I don't understand.'

Albert wasn't feeling inclined to explain that it was Flora Winsmore who'd told him about Bone being in Wenfield on the days of each murder. The fewer people who knew about his connection with Flora, the better. But she still filled his mind: he still longed for her when he was lying awake in his bed at the Black Horse and as he walked through the village he searched every approaching face in the hope of seeing hers. They had arranged to meet at seven that evening and he felt a frisson of anticipation whenever he thought about it. He'd felt like this about Mary when they'd first met; before time and death had robbed him of the woman he'd once loved.

'I telephoned Dr Bone's surgery, sir,' said Teague, interrupting Albert's thoughts. 'His housekeeper said he's due at the hospital today.'

'In that case I'll have a word with him while he's here.'

Teague's eyes widened in alarm. 'Surely you can't suspect him, sir? He's well respected round here – did a lot of good work up at Tarnhey Court during the war.'

'He wouldn't be the first member of that particular profession to turn to murder, Sergeant, and until we know otherwise, nobody's above suspicion.' For a brief moment it occurred to him that Flora's hints about Bone might have affected his judgement. But he told himself she'd been right to mention it.

'There've been all sorts of rumours flying round the village about this ghostly soldier,' said Teague, interrupting his thoughts. 'Some say it's one of the lads who didn't come back.'

'People will believe any sort of nonsense.'

'Didn't you say Lady Cartwright had seen him?'

'Yes but . . . '

'Don't you believe in ghosts, sir?'

Albert shook his head. If ghosts existed his little Frederick would have returned to comfort his grieving parents and Mary wouldn't have been left like a hollow shell, her spirit dead but her body still living and breathing.

'I think there might be something in it,' Teague continued, a distant look in his eyes. 'My sister lost a lad on the Somme and then she went to see a medium who got in contact with him. She said this medium woman spoke in her Jimmy's voice and she told her things only he could know. It's been a great comfort to her, knowing he was happy on the other side.'

Albert was tempted to tell him it was all trickery but he stopped himself. If consulting the medium had given Teague's sister some consolation, then perhaps a bit of trickery was forgivable in strange times like the ones they were living through.

In spite of Lady Cartwright's apparent vagueness, he found himself believing her claim that she'd seen her friend's dead son – or rather somebody with his face. The mask David Eames had made for Simon Plunket while he was being treated for his wounds at Tarnhey Court had been stolen during the burglary and Albert thought it likely that the killer had used it to disguise himself; to take on the identity of a dead man, uniform and all. Maybe he'd used the other stolen mask too – a different victim of the war on each occasion, perhaps.

A hospital full of sick people was no place to conduct an interview so Albert gave instructions that Dr Bone was to be brought to the police station as soon as he arrived at work. Then he went into his little office and shut the door. He sat down at his desk and stared ahead, a pencil in his right hand hovering over a notebook. Then he began to jot down ideas. He wanted to speak to Sir William Cartwright again: he'd been the lover of one of the victims and he'd visited David Eames's cottage. Was he using his position to avoid close scrutiny? Roderick

Cartwright too had a secret but was it an appetite for slaughtering women and silencing their mouths with doves from his family's own dovecote?

Sydney Pepper couldn't have killed Miss Forrest but it was possible that he'd killed the first three victims and somebody else had copied his modus operandi to dispose of the poisonous cafe owner who had, no doubt, made a lot of enemies in Wenfield over the years with her venomous gossip and anonymous letters. Pepper's injuries had left him bearing a burden of bitterness and anger and certain aspects of the crimes certainly pointed to him. Albert's instincts told him that he couldn't be eliminated from their inquiries just yet.

This case should have been easy to solve but every time he felt he was making progress it slipped from his grasp like an eel. He put his head on his desk and closed his eyes, hoping he might learn something useful from Dr Bone.

Bone was brought in at ten o'clock. Constable Wren had caught him just as he was arriving at the hospital and asked him very politely if the inspector could have a word. It wouldn't take long.

Bone drove himself the short distance to the police station and as he entered the building Albert emerged from his office to greet him, registering the mixture of apprehension and curiosity on the doctor's face. The man looked as if he had something to hide but Albert wasn't sure what that something was. But then he'd felt like that about a lot of the people he'd met since his arrival in Wenfield. The village was a place of lies and hidden vices and he suspected there were still more things to discover, hidden beneath the seemingly respectable surface.

In the meantime, Bone was to be treated as a helpful potential witness rather than a suspect. Albert invited him to sit and told the constable to fetch a pot of tea. He wanted to put the man at his ease and he watched as he sipped his tea. Bone was a handsome man and Albert suspected the adulation of grateful patients had only served to increase his natural arrogance. He held power over life and death and he knew it.

'I'm sorry to drag you away from your duties, Doctor,' Albert began. 'But as you were here in Wenfield at the time of all these recent murders, I'd like to ask you some questions if I may.'

'I've already spoken to the police and told them I saw nothing. You're wasting your time ... and mine.'

Albert prickled at the criticism but he carried on. 'But you admit you were in the village on those particular dates? You stayed overnight at the Cottage Hospital on each occasion?'

'Is that a crime? There's a room set aside for visiting doctors and when I finish my duties late I often find it more convenient to stay.'

'Do you own a bayonet?'

'Of course not. I'm a medical man. I didn't see active service ... not in that way.'

'You have access to a military uniform ... an officer's uniform?'

'No.'

'Your patients at Tarnhey Court had uniforms. You could have kept one.'

'Why would I do that? Besides, the patients there wore special uniforms. Hospital blues – not popular with the men.'

'What about the portrait masks?'

'What about them?'

Ten more minutes of denial followed. The interrogation was going nowhere and Bone was growing impatient, shifting in his chair and looking at his watch. Then, after a long silence, he spoke again.

'I don't know why you're picking on me, Inspector. I'm not the only doctor around here. Perhaps you should speak to Arthur Winsmore. In my opinion, he's never been quite the same since his wife left him ... and the loss of his only son left him very bitter.' He stood up. 'I'm getting married, Inspector. Why would I do anything to jeopardise that?'

Albert sensed that he was trying to deflect suspicion on to Flora's father and he tried his best to hide his growing dislike of the man. But he knew he'd be neglecting his duty if he didn't at least check Dr Winsmore's alibis again. He found himself longing to find something incriminating on Bone but gut feelings weren't enough. He needed evidence and he didn't even have enough on the man to warrant a search of his premises.

As Bone left with a smirk of triumph on his smooth face, Albert clenched his fist. But frustration would achieve nothing.

He looked at the telephone on his desk, knowing he ought to cancel his meeting with Flora that evening, especially now her father was about to undergo more scrutiny.

But he did nothing.

Chapter 36

The next day Albert planned to ask Dr Winsmore to attend at the police station and answer some questions. He knew that saying nothing to Flora would be a particularly despicable kind of deception but it was unavoidable. If he told her the truth, she could alert her father and put him on his guard. And that might ruin everything.

He returned to the Black Horse to eat and passed Helen Eames on the way into the bar. She gave him an absentminded nod as they passed in the entrance hall but he stopped and addressed her.

'Good evening, Miss Eames. How's your brother?'

She came to a halt and stared at him, her eyes full of suspicion. 'Why do you want to know?'

'I'm just enquiring,' he said, taken aback by her defensiveness. If David Eames hadn't had the perfect alibi of being confined to a hospital bed, he might have thought she was hiding something.

'They're letting him out of hospital tomorrow,' she said, avoiding his eyes. 'So I'll be staying here one more night and then returning to the cottage.'

'Give him my best wishes, won't you?'

She shot him a hostile look before making for the stairs and when he entered the bar he found Mrs Jackson clearing away Helen's empty dishes. She greeted him with a couple of automatic pleasantries but she seemed to be in an unusually pensive mood and there was no chatter as she served his dinner. Albert thought she looked worried and he couldn't resist asking if something was wrong.

She hesitated before replying. 'It's my Joe,' she said, looking around to make sure she couldn't be heard. 'He's not been himself.'

'What's the matter? Is he ill?'

She didn't answer the question. 'I must get on, Mr Lincoln,' she said before hurrying off.

He'd arranged to meet Flora at seven and he didn't want to keep her waiting. After a great deal of thought he'd finally resolved to ask her about her father's whereabouts at the times of the murders, trying to make his questions so subtle that she wouldn't realise she was being interrogated. If her answers aroused any suspicions, he'd then regard Dr Winsmore as a suspect, otherwise, he'd assume Bone was making mischief for a colleague. He felt pleased with himself for coming up with this solution and hoped Flora's answers would confirm what he suspected about Bone. He hadn't liked the man.

There was no sign of Joe Jackson when Albert left the Black Horse. He'd set off early to allow himself time to nip into the police station and check the routine statements Jackson had given. Everyone in that village was a potential suspect and Mrs Jackson's worries had made him uneasy.

Sure enough, when he found the appropriate reports he found that on each occasion Joe Jackson had been working at the back of the hotel, out of sight of the public in the bars. Each time his wife had vouched for his whereabouts which, in Albert's opinion, meant little. Wives have been known to cover for their husbands, if not out of love then out of a desire to maintain their comfortable lives.

But time was moving on; he had to keep his appointment with Flora so the matter of Joe Jackson would have to wait. He left the station and as he neared the meeting place, his pace quickened. He knew that what had happened between him and Flora Winsmore had been wrong and he should have stopped it before it had even begun. But he hadn't and when he saw her waiting by the gates, her bicycle propped up against the wall, he felt a new wave of desire for her. She was squatting down, examining the tyres and when she heard his footsteps she straightened herself up and greeted him with a smile of relief.

'This is my alibi,' she said, pointing at the bicycle. 'If anyone comes along, I'll pretend there's a stone caught in my tyre. It looks a lot less suspicious than just standing here waiting.'

He couldn't help admiring her resourcefulness. As he'd approached he'd been quite fooled by her act; the worried frown of annoyance at a machine that had just let her down. After making sure there was nobody about to see he led the way towards the little path leading to the boathouse.

Once there he shut the door carefully behind them

and when he turned he saw her standing there, her arms held out to him. 'I saw Helen today,' she said. 'She told me David's not being sent home until tomorrow.'

'I know. I saw her at the Black Horse earlier.'

'That means the cottage is empty tonight,' she said, the words full of meaning.

She kissed him, running gentle fingers across his scarred cheek. 'Come on, let's go.'

He didn't want to resist. He wanted to snatch his share of happiness, however brief it had to be. A little warmth in a cold place. He went with Flora to the cottage and watched as she unlocked the door, trying to concentrate on the moment. She led him upstairs again and when they made love there was an urgency about it, as though they both knew they had little time. The cottage was only theirs for the evening. After that night they'd be displaced lovers. And once he'd discovered who killed those women, they'd part and never see each other again.

Afterwards they lay together on the bed and for a while they didn't speak. Then Albert broke the silence.

'The police took a statement from your father, didn't they?'

Flora shifted onto one elbow and stared at him. 'They asked him whether he'd seen anything. Why?'

He didn't answer her question. 'I interviewed Dr Bone today.'

'Did he admit he was here in the village when those women were killed?'

'Yes. But he said that was just a coincidence.'

'I don't believe in coincidences.'

He saw that the colour had drained from her cheeks. 'You don't like Bone, do you?'

'I worked with him. He despises women.'

'What makes you think that?'

'He ... assaulted one of the nurses at Tarnhey Court. And if he's capable of something like that ...'

She didn't have to finish her sentence. If a man's hatred of women gets out of control it might escalate to murder. She was accusing Bone of the worst of crimes.

'I'll probably be having another word with him,' he said. 'But I'd also like to speak to your father.'

'There's no need,' she said quickly. 'Father was either at home or out visiting patients when those women were killed.' She sounded desperate to be believed.

'Can you be absolutely certain of that?'

'Of course I can.'

She lay down again, staring at the ceiling with frightened eyes. It was obvious that she didn't want him to speak to her father. And that she was doing her very best to deflect suspicion onto Bone.

'You don't want me to speak to your father, do you?'

'I don't want him upset. He still hasn't got over my brother's death and ...'

'It'll just be a chat,' he said. 'I'm sure he has nothing to worry about.'

They lay there for a while, Flora's head resting on his chest. He kissed her hair and held her close, feeling a warm glow of comfort. Perhaps something akin to love but he couldn't be certain. He closed his eyes, relishing the moment, trying hard not to think of what would happen when their idyll was shattered – as it inevitably would be.

'Are you going to question Sir William Cartwright again?' Flora asked after a while.

'I'd like to but I've been warned off.'

'What do you mean?'

'Someone on high doesn't want me to bother him.'

'Can they do that?'

'Yes. But if I put pressure on his son, that might make Sir William emerge from his shell.' He gave a bitter smile. 'I know all the tricks.'

'You can't believe Roderick's responsible. I've known him since we were children.'

'Then you'll know his little secret.'

He saw the colour return to her face, a blush this time. 'What secret?'

'I think we both know that, don't we? Roderick Cartwright prefers men to women.'

Flora sat up and twisted round to face him. 'Surely you're not going to arrest him?'

'No, I'm not. As far as I'm concerned, it's his business and nobody else's, no matter what the law says. But I don't have to let Sir William know that, do I?'

She looked less relieved than he'd expected, as though something was still bothering her.

'I haven't asked you how your visit to Liverpool went. Did you find your mother?'

He saw her shake her head but it was hard to read her thoughts.

'You should try and find her. It's important.'

'I don't want to talk about it,' she said quietly.

Albert knew the subject was closed. He'd leave it for another day. He leaned over to take his pocket watch from the waistcoat he'd flung onto the chair by the bed. He checked the time and said he had to go.

As Flora tidied the bed, he watched her, the policeman

in him taking over from the lover. She was nervous about him speaking to her father, that much was obvious. But had she lied about Edward Bone to shield her own flesh and blood? He reached out for her and they kissed again.

Once they'd dressed, they left the cottage, shutting the door carefully behind them. And as they walked back up the path, Albert wheeled her bicycle, only handing it back to her once they reached the lane.

'Please don't upset Father,' was the last thing she said before hurrying off into the dusk. Albert watched her go, knowing he couldn't make any promises.

Chapter 37

So far every path the investigation had taken had reached a frustrating dead end but time was passing and Albert knew they needed to make some progress. He had made an appointment to see Dr Winsmore that morning after his surgery finished and he felt unusually nervous about the interview. Perhaps it was the prospect of encountering Flora during his visit – or perhaps it was the thought of speaking to the father of the woman who'd become his lover. He wasn't sure.

The previous evening he'd called back at the police station after his meeting with Flora to take stock of what they knew. It had been Albert's idea to cast the net wider and interview everybody who lived in the surrounding countryside but he was disappointed in the results. Most of the men were too old, too young or too disabled by war to be capable of covering that amount of ground at night and killing four women in cold blood. Either that or they had people who'd vouch for where they were at the times of one or more of the murders. And none of them had any intimate knowledge of the dovecote at Tarnhey Court.

The police in nearby towns and villages had also been asked to speak to any likely suspects but, again, there was nobody in particular who'd fallen under suspicion; certainly no one who had access to an officer's uniform. Unless he was putting far too much faith in Lady Cartwright's sighting of the ghostly soldier. But he knew that the dead officer's mask had been stolen from David Eames's studio so perhaps there was something in it after all.

Albert was beginning to look forward to his hearty breakfasts at the Black Horse. Mrs Jackson was an ever-efficient presence while her silent husband rarely made an appearance. But today he was there, cleaning the bar in the saloon while his wife bustled in and out to serve the breakfast.

It was always at the back of Albert's mind that Joe Jackson had once tried to hang himself, driven to despair by the jibes of the self-appointed Society for the Abolition of Cowardice. He wondered if the affable Mrs Jackson had ever really forgiven those women for their cruelty. Or had Joe Jackson harboured resentment against them, festering over the years and bursting in a dreadful moment of violence like a lanced boil? He thought about this as he cut up the fried egg on his breakfast plate, watching the bright yellow yoke oozing out over the white plate as his knife pierced it.

Once he'd finished his breakfast he dabbed his lips with the napkin Mrs Jackson had placed on the side plate for his use. The Black Horse might be a relatively humble village inn but her standards were high. He left the saloon bar and made for the stairs, intending to fetch his coat and hat because it had begun to rain heavily outside. When he reached the passage he saw Joe Jackson opening the door that led out into the back yard and the secretive nature of this mundane act caught his interest. Once Jackson had vanished through the door he waited a few seconds and followed the man out only to find the yard completely empty.

The cobbled space had been swept clean but the scent of manure drifted from the stables at the end. He could hear the distant stamping of hooves and a faint whinnying sound so he guessed that there were horses in there, probably to pull the little cart he'd seen. He remembered Mrs Jackson saying they sometimes sent it to the station to pick up guests but it hadn't been used for that purpose since he'd been there: he supposed they had more visitors in the summer months.

He heard one of the old wooden doors on the opposite side of the yard creaking open so he shot back into the corridor. He still wanted to know why Joe Jackson was behaving in such a furtive manner but he had no wish to be caught snooping. He had never considered Jackson as a serious suspect for the murders but now he wondered why he hadn't looked into the man's whereabouts more thoroughly. Perhaps it was because he liked Mrs Jackson and felt a little sorry for her. She'd had it tough supporting her husband through his darkest time so he felt reluctant to disturb the peaceful existence she'd built up at the Black Horse since the war ended. Perhaps he was just losing his touch. He'd had too many distractions of late. Especially one. Every time he thought of Flora he felt a fresh stab of remorse.

He was preparing to climb the stairs when Mrs Jackson appeared, smiling as if nothing was wrong in her world. She produced a letter from the pocket of her apron and handed it to Albert.

'Another letter from London for you.'

He had never told her who his other letters were from and he wasn't about to do so now so he thanked her and slipped it into the pocket of his jacket to read in private.

It was another from Mary and he felt bad that he'd made no effort to write back. But often when he was away he was too busy with his case to take the time. She understood that. Besides, what would he tell her? I've met another woman and I think I might be falling in love with her? Silence was sometimes the best course of action.

He heard the chink of glass against glass as Joe Jackson came back into the inn carrying a crate of beer bottles. He disappeared into the public bar and Albert wondered whether he should go outside to satisfy his curiosity. But it was likely Jackson would return so he decided against it. Instead he took himself upstairs to his room to read his letter in private.

He opened the envelope slowly with no sense of urgency. Whenever he thought of Mary he felt as though a veil of gloom had descended in his brain. A faint aching in his heart for what he'd lost – for what could never be again.

He deciphered her neat, small handwriting.

Dear Albert, she began. *I went to see Mrs Huggins last night. I was nervous at first because she was a big woman who looked nothing like a MEDIUM and I know she got in touch with Mrs Hawthorne's Johnny but I thought she wouldn't be any use. So many of them are CHARLATANS like you always say but Mrs Huggins is different. She got in touch with Frederick and spoke in his voice. I swear to you it was HIM. He said he was happy and that there were a lot of children where he was. And there were lovely gardens. And he knew you were away because he said he wished Daddy was there. He ASKED for you, Albert. It was a MIRACLE.*

Albert stood there for a while staring at the words, noting the capitals she'd used. She only wrote like that when she was in a state of heightened emotion. She believed she'd been in touch with Frederick. She believed she'd witnessed a miracle.

He sank on to the bed. Sooner or later he would have to go back to London and face her. He'd have to listen to her going on about Mrs Huggins and he knew she'd urge him to come with her to visit the medium so that he too could communicate with their dead son. It was something he didn't think he could face. Especially when he thought of Flora Winsmore.

The only way to banish all these swirling thoughts from his mind was to bury himself in work so he walked the short distance to the police station in the rain and headed for his office, acknowledging the greetings of his temporary colleagues with a curt nod. After reading through all the statements that had accumulated over his relatively brief stay, he felt as confused as ever. The ghostly soldier, the masks, the doves from Tarnhey Court. Something was going on here he didn't understand; some dark secret the people of Wenfield were hiding perhaps.

He hadn't particularly liked Dr Bone but he'd be

316

neglecting his duty if he didn't follow up his poisoned insinuations about Dr Winsmore. He estimated that the doctor would have finished his surgery by midday and as he knocked on the Winsmores' door he felt nervous, hoping Flora wouldn't answer. The thought of her and what they'd shared unsettled him, even more since he'd heard from Mary again. The misery of his existence since Frederick's death had made him susceptible to temptation and he knew that he'd been weak. And yet the memory of Flora still excited him.

To his relief the housekeeper answered and she led him into the doctor's presence. Winsmore greeted him with that false bonhomie that people use to conceal their nervousness. Albert had seen it all too often.

'How can I help you now, Inspector?' The doctor arched his fingers at looked Albert in the eye.

'You've given a statement about your whereabouts at the times of the recent murders.'

'So I have. Why?'

'I'd like to go over your account again. It's just routine.'

The doctor nodded uneasily. 'Very well.'

Albert went through his questions again with Winsmore's original statement there on his knee in front of him to refer to for discrepancies. There weren't any and the answers were confident ... almost as if they'd been well rehearsed. If the doctor was lying, he hadn't been able to catch him out.

And yet he still had the feeling the man was holding something back, although his instincts told him that whatever it was might not be connected with the murders. Somehow Albert couldn't see Winsmore stuffing those doves into the victim's mouths but he'd been wrong before.

'I've spoken to Dr Bone.' He let the words hang in the air for a few seconds, watching Winsmore's face. He could see a resemblance to Flora there that unnerved him. 'I believe he was here in the village at the times of the murders.'

'Was he?'

'What kind of man is Bone? I've been hearing rumours that he has a history of violence towards women.'

'Who on Earth told you that?'

Albert felt the blood rising to his face. 'I'm afraid I can't say. Are you aware of anything like that?'

'Absolutely not. I have the greatest respect for Edward Bone as a colleague and a doctor.' Winsmore's words sounded convincing. 'Are you implying that he has something to do with these dreadful murders?'

'I'm afraid I can't comment on that, Doctor. Our investigation is still ongoing and we have to consider every possibility.' Albert stood up to leave but when he was at the door he turned. 'By the way, Doctor, what happened to your wife?'

Winsmore's eyes widened in alarm. 'I don't see what that has to do with your case, Inspector. Now if you'll excuse me, I'm rather busy.'

As Albert left the house, he knew one thing for sure. The subject of Flora's mother had shaken Dr Winsmore. And he wondered why.

Chapter 38

Flora

I have said nothing to Father about Edith's accusation, or about my secret visit to Liverpool and my meeting with Martin Nerrist. I know now that Edith didn't tell me the truth about the flower bed grave, but why would she lie about something like that? I grew up thinking Edith was my friend but now I'm wracked with uncertainty. Perhaps she's been our family's enemy all along. Perhaps she and Bone deserve each other.

After helping Father in his surgery all morning I go upstairs to change my clothes. The muddy clothes I wore to dig up the flower bed are stuffed in the bottom of my wardrobe. I plan to clean the boots as soon as I have the house to myself and on Monday when the woman comes to help with the laundry, I'll take the clothes downstairs and put them amongst the other dirty linen. Now I know Edith's a liar, I wonder afresh what happened to Mother. My nightmares continue, vague and disturbing, always the same. But they are something I've had to live with since my dear brother, John, left us.

I am about to come downstairs again when I hear voices. Albert and my father. For a moment my heart lurches. Has my lover come to tell him of our relationship or is he here on police business, speaking to Father as he said he would? To my disappointment, I realise it must be the latter. Albert won't be in a position to make things public until his case is concluded. And I've no idea when that will be.

I stand at the top of the stairs waiting in that same spot I'm fixed to in my dream, and as Albert leaves the house, I step back into the shadows watching him. He has a limp as well as the injuries to his face and hand. War is a terrible thing but at least he came back ... unlike John.

As soon as he's left the house I tiptoe downstairs in search of Sybil and when I find her preparing for lunch in the scullery, I tell her I'm going out to buy some hairpins from the haberdashers. I don't tell her that my true intention is to meet Albert, seemingly by accident.

However, I'm too late. When I step out into the street, there is no sign of him so I walk on towards the shops. I see the police station with its blue lantern over the front door and see Constable Wren emerging, wearing his cape over his uniform because there's a chill wind blowing in from the hills. When he passes me he nods in an avuncular fashion and I smile back. There is a wonderful innocence about the man which makes it impossible to distrust him.

I carry on until I reach the war memorial at the end of the High Street, its clean granite as yet unsullied by the soot that hangs in the air, and when I stop my eyes travel to John's name as they always do. As I bow my head I hear a voice saying my name softly.

'Flora.'

I turn quickly and see Roderick Cartwright standing there. His eyes too are focused on the memorial and I know which name interests him. James Carr. Private James Carr. The coachman's beautiful son.

'I miss him,' Roderick whispered.

'I know you do.'

'It was those bitches who encouraged him to go. The Society for the Abolition of Cowardice.'

'They bullied all the men. I remember John saying he'd rather face the enemy than that lot.'

'Well four of them have received their just deserts. Now they know what death's like.'

I look into his eyes and see nothing but bitterness.

'I'm sorry,' he says. 'It's just that I've had some bad news. One of the friends I'm going into business with has been arrested in Manchester.'

'What for?'

He gives me a strange look. 'They call it gross indecency.'

I put a hand out to him and touch his sleeve. 'I'm so sorry.'

'I don't know what Father's going to say when he hears about it. He's told me to be careful of the company I keep ... keep my nose clean. Says any scandal could finish him. He's down in London at the moment staying at his club. Between you and me I think he's avoiding that policeman they've sent up. Lincoln, isn't it?'

'Yes. Albert Lincoln.'

For one split second I'm tempted to confide in Roderick

321

and tell him Albert Lincoln is my lover. After all, I know about his hidden life so why shouldn't he know about mine? But Albert has asked me to say nothing and there's plenty of time to be open. Roderick will be the first to know when all this is over.

'Why does your father want to avoid the police?'

Roderick's gaze focuses once more on James Carr's carved name. 'Those bitches didn't only bully men into going off to be killed, a couple of them also got wind of me and James and their poisoned tongues started clacking.'

'How did they find out?'

'Servants' gossip maybe. Or perhaps one of them saw us together and leapt to the right conclusion. Then Father was sleeping with Sarah. What a scandal that would have caused if it had come out. Let's face facts, Flora, he had more reason than most to want her dead and I know he breathed a sigh of relief when he heard the news. I was there. I saw him. When he thought nobody was watching he smiled.'

'You think your father could be the killer?'

For a while Roderick doesn't answer. Then he leans close to whisper in my ear. 'Take no notice. I'm just letting off steam. I don't intend to say anything to the police. Promise you won't either. Promise.'

He suddenly looks anxious, as though he fears he's said too much. But I say he can trust me. I have no particular liking for Sir William but for Roderick's and his mother's sake I won't pass on his suspicions, although I can see there is some logic behind them. I reckon Sir William would go to any lengths to avoid facing a scandal. He's an important man with a lot to lose.

I want to put my arms around Roderick and comfort him, just as I used to do when we were children and he was upset. But now the trivial annoyances of childhood have been replaced by graver problems.

Roderick's father runs the risk of being arrested for murder ... and his son might have to face challenges of his own.

Chapter 39

Ten days have passed since I saw Roderick and I hear that
Sir William is still in London. To my disappointment
there's been no word from Albert for over a week and I
wondered whether he'd returned to the capital, perhaps
in search of Sir William.

But this morning I found out that he's still in Wenfield
because Sybil has passed on some news she gleaned in
the village. She says that Albert – or Inspector Lincoln as
she calls him – has been seen going up to Tarnhey Court.
Surely if Sir William is back and has been arrested, word
would have got about. I find myself hoping that Roderick
hasn't been taken away to languish in a cell like his friend
from Manchester. How I long to know what's happening.

Father tells me there have been no new cases of influenza at the Cottage Hospital for a few days now which is
a blessing. I've been feeling a little tired and unwell
myself and I did fear at one time that I might have

succumbed to the illness. But my monthly period didn't arrive as it normally does and this morning I felt a little nauseous. I know what these things portend and at first I was afraid. However, I know that, if my suspicions are correct, Albert will greet the news with delight. How can he not?

I have ceased to wait so eagerly for that letter from Manchester Royal Infirmary because this new thing that might be growing inside me has changed everything. Once Albert knows that our love will bear fruit, we can make our plans. I feel a mixture of nervousness and excitement, as if I am about to embark on a new journey that could be filled with delight or peril.

I've ventured into the village each day, walking past the police station in the hope of catching sight of him but now I wonder whether I should make a more determined effort to seek him out. I'm sure he's fully occupied with his work or he would not be neglecting me like this. In a way I'm relieved that he hasn't been here to question Father again but, on the other hand, I long to see him.

I've taken to going up to my room and gazing from the window like a lovelorn princess in a fairy tale in the hope of catching a glimpse of him. This morning I helped Father in the surgery before going upstairs to take up my post. I feel a little sick again now but I take deep breaths and this seems to ease the discomfort.

Then I see him walking down the street alone and I hurtle down the stairs, without stopping to put on my coat and hat. I open the front door and walk quickly after him, not wishing to make an exhibition of myself by breaking into a run. He must hear the click of my boots on the cobbles behind him for he turns and waits for me to catch up. There is no smile of greeting. He looks serious and I guess this means his investigation isn't going well.

'How are you?' he asks, his eyes darting around as though he's checking there's nobody about to overhear.

I hesitate before replying. 'I need to talk to you ... somewhere private.'

Now that David is out of hospital and he and Helen have moved back to their cottage there is no bolt hole for us except the boathouse. I suggest we go there but although he nods, I sense his reluctance and I'm gripped by a sudden apprehension.

He seems tense as we walk, relaxing only when we are out of sight of passers-by. In his position I realise he doesn't wish to attract the attention of the gossip mongers – and there are still plenty about, even now that Miss Forrest has been removed from their ranks – and yet something about his manner, the way he walks in silence without looking at me, makes me uncomfortable.

When we reach the little boathouse I see the river is in full flood from last night's rain. The water roars by over the rocks, drowning out the singing of the birds. Only the shrieking crows nesting in the nearby trees are making themselves heard above the sound. There's no sign of Tarnhey Court's white doves today. Only the darkness of the crows and their mocking cry.

We enter the boathouse and I stand tilting my face towards him, my lips slightly parted to receive a kiss. But he doesn't bend forward. Instead he stands, statue still and waits for me to speak.

'I expect you've been busy,' I say.

'Yes.'

'Have you spoken to Sir William again?'

'Yes. He's been eliminated from our inquiries.' I can tell by his expression that he's not entirely happy about this.

'What about Roderick?'

'Don't worry, he's in the clear. His friends in Manchester have vouched for him.'

'I'm glad. I've known Roderick for a long time. He's a friend.'

'I guessed that.'

There is an awkward silence but I know I can't wait any longer. I tell him that I might be having a child, gabbling the words. Then I see his eyes widen in panic then narrow. The mouth I've kissed so often falls slightly open in astonishment then the lips are pressed tightly together.

'You're not pleased? I thought that after what you went through in the war ... I thought we could make a new start. Live for the future.'

He bows his head so that I can't see his face and a sudden chill passes through my body.

'I'm so sorry, Flora,' I hear him saying. 'It's all my fault. I should have told you I was married.'

His words hit me like a punch.

'If you are pregnant I'll take responsibility. I'll sort something out.'

'What?'

He shakes his head. He doesn't know. It was just something to say.

Then he speaks again. 'We lost a child to influenza ... a little boy. Frederick. My wife Mary ... she's never recovered from the loss and ... ' He raises his head, his eyes suddenly hopeful as if he's had a brilliant idea. 'What if

Mary and I adopt the child? You can go away somewhere to have it and . . . ' He sounds breathless, as if he is fighting against some invisible foe.

Part of me knows his suggestion is sensible. But his words have robbed me of all hope. The child I'll bear will be snatched from me like the life I'd hoped to build with Albert.

I refuse to cry. I leave him in the boathouse and stumble back to the village. People greet me and I respond automatically, hoping they won't be able to tell that my hopes have just been smashed and my world lies in ruins.

The shock has endowed me with fresh courage. When I return to the house Father is about to embark on his rounds and I tell him I wish to speak to him in private.

Suddenly I feel the need of a mother to confide in and as I follow Father into his surgery, I think of her. I hear that slightly mocking laugh of hers and wish I could speak to her and make her see how much she hurt me. I feel I cannot share the truth about Albert and our baby with Father just yet, although I know a confession will be inevitable when my dilemma becomes obvious. But that doesn't mean I can't try to discover once and for all what became of my mother.

Father sits down and looks at me, his gaze impersonal as though I am just another of his patients seeking his advice. He asks if something is the matter and I allow a few moments of silence before I speak.

'A fortnight ago I travelled to Liverpool,' I begin.

He is suddenly alert. 'You never told me. What did you go there for?' I imagine the mention of that city brings back memories. Unpleasant ones of desertion and loneliness. I wonder if he hates Martin Nerrist for what he did. Or was all his bile directed towards my mother?

'I went to visit the man Mother was said to have left you for.' I know the words are brutal but after my encounter with Albert I am in no mood for kindness.

'Why?'

'Because I want to find her. He says she didn't go away with him. He has no idea where she is.'

Father doesn't reply.

'I know what you told Edith.'

I see the colour has drained from his face. He suddenly looks old. A lost old man. He'd looked like that when the telegram arrived to say that John was dead.

'Edith said you asked her to marry you and that you said you were responsible for Mother's death. She said you confessed to pushing her down the stairs. Was she telling the truth?'

He looks numb with shock but I've gone too far to stop now. 'She said you buried Mother in the garden. Is that true? I need to know.' I feel hot tears run down my cheeks. This is like those dreams when I feel that helpless anger. The dreams when I am standing at the top of the stairs begging Mother not to go and I reach out to her.

At last Father speaks. 'Some things are best forgotten. I didn't kill your mother. Let's leave it at that.'

'So why did you tell Edith . . . ?'

He looks confused. 'I don't know. She was starting to ask too many questions. She wouldn't let the matter drop. Please, Flora. I don't wish to discuss it.'

'But where is Mother? Is she still alive?'

He doesn't reply but I think I see a small shake of his

head, barely perceptible as though he can't bear to acknowledge the truth.

'Is she buried in the garden?'

He shakes his head more vigorously this time. He looks exhausted. 'I said that because I knew that if Edith told anyone and there were repercussions, I could prove it wasn't true.'

'But you keep the flower bed near the wall like a shrine,' I say, puzzled.

'That's because she used to love to sit in that spot and take tea – not because she's buried there.'

'So what happened to her? Please tell me.'

'She's gone and nobody will ever find her. I'm saying no more.'

'Do you mean she's dead?'

'Let the past remain buried. Please, Flora. Forget about her. Believe me, I've tried to all these years.'

He opens the drawer of his desk and takes out a bottle. The liquid inside is amber. Whisky. He has a crystal glass in there too and he pours a measure and downs it in one gulp. I never knew he kept strong drink in his surgery. Perhaps there are a lot of things I don't know about my own father.

Chapter 40

I am alone in the house. Father has gone out on his rounds and Sybil is visiting a friend. I sit nursing my secret and listening for the ringing of the telephone. I have promised Father I'll answer it and take any messages that come in. Whatever has happened, whatever Father has or hasn't done in the past, his patients still have need of him.

I'm sure now that Edith was lying, that she made up the story about my father to get back at me for telling her the truth about Dr Bone. I hadn't thought her so spiteful and at this moment I hate her. And yet she was once the nearest thing I had to a mother and I long to speak to her. But I'm sure that wouldn't be wise.

It's been over three weeks since the last murder and I wonder whether Albert will be recalled to London if he doesn't apprehend the culprit soon. I imagine that if the killer escapes justice, he will return home in disgrace.

The failed detective from the mighty Scotland Yard. The village still buzzes with talk and speculation and every man comes under scrutiny, especially those who have returned from the war changed in body or mind. Wenfield is not a comfortable place now. I wonder if it ever was entirely comfortable for my mother.

Every time I venture into a shop I am told by some woman to take care and it is pointed out to me that they haven't caught him yet. I nod in agreement and promise caution. It keeps the busybodies happy.

With each day that passes, I am more certain of my condition and I wonder what the village will make of it when my growing belly becomes obvious. I have no kind aunt in some place where I'm not known who can take me in when my belly grows. Nobody who will spread the lie that I am some grief-stricken young widow whose brave husband, having returned from the war, has recently succumbed to the influenza. I have been lied to. Tricked. And sometimes I think that what Albert did is almost as bad as the ordeal Bone put me through.

I hear the doorbell ring and I hurry into the hall to answer, assuming it will be one of Father's patients. But when I open the door I see Bone standing there on the step, hat in hand, as though my thought has summoned him like some demon in a pantomime. He steps forward without doing me the courtesy of asking whether he can enter the house. I stand aside automatically. The very thought of him making physical contact repels me.

He pushes his way into the hall, shutting the door behind him and says he wishes to speak to me in private. His eyes burn into me with such hatred that I'm afraid. I'm alone with him with no hope of rescue. He stands between me and the door and I feel myself shaking as I remember what happened when we were alone before. I back away but he follows and somehow we end up in the drawing room.

'You've got a loose tongue,' he says, reaching out and pulling me towards him. 'You've been talking to my fiancée. Telling her things about me. Lies.'

I summon the courage somehow to look him in the eye. 'Are they lies?'

'Of course they are. You led me on. Threw yourself at me. You can hardly blame me if I took what was on offer.'

'That's not true,' I say. I feel tears of frustration welling in my eyes.

'You said you were in love with me that night in the dovecote. It was only when I said it was just a bit of fun that you started complaining.'

I hear the door bang shut outside the room. Sybil is home – or maybe Father.

I push Bone away, disgusted with his lies.

He raises an admonishing finger. 'You'll regret spreading stories about me,' he says in a low hiss. 'Edith said it was you who told the police I was in Wenfield when those murders were committed. Is that true?'

'Perhaps they should look into your activities more closely,' I say. 'After all, you know all about doves and dovecotes, don't you?'

For a moment I think he'll strike me. But then Sybil enters the room with an apology, clearly surprised when she sees Bone. He switches on a distant smile and the speed with which he reassumes the role of respectable doctor astonishes me.

She mumbles something about not realising I was

entertaining but I can tell she's remembering my indiscreet words about Bone being no gentleman. She gapes at me as I tell her Dr Bone is just going. Now there are two of us he has no choice so he leaves, sweeping past Sybil with a curt nod of farewell.

'He's in a hurry to get to the hospital,' I explain when he's gone and Sybil gives me a curious look. She's sensed that something unpleasant has happened and I'm not sure why I lied to her. But sometimes untruths are easier than long and painful explanations.

'As long as you're all right,' Sybil says.

I know she's willing me to confide in her but I think it best to keep my dealings with Bone to myself. There is only one person I want to tell. And that is Edith. I want to convince her that her intended hasn't changed and that what happened between us at Tarnhey Court was no fault of mine.

'You look pale, miss,' Sybil says but I tell her I'm fine and she sidles out of the room slowly as though she's reluctant to leave me alone. She has a good heart but I can't take the risk of making her my confidante.

As soon as Sybil has vanished into her domain at the rear of the house, I creep out into the hall and take the telephone handset from its cradle. I ask the operator for the number of Dr Bone's house and wait for Edith to answer.

My heart is thundering as I tell her what's happened and I realise that I should have told my story face to face so that she could see I was telling the truth. I'm not prepared for the violence of her reaction.

'If you're going to spread slanders like this, I'll have to report what your father told me to the police. I mean it,

Flora. I allowed a man to get away with the murder of his wife and now I'm going to put things right. And if he's capable of one murder, who's to say he's not responsible for the rest?'

I feel numb. This is not what I intended and if I don't take care, Father will be arrested. He will be questioned about my mother's death and he might even come under suspicion for the recent murders. Although he apparently had alibis for each occasion, I have to face the fact that I didn't really know where he was. I made assumptions – I assumed he'd told the truth.

Somehow I have to retrieve the situation and now I hear myself begging Edith to hold off until we've had a chance to discuss the matter. I suggest we meet this evening, fearing she'll refuse.

But she doesn't. 'Very well,' she says. 'I'm willing to meet. But you can't come here. Edward will be at home all night.'

I ask her if we can meet in Wenfield and she hesitates before saying she'll take the train over. One stop. She says she can be there at half past seven and I assure her that, if she truly suspects my father of these appalling murders, he'll be visiting the Cottage Hospital at the time of our meeting. Eventually she agrees to meet at Pooley Woods where we're guaranteed complete privacy for our conversation because nobody goes there now. As there'll be two of us we won't be putting ourselves in any peril, I tell her. They say there's safety in numbers.

All of a sudden I feel reckless. I don't care about facing danger providing I can convince her of the truth of what I've said and make her promise to stop making accusations against Father. And I'm certainly not afraid of any ghostly soldier. He has no reason to harm me.

For the rest of the day I go about my usual work, helping Sybil with the household duties before helping Father in his surgery when he returns from his rounds. I don't tell him about Dr Bone's visit. What would be the point?

After Father and I have eaten I say I'm going to my room. But while he is reading in the drawing room, I get ready for my meeting with Edith and then sneak out of the back door, careful to let nobody see me.

Chapter 41

Albert

Conscience can be an irritation. Albert Lincoln wished his didn't make him so uncomfortable.

The previous night he hadn't slept because he was lying awake going over Flora's revelation in his restless mind. His suggestion that she give up her child to him and Mary as a replacement for their little Frederick had seemed to make perfect sense when he'd blurted the words out but then he'd seen the devastation on Flora's face. He knew she'd hoped for marriage. She'd hoped for a family of her own and he had shattered all her hopes as surely as if he had punched her to the ground and stamped on her helpless body. He had been cruel but there was no way he could make amends now without betraying Mary and the memory of their dead son.

After another day in the police station trawling through statements he returned to the Black Horse with a lonely emptiness gnawing inside him. The solution to his case was as elusive as ever but at least there had been no more deaths since Miss Forrest's and he wondered whether this was significant. Perhaps the murderer had sated his taste for destruction for the moment ... or perhaps the victims had been selected carefully. Those particular women might have been chosen because they deserved death and the killer had appointed himself judge, jury and executioner.

There was another explanation of course. The murders might have been committed to hide the disposal of one victim in particular. The lull in the killings coincided with Sir William Cartwright's absence in London and he couldn't forget that Sarah Cookham and her unborn child had been a great inconvenience to the owner of Tarnhey Court. But he had to be absolutely certain of his facts before he acted. Sir William's importance meant that the burden of proof was even greater than it would be for a lesser being. This sad knowledge made Albert angry but it was the way of the world.

As Mrs Jackson served his dinner, she seemed distracted but when he asked her if anything was wrong, she shook her head. She was fine, thank you, sir, but he could tell she was lying. He repeated the question and, after a moment of hesitation, she asked permission to sit down at his table.

She sat in silence for a while as though she needed time to collect her thoughts. After a while she took a deep breath.

'I've been thinking of those women, the ones who were murdered,' she said. 'They were all members of that Society ... the one for the abolition of cowardice. Do you think that might have anything to do with why they were killed?'

Albert suddenly felt alert, sensing that he was about to discover something important. 'Possibly.'

'Then there's something my Joe said . . . about seeing a soldier in Pooley Woods.'

'When was this?'

'A while ago . . . around the time little Myrtle Bligh was killed.'

'What was Joe doing there?'

She blushed. 'He went there to meet a friend.'

'Who?'

She shrugged. She didn't know. 'He said he'd seen a ghost . . . a soldier. I asked him about it later but he said to forget it. It was none of our business.'

'Why didn't either of you report this to the police?'

'Because I thought he'd been drinking,' she said, embarrassed. 'He sometimes gets confused.'

'Where can I find him?'

'He's in the back seeing to the horses.'

He watched her leave the room, wearing the expression of a woman who regrets saying too much. He recognised that look because he'd seen it before so many times.

He stayed at the table for a while staring into his half-drunk pint of beer, recalling how he'd seen Joe Jackson in the stable yard the other day, heading for one of the outhouses with a shifty look on his face. Perhaps the man had something to hide and that was why he hadn't reported his sighting of the soldier to the police. He hadn't believed Mrs Jackson's claim that her husband had been drunk. He'd come across a lot of innkeepers who fell prey to alcohol but he didn't think Joe Jackson was one of them.

As soon as he finished his drink he made for the back of the inn and opened the door to the stable yard. Like before, the smell of manure hit his nostrils and he could hear the inhabitants of the stables snorting, ready for a well-earned sleep

The daylight was fading fast and he could see the glow of lantern light in one of the windows at the other side of the yard; the window beside the door he'd seen Jackson entering the other day. He crossed the yard and opened the door slowly. Inside what he took for an old store room, he could see Jackson tending to a strange, steam emitting contraption made of copper and glass. Then after a few moments Jackson turned round and Albert saw a look of horror on his face, like a man discovered bent over a still-warm corpse.

'So this is what you get up to in here, Mr Jackson. I had wondered.'

Jackson stared at him, speechless.

'Distilling your own spirits is illegal, you know.'

'I only do it for friends,' the man whined. 'Am I under arrest?'

Albert took pity on him. He was there to catch a killer, not to investigate an illicit still. Besides, he'd heard how the war had affected this man and he wasn't in the business of making life harder for him, even if he had strayed onto the wrong side of the law.

'To tell the truth, Mr Jackson, what you're doing in here is none of my business. All I'm interested in is these murders. Your wife says you saw something in Pooley Woods on the night Myrtle Bligh was killed.'

Jackson nodded.

'I take it your visit there had something to do with this

little sideline of yours and that's why you didn't come forward?'

Another nod. 'I was making a delivery. You're not likely to be overheard in the woods. I handed over a few bottles of the stuff to a man I'd rather not name and I was making my way back to the village when I saw someone – a soldier in uniform. I don't think he saw me but I was close enough to see that he was a lieutenant . . . one pip. I recognised his regiment badge and all.'

'Did you see his face?'

He hesitated. 'This is going to sound a bit mad but his face didn't seem quite right – I don't know how to explain it.'

'Could it have been a mask?'

Joe's eyes lit up in recognition. 'It could have been.'

'You've no idea who it was?'

'A couple of men from the village were lieutenants in that regiment but it couldn't have been one of them 'cause he's dead.'

'And the other?'

He shook his head. 'Wrong build.'

'What were the names of the two lieutenants?'

'It wasn't either of them, I'm sure of that.'

'I'd still like their names.'

As soon as Jackson gave him the names, Albert left the Black Horse. There was something he had to do.

Sooner or later he had to face Flora so he made for the Winsmore house only to be told by Sybil the housekeeper that she'd gone out. Sybil clung onto the doorpost as she spoke and there was a worried look on her face.

'My cousin Edith rang a few minutes ago. She told me she'd arranged to meet Miss Flora in Pooley Woods but

341

she couldn't keep the appointment and asked if I could pass on the message. But when I tried to find Miss Flora, she wasn't there. I've searched all over the house but there's no sign of her so she must have left already. She'll have gone there alone.'

Growing panic was making Sybil's voice shake and Albert was seized by the kind of dread he used to feel just before going over the top. 'If I'd known where she was going I would have stopped her,' Sybil said, wringing her hands.

'You're sure it was Pooley Woods?'

'That's what Edith said. Do you think she'll be all right?'

Albert couldn't find any words to reassure her so he mumbled his thanks and walked back down the little garden path.

Dusk was falling and when he reached Pooley Woods the huddled trees seemed to form a shadowy portal into another world; a world of lost sons and lost souls. He was amazed that Flora had agreed to come to that place after everything that had happened there, but then the Flora he knew was headstrong – some would say courageous. It was something he'd admired about her when they'd first met. But now it worried him.

He began to walk, taking a well-trodden path and alert for any sounds that would betray Flora's whereabouts. The uncomfortable thought passed through his mind that, if she was to find herself in danger there, the wounds he'd suffered in the war might hamper his ability to apprehend her attacker and he suddenly felt frustrated by his weakness. But he hadn't time to summon back-up so if his fears were justified, this would be him pitched against a faceless foe. Just as it had been on the battlefield.

For a while all he could hear were the night crows mocking high up in the branches. Then as he moved on further into the trees he thought he heard the soft cooing of a dove, there for a moment then gone. He called out Flora's name but there was no answer. He called again. Then a third time. But all he could hear were the noises of the woods.

He waited, examining his pocket watch in the gloom and hoping Sybil had been mistaken and that Flora had merely gone out for an evening stroll through the village or paid a visit to a friend. The time passed slowly in the fading light and he was about to leave when he heard the crack of a twig somewhere in the distance. He froze. There it was again. Someone was treading softly through the undergrowth. Then he saw a figure flitting through the trees to his right, moving quickly and noiselessly like a phantom.

He started to follow, conscious of the injury to his leg slowing him down. It was aching now as he stumbled through the undergrowth, keeping the figure in sight while doing his best not to be seen. Eventually the figure came to a halt in a small clearing, the place where Miss Forrest's body had been found, and Albert hung back, flattening himself against the trunk of an ash tree.

From his vantage point, he had a good view of his quarry and he could see it was a soldier. A lieutenant, just as Joe Jackson had said, wearing a polished leather Sam Browne belt that gleamed in the light of the full moon against the rough khaki of his uniform. One of the names Jackson had given him was that of Roderick Cartwright but Albert was as sure as he could be that this wasn't him, even though most of the man's face was obscured by a mask.

It was a round face with a moustache and spectacles and only the wearer's chin was visible underneath. Even though the ill-fitting mask had clearly been made for someone else, it endowed this officer with another man's identity. And, from the fit of the uniform, that didn't belong to him either. The trousers had bunched up around the ankles suggesting that it had been made for somebody much taller.

The soldier turned his head slowly and Albert knew he'd been seen and the killer was now poised for flight. But he wasn't going to let him escape.

The man took off, dodging through the trees, and Albert followed. His quarry was agile, light on his feet. But the ground was still covered in last autumn's rotting, damp leaves and suddenly he slipped and fell, allowing Albert to catch up a little.

He yelled to the man to stop. He wanted a word. He knew he sounded like a policeman but he wasn't sure how else he should sound. There are no clever words for such an occasion . . . only barked orders.

The man ignored him but Albert carried on, keeping him in sight. Lady Cartwright and Joe Jackson had reckoned he was a ghost, the spirit of some unfortunate lad lost in the war. But ghosts don't run – they vanish.

He caught sight of the soldier's bayonet hanging from his belt and he saw him draw it out, clutching it in his right hand as he ran. He was armed and Albert wasn't.

But Albert was determined not to be known as the Scotland Yard man who had the killer in his sights and failed to bring him to justice. The adrenaline pumping through his body made him forget his damaged limbs and what the war had done to him and he was catching up. Slowly. It would only take one false step on those treacherous leaves, one stumble and he'd have him. Then he'd have to deal with the bayonet as best he could.

He was feet away now and he could hear the man panting, breathless. To Albert's surprise he realised that, of the two of them he was probably the fitter. Soon he was close enough to reach out and grab the officer's tunic and as soon as he clutched the rough cloth in his hand the killer fell to his knees and twisted round to stab at Albert with the bayonet's naked blade.

The weapon missed its target and Albert saw his adversary scramble to his feet and draw the blade back again. With only one good hand to defend himself he knew he needed to be resourceful and fight dirty so he gave the soldier's leg a hearty kick, sending him crumpling to the ground.

The bayonet dropped from his hand, a hand that looked surprisingly small, and Albert snatched it up and clutched it, pointing it at his prisoner. Then, to his surprise, the soldier slumped forward and began to cry, a desperate sobbing like a mother mourning her child.

It was then he suddenly realised that the figure he'd taken for a man was actually a woman. A woman had committed those atrocities. A woman had meted out a dreadful vengeance.

He threw the bayonet to the ground, reached forward and tugged off the mask.

Chapter 42

Flora

I had another dream last night, more vivid this time as if the mist had cleared at last. I was standing at the top of the stairs and Mother came out of her bedroom with Father following after her.

They were quarrelling loudly as they often did and I heard her say she was leaving. She'd fallen in love with a man and she was going away with him. She was leaving for good and she was going to take me and John with her. But Father told her he wouldn't allow us to live with an adulterous whore. He said the words in a low hiss like a snake ready to strike. I'd never heard Father talk that way before and it frightened me.

I have dreamed of Mother so often but those dreams have always been incomplete. They stopped as soon as Father came out onto the landing but now they continue, relentlessly to the close.

In my dream now I see John standing in the doorway

of his room, calling to me to go back to bed. But I ignore him because I want the quarrel to stop and I want Mother to stay. But most of all I want her to stop hurting Father.

She brushes past me, making for the stairs with no acknowledgement that her own daughter is there watching. There is a determination about her I haven't seen before and I can tell her only desire is to be with her lover and nothing will stand in her way. In that brief moment I hate her for hurting Father and I have to stop her somehow. Then, as she reaches the top of the stairs, I give her the strongest shove my weak child's body can manage. She falls. In my dream I hear her body hitting the wooden stairs again and again. Bang, bang, bang. Until she lies silent and still at the bottom.

For so many years I've blotted that terrible night from my mind but now I know that I've always been a murderer. It is amazing how the human brain can deny such horrors: Father's books on the sicknesses of the mind say that it is a kind of amnesia, a memory that is repressed because the mind can only cope with so much trauma. I understand Dr Freud recorded such cases in his research. But, in spite of this, I am still a murderer and the Reverend Bell would no doubt say that I bear the mark of Cain.

After you've killed once, I suppose the second time is easy, the third easier still and so on. Until you justify each death in your mind and you can't stop ridding the world of those who've hurt you and yours. Now I realise why Father wished to put a stop to my nursing ambitions. What use is a nurse who can kill so readily? What guarantee is there that she won't use her skills for harm? Father has kept my secret faithfully, as did John when he was alive, and nothing was ever said about the matter. They

347

protected me all those years but I realise now that they must have watched me as one watches a potentially dangerous animal, always wary even when the risk seems slight.

I now know that Father buried Mother's body by night in a newly dug grave in the churchyard and he even made his false confession to Edith to protect me when she began to suspect the truth. He lied out of love for me.

It was Albert who arrested me; Albert who questioned me in that airless room at the police station. I have rarely seen a man so shaken by events, not even in wartime. Above all he looked hurt and betrayed. And yet it is he who betrayed me. I pointed out to him that I am still the mother of his child. And I saw tears form in his eyes at the discovery that I am not the woman he thought me to be.

I am a murderer. I am set apart from the rest of humanity. And yet I consider that my actions were justified. I obtained vengeance for all those poor lads who were herded to war like terrified animals to the slaughterhouse. I did no wrong.

Chapter 43

Albert

Albert Lincoln felt as if he'd been kicked, punched to the ground by a brutal assailant. He experienced almost the same numb shock as he had when the shell hit him. But then only his body had been injured. This time it felt as if his soul had been torn in two.

After the initial struggle, Flora had come quietly, as if she knew she had no choice but to yield to the inevitable. As he was in charge of the case, there was no way he could avoid the interrogation; no way of passing the task to somebody else. Teague and Wren had no inkling of his relationship with the prisoner and he wanted it kept that way. Besides, he was the man from Scotland Yard. He had made the arrest so it fell to him to bring the investigation to a satisfactory close.

Flora was waiting for him in the interview room, still dressed in the uniform that hung loosely off her body, like a child dressing up in her father's clothes. The officer's cap lay on the table beside her, along with the mask. The greater part of a man's face, complete with moustache and spectacles. It was the face he'd seen in the gloom of the woods: the face of an unknown soldier.

He sat down opposite her and maintained his silence for a while as he searched for the words to begin. At first her head was bowed as if in shame. But when he asked his first question she raised her face and he saw no regret in her eyes, only defiance.

He had to keep the questioning professional; he had to suppress his feelings and do his best to ignore everything that had happened between them. The silent presence of a constable standing by the door would keep his mind on the task in hand which, he thought, was for the best.

'Tell me why you killed Myrtle Bligh,' he began. 'You worked with her at Tarnhey Court, didn't you?'

'Yes,' Flora answered quietly. 'But she became one of them. The Society for the Abolition of Cowardice.' She spat out the words like bitter seeds. 'She killed my brother.'

'Surely the enemy killed your brother.'

'That's one way of looking at it but I prefer to think it was those witches from the SAC. John came home wounded, you see. Only his were wounds you couldn't see. Believe me, his injuries were as real as yours. But because they weren't visible, Miss Forrest and her coven thought they didn't matter. To those ignorant, self-righteous bitches, what we now call shell shock didn't exist. They thought it was cowardice, and they bullied John, harangued him until he gave in and went back to

350

the Front. I'd taken a break from working at Tarnhey Court to look after him so I knew how fragile his mind was. He just couldn't take the pressure they put on him.'

Her eyes were brimming with tears and Albert took a clean handkerchief from his pocket and handed it to her. She held it to her eyes, half folded like a blindfold.

'My brother, John, was beautiful. He wanted to be a doctor like Father and he was kind and gentle ... until those women destroyed him. Once he started receiving those white feathers they were so fond of sending people, his mental condition deteriorated and the guilt he felt about not doing his bit ate into him. As well as the shell shock he had an injured foot so he didn't have to go back but once they saw he was capable of walking round the village, they kept on and on at him. So in the end he just gave in. He was sent back to the Front. When I saw him off he was shaking and I begged him not to go. But they made him. They killed him.'

'Is that his uniform you're wearing?'

'Yes.' She touched the cloth lovingly, brushing it gently with her fingers. 'It's all I have left of him. I'd often go up into the attic and put it on. It made me feel close to him.' She brought the sleeve up to her nose and sniffed. 'Do you know I can still smell his cigarettes on it.'

'Smoke lingers,' Albert said softly.

'Like a ghost. Do you believe in ghosts?'

It was a question Albert couldn't answer. 'When did you decide to kill those women?'

'It was when they were collecting money for the war memorial. They were making lists of the names they thought should be on it. Gloating about the dead as though it didn't matter that people had lost men they

351

loved. It was as if their deaths weren't real. Even though they'd lost men themselves, they didn't seem to understand what they'd done.'

'And that made you angry? You lost control?'

She shook her head. 'I didn't lose control. I planned it all carefully. I wanted to teach them a lesson, to take my revenge on them on John's behalf and on behalf of all those men whose names are carved on that memorial. I should have stopped those women spreading their poison earlier. Do you know Joe Jackson from the Black Horse tried to hang himself because they were tormenting him? If he'd succeeded, they'd have had another death on their hands. God knows how many other lads from this village they sent to be slaughtered. The only thing I regret is that I didn't stop them earlier while the fighting was still going on.'

'Why didn't you?'

She leaned forward, putting her elbows on the table and putting her face close to his. He could feel her warm breath on his face . . . as he had before they'd kissed the first time.

'Because I was fully occupied at Tarnhey Court, looking after all those poor suffering men. Who knows how many of them had gone to the Front because of the likes of Miss Forrest and her cronies? But at least they were out of it at Tarnhey Court.' Albert saw her look at his hand. 'Just like you were when you came back to Blighty.'

She sat back in the hard chair and Albert's eyes travelled downwards to her belly. It was flat now but he couldn't forget that it now contained the child he'd fathered. He glanced at the constable on duty by the door, wondering if he could order him to leave them alone for a few minutes because there was so much he wanted to say. But he lacked the courage.

'I can understand why you wanted to avenge your brother's death. But my mother always used to tell me that two wrongs didn't make a right,' he said lightly.

'That's her opinion.'

'How did you persuade them to meet you?'

'I sent them letters from the man they'd lost, saying they weren't dead but they'd deserted and had to lie low or that they'd been on some secret mission. The letters requested a meeting in the woods or, in Annie's case, near Fuller's Farm. Only it wasn't their loved one who was waiting – it was Lieutenant John Winsmore.' She picked up the mask from the table beside her. It seemed light in her fingers. 'I broke into David Eames's studio and took a couple of the masks he'd made ... the ones that belonged to patients who died of their wounds and wouldn't need them any more. I knew David had kept them. They're works of art, don't you think?'

Albert couldn't deny it. He nodded. 'A useful disguise.'

'Yes and I was avenging those men too.'

'You see yourself as an instrument of vengeance?'

She shrugged her shoulders and the uniform slipped a little to reveal the strap of a camisole underneath; fine cotton beneath rough khaki.

'I killed my own mother so killing again wasn't difficult.'

Her admission stunned him afresh. As far as he knew, her mother had run off with a lover. He waited for her to continue.

'Father covered up what I'd done and he buried her in a freshly dug grave in the churchyard. I was eight. I became a murderer at the age of eight. And Father's kept my secret all these years.'

'I don't believe you,' Albert said in a gasp as the horror of her confession hit him. He suddenly felt hot, as if the room had no air, even though the northern air outside was chilly.

'I suppressed the memory – blocked it out of my mind for years. Father said it can happen in cases like mine. I killed Mother because she was leaving us and I really couldn't let her do that.'

She sounded almost proud. Somehow, in her mind, she was justifying her actions. The faithless mother and those women who'd bullied young men into sacrificing their lives on the fields of France. To her, all her victims had deserved their fate.

'Why did you put the doves in your victims' mouths?' he asked. It was as if he was talking to a stranger now. The Flora Winsmore he'd known, the spirited but gentle nurse, had been a fabrication. That facade, that mask, had concealed a mind twisted by the losses in her life.

'Were those women really victims? I think that title's more appropriate for the lads they sent to their deaths, don't you? I found the first dove dead and thought it fitting to stop Myrtle's mouth with it. After all, it had been her words that killed those men. It was she who sent the white feathers. A dove is a bird of peace and I saw the irony of it. Same with the others . . . only I had to trap and kill the birds.' Her face clouded. 'I didn't enjoy wringing their innocent necks. To tell the truth, it bothered me far more than killing the women.'

'You arranged the bodies so that it looked as if the motive was sexual assault.'

'I did that to deflect suspicion. How could a woman ever do something like that?' She gave a cold smile. Then the smile vanished. 'That nurse I told you was assaulted at Tarnhey Court by Dr Bone – that was me.'

The revelation robbed Albert of speech for a few seconds. He stared at her with a mixture of pity and disbelief. 'You kept this to yourself?'

'Who would have believed me? I tried to tell Edith, the woman he's to marry, but she said it must have been my fault and that I'd led him on. I timed everything so that Bone was here in the village on the occasion of each murder. I wanted him to be arrested. I wanted him to suffer. I would have been glad if he'd hanged for it. He said he loved me – made me promises then, when he'd got what he wanted, he changed in an instant. He laughed at my naivety. Would you believe it, he laughed at me?' Her eyes lit up with fury at the memory and Albert felt his face burning.

Then she took a deep, shuddering breath. 'I had to time the murders so that the innocent would go free. I couldn't allow Jack Blemthwaite or Sydney Pepper to hang and I knew that if there was another murder while they were in custody, they'd have to be released. I knew Sir William and Roderick Cartwright were suspects too and they're both away at the moment so they wouldn't have been able to kill Edith. I can't say I like Sir William or approve of some of his actions but I had to clear both of them of suspicion, didn't I?'

'Is that why you'd planned to kill Edith?'

'She was going to accuse my father of murder. I thought she was my friend and she betrayed me.'

Albert heard a peevish note in her voice, like a

petulant little girl. He couldn't help wondering how she'd managed to hide her true nature from him when they'd been together. He'd been on the verge of love but had that blinded him to reality? Or had she just been an expert at deception? Perhaps, he thought, there were two Flora Winsmores – one the caring nurse and sensible doctor's daughter and the other an unpredictable killer who, in spite of her brutality, was unwilling to allow innocent men to suffer for her actions. He'd met a lot of murderers in his time but none had surprised him like this. None had managed to baffle him as she had.

'So you appointed yourself judge and jury? You condemned Edith to death?'

'Somebody has to put things right.'

'But that somebody isn't you, Flora,' he heard himself saying softly, resisting the urge to take her hand.

As she was led from the room, he bowed his head in despair. He no longer trusted his own judgement. Perhaps he was a useless detective. Perhaps when all this was over, he should go back to London and pursue another profession.

When he felt warm tears welling in his eyes, he was relieved that the constable had left him alone and there was nobody there to witness his fall from grace.

Chapter 44

Flora Winsmore had been too young at the time of her mother's death to be charged with her manslaughter but she was found guilty of the murders of Myrtle Bligh, Annie Dryden, Sarah Cookham and Emmaline Forrest and sentenced to hang by the neck until she was dead. The judge asked the Lord to have mercy on her soul.

Albert visited her shortly after she'd been taken to prison in Derby to await trial, but the presence of a stern female warder had ensured their conversation didn't stray into the realms of intimacy. He didn't make a second visit. The experience of seeing her in custody, dressed in the garb of a female prisoner, was too painful to repeat. It only emphasised how she'd managed to deceive him and he didn't need reminding of his own inadequacy.

Once the investigation was complete, he'd returned to London and Mary. Her mother had recovered from the influenza and no longer needed her care so she was

357

home to greet him when he arrived. If greet was the appropriate word.

The first thing that struck Albert when he saw her was how drab she looked, almost as if she had stepped out of a monochrome photograph with her pale hair, her grey dress and her pallid skin. On the train down to the capital he'd harboured a hope that his long absence would have made her eager to see him and she'd have made an effort to put aside her grief. But he was to be disappointed. If anything, she felt Frederick's absence more keenly now, although she claimed that her visits to the medium had provided her with some comfort. Frederick, she assured him, was happy and had other children to play with in paradise ... although he missed his mother. There was no mention of his father.

She spent a lot of time at the Spiritualist Church she'd joined and asked Albert if he'd like to go with her. When he declined her invitation she didn't ask again.

Albert found himself spending more and more time at Scotland Yard, volunteering to work overtime while other men, keen to be with their families, regarded him with gratitude, mixed with a slight suspicion that he was showing up their lack of dedication. But what else did he have in his life? A wife who no longer lived in this world. A dead son. And Flora's baby, as yet unborn to its doomed mother. Her execution had been delayed, of course. They do not hang pregnant women.

The thought of what would become of his son or daughter haunted him day and night. But he could speak of it to nobody. It was his secret – his and Flora's. And soon she would be in no position to betray it.

When he estimated Flora's time was near, he

358

telephoned the prison governor to make discreet enquiries, asking what would happen to her child when it was born. The answer was vague. An orphanage perhaps. Or adoption by some deserving local family. But it was pointed out to him that many would be reluctant to take such a child into their homes. Many believed in bad blood, the taint of murder passed from mother to child. And as for the father, he was told, there was a chance he was criminally inclined as well. She had declined to identify the man with whom she'd fornicated.

Albert had made the tentative suggestion that perhaps he and his wife could give the child a home, trying his best to make the offer sound as if it was made out of Christian charity, but the reply was vague. It would be up to the appropriate authorities. He was reluctant to press the matter too far, fearing it might arouse the governor's suspicion. Besides, how would Mary react to the sudden appearance of a strange baby? It was something that needed a great deal of thought.

He was almost glad when he was called to the scene of the brutal murder of an elderly man in a flat above an Islington shop. When he was standing in the victim's blood-soaked parlour, directing operations, he was no longer thinking of Flora Winsmore. And for that he was grateful.

Chapter 45

Flora

I have a son. They tell me it was a difficult delivery but all the pain I endured during those long hours in that sparse cell evaporated from my memory as soon as I held my little boy in my arms.

Then he was snatched from me and taken God knows where. I'm assured that he'll be safe and well taken care of and I suppose that is some consolation, even though my heart breaks at the thought of it.

It is time now. I have been measured and weighed. I hadn't expected a hangman to be such a dapper, businesslike little man, more like a junior bank clerk than a bringer of death.

The door opens and the governor steps in, followed by the clergyman with the long face who came to pray with me yesterday evening. He has his prayer book open, ready to begin, as they strap my hands behind my back.

I'm led the short distance to the trap door where my legs are strapped and the hood placed roughly over my head. A mask to hide my identity.

Then I hear a sound. Metal against metal. And I prepare to fall.

Chapter 46

Albert

I have a son but nobody will tell me what has become of him.

He has been taken away and, as far as the authorities are concerned, his fate is none of my concern. Even if I told the truth they might not believe me and it would ruin my professional standing and maybe cause a scandal.

But I am determined that one day I will find him. One day I will know my son and he will know his father.